Don't Forget Me Tomorrow

A.L. Jackson
www.aljacksonauthor.com

Cover Design by RBA Designs
Cover Image by Michelle Lancaster Photography
Editing by SS Stylistic Editing and Margo Lipschultz
Proofreading by Julia Griffis, The Romance Bibliophile
Formatting by Champagne Book Design

The characters and events in this book are fictitious. Names, characters, places, and plots are a product of the author's imagination. Any similarity to real persons, living or dead, is coincidental and not intended by the author.

More from

A.L. Jackson

NEW YORK TIMES BESTSELLING AUTHOR

Time River
Love Me Today
Don't Forget Me Tomorrow
Claim Me Forever

Redemption Hills
Give Me a Reason
Say It's Forever
Never Look Back
Promise Me Always

The Falling Stars Series
Kiss the Stars
Catch Me When I Fall
Falling into You
Beneath the Stars

Confessions of the Heart
More of You
All of Me
Pieces of Us

Fight for Me
Show Me the Way
Follow Me Back
Lead Me Home
Hold on to Hope

Don't Forget Me Tomorrow

NEW YORK TIMES BESTSELLING AUTHOR

A.L. JACKSON

Prologue

I STARED AT HER FROM ACROSS THE ROOM.

I could feel the walls closing in, and the need I'd had for her for my entire life growing stronger than it ever had. As if the two of us were hinged on this moment.

"Tell me I'm not too late. Tell me you still love me." There was no stopping the plea.

Pain and desperation twisted through her expression. "Do you think I could ever stop loving you?"

The second she said it, I snapped, and I was across the room.

I crashed into her in a landslide of greed.

One hand dove into her hair and the other curled around the side of her neck as I crushed my mouth against hers.

Really kissing her for the first time.

Nothing had ever felt quite like kissing Dakota Cooper.

It was flames and heat and pure relief.

I sucked it in, imbibing the feeling as I devoured her mouth.

My chest nearly blew with the power of it. With the way my heart thrashed violently at my ribs. With the devotion that surged from the sacred place that had always been meant for her.

Except I'd always known why I couldn't touch her. The reasons I'd built the walls between us.

Why she was only supposed to be my best friend's little sister.

I'd crossed a line I wasn't supposed to cross.

And I should have known I'd have to pay the penalty…

Chapter One
Ryder

WHAT THE FUCK WAS SHE DOING OUT HERE?
I slowed my motorcycle as I came upon a small white Volvo SUV pulled off to the side of the road, its hazards flashing through the dusky light as the summer day faded into grays.

My guts tangled in a knot of worry.

We were twenty miles outside of town, and the two-lane road was basically desolate except for a random car that whizzed by.

There was no mistaking that car. The rear window was a fucking billboard for the country market and café Dakota Cooper owned. It wasn't like I blamed her for wanting to advertise, but I didn't love that every fucking person in this town knew her name, either.

Where she worked and where she lived.

Not that there was a ton of privacy in a small town the size of Time River.

Everyone knew everyone.

And even if she lived in the middle of a bustling city, I was pretty sure she would have made a name for herself, anyway.

Hell, I figured every time she smiled at some unknowing fool, she carved herself into their memory.

Made her mark.

Unforgettable.

Protectiveness lined my insides in a sheet of steel.

It was nearing dark, and she was out here in the middle of nowhere.

By herself.

Any monster could roll up and catch her unaware.

Just like me.

My bike came to a rumbling stop ten feet behind her, and I killed the engine, tossed the kickstand, and swung off as I took stock of the situation.

Dakota was more than capable, but it still made me itch that she was on her knees in front of the back-passenger side tire, cranking at a handle on the jack to lift the rear-end of her car.

Looking like a goddamn vision beneath the rays of the setting sun.

I tamped the bolt of lust that stirred my dick, something I'd gotten really fucking good at over the years, and I edged toward her, my boots crunching on the loose gravel.

Awareness rippled through the twilight with my approach.

A flash of tension before it settled into something familiar and right.

"Funny, I didn't see a call or text from you," I said, words rough and carrying over a big truck that blew by, sending a flurry of debris scattering through the air.

Dakota glanced my way. The hint of a smile played through the shiny gloss coating her lush lips.

"That's because I didn't call you." Her voice was a tease as she continued to crank the handle, though her breaths were coming hard with her exertion as the back-end of her Volvo slowly hoisted.

At least she had a blanket spread on the ground to protect her bare knees since she had on one of those sundresses she always chose to wear. Black fabric dotted with pink flowers that hugged every lush curve of her body.

I thought she might have been prescribed specific attire with the sole purpose of driving me out of my mind.

"You should have."

"What, you think I'm not capable of fixing a flat tire?" Eyes the color of cinnamon and fire glinted back. "I seem to remember someone who insisted on making sure I knew where the jack and spare were when I bought this car."

She arched a brow. Her cheeks were full and high, and the threat of that tiny dimple on the left side of her chin flickered and danced like temptation.

"Yeah, that was so you would know how to do it for when I'm not around, and here I am." I lifted my tatted arms out to the sides.

Except if she had called an hour before, I wouldn't have answered. I'd have been too wrapped up in the bullshit dragging me under. A millstone around my neck.

One day it would be the reason I drowned.

The thousand shades of brown in her eyes danced as she peered up at me, and she chuckled a low, throaty sound that shivered over my skin. "Of course, you are. Tell me you're not stalking me?"

Stuffing my hands into my pockets, I let a smirk ride to my face. "You know it. It's my job to know where you are at all times."

"Is that so?" Her expression twisted in playful disbelief.

"Isn't that what friends are for?"

"Friends? Hardly. It sounds to me you're acting more like my overbearing brother. I swear, if it was up to the two of you, I'd never step foot outside by myself."

Sounded like a solid plan.

"What are you doing out here, anyway?" I asked.

"I had to pop over to Costco in Poplar to grab some things for the café. What are *you* doing out here?" She tossed it back at me like she figured I'd been up to no good.

I had been, but I doubted it was what she was thinking.

Shame locked down my throat. As close as I was to Dakota, there would always be a wall. A place I couldn't let her see. The fucking last thing in the world I wanted her to know about me.

My jaw clenched as I forced out the lie. "Just felt like feeling the wind on my face. My bike was calling to me."

"A little hot for that, isn't it?"

"Never too hot for me." The smirk was back in full force.

With the history around us, I was thankful we'd gotten to this place.

Where we could be easy together.

Friends, even though it was fucking painful being this close to her most of the time.

But I would take her any way I could have her.

She scoffed and turned her attention back to the jack, clearly picking up on the innuendo I couldn't help but slide into the conversation. Before I could let my brain spiral into depravity, I strode the rest of the way up to her.

It cast her in my shadow where I towered over her.

"Are you going to get up off your knees and let me help you, or are you just going to leave me standing here staring at you like a lazy prick?"

Leaning back, she swiped a bead of sweat that trickled from her hairline with her bare shoulder.

My fingers itched with the urge to reach out and trace the spot. But touching her was the last thing I could do. I wouldn't taint her goodness with the sickness of me.

"Haven't you learned yet that you don't need to ride in like the cavalry, Ryder?"

"I already rode in, Cookie, so you might as well let me."

I'd started calling her that years ago.

Now there was no way I could stop.

Pushing to standing, she waved at the flat tire. "Fine, if it makes you feel more like a man, then go for it."

I shook my head at her. "Are you trying to bust my balls?"

"Someone needs to." She punted me a grin.

I started to move to take her place, but she bent over to straighten the skirt of her dress.

It speared me to the spot.

Her tits were heavy and spilling out of the scooped neckline.

Her hips full and wide and perfectly hugged by the fabric.

Hair a warm brown that was streaked with honey, and she wore it in a high ponytail, the same way as she did most days, the lush locks wavy and draping over one shoulder.

I couldn't help but envision wrapping my hand around it, tugging her head back, and devouring that lush mouth.

I swallowed hard, doing my best not to ogle my best friend's baby sister.

Dude would fucking gut me if he had an inkling of an idea about the thoughts I had of her.

Too bad he was the least of my worries.

She moved a foot to the side, and I took her spot, reining that bullshit in.

I knew better.

Dakota was a friend. Like a sister to me. And I'd do well to remember it. Because I would never fucking drag her into the mess that was my life.

I cranked through the lug bolts, removed the tire, then was quick to replace it with the spare.

The whole time, I could feel her attention on me. Eyes tracing.

"You enjoying yourself, Cookie?" I canted a glance up at her. The last of the light caught her in its hazy rays.

Brown hair and mesmerizing eyes.

So goddamn pretty my stomach clutched.

Raking her teeth over her bottom lip, she tried to contain her laughter. "Guess I like you on your knees for me."

A snort left my nose. I'd been for years, and she didn't have a clue.

Giving a final tug at the lug nuts to make sure they were tight, I shifted to fully look up at her. "You need to make sure you're not driving on this for long and take it in to get the original tire repaired or replaced."

The cock of her head was nothing but a razzing challenge. "I am a capable adult, Ryder. I even own my own business."

"Know that, Dakota." The words were low.

"Then you can stop treating me like a little girl." The barest flash of annoyance hit her expression.

If only that was the way I saw her.

"Go ahead and tell my brother while you're at it," she tacked on, rolling her eyes though there was affection woven through. "The two of you are ridiculous."

"I just care about you, Dakota. About Kayden." The admission came rough, and the sweat that suddenly slicked my skin didn't have anything to do with the summer heat.

Thinking of Dakota's son always got me that way. He was two, and the cutest fucking thing I'd ever seen.

I didn't know if it was loyalty or jealousy that hit me hardest, not that I had any right to the last.

Softness radiated from her as she gazed down at me, that sweetness that was always lingering beneath the surface riding from her tongue. "You know I can't call you every time some little thing goes wrong in my life and expect you to come running, Ryder. You've already done enough for me. Too much."

Gratitude tinged with unease infiltrated her tone, her eyes dropping for a beat. I knew exactly where her mind had gone.

The money I'd given her to help start her business.

I released the jack and stood. There was nothing I could do but take her by the chin. More tender than I should. I towered over her, searching her face like there was a way I could get her to understand.

"That's where you have it wrong, Dakota. You can. I expect you to call me. Whatever you need. And there is no such thing as *too much* when it comes to you. Do you understand?" The words left me like a tumble of stones. A plea and a demand.

Because I'd wanted to give her everything I had, but the only thing I had been able to do was give her the one gift that I could.

She viewed it as a debt. Like something she needed to repay.

She could never understand that what I'd given her was my heart.

Those pink lips parted, and fuck, greed twisted through me like a hurricane, cock pushing at my jeans like I might be able to possess the one woman I could never have.

"I don't want you to waste your time on me," she whispered. "I know you have your own life. Things you need to take care of."

A puff of disbelief escaped between my lips. "You could never be a waste, Dakota Cooper."

The air thickened. Growing dense and pushing in. Heavy and hot. A dragging pull between us.

My phone pinged in my pocket, and both of us jumped back like it was a warning going off that we were about to cross a line we couldn't cross.

Blowing out a steadying sigh, I dug into my pocket and thumbed into my phone like it was the most important thing in the world, then my chest clutched with the reminder of why I could never get too close to Dakota.

Why she'd hate me if she knew.

Dare: Where the fuck are you? You're late.

Swallowing around the barbs in my throat, I looked up at the woman who stood three feet away shifting on her feet.

Innocent and right and every good thing in this life.

I roughed a hand over the back of my neck, attention on my boots when I said, "I need to get going."

I felt the weight of her nod. "Yeah, I need to get to my mom's and pick up Kayden before they get worried."

I hoisted up her flat tire, opened her trunk, and tossed it in. Dakota came to my side, her presence close to overwhelming as she placed the blanket she'd had on the ground on top of it.

For a second, we hovered in each other's space. So close but where we could never belong.

Lost to a beat of greed.

The kind I could never give into.

I pushed the button to close the hatch then took a step toward my bike. "Be safe, Dakota."

Cinnamon eyes watched me like they could see through to my sins. "You, too."

Chapter Two

Dakota

RYDER STRODE BACK TO HIS MOTORCYCLE.

I watched.

Unable to look away as blinding rays of sunlight slanted through the sky, riding in from the edge of the horizon where the sun melted away.

The man was lit in a backdrop of vibrant pinks and purples and blues.

He was midnight in the middle of it.

Black hair that shone like silvered onyx, shaved all the way around on the sides before it faded into the longer, wavy pieces that angled forward in the front.

He wore black jeans, a worn leather jacket, and boots, even though it had to be close to a thousand degrees outside.

Shoulders wide and his chest hard and packed, the rest of him sinewy and lean, so tall he cast a shadow wherever he went.

The man was chiseled strength and constrained danger.

Hotter than any sin I'd ever dream of committing.

He had to go and do it all with a sly smirk on his gorgeous face, so cool and casual you'd think he didn't have a care in the world.

I wondered if I was the only one who noticed the disorder that writhed beneath his blasé exterior.

If they felt the current of goodness laced with corruption.

If I was the fool who always looked too close, wanting to sink inside and disappear when he was the last guy on the face of the earth I should want.

I'd been in love with Ryder Nash since I was nineteen, probably earlier than that if I was being honest with myself.

I was working on getting over that, though.

Moving on.

Because I cherished the friendship we had. This closeness that I didn't share with anyone else.

I couldn't imagine there would ever be a day that a part of me wouldn't hang onto the fantasies of him looking at me the way I looked at him. The part that would get tripped up when he got close to me, the way he just had.

When the air seemed to shimmer with light and the edges of my consciousness got pulled toward his darkness.

When I got stuck in something that felt like the swelling of need.

A blaze of something that could scorch me to the bone.

The part of me that couldn't help but wonder if he felt it, too.

But there was a bigger part of me that had accepted him as my friend. The guy who was always there, riding in like a dark knight. The part of me that didn't want to hurt anymore when I looked at him.

The part that was ready to love and to find the one who would love me back.

Still, I couldn't look away as he turned and slung a leg over his bike and straddled the metal.

Tatted hands curled around the handlebars. Waves of black hair billowing in the breeze.

But it was the gunmetal eyes staring at me through the fading light that sent chills scattering down my spine.

The man *midnight* at the helm.

He kicked over his old bike and it grumbled to life.

He just sat there, waiting on me.

Right.

I was supposed to be getting in my car.

I shook myself out of the haze he'd cast and forced myself into action. I checked both directions before I rushed to the driver's door and climbed in.

I started my car, checked the lane beside me again, then eased onto the road, keeping my speed far less than I normally would travel.

With the look on Ryder's face when he'd received that text, I'd figured he'd blaze around me and burn a path back into Time River.

Someone was waiting on him.

I knew it.

The thing was, there was always someone waiting on Ryder. His phone pinging off with the slew of women he seemed to have at his beck and call.

I didn't let it bother me anymore.

But he didn't fly around me the way I'd expected.

No.

He followed.

Followed me to the end of the highway and through the small town that I loved.

Time River, Colorado was hidden at the base of a gorgeous ridge of mountains with a river running through.

Cozy cottages and two-story buildings with colorful awnings ran along Manchester, the main street that cut through the middle of town. The sidewalks were decorated with planters that overflowed with flowers, and old-style lamps had flickered on with the setting of the sun and now burned a yellowed glow.

I drove by shops, restaurants, and boutiques.

A couple hair salons and a new day spa, plus an old-timey hardware store and a renovated hotel.

The whole time I traveled, I could feel the weight of the single headlight of Ryder's bike covering me in some kind of shield.

Satisfaction hummed in my being as I passed by Time River Market & Café, my restaurant and country store. There were some days I still couldn't believe that I'd built it into what it was today.

A focal point of our community where locals and tourists alike flocked to meet. I was thankful I'd found people I could trust to help me run it, and tonight, the parking lot was packed to overflowing with our dinner guests.

None of it would have been possible without Ryder, and sometimes I still didn't understand it. Couldn't comprehend why he would offer me something so great and expect nothing in return.

Ryder who remained close behind.

It wasn't until I slowed to make a right onto my mother's street a couple blocks up that he finally gunned it and wound around me, the engine roaring as the streak of metal flew down the street.

I reminded myself it was none of my concern where he was going, or more importantly, who he was running to.

Ryder was my *friend*. And I could rest satisfied in that, even though that friendship was always going to be bittersweet.

⁓

"Mommy, I see you!"

My heart nearly exploded as I hurried up the walkway toward my mother's porch, my spirit as eager as my feet as I climbed the two steps to where Kayden was at the screen door.

His little face was smooshed into the mesh, a distorted smile grinning back at me.

"I see you," I sang in return, and I reached down to caress his cheek through the screen.

My mother's soft laughter filtered through, and she appeared behind him and reached over to flick the lock. "He's been standing here waiting for you for the last thirty minutes."

Affection swelled. So intense as she opened the screen door and Kayden came rushing out, his arms thrown in the air. I picked him up, and he squealed and kicked as I lifted him high, before I brought him down to smother his adorable face in a thousand kisses.

I made sure to add in a bunch of smooching noises for extra effect.

Little hands gripped me by the cheeks, the child giggling like mad.

This.

This was my meaning.

Where I'd found the greatest joy, as unexpected as it'd been.

"Hey, Mom. Sorry I'm late," I told her.

"No need to apologize," she said as she widened the door for me to enter. "You're just in time. Dinner is almost ready."

"How was he today?" I asked as I tucked my squirming toddler onto my hip and followed her into the house.

"Tasmanian Devil, that one," she tossed over her shoulder as she walked through the living room that was a complete disaster, thanks to my little bit of mayhem, and into the kitchen.

I set him down in the middle of the mess he'd made. "It sounds like you have some cleaning up to do." My voice was gentle as I knelt in front of him and dragged the basket for his toys over.

"I *hungee*." He grabbed his belly in both hands.

A soft chuckle got free, and I brushed back the same rebellious lock of brown hair that always fell over his eyes. "You have to clean up before you eat."

"Do I has to, Gammy?" he hollered like his grandma was going to come to his rescue.

She moved to lean against the jamb of the wide kitchen entryway, crossing her arms over her chest with a tease dancing on her face. "Um, yes, you *has* to. You destroyed Gammy's house. Blew it down like you are the Big Bad Wolf. Now you have to put it back together again."

He howled with laughter, and he started running in place and puffing out his cheeks, spluttering as he blew between his adorable full lips. "I *bwow* it down! I *bwow* it down!"

I glanced at my mother.

Tenderness was knitted into her expression, woven with the lines that were just beginning to show on her face. Her eyes a warm brown that always met you with a sweep of soft encouragement.

Love squeezed me in the deepest place.

"You'd better get at it so I can help your gammy finish dinner. It looks like you've worn her out," I told my son, glancing at my mother again.

Her curly brown hair was frizzy, her white tee dappled with stains. But she still always managed to have a smile on her face.

"Okay, Gammy, I hurry and help you." Kayden shot into action, grabbing his toys and tossing them into the basket, only he was doing it so fast, half of them tumbled out on the other side. I picked those up and put them inside while my mother hovered at the entryway.

"How was your trip into Poplar?" she asked.

I blew out a sigh. "Fine until I ran over a nail or something on my way back. Got a flat about twenty miles out."

Worry pulled through her features. "Why didn't you call?"

It seemed everyone was asking me that.

"I had it handled. Besides, Ryder happened to be out for a ride, so he stopped and finished the job."

She tsked a sound of surprised disbelief. "That boy always seems to know when you're in trouble, doesn't he?"

I couldn't keep from rolling my eyes. "He didn't know I was in trouble. We just happened to be in the same place at the same time."

It wasn't like he had some sort of sixth sense about me.

"Which you two always seem to be." Something curious traipsed through her demeanor, her head angling to the side in speculation.

"Because we live in a town the size of a shoe box. I'm in the same place with a whole lot of people a whole lot of the time."

Okay, fine. It wasn't *that* small. There were plenty of people here I hadn't met before, especially since Time River had gone through a boom.

No surprise since in my humble opinion it was the most beautiful town in the country. I honestly couldn't imagine living anywhere else.

"Well, at any rate, it was good he was there. You aren't exactly dressed for working on cars. You sure look beautiful, though."

I always tried to dress up a little bit when I was in the restaurant since I was the owner.

I'd warred for a lot of years with my appearance, but I'd gotten over that a long time ago.

The comparison game.

Thinking I was less.

Sure, sometimes the scars from the taunts when I was younger got the best of me, and those insecurities still snuck up on me every once in a while, but not today. Because I did feel beautiful, and I freaking loved this dress. "Thanks, Mom."

"I mean it," she rambled as she turned back into the kitchen. "Now are we going to eat or what? I invited your brother and sister, but both have plans tonight, so it's just us."

"As long as it's as good as the pot roast that was the special at the café tonight," I teased as I finished straightening the pillows on the couch then took Kayden's hand to follow her.

She tossed me a big smirk as she stirred something that smelled delicious on the stove. "And who was it who helped you create that recipe? Now sit your cute butt down and let your mom take care of her little girl."

Moving to her side, I wound my arm around her waist and set my head on her shoulder. "Thank you. I hope you know how much I truly appreciate you."

She pressed her cheek to mine. "I know that, Dakota. And I hope you know how much I love you and want the best for you. The only thing I ask in return is that you keep chasing after joy, and don't you dare ever stop. And I'll be right here with you every step of the way."

I gulped around the knot that suddenly felt heavy at the base of my throat. "I won't."

Chapter Three
Ryder

I EASED MY BIKE INTO THE PARKING LOT OF MY SHOP. NIGHT HAD taken hold, the sky strewn with a smattering of stars, the moon barely climbing from the horizon and casting a faint glow over the earth.

The industrial building was set back from the road, nothing but a big metal box backed by trees that extended beyond the property line.

Black windows fronted it, and a large sign hung above the double doors that led into the front office.

Nash Metalwork Designs.

Disgust pulled so hard at my ribs it was a wonder I didn't bust apart.

I was so fucking proud of what I'd built.

Of the beauty I created with my hands.

But it was the underbelly of it that made me sick.

The chains that held me hostage.

Chest feeling like it might cave, I wound my bike around the right side of the building. The grumbling engine broke through the quiet that clung to the dense air, this side of town that housed manufacturing shops and warehouses pretty much shut down for the night.

Three massive garage doors lined this side, and the pavement extended out so trailers could be backed into the bays so customers could pick up whatever custom pieces they'd ordered if I wasn't the one delivering it.

Anything metal was my specialty.

Mostly I made custom doors, gates, and fences plus different types of displays, shelves, and counters for local businesses. Every once in a while, I designed special pieces for cars and motorcycles, and it wasn't rare that I worked on horse trailers and the like, designing something to turn heads for the horse dealers and rodeo stars to haul their prized possessions around in.

Tonight, a pickup truck and trailer waited near the far door at the end of the side lot.

Blood pounded through my veins as I eased my bike to a stop beside it. The spray of my headlight tossed a murky light over the man who was leaning against the building next to the door.

Dressed in dark jeans and a tee-shirt like he was a legit customer here to do business.

Hands stuffed casually in his pockets and head rested back on the metal.

But there was nothing about him that was legitimate.

Hatred lined his face and greed was set deep in the brown of his eyes.

Animosity thumped through my bloodstream. Adrenaline that surged and rushed as I nudged out the kickstand and killed the engine of my bike.

Silence swept in behind it, eerie and thick while the two of us stared each other down through the wisping shadows that played across the lot, the falling darkness barely cut by the dingy light that hung at the side of the door.

It lit one side of Dare's face, his jaw grinding as he chewed at the edge of his lip where he remained kicked back against the wall like a bad fucking memory.

The asshole was massive, tossing a vibe of burly intimidation. No doubt, it worked on plenty of people. Dude looked deadly, and he had the history to back it.

But I was having a hard time continuing to give a fuck.

"You're late," he said, vibrating with irritation.

I swung myself off my bike and canted him a grin like the sight of him didn't leave me shaking with hostility. "Had something I needed to do."

Like I'd just leave Dakota stranded on the side of the road.

A scoff rolled up his throat. "Is that so?"

I strode up slow, voice dripping with bitterness as I angled toward him. "You think I sit around waiting for your texts?"

He lifted his chin, eyes flashing with a warning. "Think you know they're the only ones that matter."

I wanted to tell him to fuck off.

Push back.

But how the hell did I do that when this bastard had me in chains? When I knew what he would do if I didn't comply.

Visions flashed.

Cold. Limp. Lips blue.

Sucking down the rage, I forced myself to move, edging around him to punch in the code next to the door.

Stepping inside, I tapped the button to open the farthest garage door. The engine whirred as the massive metal door rolled up.

Dare hopped into his truck and backed the trailer inside, and I was already undoing the latch and opening the tailgate before he'd gotten back out.

Whatever it took to get this fucker out of here faster.

Did it even matter, though? Once he was gone, he still might as well be standing in front of me with his hands wrapped around my throat, squeezing the life out of me.

Slowly bleeding me dry.

He climbed into the trailer and carefully backed out the car sitting inside.

It was on me to modify it, load it at the safehouse, and get it to its drop-off point.

I watched him as he eased it down the ramp. He left it sitting facing out in the middle of my shop, and he climbed out and tossed me the keys. "Ty will meet you at the safehouse at ten on Tuesday. Have it ready and don't fucking be late."

Old rage stormed, shockwaves of bitterness and hate. I looked at his face. At the man who had me by more than the balls, because it was my fucking life in his hands.

My shame and the chains and this debt that had stolen every good thing from me.

Fuck, I wanted it back, and if I ever was going to, I was going to have to fight for it.

"About finished with this," I told him, lifting my chin.

He chuckled a dark sound as he closed the tailgate and locked it, then moved to the driver's side of his truck. He looked back at me, a warning lining his face. "Think you know what happened the last time you started spouting shit like that."

Without saying anything else, he climbed in and slammed the door.

I watched him pull out.

A gnarl of fury burned my insides.

A blaze of spite.

The second he was gone, I pressed my palms to the table next to me, struggling to take in a breath around the mayhem that battered my insides.

Because I meant what I'd said.

I was about finished with this bullshit.

And it was on me to figure out how to get myself free.

Chapter Four

Dakota

I TUCKED KAYDEN'S GLOWING NIGHTLIGHT BEAR UNDER HIS ARM AND tiptoed out of his room. The child went and went until he basically passed out. Tonight, he'd ended up facedown, spread-eagle in the middle of our living room floor surrounded by every piece of his train set.

He hadn't budged when I'd carried him upstairs.

Blowing out a contented, albeit exhausted sigh, I crept downstairs to the first floor of my house. It was attached to the back of Time River Market & Café and had once been a warehouse from when the café used to be a traditional diner.

Upstairs, the storage rooms had been converted into two bedrooms and a small loft that overlooked the big, open space below.

It was as quaint and cozy as my café.

The walls exposed brick that I'd whitewashed, the floors the original wood and concrete, stained different shades of gray and cream.

The fabrics were soft and lush, the furniture comfortable and unique.

My best friend Paisley had dubbed it country luxury.

It wasn't large by any stretch, but it was mine, and I loved every square inch of it.

I picked up Kayden's things before I headed for the kitchen. It sat against the far wall of the room, and I'd painted the distressed white cabinets myself and the counters were topped with butcherblock.

I popped onto my toes so I could grab a wineglass from the cupboard then filled it to the brim with merlot.

Kosher, it was not, but since I was drinking alone, I made the rules.

Each night, I gave myself a few moments to unwind.

Heading back into the living room, I plopped onto the plush dark gray couch. I nearly jumped out of my skin and sloshed the wine over the rim when my phone suddenly rang.

A massive grin slid to my face when I saw Paisley's name lighting the screen, and I quickly answered, speaking before she got the chance.

"Oh, you do remember me after all. Someone has been too busy getting herself loved up by their man to remember their bestie even exists." I feigned a pout.

Laughter rippled from the other end of the line. "As if I'd ever forget you, but since you gave me explicit instructions to never call you when I was getting loved up again, it's been hard to fit it in."

My best friend had gone and fallen hard for her new man, Caleb. Caleb was Ryder's cousin who'd been living in Seattle and had bought a giant ranch here on the outskirts of Time River. He was crazy rich, and Paisley had been hired to train his little girl how to ride her horse.

Sparks had flown the moment they'd met each other, even though at first, they'd been mistaken for fiery darts of unmitigated hate.

I guess it was true that sometimes enemies made the best lovers.

It hadn't taken long for it to turn into so much more than that.

"I might love you and Caleb together and all, but I don't need to be present for your sex-capades." I let the tease wind into my words.

She'd tried to play it off that day, answering when I'd called, pretending like she could barely talk and mewling like a cat in heat because she was out working with the horses, but I knew better.

The two of them were insatiable.

Paisley laughed again, though it was throaty and low, even deeper now after the injuries she'd sustained with everything that had gone down at the ranch at the beginning of the summer. "Caleb's a little on the adventurous side, but I can promise you, we aren't going there. I don't share my man."

"Eww," I told her, grinning as I took a sip of my wine. "Don't even make my poor brain go there."

"Well, your poor brain needs to go somewhere and find yourself some action. I know you're sitting over there by yourself in the dark, drinking a giant glass of wine."

I pulled the glass away from my lips, frowning at it in the lapping shadows of the room.

Damn, she totally had me pegged.

"I have plenty of action," I argued. With my hand and vibrator, but sometimes that's all a girl needed. "And sitting here in the dark with my wine is called *relaxing*. You should try it sometime."

"I can tell you what really relaxes you..." She drawled out the innuendo.

"Shut it," I said, fighting the amusement that wanted to come flooding out.

"Fine, fine, I'll quit pestering you. *For now*. But pretty soon, we're going dick-hunting."

I nearly choked on the sip I'd just taken. "Dick-hunting?"

"That's right. Dick-hunting. When one embarks into the wild jungle called dating."

"Eww," I said again. "The visual, Paisley."

"If your response is eww, you've obviously been looking at the wrong ones. Caleb's is drool worthy."

"Stop right there," I said through the snickering that wouldn't stop coming.

Anytime I talked to her, she left me a giggling mess.

"Oh, Dakota, we know you are missing out, my poor, dear friend. It's high time we found someone to love you up. Don't think I haven't noticed you haven't gone out once with a man since I moved back from Arizona."

I blew out a strained breath. "I know. I've just been...*busy*."

It wasn't like I didn't want to find someone, but I guessed I didn't know how to start. How to truly move on the way I'd been trying to do.

How to trust I would find someone who loved me the way I wanted to be.

How to find someone who would *choose me*.

"Sitting on your couch at night alone?" It overflowed with disbelief. A nudging beyond the playfulness.

Soberness took over. "I think I'm almost ready."

I could hear her warring thoughts. Not even she knew about Kayden's father, and the one time she'd asked, I'd flat out told her I didn't want to talk about it. I figured most people thought I'd gotten my heart broken, but the truth was, I'd barely even caught his name.

It was the circumstances that had driven me to it that still lingered like old wounds.

"You know the only thing I want is for you to be happy, and I'd leave you alone about it if I didn't know you really well. And I know you're missing something."

Before I could respond, she cracked, "Like some of the good D."

"Did you actually call because you wanted something?" I tossed the question out like I was actually mad.

She chuckled. "Oh, right yes."

She lowered her voice to keep her words a secret. "I want to plan a big surprise birthday party here at the ranch for Caleb. He's been showering me with so much love and attention, and I want to make sure he knows how much he's loved, too."

She hesitated before she asked, "I was hoping you'd cater it?"

Warmth spread through me. "Like you even have to ask. Of course, I'll do it. It'd be an honor."

"How do I have the bestest bestie in all the land? My Doodle-Boo always has my back."

"Like I'd leave my Paisley-Cakes hanging?"

We'd started with the ridiculous nicknames in second grade and they'd forever stuck, neither of us outgrowing them, even in the time we'd been separated with her living out of state.

Her tone softened. "Seriously, thank you so much. I really want it to be special for him."

"We'll make sure it is. When are you thinking?"

"The third Saturday of next month?"

I glanced around like I actually had a calendar to check. "I think I'm free. I'll get a couple staff on hand to help with service and all of that."

Paisley squealed. "Seriously the best. I cannot wait. I'll stop by soon so we can go over details, if that's okay?"

"Absolutely. Any time."

"You're grade-A amazing, Dakota. Don't you ever forget it."

"How could I when you won't let me?" I teased.

"Crap, Caleb is calling from the other room to come to bed. I better go before he gets suspicious. Thank you again."

"Go on and get yourself some of that deliciousness."

"Don't mind if I do." She suddenly squealed, and I was pretty sure Caleb had sneak attacked her from behind. "Bye, Doodle-Boo. And don't you dare put on one of those true crime podcasts the way you like to do. I don't want you to be having any nightmares."

She barely got it out before the line went dead, and I sat there, grinning at my phone like I was actually looking at my best friend.

She was wild and reckless and fun, and I loved every crazy thing about her.

Silence washed in behind it.

A hint of loneliness that crept into the recesses.

A quiet hum that reminded me I was alone.

I sipped at my wine while I fiddled with my phone, heart a little heavy, then I breathed out a short breath when a text buzzed through.

I fought the flutter in my chest when I saw who it was.

I'm moving on. I'm moving on. I'm moving on.

I had to remind myself of it when he got to acting all concerned, which was really often. But he'd always been concerned, ever since I was a little girl. I needed to remember that was because he would forever look at me like a sister.

Ryder: What's up, Cookie? You get home safe?

I tapped out a quick response, refusing to make it weird. This man was a constant in my life, and I didn't want it to bring me pain any longer.

Me: I did, and a whole lot earlier, thanks to you.

It didn't take long for another text to come through.

Ryder: See, you did want me riding in like the cavalry after all. Admit it.

I could almost see the smirk lighting on his face.

Me: Pssh. I just didn't want to make you feel like a lazy prick. I would have done fine without you.

Ryder: Ouch. Way to stab at a man's ego.

Me: I thought I was feeding your ego by letting you play white knight? Besides, I think your ego is plenty big. I've seen you in action.

It took a second for him to respond.

Ryder: You watching me?

My stomach tightened. Sometimes, I swore he was flirting with me.

Me: Just to keep an eye on you to make sure you're not making a fool out of yourself.

His response was almost instant.

Ryder: Damn, Dakota. You really are stabby tonight. Something have you on edge?

Ugh. If he only knew how many times he'd had me exactly that way.

Me: No edge here. Just telling you like it is. You watch out for me, and I watch out for you 😊

Ryder: That's right. That's what we do.

Another text popped in behind the last.

Ryder: How's that little man?

Me: Sleeping like a rock. After he single-handedly destroyed both mine and my mom's houses, of course.

Ryder: Tiny Tornado.

Affection pulsed. Ryder had always been so sweet to my son. And Kayden adored him, claiming him as Uncle.

Ryder: Listen, I better call it. Just wanted to check in. Sleep well, Cookie.

With the dismissal, I let my phone slump to my lap, almost wanting to say more but knowing I couldn't.

But one thing was for sure.

I couldn't keep pining after him my whole life.

It was time to let go.

Chapter Five

Dakota

There was always a certain energy in my café.

The bustle of people coming and going, the bell dinging over the door, the clatter of dishes and the lilt of voices and laughter.

Wound in it were the scents that floated through the air like temptation—the sweet smell of baked goods, the rich aroma of gourmet coffee and cream, and the savory meals served piping hot.

Sometimes I squeezed my eyes closed with the urge to pinch myself, unable to believe that it'd come to fruition.

Twenty-six, and I owned the busiest restaurant in town, not that it was about obliterating the competition. It was just validation that people wanted what I had to offer.

Time River Market & Café was split into two sections. The front boasted a country store and, just beyond that, was the dining room, bakery, and coffee shop.

I was currently in the store, writing the lunch specials on the chalkboard that sat on a white easel. I kept it situated at the side of the big double doors that opened to the dining area so people would see what we had to offer as they were being led to their tables.

I always used a bunch of different colors of chalk, and my hand swirled across the black surface, weaving the words into an elaborate design.

The bell over the door dinged, the same way it'd already done a thousand times today, but with it came the shift in the air that would forever tug at my spirit.

A scant tightening of awareness.

A dense sensation that whooshed and whispered as it brushed across my flesh.

I already had a bright smile pinned on my face when I shifted to look over my shoulder. Caleb and Ezra came in first, Ryder's cousins who met here for lunch at least once a week.

But it was the man who stepped in behind them that tilted the ground a fraction of an inch.

Setting me off-kilter.

Just barely.

But I always felt the wobble of the earth.

Gunmetal eyes seemed to find me in a flash, like he already knew I was there. The hint of one of those sexy smirks tipped at the edge of his mouth as he lifted his chin at me in a silent hello, then he roughed a tatted hand through his ebony hair as he took in his surroundings.

Midnight in the middle of the day.

Ezra strode my way first, dressed in his sheriff's uniform. The man was a heaping stack of muscle and brawn. His sandy blond hair was cropped short, and his beard was barely more than a five o'clock shadow.

He looked intimidating, but he was as nice as could be.

I'd known him forever considering he was Ryder's cousin and he'd hung out with Ryder and my brother, Cody, through the years.

"Hey, there, Dakota. Are you whipping up something special for us today?"

"As if I would be doing anything else," I told him, giving him a coy curtsy as I waved a hand at the sign like I was offering up a prize.

A low groan emanated from him as his gaze swept over the specials. "A Monte Cristo. How's it you always know exactly what I'm craving?"

"Food *is* my love language," I tossed at him with a grin.

"Which is why we always come running." He wrapped his muscled arms around me in a warm hug. "Good to see you. How have you been?"

"Great," I told him, squeezing him back before I turned to hug Caleb.

"Are you taking care of my bestie?" I filled it with as much teasing accusation as I could muster.

Arrogant satisfaction jumped into every line of his face. "You don't think I wouldn't be, do you? Taking care of her is what I do best."

"You better, I wouldn't want to have to hurt you."

Caleb smiled, all the sharp angles of his face softening as his eyes crinkled at the sides. The man had been so hard and rigid when he'd first shown up in town.

Loving someone looked good on him.

"I won't ever give you a reason to," he promised.

The whole time, I could feel Ryder loitering behind them, so casual as he let his gaze sweep over the shelves situated around the store. The different displays of jewelry and soaps and handmade goods. I tried to showcase as many local artisans as I could. Our community would always be better if we were supporting one another.

Finally, he eased up, and I fought the tremble that shook my insides when he raked his teeth over his bottom lip, his aura hitting me full force.

Warm leather and deep, decadent spice.

"What's going on today, Dakota?" he asked.

"The usual. Keeping people fed."

His attention traveled to the specials, quick to land on the dessert of the day.

Molten Midnight Chocolate Cake.

Did I imagine the twitch of his mouth?

Did he know?

I cleared my throat. "I hope you're hungry."

"Starving," he said.

Funny, it was my stomach that rumbled, standing in his space this way.

I rocked back on my heels like it could put some distance between us. "Then you came to the right place."

"Came to the best place." It was grumbly and low.

My heart kicked.

You are moving on, Dakota. No more getting all swoony and sweaty every time he comes around.

I angled my head to the open doorway while I grabbed them menus. "Let's get you seated then."

They followed me into the dining room.

To the left, booths lined all three walls. Each were high-backed and done in gray wood. Blue and cream-colored checkered cushions made them extra comfy, and I'd adorned the tables with a spray of cream-colored flowers in metal containers.

The middle section was set with long tables, done community style with a bunch of chairs on each side.

I wound them through the mess to an open booth that overlooked Manchester.

Caleb slipped into the booth on the left, and Ezra slid in on the right, moving to the window so Ryder could sit next to him.

Ryder who tapped his long, thick fingers on the tabletop in a mesmerizing rhythm as he slung his long body back in the booth.

Not that I noticed or anything.

Clearing my throat, I tucked a loose strand of hair behind my ear. "What can I get you to drink to get you started?"

"I'll take one of those strawberry iced teas." Ryder said it without hesitation.

"I wasn't even asking you," I teased. "Don't you ever get bored of having the same thing?"

Gunmetal eyes gleamed. "Never."

I got the order for Caleb's coffee and Ezra's regular iced tea, then wound my way back toward the kitchen area.

On this side ran a bar, done in the same gray wood as the booths, one half with six high stools where patrons could sit, and to the left of it was the bakery display case and coffee bar. Behind it were counters and the swinging door that led into the kitchen.

I went behind the bar and got to work on their drinks, taking a quick glance at Beth, my manager on staff today and also one of my best friends. She was leaned into the display case, restocking chocolate chip cookies that had just come out of the oven.

"Do you need anything?" I asked her as I worked.

"Nope," she said. "Think we have everything handled. Food is coming out fast and customers are happy and these cookies smell like heaven. Can't get better than this. I don't know how you do it, but what comes out of your oven is pure magic."

"I need to have something going for me," I teased.

"Oh, you have something going for you, all right. And every day they just get better. Think half the restaurant is hypnotized by the smell. You just keep doing the good work, and I'll take care of the rest. Well, except for your man over there. You go take care of him because I don't think there is anyone else who can do it."

She angled a waggish brow at Ryder's table, her dark eyes gleaming and her red lips pulled into a massive smirk.

I groaned at her. "Don't you even start."

Beth never failed to give me crap about Ryder.

"Don't *you* start. That boy is here every other day, hanging around like a puppy dog, nothing but a mutt begging for *food*."

"Um, yeah, he does come to eat," I drew out.

"Looks to me like you're feeding him the wrong thing."

I followed her line of sight to catch Ryder staring our way before he turned his head back to something Caleb said.

"Hardly." I scoffed it as I focused on organizing their drinks on a tray because what she was insinuating was totally absurd, all while I fought the tingly sensation that billowed across the room.

Picking up the tray, I started around the counter, and she hollered after me, "You keep trying to convince yourself he's not salivating for a taste of that cute butt of yours."

I cringed.

Awesome.

She'd announced it to half the restaurant.

No doubt, someone was currently calling my mom to speculate just who was salivating.

And I wasn't sure my butt could be called *cute*. There was a whole lot of junk in my trunk, but I did have to admit it looked pretty damn good in this dress. The red fabric shifting around my thighs and the v of the neckline dipping between my breasts.

My gaze fixated on the table I was walking toward. The three of them were some of the closest people to me in my life. Still, I always felt like I was chasing down a storm every time I stepped into Ryder's vicinity.

The man his own brand of chaos where he sat there looking both raw and smooth.

I didn't know how it was possible, but he made it look easy.

Stepping up to their table, I passed out their drinks. "Here we go."

A round of thanks went up, and I eased back, doing my best to ignore the energy that forever vibrated from Ryder.

Intense and severe and somehow effortless.

Enigmatic.

Entrancing.

I cleared my throat. "Do you know what you want to eat today?"

"Tell me more about that Monte Cristo," Ryder said, turning the full force of his attention on me.

I fiddled with the end of my ponytail. "Well, I can't take credit for this recipe since it's pretty traditional—ham and swiss stuffed between two pieces of French toast, dipped in batter, and deep fried, then coated in powdered sugar and served with a side of homemade raspberry jam."

Even still, it was freaking delicious. Done my own special way because I'd never serve something mediocre or mundane.

Apparently, Ryder agreed with the philosophy, because he groaned and scrubbed an inked palm over his face. "Fuck me. Sounds so good, Dakota."

I had to hold back the whimper that threatened to escape.

Why did it always have to come out like sex on his lips?

"It seems like you want me to feed you."

So maybe I was going to keep some of those fantasies, and I couldn't help but play off what Beth had said, loving the way those eyes were taking me in like he didn't want to look anywhere else.

He let go of a rough chuckle. "Thinking that's exactly what I want."

Tingles spread, prickles that kissed along my flesh.

Sometimes he made me think...

A menu suddenly slapped down on the table, and I jerked to find Ezra grinning my way. "Hell, yeah, give me one of those, too. I'm not about to pass that up."

"No reason to change a good thing," Caleb agreed.

I gathered their menus then dipped my head. "All right then, three Monte Cristos are on their way."

"Thanks, Dakota."

"Always," I said as I turned to head back to the kitchen to put in their order.

I wasn't exactly sure what it was, but there was something that tripped me up.

Stalled me out.

Something I caught out of the corner of my eye at the very edge of the windows that ran the far side of the building.

A shadow or a shape or a figure.

Disquiet washed through me.

This penetrating awareness that covered me in a sticky film of dread and sent a cold shiver curling down my spine.

One blink later, it was gone.

I blinked more, uncertainty filling me as I stared out the window overlooking a grassy area backed by trees.

Nothing was there.

I shook myself out of it, realizing I had to have been seeing things, making it up, and I wound back through the tables, pushing through the kitchen door to the bustle of activity on the other side.

Paisley was right—I was really letting those true crime podcasts get the best of me.

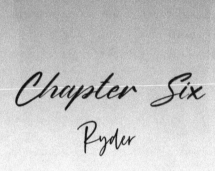

Chapter Six

Ryder

I COULDN'T HELP BUT WATCH DAKOTA WALK ACROSS THE DINING ROOM, the way she weaved between the tables, offering smiles to the customers she recognized as she went.

Red fabric flowed around her hips and swished around her lush thighs, the woman this force that was hard to look away from.

But I hadn't missed the shift in the air. The way she'd stumbled and froze a beat.

But when I'd looked behind me, I couldn't find anything amiss.

I shouldn't worry so much, but I guessed I'd spent so much time in that role, thinking I needed to watch over her, that it came as second nature.

She was more than grown, though. She was strong and fierce and successful, and I needed to remember she could do a whole hell of a lot better without me.

"So, how's it going?" Caleb's voice jerked me out of the trance, and I returned my attention to the table as I took a swig of my iced tea. Swore to God, my mouth nearly exploded with the taste, chunks of fresh strawberries coming up through the straw, the perfect blend of sweet and sour.

Thought that it was the perfect analogy of Dakota. The woman who was all shy blushes then could turn around and knock you flat with the teasing glint in those cinnamon eyes.

"Good," I told him. "Things are going great at work."

It was true.

I'd gotten a ton of legitimate contracts recently. Custom pieces I was proud to create.

A burning need had lit inside me to turn all my focus to that.

To end this sentence.

This penalty.

My mind spinning with possibilities on how to break the bonds.

But I knew what it would take.

It would be the fight of my life.

That I'd be putting it all on the line.

Risking everything.

Likely signing my own death certificate.

But I couldn't go on this way.

Ezra shifted in the booth next to me, the cushion creaking with his large frame. "Nice to hear you've been busy, brother."

"Yeah."

"Good thing. Keeps you out of trouble." He arched his brow as he took a sip of his tea.

If he only knew.

Having a cousin as a sheriff and living the life I'd lived wasn't exactly easy. I always felt like scum, lying to him the way I did.

Hiding.

Pretending.

For years, I'd believed I didn't have another choice, and the only thing I could do was keep him in the dark.

So, I played this role the best that I could.

I was so fucking ready to stop faking.

I jutted my chin at Caleb to get the attention off me. "How about you?"

Caleb grinned, fucker so happy now that Paisley had come into his life that he was a different man. Dude had waltzed around looking like a rich prick for years, wearing suits and a chip on his shoulder.

Now he had on a Henley and a pair of jeans, the edge he'd always worn erased by the woman who'd changed everything.

"Better than would be prudent to discuss at the lunch table." Suggestion filled his voice.

Ezra groaned though he managed to keep a smile on his face. Ezra was still grieving the loss of his wife, but he was finally getting to the point where we could joke around, where we didn't have to tiptoe and worry he would lock down the way he used to.

"Rub it in, asshole," he said, wry amusement tugging into his features.

Caleb lifted his hands in feigned innocence. "I didn't say anything."

"Yeah, but it is written all over your smug face." I pointed at him.

His grin just grew, and he shrugged. "Can't help it."

Then his brow lifted as he angled toward me and lowered his voice, "And it's not like you're not out getting your dick sucked every night of the week."

"I'll have you know I skipped last night." I pitched him a smirk, the distaste of what really had gone down last night burning like acid in my guts.

I hadn't slept at all.

Trying to figure out my angle.

How the fuck I was going to get myself free.

Feet pacing the ground as I'd wrestled through every scenario.

I should have gone and blown off some steam. Found a willing body. Fucked it out of my system. But I'd ended up lying in bed instead, texting Dakota because she was the one woman I couldn't get off my mind.

Then I'd jerked myself to the memory of her tits spilling out of that dress when I'd found her stranded on the side of the road.

Clearly, my willpower sucked.

"The travesty," Caleb taunted.

"While I was at home watching *Minions* for the hundred-thousandth time with my kids." Ezra let go of a self-deprecating chuckle.

He had three adorable kids.

His twins, Owen and Oliver, were four, and he had a little girl named Olivia who was six.

"Hey, man, it's a good fucking movie," I told him. "I don't know what you're complaining about."

Ezra laughed an incredulous sound, and he roughed a hand over his short hair as he sat back and challenged, "And you've seen it?"

Of course, I'd seen it.

"It's one of Kayden's favorites."

"Right." Caleb shared a look with Ezra.

"The fuck is that supposed to mean?" It came out a scoff undercut with a warning.

Knowing exactly where they were going to take this.

Too bad my mind was already there, or maybe my subconscious had made the leap.

Racing out, drawn toward her the second she came out from the kitchen through the swinging door, carrying an order for another table.

I immediately looked her way.

She might have owned the place, but she never hesitated to jump in, to get her hands dirty, in the middle of every facet of her restaurant.

My attention got stuck there—on her face that lit up in one of her earthshattering smiles, those plump lips coated in a shiny, glossy pink as she laughed at something a customer said.

Pink hitting her cheeks.

No doubt, she was getting a compliment, the way both humbleness and pride radiated from her.

She was facing me, so this time, I had the vantage of the front of that red dress. Her tits were pressed up, cleavage barely exposed at the neckline that tipped down. Hair in one of those high ponytails she loved to torment me with.

My stomach twisted, and I had to force myself to look away.

Too bad my gaze tangled with Caleb's when I did.

He smirked. "As you were saying…"

My head shook, voice low. "Dakota and I are just friends. Hell, she's like a fucking sister to me."

"That's some kind of fucked up *sisterly* relationship you have then." Pure insinuation rolled out of Ezra.

I sent him a glare. "You don't know what you're talking about."

Disbelief filled his expression. "Dude, I could literally hear your heart taking off at a sprint the second she came out the door." His voice twisted with the prodding. "Tell me you weren't just thinking about spinning her around, pressing her over the counter, and hiking that dress up around her waist so you could get to the sweetness underneath."

My teeth ground, visions of it assaulting my mind. "I don't appreciate you talking about Dakota like that."

The words were stones.

Ezra's mouth split in triumph. "Exactly my point."

"Just because I'm protective of her doesn't mean I want her."

"So, you wouldn't mind me going for her?" he pushed.

Unease spiraled through my senses. It was exactly what I should want. For her to be with someone good.

A nice guy.

Someone who was stable and honest and had a fucking future that he could offer.

A guy someone like me could only hope to be.

Too bad I could hardly stomach the thought of him with her.

"You want her?" I shrugged like the thought of it didn't make me want to puke. "Go for it."

Laughing, he clapped me on the shoulder, squeezing tight and shaking me. "You are so full of shit, Ryder. You're literally about to levitate off your seat, head spinning around. Demon-possessed. I'm actually scared."

Caleb let go of a chuckle. "You should be terrified, Ezra. Turn your back, and you're bound to wind up missing tonight. Fucker's going to have you buried in a shallow grave for even thinking about going after his girl."

"And we're blood," Ezra drew out, the razzing completely at my expense. "You wound me, Ryder."

I shook my head, fighting a grin that didn't know whether to be frustrated or amused. "Just care about her, okay? And she's Cody's little sister, so let's all have a little respect, yeah? It's him you have to worry about. You look at his sister wrong, and it's not going to turn out pretty."

Caleb and Ezra were sharing a glance again, not buying for a second the shit I was tossing out.

Fuckers.

But I couldn't give any more of my attention to that because I felt her coming.

A windstorm that whipped through the room, stealing the breath from my lungs when she returned, this time with our food.

"Three Monte Cristos for my favorite customers." She set a plate in front of each of us, and I wasn't entirely sure of the reason my stomach twisted in a needy knot.

If it was because I had the urge to reach out and touch her from under the table, glide my hand up the side of her leg to get under that skirt.

Or if it was because I was punched in the face with the mouthwatering scent.

Warm sugar and pure sweetness.

I wasn't the only one, though, because both Ezra and Caleb moaned.

"Good God, woman, what are you trying to do to me?" Ezra said as he drove a fork into the deep-fried deliciousness. It came up steaming, melted cheese and gooey jam.

I took a bite, too, not even caring that it was so hot it nearly seared my tongue.

"Good?" she asked, more of that humbleness riding free.

"Best thing I've ever tasted." That was from Ezra.

A giggle escaped from her, and she shook her head. "You say that every time you come in here."

"That's because it's true, each time better than the last."

"The pressure," she deadpanned.

I turned my eyes up to hers. "You've got nothing to worry about, Dakota. Not one damned thing."

⌒✲⌒

Twenty minutes later, I was swiping a napkin over my mouth and slumping back in the booth.

Knocked the fuck out from everything that was Dakota Cooper.

My stomach overfull, but I couldn't help but indulge in whatever she fed me considering I could never take a bite of what I was really hungry for.

She cleared our plates, stacking them high in one hand, before she pulled the bill from her pocket. She set it facedown in front of me before she grazed a gentle brush of those fingers across my shoulder.

Sparks lit.

A faint glimmer.

A glow of what could never be.

"You guys have a great day," she said, cinnamon eyes jumping around to land on each of us.

"Bye, Dakota. See you soon," Caleb and Ezra both said.

I turned over the slip, pulse catching when I read what was on the other side, her swirly handwriting woven deep into the paper.

I shouldn't be surprised. Shouldn't take it as something it was not.

But it never failed to stab me in the guts.

Love is on the house.

Chapter Seven

Dakota

"WHAT DO YOU THINK YOU'RE DOING?"

I didn't whirl around or gasp with the gravelly voice that hit me from behind. Why, when I already knew he was there? That dark intensity wisping through the air and curling over me like a blanket.

Both comfort and something so utterly uncomfortable I wasn't sure I could ever make sense of it.

I already knew he'd come, the way he always did, so I chucked him a saucy grin from over my shoulder where I was bent over the front of my desk, my laptop shifted around so I could look up a sales order to check for when it was scheduled for delivery.

"Working," I told him, and I tried not to get hung up on the way he had a shoulder leaned against the jamb of my office door, every sinewy inch of him cocked in an easy casualness that still looked like you might get electrocuted if you got too close.

His edges so sharp they could cut with a glance.

Not that or the way his gaze seemed to snap up from where it'd been locked on my backside. I just hoped my dress wasn't hiked up so high that my underwear was showing.

He scoffed, stuffing those tatted hands into the pockets of his jeans. "You have to stop doing that." It grated from those plush lips.

"And what would that be?" I asked, shifting around and propping myself against the wood of my desk.

He pushed off, coming closer, the ground doing that trembling thing as he took a step my direction, then another until he was right in front of me.

Towering tall.

Sweet severity dripped from every inch of his flesh.

"You know exactly what I'm talking about," he grumbled, though there was a softness to it. "Thinking you have to comp my meal every time I come in."

My head barely shook. "Why wouldn't I?"

Something flashed through that gunmetal gaze.

Something stark.

Potent.

"We are like family," I rushed to clarify, holding back the automatic response that I really wanted to give.

The truth that this restaurant wouldn't exist without him.

But every time I brought up the money, he got angry and insisted it was mine.

A gift.

But there was no way I wasn't paying him back. It just didn't feel right. I was getting close to being able to.

He exhaled a short breath, and he angled in closer, his whispered words breezing across my face. "Yeah, we are. But that doesn't mean you need to be tossing out what you have to offer for free. You worked hard for this place, and I want to support it." He hesitated for a beat before he muttered, "I want to support you."

Did he have any idea how much he'd already done that?

That I could never ask him for more?

"And maybe I just like feeding you." Somehow my voice had gone choppy where I was pinned to my desk with an inch separating us, shallow as I stared at him as he gazed down at me.

His gaze drifted, landing on the metal box I kept on my desk. My nickname was etched on the lid, and I wondered if it made me pathetic that it was my most prized possession, every recipe I'd ever created tucked inside like a treasure.

"You've always liked feeding me, haven't you? Taking care of me?"

"I thought that's what we do for each other." It came out a rasp.

A breath.

Air that stirred and danced.

An entrancing vapor that I'd gotten sucked into.

I screeched when another voice came from out of nowhere.

"Hey."

Caught off guard, I fumbled and gasped, flustered as I tried to push out from under Ryder while angling far enough around him to find my brother standing in the doorway to my office.

Ryder peeled himself back, totally unaffected, so cool as he shifted to face my brother while I fidgeted as if I'd been caught doing something salacious.

But I was pretty sure mine and Ryder's versions of *salacious* were entirely different.

Cody had both hands pressed to either side of the doorway and was leaning in. My brother was 6'2", wide and thick, wearing worn jeans and work boots and a thin button-up flannel. His hair was short and the same color as mine, a full beard on his face.

"Hey, man. What's up?" Ryder asked him, crossing his arms over his chest while I clung to the edge of my desk, worried my knees might not be strong enough to keep me upright if I let go.

Especially when my brother's gaze jumped between us, narrowed and full of speculation.

I didn't know what he thought he needed to be worried about.

Just because my mind kept dreaming it up didn't mean there'd ever been anything going on between us.

Cody must have realized it, too, because he grinned at Ryder. "Was just grabbing a to-go order and wanted to say hi to my sister. Didn't know you were here."

"Yeah, had lunch with the cousins," Ryder said. "I was telling Dakota goodbye before I head out."

I finally gathered myself enough that I could pry myself from the desk. "Hey, Cody. How's it going?"

A full smile climbed to his mouth. "You know how it's going. Got word it was Monte Cristo Day, which we all know really means Best Day Ever, and I came running."

I couldn't stop the affection-filled giggle. "It means that much to you, huh?"

He shrugged, the man nothing but a burly brute. "Sure does. Because my baby sister loves me and knows her Monte Cristos are literally the sustenance of life. I was about to die, it's been so long since I've had one."

So yeah, I had a thing about making my family's favorites.

It was the way I expressed how I truly felt about them.

The way I showed them my love.

I eased around Ryder, ignoring the buzz in the air, the vestiges of his close proximity still flickering across my flesh as I moved to my brother.

I popped up on my toes and pressed a kiss to his cheek. "You know I only bring them back around for you."

"That's right."

"Excuse me, I like me a good Monte Cristo, too." Ryder's playful voice hit me from behind.

Cody's grin turned smug. "That's because you don't count, my friend. Hell, this place wouldn't even exist if it weren't for me. Who was it that Dakota continually baked for when she was a little girl, testing her recipes out on? Who encouraged her to step out and take the chance and make it happen when she got older? Who tells her every damned day she's the best baker who ever lived?"

I bit down on my lip.

Ryder, Cody. It had always been Ryder.

Because Cody might have always supported me, but it was Ryder who'd given me the courage to chase my dreams.

Chapter Eight

Dakota

Six Years Old

DAKOTA STOOD ON A STOOL AT THE KITCHEN COUNTER NEXT TO her momma. A big silver mixing bowl was in front of them, and Dakota's momma helped her hold up the big bag of flour so she could pour it into the measuring cup.

Her arms strained from the weight, but Dakota knew she was big and strong, and she totally could do it. Her tongue poked out the side of her mouth as she concentrated. "All the way to the two, right?"

"That's right."

When it hit the line, Dakota grinned and let go of the bag. "There."

Soft laughter rippled from her momma.

Dakota loved that sound.

It was warm and made her feel as squishy and comfortable as it did when she snuggled up in her bed.

Her momma said since she was six, she was finally old enough to cook, even though she was constantly telling her to be careful so she didn't burn herself.

Dakota had only done it once, and she thought she'd learned her lesson and she wasn't ever gonna do it again.

"Okay, now dump it into the bowl and then we crack two eggs on top."

Dakota picked up the measuring cup with two hands and dumped the flour into a bowl that already had a bunch of sugar inside. She giggled when a plume of white dusted the air. "We're making a cloud."

More gentle laughter touched her ears. "Baking isn't usually the cleanest activity in the world, but you can be sure it's the yummiest."

"And yummy is the best."

"That's right."

Her momma handed her an egg, and she wrapped her hand around Dakota's, guiding her to gently tap it against the edge of the metal bowl. "Okay, real gentle, now."

It cracked open and the yellow yolk and gooey clear stuff oozed out onto the flour. They did the same with the second, then added chocolate chips, butter, and oil.

"I get to mix it now?" Mixing was her favorite part. Other than eating it at the end, of course.

"Yep. Put the mixer in and start it really slow."

Concentrating, Dakota put her finger on the button, and she carefully moved it to the right speed like her momma had taught her to do. It whirred to life, and the metal arms clanged against the metal bowl.

"Okay, you can turn it up faster now."

Dakota did as she was instructed, and she watched the ingredients whip together, becoming a brown dough.

They used a spoon to make little balls, lining them in three rows on the sheet. Then her momma carried it to the oven since Dakota wasn't allowed to do that part yet. "In they go. Ten minutes, and they'll be baked to perfection."

Then her momma shut the door and set the timer on the clock.

"Do you think I did a good job?" Dakota asked, dusting off her hands.

Her momma nudged Dakota's chin with her index finger, sending her a smile. "I think you did a great job."

Excitement widened Dakota's eyes. "Like I'm the best baker in the world?"

A quiet chuckle rolled from her momma, and she ran a tender hand through Dakota's hair. "Well, I would say you are pretty dang close. Just remember to always do it with love, and you can't go wrong. It will always be delicious."

When the timer dinged, her momma used the mitts to pull the cookies out, and she set them on the counter to cool. Once they were, she let Dakota use a spatula to put them on a plate.

They smelled so, so good, and it made Dakota's tummy rumble.

A minute later, the sliding glass door to the backyard whipped open, and Cody and Ryder came running in from where they'd been kicking the soccer ball on the lawn out back. Shoes banging on the floor and their arms and legs flailing as they fought each other to make it in first.

Ryder was Cody's best friend, and he was over a whole lot.

"Wild boys," her momma tsked, like the words might be mad but her voice was too soft for that. "You two settle down while you're in the house. You're liable to tear the whole thing down, and you know I don't have the time to deal with any of that."

Cody and Ryder both straightened, though Cody gave his friend a shove from the side at the same second Ryder was saying, "Sorry, Ms. Cooper."

Then Cody's friend inhaled a big breath and his chest puffed out. "Did someone make chocolate chip cookies?"

He pushed his shaggy black hair from his eyes. Eyes that were the same color as the night went wide when he saw the plate of them.

"Can I have some?" he asked their momma.

"You'll have to ask Dakota. She's the one who baked them." Dakota's mother's smile was crooked when she looked between them.

"Can I have one, Dakota? They smell better than anything I've ever smelled before."

Dakota's chest filled with pride, something like feathers that tickled in her heart and floated in her belly. Her shoulders went up to her ears. "I made 'em for you. You like the chocolates the best."

He smiled even bigger.

"Well, go on then," her momma said. "How about some milk to wash it down?"

"Yes, please," Ryder said right away.

He and Cody grabbed two cookies each.

Cody gobbled his down in a single bite.

Ryder took his to the table and sat down, slowly eating each one, like he wanted the taste of them to last forever.

Dakota couldn't help but watch.

"Was it good?" she finally asked because they needed to be if she was going to be the best baker in the world.

Ryder grinned with his big red lips. "That was my favorite thing I ever ate."

Chapter Nine

Dakota

MY EYES BLINKED OPEN TO THE LAPPING DARKNESS OF MY ROOM. It might have been peaceful, but instantly, my ears were attuned to what had pulled me from sleep. A sense that there was something out of place in the quiet.

My first thought was it was my little man waking in the middle of the night.

We'd been working hard on getting him to sleep in his own room, but there were times when he woke, whimpering and crying for me.

But tonight, a bulky hedge of silence echoed back.

So thick I tasted it.

A sour lump of dread.

It clung to the darkness as if it were its own entity, dripping from the walls and crawling across the floor.

My skin slicked with sweat, and my flesh pricked with those goosebumps you get when you're being watched.

I didn't know what it was. How sometimes you just knew, instincts kicking in that something wasn't quite right.

The energy off and hinting at something sinister.

Unease stirred through my senses as I strained to listen, keeping as quiet as I could as I eased from my bed. I grabbed my phone from where it was charging on my nightstand and tiptoed across the room.

I pressed my ear to my bedroom door that I'd left open an inch.

The only thing I heard was the wind as it rustled through the trees, a long branch scraping at the glass outside my window. That and the lulled vacancy of the night that whispered through the atmosphere. The chirp of crickets and the random bark of a dog from somewhere in the distance.

Still, a slow slide of chills crept down my spine like the melting of ice, sinking to the bone.

But I couldn't remain frozen in it.

I edged out of my room and ran on my tiptoes down the short hall to Kayden's on the right.

My child was the only concern.

I slipped through the crack in his door. The darkness was cut by the nightlight bear that glowed from his crib, and I quickly scanned his room to make sure everything in there was okay.

Kayden was face down and fast asleep with his arm wrapped around the glowing bear, his little lips pursing with each breath as he dreamed whatever beautiful dream was in his head.

Relief hit me, and I turned to quickly shut his door and lock it. I leaned against the wood, taking in several breaths to process what to do.

At war with it being nothing but also unable to shake the feeling that something had been there.

I was also fully aware of how easy it was to convince yourself of the boogeyman in the middle of the night.

I could go and investigate things myself, but I didn't want to leave Kayden's side, and I sure wouldn't take him downstairs if there was a chance there could be danger.

There probably wasn't. Most likely it was a false alarm. My mind conjuring a bunch of terrible scenarios there was little chance it would turn out to be.

But still, I wouldn't take the risk.

I contemplated, turning the options over in my head.

I could call my brother, but he lived twenty minutes out of town.

And if I called Ezra, he'd be liable to send over a cruiser or two.

Definitely not necessary.

The solution landed directly on Ryder.

Ryder who lived super close.

His house was only a mile away.

He was the obvious choice even though there was a part of me that hesitated. The last thing I wanted to do was wake him in the middle of the night for no reason.

Or worse, interrupt something that I sure as heck didn't want to interrupt.

But I bit back the worries because what really mattered was making sure that Kayden was safe, that our home was secure without sending the local law enforcement on a wild goose chase.

I made the call, and my stomach did summersaults as I waited for him to answer.

It took him to the second ring, his voice groggy with sleep, though there was no missing the concern embedded in the roughness. "Dakota?"

"Hey, Ryder," I whispered. "I'm so sorry to wake you."

"It's fine." I could hear shuffling on the other end of the line, and I pictured him sitting up and raking one of those hands through his hair that was assuredly a mess. "What's going on?"

The words started to form on my tongue when my entire being froze.

Held in the bang that thudded downstairs.

I whipped around to face the door, heart hammering in my chest, so loud I was sure Ryder could hear it.

"Dakota, tell me what's happening."

His demand cut into the anxiety that surged, my response dipping so low I wasn't sure he'd be able to make out what I said. "I don't know what it is, but something woke me up, and I just heard whatever it was again. It's probably nothing, but I didn't want to take the chance."

"Where is it coming from?"

"Downstairs. A banging of wood or something. It's probably nothing, but I just...got a weird feeling."

A harsh sound left him at that. "Where are you right now?"

"Locked in Kayden's room."

"Good. Stay there. I'm on my way."

Air heaved from my nose, relief and this worry that wouldn't let me go. "Be careful, okay?"

I would never forgive myself if I dragged him into danger.

"Don't even give me a thought, Cookie."

As if he didn't possess most of them as it was.

The line went dead, and a sigh pilfered out before I began to pace, waiting for…anything. Another bang or for some creep to go hacking at the wood of the door with a butcher's knife.

And I really hoped the last was just a figment. Before I'd gone to sleep, kept company by my overflowing glass of wine, I had listened to a particularly horrific story of a poor woman who'd moved out into the middle of nowhere to start her own farm, all by herself, and her deranged neighbor had done just that before he'd taken that knife to her.

But that was out in the middle of nowhere.

And this was…here.

In my adorable house.

In Time River where it was safe.

And I was pretty sure any craziness this town could contain had already been used up by what Paisley, Caleb, and Evelyn had gone through at the beginning of the summer.

Still, I shivered, unable to settle, relaxing only a fraction when headlights brightened against Kayden's window, and I heard the grumble of an engine pull up to the front of the house. I could tell by the distinct sound of it that Ryder had driven over in his car.

Or maybe I just noticed everything about him.

Recognized him.

The pieces of who he was entrenched in my psyche.

His presence thick.

Powerful as it curled through the atmosphere.

The headlights cut out, and I rushed for the window, pulling back the drape to find him coming through the gate.

A silhouette beneath the star-studded heavens. His body lithe and smooth, slinking in like he was a predator on the hunt.

A slip of midnight moving through the darkness.

My heart panged at my ribs as he eased down the walkway. I couldn't make out his features, but he moved slowly.

Carefully.

With purpose.

A moment later, he disappeared under the awning of my porch.

The second he was gone, I moved back to the door, pressed my ear to the wood, and craned to listen.

I sensed him stronger then, his footsteps heavy as he moved around downstairs, and I took a measure of comfort in the fact they were steady, no commotion or sudden attack coming from out of nowhere.

My pulse thudded a little harder as his footsteps echoed up the stairs, and a second later there was a light tapping at the door. "Dakota, it's me. Open up."

Breathing out a sigh, I turned the lock and opened the door.

I hated the way my breath left me on an audible rush.

A heave of relief.

The man stood there in tight black jeans and a black undershirt. Black hair a wild mess. No shoes on his feet because he didn't take the time for that.

Was it wrong my spirit fluttered at the fact? That he'd come running for us?

But it was his gunmetal eyes filled with a worry I couldn't quite process that sent a brick of trepidation sinking to the pit of my stomach.

"Did you find anything?" I whispered.

Ryder peered in over my shoulder, checking on my son, as if he needed to reassure himself that he was safe. Then he returned his attention to me, a sigh pilfering from between his full lips, keeping his voice lowered so he didn't disturb Kayden. "The sound you heard was the front door banging open against the interior wall."

A frown pulled to my brow. "I'm positive I locked it before I came upstairs."

I mean, I'd locked it the second I'd come inside then had double checked it before I'd come up to go to sleep.

I was positive, positive.

Disquiet pulled through his expression. "Looks to me like someone fucked with the lock."

Alarm pulsed, and that frown was pulling deeper, in confusion and disbelief. "Are you sure?"

"Yeah, Dakota, I'm sure. Something like that doesn't happen by accident. But whoever it was is long gone."

Fear sped through my senses, and I looked back at Kayden, a knot so thick in my throat I was having a hard time breathing. "I can't believe this."

Ryder's words pulled me back to him. "I'm going to give Ezra a call to get someone out here to check on things, but not until I get you two out of here."

That time my furrow dug so deep I was pretty sure I was seeing double. "Excuse me?"

"Getting you out of here…taking you to my place."

"I don't think that's necessary, Ryder."

He stepped forward, towering over me like a dark storm, that mayhem I could always feel vibrating beneath the surface surging through the room and ricocheting from the walls. "It's very necessary, Dakota. You think I'm going to leave you here knowing some asshole might have been trying to get into your place? Not going to fucking happen."

"We're not your responsibility."

"Yet I'm the one who's here." His words were close to a growl, sharp as they raked over me.

Chills lifted, and I fiddled with my phone like it was an 8-Ball and would spit out the proper answer on how to handle this.

"Aren't we overreacting a little bit? I mean, this has to be a false alarm, right? It's probably Mr. Chainfeld next door, thinking he was locked out of his place and needed to break in."

The poor old guy had started getting disoriented lately, and I'd had to call his wife from the restaurant the other day when he'd gotten distressed over his bill after Beth had asked for his credit card to pay for it. He'd started shouting that she was trying to rob him.

Because I couldn't stomach the alternative.

That it might actually be dangerous to stay here.

Nerves rattled, and I inhaled a shaky breath.

"Not taking that chance, Dakota. Not with you, and not with your son. Of course, I could always take you to your brother's if you'd prefer."

Something wry infiltrated that.

"No." It shot out in a bolt of horror. I mean, not that I didn't love my brother, but that was not going to work out. Cody might have good intentions, but he drove me insane with his overbearing ways. He'd be so far up my ass about every little thing that I would go nuts.

I definitely didn't want him to catch wind of this.

Not until we knew for sure.

But staying with Ryder? There had to be a better solution.

I wasn't sure I could handle that. Being in his space.

Close quarters.

Watching him do his thing.

It was bad enough to have to witness it when we were out, but it would be so much harder with it paraded right in front of me.

"Then let's get your things." He gruffed it like it was a done deal, not waiting for a response before he angled around me, going right to Kayden's dressing table where he started tossing a bunch of things into his diaper bag.

It took me a second to wrap my head around it, and I moved for him, reaching out to touch his forearm to stop him. "This is a bad idea, Ryder."

He whirled around, and shock spiraled through me when he suddenly had me by the jaw, fingers soft but sure before his hand slid up to my cheek.

His hot palm burned into my flesh.

My stomach tipped onto the floor.

What the hell was he doing?

My feet had turned to putty as he stared down at me. "Call it what you want, Dakota, but I'm not leaving here without you and your son." The pad of his thumb traced along the hollow of my eye. "I won't take that risk."

I blinked at him, hardly able to press out the question. "Do you really think we're in danger?"

His hand tightened on my face, that gaze darkening and deepening, swilling with something harsh and severe. "I'm not sure, Dakota, but if you are? I promise I will take care of you. Protect you."

"Why?"

"Because protecting you is what I was created to do."

I swallowed around the jagged rocks that littered my throat. I had to set aside the questions and worries. Set aside the desperate need to ask him what he meant when he claimed things like that.

None of that mattered right then.

Bottom line, I couldn't take that risk with my son, either.

And it wasn't like this was forever. It was just for the night. Ezra would check things out and find it was all good, tell me there was nothing to worry about, and I'd be right back home.

One night.

It wasn't like I hadn't spent the night under the same roof as Ryder before.

But it'd been a long, long time ago, and it'd always been wrought with that crush that had made me feel like I couldn't breathe, like the walls had closed in.

Made me toss, awake but never fully alive.

Wanting with a need that would never be met.

I forced a big smile to my face. "Fine. But know Kayden is going to destroy your house."

Ryder chuckled. Low and deep and dark, and still, the man somehow made it seem easy and light. "You think I'm afraid of a two-year-old?"

Softness filled his gaze, but there was also something deeper. Something that spoke of a hidden fear that loitered in the depths.

"Are you sure it's not a bother?" I asked.

"Like I said, taking care of you is what I was meant to do, Dakota."

Confusion bound, and I couldn't get free of the snare of those eyes that were watching me.

I had to refuse it. Not allow my head to go tripping into fanciful things.

It'd hurt too damn much when I'd learned Ryder would never love me back. Not the way I'd wanted him to.

So, I found the will that I'd come to find then, the strength, and I pulled back up some of those walls that sometimes threatened to slip, remembering that Ryder would never be anything more than a friend.

A friend that growled, "Now pack your things before I do it for you."

Chapter Ten

Dakota

TWENTY MINUTES LATER, I WAS PULLING OUT OF MY DRIVEWAY that wound around the side of the café that dumped into its parking lot. Ryder followed close behind, his headlights covering us as we eased out onto the main road in the dead of night.

Kayden had barely stirred when I'd picked him up to carry him downstairs and buckled him into his car seat in the back of my car.

Ezra was on his way. He'd insisted he would come himself, along with one of the other deputies on duty.

I made them both swear not to tell my brother or the rest of my family until we were certain of things.

I didn't want them freaking out for no reason.

I glanced in the rearview mirror.

Appreciation washed over me.

Once I'd let the panic subside, I realized how lucky I was to have an incredible group of people surround me when I needed it.

Ones who supported.

Without question or reservation.

People who truly cared and would drop everything and come running.

Not everyone had that.

It was the whole point of family, wasn't it?

And I guessed I had to admit this was Ryder offering his own personal strength.

His own type of dedication.

Swooping in. Forever the protector. The one who'd step in front of a car spinning out of control to push their loved one out of the way.

The one who'd fight if it came down to it.

Oh, and Ryder would definitely fight.

He might come off as easygoing, but I'd seen him come unhinged a time or two.

The scraps he and Cody had gotten involved in when someone had said the wrong thing or acted the wrong way.

The aggression that had taken over a year ago when some douchebag had gotten too friendly with me at the bar and wouldn't listen after I'd told him to keep his hands to himself.

My stomach tightened when I thought back to what he'd done when I was nineteen. The turbulence of his assault and the aftermath of what he'd left behind.

No, Ryder was not to be toyed with, which I guessed was part of the reason I'd called him in the first place.

It was the rest of this that was difficult, making the two quick turns required to get to his house and pulling into the driveway.

I couldn't shake the sense that I was traveling into forbidden terrain.

Rocky, unstable ground.

The neighborhood was completely quiet at this time of night. The windows blackened. A calm so intense you could almost see it hovering over the roofs.

His neighborhood was in an older area in Time River. Some houses were large estates and others were smaller, though each sat on two acre lots.

Most had been renovated, their values skyrocketing, though there were still a couple that were run-down and gave off a creepy vibe, especially at two in the morning.

Ryder's was smaller, though fully redone, as quaint and gorgeous as could be. White and two-story with a big, elevated porch out front.

It had been his childhood home, where he'd grown up, just him and his mother.

It made my heart soar that he'd been able to buy it back once he'd had the means.

Knew what it meant to him.

He was the one who'd had the remodel done, bringing it back to life when it'd once rang with death.

Ryder pulled in directly behind me, boxing me in, and I exhaled a shaky breath.

I could handle this.

It wasn't any different than hanging out with him at Mack's or at my brother's or at my mom's. Or any of the times he'd come by my house to help with things, or when I'd pop over here to drop off some special recipe I'd made.

It was totally, completely the same.

I didn't know why I was making such a big deal about it.

I worked at convincing myself of that while I climbed from my car. Ryder was already there, striding up to the back passenger door and opening it.

I stalled out for a fraction of a beat.

This dark, casual mayhem that stirred the air and sent it skittering across my flesh.

Midnight.

He dipped in, unbuckled Kayden, and pulled him into his tattooed arms.

God, why did a man snuggling a baby have to look so good?

But even contemplating that was dangerous, so I started for the tailgate to grab our things. Only Ryder snagged me by the wrist as I started to pass. "Leave it. I'll get everything once we get you settled inside."

"I'm not incapable of carrying in a few bags, Ryder."

He smirked one of those smirks that danced through my insides.

"Clearly. But why would you go and do that when I'm here to do it? Use me up, Dakota."

He had the audacity to wink.

"You're asking for it." I forced lightness into my voice as I yanked a little to free myself from his hold. The connection was just too much. "I'm going to get used to this pampering, and you're never going to get rid of me. Lugging around that kid is getting tough. He's heavy."

I rambled it as I turned to move up the walkway that wound around the front of the house to the five steps that led to the porch.

Ryder followed close behind.

That energy vibrated.

Entrancing.

Hypnotic.

Our footsteps thudded softly across the planks.

Ryder edged around me when we got to the door, and he held Kayden in one arm while he worked the key into the lock with the other. Wrangling all of that, he still managed to glance back at me with that sly expression on his face. "Who said I wanted to get rid of you?"

Doing my best not to choke on his words, I scoffed out a tease, giving into the playfulness he seemed to have gotten lost in as he held the door open for me to enter.

"I'll give you until tomorrow morning for you to be hauling us back to my place and dumping us on the doorstep. He looks harmless now..." I drew out.

I cast a soft glance at Kayden held in the safety of the man's arms as I stepped passed them.

Affection inflated my chest.

Chuckling, Ryder rubbed his hand over my son's back. "You act like I don't know a thing about this tiny tornado. Think I can handle it."

"You are begging for trouble."

Okay, the one who was really begging for trouble was me.

"Guess I am, aren't I?" The mumble was so quiet I wasn't sure if I imagined it, and Ryder angled around me and headed for the stairs. "Come on. Let's get you two settled so you can get some rest."

He bounded upstairs and I followed. His room was on the left, and two additional bedrooms were down the hall to the right. Ducking into the first one, he flipped on the light. "Why don't we set you both up in here tonight, and tomorrow we'll get Kayden situated in the room next door. I don't want him to freak out when he wakes up in an unfamiliar place."

My stomach twisted with an onslaught of too many things.

The fact that he was always so thoughtful. I mean, what man would think of that?

It got all knotted with the fact that Ryder was talking like we were going to be here for a bit.

"We won't be staying more than one night, Ryder, so this is great, thank you."

He laid Kayden down in the middle of the massive bed that took up half the room. The covers were a satiny sheen of black. Not surprising since that's what most of his house was decorated in.

Then the ground shook when he shifted around, tall and dark as he erased the space between us, and he backed me into the wall. Eyes flashed as he angled down, words harsh and jagged. "You'll stay here as long as needed, Dakota. Until we know you're safe, and I won't let you go a second before that."

⤖

I'd probably only been asleep for an hour when I woke, needing to pee. The room was still hedged in darkness, the only light a wedge of it slanting through a gap in the drapes that covered the window. I tossed off the covers and stepped onto the worn, wooden floor.

Kayden was asleep in the portable playpen we'd brought, and I leaned over it to check on him. He was face down the way he loved to sleep, his glowing bear tucked under his arm, his back rising and falling with each steady breath.

Relief left me on a sigh, the dregs of the fear I'd felt earlier at home easing more.

As long as he was comfortable and safe, then I couldn't complain.

Careful not to wake him, I tiptoed the rest of the way across the room on bare feet, slipping out and into the short hall where I edged toward the bathroom that sat between Ryder's room and the guest rooms.

With how old the house was, I guessed Ryder was lucky that he even had a bathroom upstairs.

I kept my footsteps quiet as I crept for it, then I yipped when the door suddenly flew open.

Bright, blinding light blazed out from the opening and cut into the duskiness where I stood chained to the spot.

Or maybe I was just dumbstruck by the sight.

Ryder had been on his way out, and he halted in the doorway, standing there in only a pair of gray sweatpants, black hair wild and his chest bare.

So tall and imposing and perfect that the breath fled from my lungs.

It left my chest feeling empty and achy.

There was nothing I could do. My eyes roved. Drinking in every inch of him.

It wasn't like I'd never seen him without a shirt before.

It didn't matter.

Every time it knocked me upside the head.

Made me stupid.

Mouth watering, and my wayward heart hammering a thousand errant beats.

I barely even registered his gruff, "Dakota."

I was too busy ogling the mantrap in front of me.

Literally, I couldn't tear my gaze away.

His skin was taut and tanned a golden brown, all his corded muscle bristling with that power that vibrated beneath his cool exterior.

Though tonight, there was nothing cool about him.

He was heat.

Flames.

A freaking fire that would consume me in a beat.

A dark tower that loomed in the doorway.

His chest and shoulders an expanse of strength, wide and coarse and thick. Pecs hard and his abdomen cut in a severe line. A tease of his hip bones were exposed over the top of his waistband, and God, there was no stopping myself from peeking at the outline that pressed beneath the fabric of his sweats.

But what I could stare at for days were the designs that covered almost every inch of him.

He'd gotten them throughout the years, as if he'd used the designs as an album of his history.

Symbolic.

Graphic.

Explicit.

A tree grew up his right shoulder, the spindly branches stretching out to cover his right pec. A crow sat on one of the branches, ready to take flight, though there was a chain around its leg, keeping it from flying.

On the opposite shoulder was the face of his mother. A stamp of grief. The first one he'd ever gotten when his mother had passed when he was sixteen.

So much pain surrounded it. Her death so horrible. A wound that would never heal.

My eyes traced and foraged through the intricate designs interwoven with nonsensical things.

Hearts and skulls hidden in vines.

A scroll ran up his left ribs.

Meet me in the place of the forgotten.

And I wondered so many times if that's the way he felt. As if he'd been forgotten. Left behind.

It made me freaking blush that he had a chocolate chip cookie tattooed just above his right hip.

But what always reminded me of my place was what sat in the center of his chest.

It was a broken clock.

Distorted and warped.

The bottom of it was crumbling, and a bleeding human heart had fallen through the hole. A hand held it up, crushing it while it struggled to beat.

My throat nearly closed off as I looked at where its fractured hands were forever stuck at five o' four.

A moment in time that had marked him.

Scarred him.

Destroyed him.

A time that had crushed me, too, though I doubted he truly knew how deeply it had.

It was when I'd realized that I was just a foolish girl chasing down a fantasy.

Shame pressed down on my chest.

How damned selfish to make his loss about me.

Forcing myself out of the stupor, I cleared my throat and shifted on my bare feet, realizing I'd been staring at him awestruck for God knew how long.

"Hey," I finally croaked.

"Did I wake you?" It was a rough, groggy grumble, like he'd wandered in here still half asleep.

"No. I just needed to pee."

"Sorry there aren't two bathrooms up here."

Our voices were held, whispered on the same volume of the hum that resonated through the hall, and I felt him waver, hovering there like he wasn't sure what to say.

"It's not a problem. You're the one who opened your house up to us."

His expression flashed in intensity. His eyes raced over me so fast I had to have imagined it.

"My house is always open to you, Dakota."

Everything tightened, glowed and pressed and burned.

I blamed it on the night.

The way everything seemed to become compressed.

Dense and thick.

I forced a tease onto my lips. "Ah, I'm pretty sure it's not *always* open to me, Ryder. You wouldn't want me waltzing in here when you are *entertaining*, now would you?"

I put as much razzing suggestion into it as I could.

As if it didn't matter.

Like I was just another one of the guys giving him crap for being a player.

"Now get out of my way, this girl needs to pee." I nudged him in the chest.

I swore my fingertips sparked.

He angled an inch to the side, like I was going to fit through the tiny spot left between him and the doorjamb.

Hardly.

"Ryder." Exasperation filled my tone as I hissed low, "Get out of the way before I pee my pants."

He did, stepping farther to the left, only he took me by the elbow when I went to step by him, and he pressed me to the door. Caught off guard, my back flattened against the wood, mouth gaping at whatever he thought he was doing.

He loomed over me, illuminated in the light but still dark as midnight.

My breaths went short. Shaky and confused. The desire I shouldn't feel had to be palpable in the fraction of space separating us.

Eyes ablaze, his head cocked to the side, and he continued to hold onto my elbow like I might suddenly disappear. "You think any of those women could ever be more important than you?"

My chest nearly caved with all the times he'd hurt me doing just that.

A sharp blade dragged across my flesh every time we'd been at a bar, and he'd walked out with someone else.

"More than that, you think I've ever brought one of them here?"

A scoff quivered free. "I might not know *where* you spend your time, Ryder, but I know how you spend it."

There was no keeping the hurt out of it.

No faking it.

A thundercloud cracked through his expression.

Shame and regret.

Tears stung at the back of my eyes, and I turned my head away, dipping my chin in embarrassment.

God, the last thing I wanted was for him to feel sorry for me.

With his free hand, he reached out and forced me to look at him. "But that time isn't important, Dakota. It's wasted. Squandered. Told you before, if you need me, I'm there. It doesn't matter *what* I'm doing. I would never forget you. Do you understand?"

Meet me in the place of the forgotten.

I gulped, and I could barely nod.

"Good." He grunted it right before he turned and walked out without saying anything else.

He left me there, half pinned to the door and trying not to drop to my knees.

Wondering what the hell had just happened.

Chapter Eleven

Dakota

Eight Years Old

DAKOTA MOVED DOWN THE NARROW AISLE, TRYING TO PRETEND like she didn't hear the snickering coming from the few kids who remained on the bus. With every step she took, her backpack swished on her back, hitting the sides of the seat, only making the kids snicker more.

Tears burned at her eyes, and her throat tingled, and as hard as she fought to hold them back, one had already gotten free by the time she made it up to the bus driver.

Ms. Sally smiled at her, though there was a bit of a frown on her face. "Are you okay?"

Dakota nodded quickly, trying to swallow the ugly feeling, to keep it hidden when it felt so big and yucky it fought to burst out.

Ms. Sally's worry deepened, though she just angled her head and said, "All right. You take care of yourself, Dakota. Tell your mom I said hi."

Dakota could hardly nod again as she scrambled down the steps as fast as she could. The soles of her tennis shoes hit the gravelly pavement, and they thudded hard beneath her as she made a beeline in the direction of her house without fully running.

If they saw her running, they'd know why.

The loud engine of the bus churned, and the axles squeaked as it began to roll up the road. The second it disappeared over the hump up ahead, she started to run.

This was just as the full impact of her tears began to fall.

She looked at the door of her house, and she knew it'd be safe inside, that her mom would take her in her arms and hug her tight, but there was something that wouldn't let her do that. She didn't want her mom looking at her that way.

With that sadness that swam in her eyes and the way her voice always shook when she promised, *It will be okay. Kids at school can be really mean. They don't know what they are talking about, and you can't let them get to you. Not when you're so wonderful.*

And maybe they were really stupid and dumb, but that didn't mean it didn't make Dakota's stomach feel sick every time she overheard the whispers.

Those were bad enough.

But it was the loud ones that hurt the worst.

When someone said something like Mason did and everyone laughed, half of them in her face and others trying to pretend like they hadn't.

She didn't take the walkway up to the house, and instead, she wound around the side of it, following the path that ran along the back fence and led to the small stream in the woods behind their property.

There was a big tree with a branch that hung close to the ground, so low she was able to crawl up and sit on it.

She unwound the straps of her backpack from her shoulders and let it fall to the grass, then she began to carefully climb up the slanted branch, finding the spot where she could wedge herself into a nook and use it as a seat.

She closed her eyes tight and listened to the babbling of the water and the birds in the trees. Hugged herself hard as she focused on the soft breeze skimming over her hot, fiery skin.

Here was where she could pretend like she could just disappear.

Only she startled when she heard the snap of a twig behind her, and she whirled around in shock, a sound squeezing from her throat when she did.

Then she whipped back around when she remembered her entire face was a mess of snot and tears. She couldn't let him see her like this.

Yet he didn't go away.

He climbed up beside her.

Sniffling, she ran the sleeve of her shirt over her face like she could mop up all the evidence.

"What's wrong?" Ryder asked, trying to peer around her to look at her face.

She shifted farther to the side and mumbled, "Nothin.'"

"I don't think it's nothin' if you're crying."

She sniffled again, wishing he would go away all while wishing he would stay. She both hated and liked being around him. Hated and liked the butterflies that flew in her belly when he looked at her. The heavy, strange sensation she got in her chest.

It made her feel shy, but also like she didn't want to be anywhere else.

"Hey," he said when she didn't answer, and he set a hand on her arm and tried to turn her toward him. She finally gave in, looking up at his eyes that were the same color as the night. Twinkling like they had stars in them, but so dark she couldn't tell how deep they went. "Tell me what's wrong. You know you can tell me anything. Is someone being mean to you?"

Her teeth grabbed onto her lip, and she bit down to stop herself from admitting it.

"It's fine," she said.

"No, it's not fine if someone is being mean to you, Dakota." His voice got hard.

She turned away and drew up her legs, hugging her knees to her chest. "Lots of people are mean." She mumbled that like a dirty secret.

"Who?" he demanded.

"Mostly this dumb boy in class." She choked over that, and the tears started coming harder again.

"What's he saying to you?"

She buried her face in her knees, hating the way it hurt to breathe. "I brought cookies into class to share for Paisley's birthday."

"That's cool."

She shook her head. "At lunch, Mason said I was a fat Betty Crocker."

Anger moved through him. She could feel it. "He's nothing but a jerk, Dakota. Everybody's got their own size. Look at your brother. He's two times the size of me. You don't listen to people like that. Besides, my mom says you're the prettiest girl she's ever seen."

"Really?"

Did he think that, too?

"Yeah. He's probably just jealous of you because he doesn't get to have all the awesome stuff you make. And who the heck is Betty Crocker?"

She almost laughed, but she was still crying full force, and it made her hiccup instead. "She's a baker. My favorite one. My mom gave me her old cookbook."

She'd learned every single one of the recipes inside, and she'd started changing them a bit, making them her own.

Her mom said she had a special talent.

A gift to share with the world.

She wasn't so sure about that right then.

"Well, whoever this Betty Crocker is, I bet she's not half as cool as you."

She knew he was just trying to make her feel better, but he didn't get it. How everyone had laughed. Even some of her friends.

Not Paisley, though.

Paisley had threatened to punch Mason in the nose. Dakota had kind of wanted her to.

She hugged her knees tighter and whispered, "I think everyone just wants me to disappear. Go away. Forget all about me."

"Well, that's not going to happen, Dakota. I could never forget about you."

Her heart did that throbbing thing where it felt like it might blow up from the pressure.

"You have to say that because you're like my family."

"No way. I'm saying it because you're probably my favorite person in the whole world."

She peeked out at him, trying to catch his lie. "Not better than you like Cody," she challenged.

"Ha. I like you ten times better than I like Cody." He smiled at her with his big red lips.

That was always when the butterflies fluttered the hardest. Well, that and when he was eating something she'd made.

"Why do you think I came looking for you and left him inside playing Xbox?" He knocked his shoulder into hers. "Forget that idiot Mason. You're way too awesome to be out here crying by yourself."

She sniffed and ran her sleeve over her face again.

Without climbing down, he hopped off the branch and landed right on his feet. He stretched out a hand for her, and his black, black hair blew in the breeze. "Come on, I've got you, Cookie."

And she knew she didn't want to be out there alone. She wanted to be with him.

So she reached out and took it.

Chapter Twelve

Dakota

SUNLIGHT BRIGHTENED THE WINDOW, NUDGING ME FROM A DEEP, restful sleep.

With a groan, I rolled onto my back, and I blinked to pull myself out of the grogginess. I was honestly surprised I'd fallen asleep at all, let alone that I'd sank like a boulder to the bottom of the sea.

Both heavy and weightless.

But I guessed I felt safe here, as if whatever was going on back at my house couldn't touch me, though with the clarity of the morning, I was pretty sure the entire thing had been an overreaction.

I sat up, ran my fingers through the knots that had taken to my long hair, then slipped off the bed.

Kayden was still out, which brought a soft smile to my face, a tug at my heart that he was so comfortable he'd yet to even notice anything amiss.

The rest of the house was silent and still as I crept out and headed for the bathroom. I was thankful I managed to avoid Ryder when I found it empty.

It was one thing for him to see me in the middle of the night like this. It was a whole different story for him to see me in the light of day.

I used the restroom then washed my hands and splashed water on my face, deciding I would head home to take a shower and get ready for work.

Still, I rummaged into the toiletry bag Ryder had left sitting on the counter so I could brush my teeth.

I tiptoed back out, though this time the house wasn't still.

That energy hummed.

Alive.

I followed it to the doorway of the bedroom where I'd slept.

Ryder was in the room, wearing the same pair of gray sweatpants he'd had on last night, though he'd pulled on a tee-shirt. I couldn't tell if I was mourning the travesty or breathing a sigh of relief.

My stomach fisted at the sight of him, so rough and menacingly beautiful.

The angles of his face sharp and hewn in severity.

His lips so red.

A cool, dark king.

But it was the sight of him lifting my son from the playpen that contracted my chest in a need so intense that I felt like I was being crushed.

Midnight eyes flashed to me where I stood just outside the room.

I swore, he dragged them over my body, riding from my face, all the way down to my feet, and back up again.

Searing and singeing every spot they passed.

My skin buzzed, and I shifted on my feet, unable to stop the old insecurities that flared when he looked at me that way.

I had on sleep shorts and a long-sleeved matching tee. The black fabric was loose and draping at the shoulder, but it didn't do a lot to conceal anything.

Long ago, I'd accepted my body.

No longer saw it as an imperfection or a blight.

Had come to love it.

But the one person in this world I'd ever wished I looked different for was Ryder.

He had a type, and I definitely wasn't it.

He might have stuck up for me when I was growing up, but it'd been because he truly cared about me. Loved all the things that were on the inside…but the outside?

Unease rippled.

I'd once thought that he maybe could get over that. See me for me, the way his words had always expressed.

But there'd always been a wall.

An obstacle.

I'd tried to knock it down, and I'd taken the chance, placed myself at his feet.

He'd rejected me.

I'd never forget his words.

Sweet and tender and so horrifyingly painful that I still carried them like a scar.

I love you, Dakota. So fucking much. But not like that.

Which was why it was time I moved on, but God, it was hard when his expression softened as he pulled my son closer to him and sent me this smile that trembled through me.

"Good mornin', Cookie."

I cleared the memories that had manifested as jagged rocks from my throat. "Good morning."

Kayden pointed his little index finger at me. "Mommy, I see you!"

Affection rushed, so acute it pulsed in every cell. "I see you, too, sweet boy."

Ryder hooked Kayden to his hip. "Guess who I heard calling for you while you were in the bathroom?"

"Me!" Kayden smacked his chubby hand against his chest. "We go Uncle Rye-Rye's house?"

He dipped his head in one of those cute nods.

He definitely approved.

"We did."

My son snuggled deeper into Ryder, pressing his head on one of those pecs. "I stay *wight* here."

You could say my son was obsessed with Ryder. I didn't blame him for the affliction.

Ryder kept hugging him, though his attention was on me. "Why don't you get dressed while I take him downstairs to get him something to eat?"

"You don't have to do that."

"You say it like spending time with my little K-Bear is putting me out."

"Don't you need to get to work?"

Something grim sobered his expression. "Going to take the morning off. Was hoping you'd do the same."

I fidgeted through the sudden disquiet. "Did you hear something?"

Ryder's thick throat bobbed when he swallowed. "Let's get this guy fed then we'll talk. Ezra called and said he's going to swing by and give us better details."

"Oh." It wheezed out. Surprise riddled with a shot of dread. I didn't like the feeling of whatever he was implying.

He came my way, and he paused where I stood, angling in close as he grazed his fingertips along the edge of my hand. "It's going to be okay, Dakota."

Then he wound around me, and I shifted to watch them as they headed down the hall.

Kayden peered at me from over his shoulder, waving his little hand, his brown hair a total mess, his chubby cheeks red and oh so sweet. "I go my Rye-Rye. Bye, Mommy!"

I choked out a rough laugh, waving, too, before I rushed into the room. Nerves rattled through my senses, and I went for my phone on the nightstand. I stared at it in contemplation for one second before I sent a text to Beth.

> **Me: Hey, something came up this morning and I'm going to be a couple hours late. Can you handle the morning rush?**

My cooks and baker would have arrived super early this morning to get everything prepped for opening, and I always planned the menu and prepared the next day's desserts as best as I could the previous afternoon so they could go right into the oven first thing, so I didn't have to worry about that.

It was when things got crazy with the customers that made me feel like I was leaving my employees hanging.

It took Beth a minute to respond.

> **Beth: Have you even met me?**

Amusement shook my head, and another text came in quickly behind it.

> **Beth: Please tell me what came up was a delicious man who kept you up all night and you're so sore this morning you can't get out of bed.**

Rolling my eyes, I tossed her words right back at her.

> **Me: Have you even met me?**

> **Beth: Ugh, so boring. You're breaking my heart over here. So, what happened then?**

> **Me: I'll explain it when I get in.**

I hated to worry her, even though I knew she would since it was unlike me not to show up when I said I would be there, but I also didn't want to say anything until I knew for sure what was going on and what the plan was.

Beth: Okay. Don't worry about things here. I've got it covered.

Me: I know you do. Thank you so much.

Beth: Always.

I changed into a pair of jeans and a cropped tee, one of the two outfits I'd stuffed into my bag last night, then threw my hair into a ponytail and took a few steadying breaths before I headed downstairs.

Ryder's home was decorated in leathers, steel, and stone. The walls a grayed, flat white and the original wooden floors stained the deepest black. His cabinets were ebony, and the countertops were stainless steel.

He'd fabricated them himself, and they stood out, a gorgeous piece of art.

The entire house was unique and manly and oozed his aura so profusely that I felt as if I were wading through a torrent of him as I tiptoed through the living room and into the opening to the kitchen.

Ryder had Kayden propped on the countertop, a hand on his side to keep him safe while he held a spoon with the other, flying it around and making zooming noises as he brought the scrambled eggs to Kayden's mouth.

Kayden howled with laughter before he opened wide so Ryder could fly the spoon into his mouth. "That was the biggest bite I've ever seen, K-Bear."

"I *gwow* big," Kayden said, so proud, his grin so wide.

"That's right, you are."

Love rushed, and I suddenly felt rawer than I had in years.

I knew it was because I'd been shaken up. The stir of last night and staying in such close quarters with Ryder had left me feeling unsettled.

But it only swelled higher when Ryder shifted to slant me a look from the side when he sensed me standing there. "You want some eggs, too?"

"No, I think I'll just have some coffee."

A frown dented his brow. "You should eat, Cookie."

"I'm fine," I told him, deciding I needed to suck it up and stop tittering around him, so I strode into his kitchen like I did it every morning. I went for the rack of black mugs that sat next to his coffee pot and filled myself one, dumping a dose of cinnamon creamer into it. "Thank you for taking care of him."

"No thanks needed, Dakota. I love spending time with him."

"Me!" Kayden smacked both hands to Ryder's cheeks, holding on tight as he curled up his tiny nose in the most adorable way.

"How did you know?" Ryder drawled in his deep voice.

"I a smart boy." Kayden gave another of those deep dips of his head.

Ryder reached out and ran a tatted hand through Kayden's hair, affection pouring out. "That's right. You are a smart, sweet boy."

The doorbell rang.

"That will be Ezra," Ryder said.

"Why don't you get it, and I'll take over here?" I edged in close so I could put a hand on Kayden.

It put me in his atmosphere.

His scent slamming me.

Leather and decadent spice.

He stayed there for a moment like he was stuck in it, too, before he seemed to peel himself away, and it wasn't until he disappeared through the opening that I was able to take a full breath. I pulled my giggling son into my arms and carried him to the sink where I shifted him around so I could clean the egg from his face.

He kicked and squirmed and howled like it was pure torture before he was giggling again when I swiped a clean hand towel over his face.

"I all clean." He beamed at me with his dimpled cheeks.

"That's right. And with a full belly," I said as I set him on his feet then poked his stomach with my finger.

A rush of wild laughter left him, and he grabbed his tummy and squeezed. "Mommy, you get me!"

My heart thudded, and I smiled down at him softly before I slowly turned when I felt the tamed disorder ripple through the air.

Ezra followed Ryder in.

I didn't love the grimness held in his demeanor.

"Hey, Ezra."

"Morning, Dakota." His voice was quieter than it normally was, and I knew from experience it was the one he used when he was delivering bad news.

"Let me get Kayden situated really quick."

"Sure."

I pulled up Kayden's favorite show on my cell. "Why don't you watch your show while Mommy talks to your uncles for a minute? You sit right over here."

I wound around them and into the living room to a lounger. "Hop up there, sweet boy."

Kayden climbed up, and I handed him my phone. "You get one show."

He squealed, puckering his adorable lips, and I reached out and caressed down his cheek.

"Love is on house." He slurred through the words, and my chest fisted, so tight I thought it might cave, and I leaned down and pressed a kiss to the top of his head.

"That's right. Love is on the house. Free and forever."

Because he would never have to ask for it.

When he was situated, I moved back into the kitchen where Ezra and Ryder were leaned toward each other, their words hushed.

I cleared my throat. "Do you two want to let me in on whatever you're whispering about over there?"

Ezra scraped a hand through his short hair while Ryder looked like he was about to go on a rampage.

I strolled in as casually as I could, going for the coffee mug I'd left on the counter. I turned to lean back against the counter and took a sip, looking at Ezra point blank. I wasn't about to tiptoe. "What did you find?"

He hesitated for a second before he blew out a sigh. "Someone definitely tried to break into your place. Lock had been jimmied. By the damage to the wood, it looks like some kind of large screwdriver had been used."

Apprehension gusted, rising up from the east like a blowing gale that ushered in a summer storm.

Every one of us in that room knew something like that didn't come by accident.

I blew out the unease, my mind ticking through the different possibilities and scenarios.

Because the question was why?

Why would someone be trying to get in?

"And you don't have any idea of who it might have been?" I asked.

Ezra wavered, contemplating his words before he finally spoke. "There have been a few break-ins lately. Some theft over at the new builds on Clifton, plus someone had their shed broken into and had some expensive tools stolen a couple nights ago. Another vacant house on Plight St. that's for sale was also completely stripped of everything inside. Thinking it might be related to that…someone looking for something of value that they could strip and sell. Might have thought your place was a part of the restaurant and empty that night."

I'd heard of a couple break-ins, but I didn't know they'd gotten so severe.

As much as I hated the idea that someone might want to steal from me when I'd worked so hard for what I had, it was much better than the alternate intentions that had been trudging through my brain.

I nodded. "I guess that's good news then."

The rumble of a growl vibrated from Ryder. "Good news?"

"It's better than the alternative," I told him.

The implication of what remained unsaid pulsed through the room, bouncing between the three of us. I could rest in the knowledge that no one had been there with the intention to hurt us.

Did the situation suck?

Sure.

But I could handle it.

"That doesn't mean you shouldn't be careful, though. Keep an eye out," Ezra added. "It worries me they might come back sniffing around the restaurant thinking you might keep money in there at night. I'm going to add another deputy to patrol downtown during that time." Then he gave me one of his tight smiles. "Don't worry. We're going to find this guy. It's happening so often, whoever is responsible is bound to slip."

"I'll be sure to remain vigilant," I promised.

Ryder grunted again, and I ignored him, keeping my attention on Ezra.

"I'm going to have to file the report, which means your brother is likely to find out." Ezra cringed on my behalf.

I let go of a small laugh. "That's fine. I just wanted some actual information on the situation before the gossip started. You know how he is."

"That I do. And I already sent someone over to get your door reinforced."

"I appreciate that."

"Of course. That's what I'm here for." He glanced between me and Ryder. "I'm going to head back to the station. Let me know if you see or hear anything."

"I will." Ryder and I followed him to the door.

"Thank you, Ezra." I gave him a quick hug.

"I'm always here."

He tipped his head at Ryder. "See you later, brother."

"Yeah," was all that Ryder said, and Ezra snapped the door as he left.

Tension suddenly barreled into me from behind.

Tacky and tight.

The air thinned.

The only sound the quiet volume of Kayden's show from across the room and the thud of my heart that pounded in my ears.

I felt like I could hardly move as I slowly shifted around. Ryder stood five feet away, all menacing glowers and huffing like a bull.

"I don't like it, Dakota."

"I don't like it, either. Some people suck, but there's not a whole lot we can do about that other than let Ezra do his job."

Ryder stepped forward. "There is plenty I could do about it."

Barely contained fury slipped from his tongue.

I shook my head. "Don't be an idiot, Ryder. Ezra has this handled, and the last thing I need is you getting involved in something that doesn't even concern you."

He slowly approached, closing the distance until there was no space left between us. "Doesn't concern me? Believe me, Cookie..." His words scraped, low and gruff. Edged with a razor. "It absolutely concerns me."

Rigidness clenched his jaw, and he seemed to war with what to say, the words he released cut with a severity so sharp I felt them raking across my skin.

"I don't want you going back to your place until this asshole has been caught."

I struggled to get my bearings. "And I'm not going to live my life scared over some jerk who's going around stealing stuff. I've lived by myself for a long time, Ryder, and if Ezra doesn't have an issue with me going back to my house, then I don't, either."

"Yeah? Well, I have an issue."

Air puffed from my nose. I swore, he was worse than my brother sometimes.

"I'm a big girl, and I get to make that choice."

He had me backed to the wall so fast I couldn't comprehend how I'd gotten there.

Pinned.

Gunmetal eyes flamed in a way I didn't think I'd ever seen them do before. But his voice was pained. "I can't take that risk with you, Dakota, and not with Kayden, either. Please. Stay with me."

"We each have our own lives, Ryder." I forced it out around the tumult.

His teeth ground. "You are my life, Dakota."

Chaos whipped.

A muddled confusion.

My brow drew tight, tugged together by the string of uncertainty and old wounds that yanked at the middle of my heart. It was on my tongue to ask him exactly what that meant when he suddenly swore and tore himself away, fumbling back two steps as he dropped his attention to the ground.

Scrubbing a palm over his face, he stared at the grains of wood like they might hold every answer he was looking for.

Then he seemed to gather himself enough to look back at me. A plea was driven into every line on his expression. "Just stay, Dakota. Please."

Chapter Thirteen
Ryder

"**I**S THIS REALLY NECESSARY?"

Dakota grumbled the whole way up the stairs even though she wasn't the one who was carrying the boxes. Not that I minded. I only minded that she thought it was a waste of my time or putting me out. For thinking for one second that she was a burden.

I glanced back at her when I made it to the top-floor landing, ignoring the ripping at my chest with how fucking pretty she was, those full lips in a constant pout as she followed me up, carrying a couple bags that I'd also insisted on buying.

"Yes, Dakota, it is necessary. You think I'm not going to have a comfortable place for Kayden to sleep while he's here?"

A comfortable place for her?

Too fucking bad it wasn't in my bed.

But I couldn't let my mind go traipsing into thoughts like that, so I shifted the massive box and sent her a grin. "Besides, I've been wanting to put a kids' room together for all my nieces and nephews, and you know with the way Caleb and Paisley have been going at it, we're bound to have a little Caleb or Paisley running around here soon."

Okay, they had no plans for that, but I needed the excuse.

That throaty laugh rolled through the air.

I had to suppress a groan.

How much my dick loved the sound of it.

"We would be in so much trouble then. I'm not sure Time River could handle the likes of that."

I chuckled. "Kid would be so full of sass we wouldn't know what to do."

"So cute, though, right?"

"Oh yeah." I shifted the box so I could maneuver it down the hall and through the door. Kayden was already in the room where we'd left him in his playpen so he'd be safe while we brought everything in. Holding onto the sides, he started jumping when he saw us enter. "Rye-Rye! Mommy! I see you!"

Dakota laughed that tender laugh. The one reserved for her son. "I see you, too," she sang, angling around so she could actually see him from behind the box.

"I get new bed?"

"That's right, K-Bear, you're getting a new bed so you always have a place to sleep when you come to my house."

"My house." Kayden smacked his little chest, and a rough chuckle got free, affection so fierce it was almost painful.

But love was like that a whole lot of the time, wasn't it?

Painful.

Unfulfilled.

Unrequited.

That or you were terrified you were going to lose it once you had it.

I leaned the box on the wall then moved to run my hand through his hair. "You like it here, huh, buddy?"

"I *wike* it *wots*," he agreed, chubby cheeks denting with those dimples, his little nose scrunched.

A throaty sound came from behind as Dakota leaned down to set the bags on the floor. "Don't get too comfortable, sweet boy. We're going to have to go back to our house soon."

My insides clutched at the thought of it. Couldn't stand the idea of her there alone. Fucking hated that someone had been lurking around her place. Thoughts plaguing me. Wondering what might have happened if I hadn't been there. If I'd been too late.

Had I scared the fucker away? Or had he been long gone once he realized it was actually a house, the way Ezra suspected?

But I couldn't take that fucking chance, and I was angling in Dakota's direction. "You don't have to go back to your house *soon*, Dakota. My place is yours for as long as you want it."

Forever if need be.

Hell, I'd be a lucky bastard if I could have that. But I wasn't lucky, was I?

Redness rushed her high, full cheeks, and she fought with rolling her eyes like she thought I was messing with her the way I used to when we were kids.

But I'd stopped looking at her like a little girl a long time ago. The day she'd come back from Boulder where she'd gone to college to study business. It was like every fucking thing I'd known had been demolished that day. Every moment of our pasts coming together to add up to that very second.

Every minute we'd ever spent together had gone through my mind in both a blur and in vivid color. Every time I'd taken care of her, and every time she'd taken care of me. The way we'd just...find each other when the other was in need.

Every interaction purposed. Every moment a building block.

In that one second, the instant I saw her after she returned, every single one of those things had come rushing back at me, and my soul had known.

But I'd been a fool. Made a deal with the devil, thinking I wouldn't get played.

So now I was left doing my best to pretend like what I felt for her didn't exist.

"You know I can't stay here forever." Her words had dimmed to wisps, and I reached out and brushed back a lock of soft, brown hair from her face.

"You can do anything you want, Dakota."

She choked out a laugh, and I could feel the way she pulled back a fraction, like we were getting too close.

"Anything, huh?" She fronted the tease.

A grin climbed to my face, and I touched the edge of her mouth, right in the little divot on the left side of her chin that drove me out of my mind. Not quite a dimple but the sexiest thing I'd ever seen.

I wanted to lean in and lick it.

"That's right, Dakota. Anything."

She gave me a feigned scowl. "You sure have a way of trying to boss me around when you say I can do anything."

A rough chuckle skated free. "Anything unless it'll hurt you. How's that?"

I was number one on that list.

"It seems to me like you're trying to take the fun out of it." There was her sweet sass, and a rumbly sound vibrated in my chest, and I knew I had to get out of there before I did something that I was going to regret.

"I need to run down and grab the mattress. I'll be right back. Hold down the fort while I'm gone?" I smirked as I paused to look at her in the doorway.

She shook her head with a slight laugh. "I'll do my best to survive without you for five minutes."

"It'll be rough," I told her, loving the way she got flushed anytime we went to teasing like this.

Then she rolled those cinnamon eyes, even though they were flashing with warmth. "It'll be a breath of fresh air, is what it'll be. Get out of here, I'm already sick of you."

Low laughter tumbled from me, and I sent her a cocky grin. "Whatever you say, Cookie."

I started out, only her voice froze me, all the teasing gone as she looked at me from across the space. "Thank you, Ryder. I don't know how I'll ever fully repay you."

I knew what she was referring to. That it wasn't just her staying here while she was in need. The money I'd given her. It'd been my biggest pleasure and my greatest downfall.

But I knew, standing there looking at her right then, that I'd do it a thousand times over.

"What's that you always say? Love is on the house." Then I tapped the heel of my fist on the doorframe before I walked out.

Chapter Fourteen

Dakota

ON SATURDAY MORNING, I WAS ON THE ENORMOUS RUG THAT took up half of Ryder's living room, playing dinosaurs with Kayden. I'd finally gotten the café to the place that I didn't work on the weekends.

I loved it.

The time to spend with my son.

The time to breathe.

The time for myself that I'd had to sacrifice to build the restaurant to what it was today.

It'd been worth it, but I was definitely relishing in the reward of it.

Roaring, Kayden clashed two dinosaurs together. "I get you," he shouted, banging them together again.

"Don't you think the dinosaurs should get along and be friends?"

"No! Fight!"

Soft laughter rolled. Apparently, Kayden couldn't be bothered with my lesson about cooperation and unity.

Yesterday, I'd ended up taking off the rest of the day, and Ryder had gone with me to pack more of our things before he'd insisted we go to Wal-Mart to purchase a bunch of stuff for Kayden's temporary room.

Whether it went against my better judgment or not, I'd decided to stay here for a while.

The thing was, when I'd gotten to my house and had seen the old door that had been removed and sat propped on the wall as the carpenter installed a new one, I'd had zero regrets about agreeing to spend a little more time here.

All it'd taken to get me firmly on Ryder's team was seeing the way the wood had been torn up at the edges, deep grooves gouged into it where a metal object had been shoved in and the actual lock had been pried out.

I'd realized that person could have come the rest of the way in, that my son was there, that we were vulnerable, and I'd known I was making the right choice.

Ezra would find whoever was responsible and everything would go back to normal.

Plus, last night after I'd put Kayden down to sleep, Ryder had sat at the table in his kitchen with me and had designed a metal security door that he was going to fabricate and install.

Once we had that extra security in place, we'd go home.

Taking extra precautions to protect my son didn't make me weak.

It made me smart.

I grinned when the raucous rapping suddenly sounded at the front door. There was only one person I knew who could create a stir as wild as that one.

Paisley had texted me yesterday demanding to know what had happened Thursday night before we decided she was going to come by to start planning Caleb's party this morning.

She was only ten minutes late.

She deserved a medal.

"I'll be right back," I told Kayden, pushing to stand before I walked to Ryder's front door.

I peeked out the window and onto the front porch.

Paisley frantically waved back at me like a goof.

I worked through the lock and let her in, and she came flying at me, long hair so blonde it was almost white, wearing a red tank and cut-off shorts and her signature cowgirl boots.

She threw her arms around me and swayed me back and forth, squishing me and making me laugh as she clung to me like she had thought she would never see me again. "Doodle-Boo."

Then she released me so quickly to take me by the outside of the upper arms I thought I'd get whiplash. She gave me a small shake. "Why in the world didn't you call me? I'm so mad at you right now."

My brows rose to the sky. "And you wanted me to call you in the middle of the night, when you're all the way out in the middle of nowhere?"

"Um, yes, isn't that what I'm for? To come running when you need me? But okay, fine, I know Ryder is closer and it was the actual wise choice, but I'm still mad." It was a pout and a tease.

Then her expression deepened as she searched my face. "Are you okay? I can't believe that happened."

"I'm fine. I mean, it was scary while in the middle of it, but I know Ezra's going to find whoever it was."

"I'm glad Ryder was there."

My stomach tipped, and I tried to ignore the fact that I could hear his footsteps echoing from his room above. The way I constantly felt him, his movements and his breaths.

The way he was all bristly and rough.

The way he was so caring and sweet underneath.

"Me, too."

"Auntie *Paisey*." Kayden climbed to his feet, and he bounced over in all his roly-poly adorableness.

"My K-Bear." She sang it as she swept him into her arms. She spun him in a circle, making him squeal, before she hooked him on her hip.

"Evie?" he asked, smacking his chest in a clear demand for Paisley to bring her little girl to him.

Paisley laughed her deep, throaty laugh. "Not today, K-Bear. She went on a special ride with her daddy, just the two of them."

"Aw, that is really sweet," I said.

"I know." I swore she swooned. "They're so precious together, I can hardly stand it."

"That makes me so happy."

Joy radiated from her. The genuine, real kind that you could almost reach out and touch.

"I'm so thankful for it," she admitted.

Emotion crested before she seemed to shake herself out of it and set Kayden back on his feet, then she lifted the strap of the bag she had draped over her shoulder. "Are you sure you're up for working on the menu?"

"Do you think I'd let anyone else cater Caleb's special day?" And honestly, I was glad for the distraction.

She giggled. "True. Besides, no one could compare, and I'd have to spend the next two weeks weeping in bed before I could heal enough to even begin to look for someone else."

I touched my chest. "The atrocity. I would never let that happen to my bestie."

"You better not."

I let go of a soft laugh. "Why don't we get set up at the kitchen table?"

I picked up Kayden and carried him into the kitchen where I put him in his playpen with a bunch of his toys to keep him occupied.

Every part of me tightened when I thought about why it was down here rather than upstairs. The way Ryder had insisted on buying that crib, then had spent two hours putting it together.

I bit my lip, taken back to how hot it'd been in that room. The way his skin had become damp as he worked, the way his black tee had clung to the sweat.

Watching him put that crib together was like watching my own personal porn.

Paisley pulled her laptop from the bag and opened it, and she also took out a notebook and a bunch of different colored pens.

"Do you want something to drink?" I asked her.

"Iced tea?"

"Coming up." I went to the refrigerator so I could pour each of us a glass from the pitcher, ignoring the way I could feel the curiosity in her eyes as she followed me with her gaze.

"So, where is Ryder, anyway?"

I cleared my throat. "Upstairs."

"Hmm…" was all that came out of her.

I set the teas on the table then took the seat next to her and turned the focus on why she'd come here. "So, do you have any ideas about what you'd like to serve?"

She tapped into her computer, and she brought up a Pinterest board with about a thousand different of those ideas.

I laughed. "Uh-oh, we are serious about this."

She cast me a side-eye, only the hint of a tease remaining there. "We are definitely serious about this, Dakota. Really serious. I want him to know how much he means to me."

"I promise he already knows that, but I also promise we're going to make this incredibly special. A night he will never forget."

"You can bet it's going to be a night he'll never forget," she said out of the side of her mouth, letting go of the innuendo.

I faked disgust. "You can keep those plans to yourself, thank you very much. I'll just focus on the food."

"That's an entirely different board you probably don't want to see." She wagged her brows.

Giggles flooded out. "Um, yeah. You'd better have that set to private. I don't think I need that visual in my head."

"You need something—"

"Shut it," I said, letting go of the razzing warning before I sat forward so I could study some of the ideas she'd pinned.

There were a bunch of appetizers done in elaborate ways, and a few hearty entrees that had been set in pretty dishes, plus she'd pinned a ton of different ideas on decorating the trays and displays.

"It looks to me like you're thinking mostly heavy appetizers."

"Yeah, I'd like to set up a big buffet table with an array of yummy things that we can pop into our mouths. I don't want to do the whole sit-down thing. I think Caleb will like it better if he can just hang out with his family and friends."

I snagged her pink pen so I could jot some notes in my own notebook.

"Hey, that's mine." She feigned a whine.

"I like it, and I want it, so it's mine," I told her with a sly grin. "And am I not volunteering my time, energy, and resources to make this happen? You'd think you wouldn't mind sharing your pen with me."

"What I think is you're a dirty thief and I'm never going to see my favorite pen again. I bet you're actually the one responsible for these break-ins and you set the whole thing up at your house as a decoy."

I gaped at her. "You caught me."

She didn't even fight her grin, knocking her shoulder into mine. "You know anything that's mine is also yours, Doodle-Boo. I mean, except for my man."

Another giggle slipped free. I always felt like I was back to being thirteen when I was around her.

We went through some different options and settled on a theme of country chic. From there, we made detailed lists.

Appetizers and desserts.

Drinks and decorations.

We were almost finished when I heard footsteps echoing on the stairs. A minute later, Ryder appeared in the doorway.

Paisley and I both looked up, but I was pretty sure it was only me who felt the earth shift.

That slight tilting that always shivered through me whenever he came into my space. Only this time, I swore I felt the world canting farther to the side than it ever had before.

The man stood there in dark jeans and a fitted black tee, black hair shining and damp from his shower. Every line of his face was sharp and edged in severity, though those gunmetal eyes were tender when he found us all in his kitchen.

"My Rye-Rye," Kayden called, scrambling to stand and holding onto the sides of the playpen as he jumped.

"Hey, my little K-Bear." Ryder strolled over to Kayden, and he ran one of those tatted hands over the top of his head. "How are you today?"

"I *pway*," Kayden told him, holding out a big, chunky truck that he'd been zooming over the walls of his playpen. "*Wook it.*"

"What? Is that a monster truck? That's awesome. You've got the coolest cars around." He was all soft smirks, and I was having a hard time with the way my belly flipped at the sight.

Maybe staying here really was a bad idea. God knew how hard it was to constantly be in his space. But I'd make it through this. He was my friend first, and that was what I needed to remember.

He moved to Paisley and pulled her out of the chair, hugging her hard and swinging her around. "Paisley-Cakes. Are you staying out of trouble?"

"Who me?" She said it like him asking it was an offense when he set her onto her feet.

Playfulness danced through his features. "Looks to me like you two are up to no good in here."

He slanted me one of those grins.

The kind that dripped sex.

I doubted he even knew it. The impact he had.

I shifted on the seat.

"Never." Paisley touched her chest before she sat back down.

Ryder chuckled one of those raspy sounds as he wandered over to the coffee pot. "If I've ever seen any trouble, it's you two."

"Oh yeah, we're total troublemakers. Sorry you have to bail us out of jail every weekend." I rolled my eyes.

His laughter was quiet, scraping the air like a jagged lullaby, and he glanced over as he stirred creamer into his coffee. "What *are* you guys up to?"

I opened my mouth to tell him about catering Caleb's party, only Paisley beat me to it.

Except what came out of her mouth was not what I expected.

"Oh, I'm just helping Dakota get set up on a dating app." She turned to look at me. Mischief pranced all over her lips. She cocked her head to the side, her fingers poised at the keys. "Do you consider yourself more of a dominant or a submissive?"

Me? Not so much a troublemaker. But Paisley? She loved standing at the pot and stirring it.

I was going to strangle her for it.

Only I didn't get the chance to before the growled words sawed through the air.

"Excuse me?"

All the softness Ryder had been wearing evaporated.

Poof.

Gone in an instant.

In its place was a vibrating hostility that made my stomach quake.

He came our way, head cocked to the side as he approached.

"I'm setting up Dakota's dating profile on this new app," Paisley acted like she was clarifying. "It's really detailed. It turns out our friend here is into some crazy kink."

Embarrassment flooded me.

I was going to kill her.

"Paisley," I snapped low. "Don't you dare—"

Ryder slamming down the lid to her laptop trapped the words on my tongue.

"Absolutely not," he snarled.

Paisley blinked up at him. Completely innocent when she was as guilty as could be. "And why not?"

That fierce gaze slanted to me. "Because I said no."

I didn't know if I was irritated or turned on.

Both, which pissed me off, too.

"Sorry to break it to you, Ryder, but I'm pretty sure you don't have a say in the matter." Paisley shook her head at him where he was still leaning over the table with his hand holding her laptop shut. "Our Dakota here is ready to get out and have a little fun. She's on the hunt for the good D. You wouldn't want to get in the way of a woman in need, would you?"

Something like fury brewed across his face.

The man was grinding his teeth so hard it looked like his jaw was going to crumble when he turned his attention to me. "Do you really think I'm going to let you out of this house to go meet some random guy? I don't think so, Dakota. It's not safe."

"Ryder—"

"Oh, I see," Paisley cut in, "because she should probably at least know anyone she might want to date first?" Paisley pressed. "Like, because of this whole break-in biz?"

That was it. My best friend was forever dead to me.

Aggression rolled through Ryder, and he eased back to standing and tossed his head to the side, making his neck crack.

"If that's what Dakota wants, then yeah." Something in his tone sounded of regret.

"Oh, right, good to know," she drew out.

Ryder looked at me in what appeared to be disappointment.

Or maybe it was pain.

Then he turned and walked out.

Chapter Fifteen
Ryder

I WAS GOING TO LOSE MY GODDAMN MIND.

Being in that house with her.

Knowing she was in the next room.

Sleeping in that bed.

Or in the shower with water streaming over her bare skin.

Or downstairs, padding around on those cute feet.

Or just fucking everywhere.

She'd infiltrated every crevice and had seeped into every crack.

Her warm spirit and that giving heart and that sweet body I was dying to get lost in when I knew it was the last thing I could do.

After a couple days passing with her being there, it was becoming clear that having her stay at my place was probably a terrible idea. It was something I wasn't sure I was going to make it through, but I couldn't stomach the alternative, either. Couldn't stomach her alone and vulnerable.

But what had nearly sent me over the edge was walking in to find Paisley setting Dakota up on that dating app. The idea of it knocked through me like a hammer to the head.

The truth that one day, she was going to find someone else.

As she should.

That didn't mean it didn't nearly spin me into violence.

And kink?

"Fuck," I grumbled under my breath and rubbed a hand over my face to keep the visions from assaulting my mind. I was at the shop, leaned over the drawing table and trying to focus on transferring the design for the security door for Dakota's house into a more detailed sketch.

Working through the dimensions to ensure everything would line up right.

All while trying to get the painful visions out of my mind.

Before Dakota and Paisley could continue on about that bullshit, I'd left. I'd had to get the hell out of that house before I did or said something that I couldn't take back.

So, I'd found myself here.

In my shop.

Where I could let my mind go and pour the tension into the art. Where I could believe I could build something better. Be something better. I wondered if that could ever be the truth.

If what I'd done could ever be eradicated or erased.

If the purpose behind it was enough or if it was just another pathetic excuse.

I had one of the rolling garage doors opened to allow for fresh air to flood the space, and I stilled when I heard an engine wind around the side of the building. A truck pulled up next to where I'd parked my bike.

I did my best not to cringe. I should be excited to see the guy, but after what I'd walked in on this morning, I felt frayed at the edges, the turmoil from what had happened at Dakota's house making it ten times worse.

Still, I found a grin as I looked at my oldest friend as he slipped out of his truck.

"What's up, man?"

I'd talked to Cody on the phone yesterday after he'd found out about the break-in at Dakota's. I was surprised he hadn't come running, but I knew he had a big job he was working on in the next town over.

I'd promised him I had it handled, and he didn't need to worry, but that sure as hell didn't mean he wasn't going to.

"Not much." He pulled his cap from his head, squeezing the brim between his hands. It was his tell. Something that he always did when he was irritated. "I stopped by your place and talked to Dakota. She said you'd needed to go into work for a bit, so I thought I'd swing by."

"Glad you did." I tossed the pencil to the slanted table, and I shifted to lean against a regular height one that sat to the side of it. I crossed my arms over my chest, watching him as he weaved his way through my shop.

Dude was a giant in the middle of the orchestrated mayhem, which was the way I worked best.

There were projects in varying stages of progress littered about, metal propped on workbenches and tables, raw pieces set in the stands for when I needed them. Every kind of welder known to man were set up at different stations, and there were a bunch of industrial saws and an elaborate paint station at the back.

There were functional pieces and others that were only meant for art, a sculpture that was going to stand eight feet tall and a big wall piece that someone wanted to hang in their living room.

Pride thrummed as I took it in.

All except for the car that still sat like an omen in the far bay.

Cody rounded a workstation, running a shaky hand over the top of his head, and he blew out a sigh as he gave voice to what had really brought him here. "This is fucked, man."

I swallowed. "Yeah. Don't like it at all."

"And Ezra doesn't have any hunch of who this prick is?" He leaned against the table opposite me, crossing one ankle over the other, his beefy frame taking up the space.

My head shook. "He told me the only thing they got was a partial print out at one of the new builds. So far, they haven't been able to pull it up against anyone in the system, but he's confident it's going to lead to something."

Anger rippled from Cody, and he gnawed at his bottom lip. "And so what? That's just it? We have to sit around and wait for that to happen?"

"Guess so."

Only I was feeling the exact thing that was clearly rolling through Cody.

The need to hunt.

Track this fucker down.

End him before he had the chance to taint the beauty that was Dakota.

"That's bullshit." His words were shards.

I huffed out a raw sound. "If I had any idea which direction to look, you could bet your ass I'd be looking."

His nod was tight. "Know you would. Always can trust you to have Dakota's back. Her best interest at heart."

He was back to looking at me the way he'd been in her office the other day. Like he might be speculating there was something that went deeper than that.

"Pretty cool of you to let her stay at your house until this blows over." How he made it both come out as gratitude and a threat, I didn't know.

"You know I'd do anything for her."

He barely nodded, but there was something disbelieving behind it. "She looks at you like you're a fucking saint walking on water."

I tried to ignore the insinuation. Refusing to take it in as truth. But I'd be a liar if I denied it. The way she did look at me. The way she felt. The way she'd let me crawl all over her if I asked. The way she'd let me take.

But I wasn't worthy of that, and Cody never hesitated to point that out.

He didn't know the details.

But he knew I was dirty.

And I would never be fucking good enough for his baby sister. I was well aware of it myself without him needing to remind me.

I scrubbed a palm over my face. "No, man. We've just always been close. You know that."

Air puffed from his nose, and he pushed from the table. "Just keep it that way, and we won't have a problem, yeah?"

Fuck.

"Don't have to tell me, Cody."

He gave a quick nod and released a heavy breath. "Sorry, man. I'm just… twisted up over this. Can't stand the idea of something bad happening to her."

"Neither can I."

That time, his nod was accepting. "I appreciate you always being there for her. For always being there for me."

"Of course. You're my best friend. We're family."

At least that's what I'd always considered him. All of them.

"All right, I'll let you get back to work. I just needed to see if you had any different thoughts."

"If I hear anything different, I'll keep you posted."

He stepped forward and gave me a quick hug with a clap to the back. "Love you, brother," he said.

"What's not to love?" I had to get in the ribbing.

Cody laughed. "Always so fucking cocky."

I pucked him a grin before I returned his hug, voice turning low. "Love you, brother. Always."

He clapped me on the back once more before he turned and weaved back through the shop.

I scratched at the back of my neck as I watched him go. It wasn't like it was the first time we'd shared words like this.

But it might have been the first time I wanted to tell him to fuck off. Tell him he didn't have the first clue what I would really do for her.

I glanced at the car sitting in the third bay.

What I needed to remember was he was right. I couldn't have her. Not when I'd already given it all away.

My heart thudded an erratic beat.

Not unless I could fucking get it back.

Chapter Sixteen

Dakota

"H ERE YOU ARE, TWO STARLIGHT SPECKLED SUGAR COOKIES and a large coffee."

I handed the white paper sack and disposable cup to the man who waited for his order at the bakery counter. I always added the daily bakery specials to a smaller version of the same chalkboard that sat out at the front of the dining room, only this one was tiny enough that it sat on top of the counter next to the register.

Today's Cookie: Starlight Speckled Sugar Cookies.

It was written in the swirling font I loved to write with, and I'd drawn a big tree with a moon hanging above it and had dotted the sky with stars. Then I'd added three squiggle lines of a stream running through.

My chest constricted as I thought of those nights, the way I'd believed Ryder was the only person in the world who could really understand me.

The only one who could really see.

I'd thought that maybe I'd been the same for him.

"Thank you," the older gentleman said.

"Any time. I hope you come again." As soon as I was finished with his order, I eased back along the counter to find I had two new customers sitting in the stools at the bar.

Paisley was grinning at me, as smug as could be, and Evelyn was propped on the stool next to her.

"I figured you would be missing my face by now. I mean, how could you not?" Paisley waved at herself.

"It's been two whole days, and you know I have most definitely not been missing your face." I sent her my best glare, even though it was hard to back it with any real anger.

"Did you miss my face, Auntie Dakota?" Evelyn peeped up, a little concerned and not understanding the playful animosity. The little girl sat on her knees so she could see over the counter, her brown hair a mess the way it always was, wild and falling in her eyes. She used both hands to try to shove it out of the way as she peered up at me.

The child could melt you with a glance.

I reached over the counter and tapped her nose. "You bet I did."

Her smile was so big it took over her entire face. "That's really good because I missed you, too. All the way to the moon. Did you know I got to take my horse Mazzy for a ride today? Four whole miles."

My eyes widened. "No way."

"Yes way." She gave me an emphatic nod. "I went with my mom, and she rode her horse, too, and we had the most fun we've ever even had, and then she said we could come here for lunch since it's our favorite."

Love rushed from my best friend.

A torrent.

So intense it nearly swept me from my feet, so I could only imagine the magnitude of what she was feeling.

Evelyn had just started calling her *mom* in the last couple weeks, ever since Caleb had proposed to Paisley and Evelyn had in turn asked if Paisley could be her mother. Paisley and Caleb had tried to be casual about it, allowing Evelyn to make the progression herself as she felt comfortable.

No question, Evelyn coming to that point had touched Paisley in a profound way.

I was so happy she'd found this piece of her heart.

That didn't mean I wasn't still crazy annoyed at my friend who was always up to no good.

Still, I told Evelyn, "It sounds like a wonderful day."

Paisley cleared the roughness from her throat and pinned on that easiness she loved to wear, tossing a lock of her nearly white hair over her shoulder. "Are you going to feed me or what?"

I scoffed. "Feed you? Didn't you see I'd pinned a picture of you on the front door saying you're banned from the restaurant?"

The gasp she let go of was ridiculous. "Ban me? The greatest friend you could ever ask for? The one who promised to help bury the bodies if ever necessary? Your ride or die?"

"My ride or die who keeps trying to throw me under the bus," I grumbled.

"I'm just trying to get you a *ride*, Dakota. You should be thanking me."

"Thanking you for what? Insinuating something you know isn't there? You have to stop that. The only thing you did was make Ryder go all big-brother bear on me while I'm having to stay under his roof. No thank you very much."

"I was just feeling out the waters…and believe me, they were *hot*. Scorching, Dakota." She dragged out the last.

Disbelief puffed from my lungs, and I kept my words low to keep them from any eavesdroppers hanging out in the restaurant. In Time River, there were bound to be plenty of them. "Hate to break it to you, but those waters are *freezing cold*. He's just in a stir over this whole break-in thing. You know there is nothing there, so drop it, okay?"

Ever since she'd moved back, she'd been watching Ryder and me a little too closely. Looking for something that didn't exist.

But my bestie was a dreamer.

A romantic of the highest sort.

A believer of white knights and twisted fates and fantasies that always came to fruition.

She sat back, a challenge written on her face. "So, are you telling me you don't want a ride?"

I started wiping down the counter a little more aggressively than necessary. "The only thing I'm telling you is I'm never getting a ride on *that*, so I'd appreciate you not needling it."

"Are we going to the fair?" Evelyn asked, far too excited by the prospect.

I choked over a laugh, and Paisley cracked up, and she reached over to wrap both arms around her and squeezed her tight. "Absolutely, in two months."

"Yay." Evelyn bounced on her knees, rocking the stool a bit.

"You be careful. We don't need you to fall over and bonk your head.

Your dad is liable to lose his whole mind if you end up in the urgent care." Paisley winked at her, like she wouldn't be losing it, too.

"I will be the carefulest," Evelyn promised.

Blowing out a sigh, I tossed the rag into the bucket under the counter. "Alright, you two, what do you want to eat?"

"I'm going to need one of those burgers and fries." Paisley moaned in anticipation. "I cannot handle how good they are."

"Samesies," Evelyn said, nodding. "We got all the same favorites."

Affection gushed from Paisley.

Relentless and unending.

"So, I'm guessing we're going to need two of my famous strawberry iced teas?" I asked.

"That's right. And make it a double," Evelyn piped up.

Paisley and I shared an amused glance before I said, "On it."

I punched in their order then moved down the counter to prepare the iced teas, adding double the amount of muddled strawberries into the fresh brew before I passed them out.

"One for Evie-Love and one for Paisley-Cakes."

Then I lowered my voice. "Who is still on my hit list."

Mischief was clear as she sat back and canted her head. "So, if you're not over there waiting for Ryder, I guess that means you're open to dating someone else."

Apprehension gusted, but I shrugged like it didn't matter. "I'm too busy to date."

Paisley's green eyes widened in horror. "No one should ever be too busy for love."

"That's right. Love is really the most important, and we can't get too busy for that," Evelyn agreed.

"I've got plenty of people who love me."

"But not the loved-up kind." Suggestion glinted through her overexaggerated gaze.

"Loved-up only leaves you messed-up."

There was no missing the questions that swirled through Paisley's mind. No doubt, she was itching to ask me about Kayden's father again. But what would I tell her?

One-night stands didn't count for much, except that one had counted on changing my entire life.

Regret clutched me by the throat. Not over Kayden. He was the biggest surprise blessing I'd ever received. But it was what had driven me to it that still left a bitter scar cut down the middle of me.

"You're only saying that because you haven't gotten loved-up right. But don't worry, your bestie is on the job."

She swiveled on her stool, her gaze bouncing around the café, searching for the perfect target.

Thank God everyone there was either married or double my age, though I doubted much the latter would stop her.

Then her grin split to straight glee when she noticed Brad come striding through the double doors into the café.

Brad who was admittedly hot in a business-y, straight-edged kind of way.

He'd opened an investments firm two blocks up on Manchester, and he came in at least once a week to eat.

He'd also asked me out twice before, which of course I'd declined.

"Don't you dare," I hissed under my breath, reaching clear across the counter to try to grab her by the wrist.

I knew exactly what she was thinking.

With me hanging onto her left wrist, she swiveled and lifted her right into the air. "Hey, Brad!" she called.

The menace slanted me a smirk from the side.

I will kill you, I mouthed, but I was pretty sure she could feel the force that came out behind it.

"Don't be so dramatic. You'll thank me later," she whispered back, trying to hide the words coming out of the corner of her mouth when Brad started our way.

His smile took up half of his handsome face, his blond hair short and perfectly parted. "Hey, Paisley."

His attention drifted to me, lingering a little longer, his brown eyes soft. "Dakota, how are you today?"

I forced myself to straighten, the smile I put on so brittle I wasn't sure how it didn't crack.

"I'm good. How are you?"

"Good, good," he said, though concern colored his expression. "I heard about the break-in at your place. I'm really sorry to hear that. I thought I'd pop over to check on you."

I did my best to shrug. "Thanks, Brad. It wasn't a big deal. Whoever it was didn't come inside and probably got scared away when they realized someone was home. Ezra thinks it's someone out stealing whatever they can find of value, and they stumbled on my place not realizing we lived there."

He shoved his hands into the pockets of his slacks and rocked back on his heels. "I hate that for you, though."

My smile slipped into something genuine. Brad really was a great guy.

"That's so nice of you, Brad." Paisley drew it out, tilting her head, my *ex-bestie* laying it on thick.

He chuckled, glancing between us like he was trying to figure out what was up. "I'm sure everyone in town is worried about our Dakota."

Excitement split her face with the way he phrased it, and there was no way to stop her from continuing without appearing like I was a crazy person flying over the counter to press my hand over her mouth. Still, I was gaping in some kind of horrified shock when she didn't just throw me under the bus again, she dragged me out into the middle of the road and chained me to the pavement.

"Maybe you should take her out for dinner to get her mind off it?"

Brad's gaze skated to me, though he'd kept his head down a bit, unsure. "I'd like that."

I inhaled a frazzled breath. Backed into a corner.

"Sounds great." I regretted it before it was even out.

"Wednesday?" he asked.

Air heaved from my nose, and I nearly told him I was busy for the next eternity. Instead, I said, "Sure."

Pleasure hinted at the edge of his mouth, lips quirking up a fraction. "I'll pick you up at seven then."

"Great."

Not great.

It was so not great.

He started to walk away when Paisley fully turned her stool around and called, "You're going to have to pick her up at Ryder's place. She's staying there for the time being."

A tight frown formed on Brad's brow before he dipped his head in acceptance. "Got it."

Then he turned and weaved through the dining room to one of the long tables where he sat opposite Mitch, one of the two accountants in town.

"I cannot believe you." The hiss was out the second he was out of earshot.

Paisley slowly swiveled back around, far too proud of herself. "You can't believe me? I thought we already talked about you starting to date."

"No, I said I was too busy to date."

"No one should ever be too busy to get loved-up by his fine a-s-s." She leaned forward to whisper-spell it. Doubling up on the precautions so Evelyn wouldn't understand.

"You are the a-s-s. I don't need you to go setting me up. I have enough on my plate." My voice was just as low where I was inclined her direction.

Sure. I was trying to get over Ryder. But I didn't think I was ready to fully date. It just didn't…feel right.

She reached over and covered my hand, squeezing it in emphasis. Soft sincerity flooded her features. "It's okay to have a little fun, Dakota. To get out and enjoy yourself. Open yourself up to the possibility because while you might deny it, you and I both know you've been closed off to it. I hate that you won't let me in and tell me why, but the last thing I want is for you to close yourself off. I just care about you and want the best for you."

Resignation had me blowing out a sigh. "I know you do, I'm just not sure—"

Her head shook. "Brad might not be your love match, but you're never going to know unless you try. It's just one date. That's all I'm asking of you. What could it hurt?"

The problem was, there was that achy spot inside me that promised it would always hurt. This hole that could only be filled by one person.

Shaking my head, I mumbled, "Fine."

Paisley threw a fist in the air. "There is my fabulous, ferocious, Grade-A, amazing bestie."

"You are amazing, Auntie," Evelyn sang, looking up at me from where she was slurping her tea from a straw with that sweet smile on her face.

Paisley looked at me like she dared me to refute them.

"Manipulators, the two of you." The tease came out lighter than I'd expected.

Evelyn lifted her hand to give Paisley a high-five. "We're a really good team."

"That we are, Evie-Love."

Shaking my head, I went into the kitchen and picked up their burgers, then returned with them.

Paisley groaned as she wrapped both hands around the enormous burger.

"Now there's no denying you love me. We all know food is your love language, Doodle-Boo. And I feel it right here…way down deep in the pit of my stomach."

She took a massive bite.

I couldn't help but laugh. "You are such a dork, Paisley Dae."

A meddling, wild, wonderful dork.

Tenderness moved through her gaze, remorse and worry making their way to the top. "But you really do love me, right?"

I glanced over to where Brad sat. A new heaviness pressed down on that empty spot that throbbed inside. I turned back to her. "You know I do. I just hope you're not bringing trouble to my door."

Paisley smirked. "Nothing is quite as much fun without a little trouble splashed in it. Now let's talk about what my hot AF BFF is going to wear…"

Chapter Seventeen

Dakota

Thirteen Years Old

THE TIMER BUZZED ON THE OVEN AND DAKOTA PADDED OVER the linoleum floor to open it. She covered her hand in a mitt before she reached in and pulled out the tray of chocolate chip cookies. The only light illuminating the kitchen was the one that glowed from the hooded vent above the stove, cutting into the darkness that pressed in from the windows and hovered heavy in the night.

Baking always made her happy.

Chased away every bad thought.

A place where her mind drifted, and her heart beat free. Where she was safe. Where she found comfort.

Where she found that feeling that made her believe she was something special, or at least that one day she was going to be.

Tonight, though, as she set the tray on the cooling rack, it was filled with sadness.

With a grief so distinct that the air felt clotted. Like a thick cloud of it had come to blot everything out.

It crushed down around her as she transferred the cookies into a tin and covered them with a lid, and it weighed down her steps as she quietly edged through the sleeping house and slipped out the front door.

She cringed when it snapped a little too loudly behind her, then she breathed out a relieved breath when she heard no movement from inside.

Keeping her feet as quiet as possible, she eased down the steps, and she stayed low as she crept along the front of their house to the side. The second she made it to the path that ran the length of their fence, she increased her pace, hurrying along it under the cover of night until she slowed at the edge of the woods that rose up behind their backyard.

She could hear the trickling of the stream as it rolled over the smoothed rocks, the hoot of the owl, and the rustle of the branches as the crisp fall air breezed through the leaves.

But more than anything else, she could taste the sourness of the sorrow that sat like a blanket that sagged from the heavens.

She eased up to the tree, her eyes tracing the silhouette that she saw from behind.

That shaggy mop of black hair had gotten long and even more unruly over the summer. He'd grown tall during that time, when he'd gone away to spend the summer with his cousin in Washington. He was no longer the gangly boy that she knew, the one who laughed at everything and was always joking around.

The one who devoured every single thing she baked and never failed to tell her it was the best thing he'd ever eaten.

The one who had met her out here so many times when he somehow knew that she was sad.

But this time, she was coming for him.

She eased forward, trying to keep her footsteps light, like she didn't want to interrupt but didn't know how to stay away, either.

Ryder didn't say anything as she crawled onto the branch where they always sat below the star speckled sky.

She didn't know how long they remained there in the silence, his breaths choppy and strained, his knees hugged to his chest. He had his chin propped on them as he stared out into the nothingness, but she doubted much he could see very far through the fog of pain.

She didn't want to say something stupid like she was sorry, so she finally whispered, "I brought you something," as she popped off the lid.

The scent of chocolate and sugar and spice wafted up to her nose, and Ryder made a grumbled sound. "Of course, you brought me something."

He shifted his face to her. It was red and splotchy, and his eyes were nearly swollen shut from the tears.

She'd known his momma was dying for a long time. She'd been sick for years. But to her, it'd seemed like it'd been that way forever, and she guessed there was a part of her that had imagined that it would just continue to stay that way.

But she'd learned two days ago that death had a way of catching up.

She passed him the tin, and he reached in for a cookie and took a bite. He tipped his head up to that starlit sky and chewed slowly, sniffling as he swallowed. He continued that way until he'd eaten the whole thing.

Then he turned back to her.

His big red smile was crooked.

All wrong.

"How's it that just tasting something you baked could make me feel better?"

She thought it was kind of a tease, and she rolled her eyes and faced forward. "I know it doesn't make it any better at all, but I just wanted you to know that I was thinking of you."

That he wasn't forgotten.

He'd always made her feel like she was important, and she wanted to do the same for him.

His smile tweaked a little deeper before he grabbed another cookie and took a bite, whispering around it, "No, Dakota. You're right. It doesn't feel better. I don't know if it ever will. But I'm still glad you were thinking of me."

Her chest felt achy, and her stomach felt hollow. She couldn't imagine what it would feel like if it was her mom. Her dad had died when she was two, and she couldn't remember him at all. She only recognized him from the pictures her mom had shown her through the years and the ones that were plastered all over the house.

She wondered if there was anyone who would be there now to help Ryder remember.

"What's going to happen now?" she whispered. "Where are you going to live?"

The last two days had been hurried. Her mom and Ryder's aunt had put together the funeral and the reception, which they'd had here at Dakota's house. Dakota had spent all that time baking and preparing, too, knowing it was the one thing she could do.

More tears fell down Ryder's cheeks. "I'm going to live with Ezra, I guess."

Behind it came an angry sound.

"That's not where you want to be?"

His head shook as he stared out into the night. "No. I want to be home. With my mom. But she's not there any longer, is she?"

He choked that with an ugly fury, and he yanked at the locks of his black hair, making a sound so low and deep that she knew it came from a place that was rarely seen.

A place people only knew in times like these.

A place filled with agony. A torment that felt like it would suck you under.

She knew he was hurting so bad, but there wasn't anything she could do to stop it. Not the same way as he'd always been able to do for her.

"I told my aunt I wanted to stay at my house. That I'm sixteen, and I can take care of myself."

"She won't let you?"

His laugh was dark. "Maybe she would have, but she told me she has to sell the house. There are all these medical bills that need to be paid. So, that fucking cancer didn't just steal my mom, it stole my home, too." He spat it through clenched teeth.

Then he was on his feet in a flash.

Jumping off the branch without saying anything.

A storm where he raged below her.

"You should go to bed, Dakota. It's too late for you to be out here."

Her heart panged. She hated that he was treating her like a little kid.

She was compared to him, but it was the first time he'd ever made her feel that way.

"I have to get out of here." He croaked it, disoriented as he looked around as if he were searching for something that had gone missing.

"Where are you going to go?" Fear clotted her whispered words.

His head shook harshly. "I don't know. Anywhere. Just…away."

He turned and started to walk, disappearing into the thick bushes and trees.

And she wanted to call out to him.

Beg him not to forget about her.

But she got the sick feeling in her stomach that he would.

Chapter Eighteen
Ryder

WHEN I HEARD THE CAR PULLING INTO THE DRIVEWAY, A SMILE crept to my mouth. I shouldn't get used to it, but there was something about it that sent a roll of comfort gliding through my senses.

Something that was becoming familiar.

The sound of car doors slamming before there were footsteps on the porch and then the turning of the lock on the door. But the best part was the clatter of feet and the explosion of excitement that suddenly burst through the quiet and shot everything into this sweet, perfect chaos.

"My Rye-Rye, I find you!" That little voice rode on it as he came running through the house, tiny feet pounding on the hardwood floors before he appeared in the entryway to the kitchen.

The grin splitting his face nearly did me in, his chubby little hand in the air and the way he was pointing at me. "I find you!"

"You did find me, didn't you? How did you even know where I was hiding?" I set the big spoon on the counter and eased his way, hiking him up into my arms.

"I a big boy," he told me, so proud with that dip of his head.

"That's right, you are, and you knew exactly where to go, didn't you?"

I wondered if he'd always know it. If he'd know when he got older that he could come to me for anything. That I'd give it all.

I was pressing a kiss to his temple when the air shifted again.

Warmth skating like rays through the late afternoon light.

I lifted my gaze to find Dakota stalled out at the entryway.

There was no stopping my hungry gaze from roving over her. Devouring her where she stood across the room.

All that light and goodness radiating around her. The force of it stabbed me right in the chest.

She wore this light pink and blue floral dress that should be modest, but she made it look like she was in a nightie, the spaghetti straps showing off the soft slope of her neck and shoulders and the fabric swishing down to caress every delectable curve of her body.

But what got me was her expression as she took me in where I held her son. Cinnamon eyes shimmering with something so right. Like maybe she'd stepped in on her meaning, too.

Fear sliced into the peace, and it bound with the resolution I kept trying to find.

Standing there, I had no question that I had to make a change. But I wasn't going to lie—actually taking the step and doing it terrified me.

The risk I was taking.

And that risk should only land on me, but I knew from experience how low that motherfucker would stoop.

Bile thickened in my throat at the thought.

My regrets were so thick that sometimes I wondered how I got up each morning.

Dakota seemed to shake herself from whatever trance we'd been under and sent me a gentle smile. "Why does it smell so good in here?"

I walked back to the stove with Kayden in my arms. Picking up the spoon, I began to stir the sauce I had in a pot. "Not half as good as it does when I walk into your café, but I figured you'd had a long day and might want someone to cook for you for a change."

Surprise rippled through her features before she slowly wandered deeper into the kitchen. She stopped at the end of the counter, and she leaned her hands on top. Three feet down from us, hovering there like maybe she was worried to tread any closer.

"You didn't have to do that." Her voice was a wisp of appreciation.

I eyed her with a smirk. "What, are you scared of my cooking? I might not be a pro, but I'll have you know I can make a mean spaghetti sauce."

A tiny giggle slipped from her lips, and she shook her head. "I don't doubt you, Ryder. You spent enough time with me in the kitchen when we were growing up, I'm sure you learned a thing or two."

It was a tease. Still, it rolled through me like seduction.

There was an easiness in it, though. That familiarity that Dakota and I had found over the years. Because if I couldn't have her the way I wanted, I at least had to have her like this. "Awful sure of yourself over there, are you?"

I let the razzing play on my tongue.

Another giggle, and a flush was rising up from her gorgeous tits and climbing her throat. "Well, what do you expect when you and your cousins always come in singing my praises? A girl is bound to let it go to her head."

I set the spoon down, unable to do anything but move her way. I reached out and tilted up her chin. "It's not only me and my cousins who are singing those praises. It's the whole damned town. And you earned that pride, Dakota Cooper. Don't ever question it."

"Mommy." Kayden reached out his arms, deciding he wanted his mom to hold him instead of me.

Didn't blame the kid a bit.

Tenderness billowed from her as we traded, and she ran a hand over his head as he snuggled into her chest, but she was still looking at me when she said, "Thank you for that."

"Mean it," I rumbled as I went back to the second pot that was just beginning to boil with water. I put in the noodles and stirred them, then set the timer.

"Why don't you sit and relax?" I gestured to the stools on the other side of the counter. "Dinner will be ready in about fifteen."

"I *hungee*," Kayden told me.

I sent him a slow grin. "Of course, you are, K-Bear. You've gotta eat so you can grow even bigger."

"I be big like my Rye-Rye!" He tossed his little hand above his head like he was aiming for the stars.

Affection pulsed thick. Both from Dakota and me, and I couldn't look away as she moved to set him in his playpen then took the high-backed stool across from me.

"Do you want a glass of wine?" I was already moving for the cabinet to pull her out a glass before I grabbed the opener for the bottle of red that I'd picked up when I'd swung by the store after I'd left the shop.

I was going to have to make that delivery tomorrow night, and maybe it'd just been that I needed to do something normal tonight, so I'd decided to make dinner. Maybe I needed something to remind me of the good before I devolved into depravity.

Or maybe I just needed an excuse to be close to Dakota. It seemed the more I was around her, the more I wanted it.

To be in her space.

To experience her goodness, inhaling it like secondhand smoke.

Or maybe it was the idea of her signing up for that dating app that had set me off-kilter. Made me feel like I was going mad.

She groaned a throaty, deep sound that spoke directly to my dick. "Are you trying to spoil me, Ryder Nash?"

A smirk hitched at the edge of my mouth as I began to twist the cork-screw into the cork.

"Maybe just a little," I told her as I poured her a glass and slipped it across the counter to her.

A giggle rolled from between those pouty, shimmery lips, and she picked it up and took a sip. "If this is a little, then I need to see what it'd be like if you really wanted to spoil someone. I bet you have all those women completely on their knees."

She twined her fingers through the end of her ponytail, the razzing drifting off a fraction at the end.

I guessed neither of us could help but cringe with what she'd implied.

"Do you think I'd take the time to spoil anyone else but you, Dakota?" It was out before I could stop it, no way to reel the confession back before it'd hit the air.

Fuck.

I focused on stirring the noodles rather than taking in the confusion that tripped through Dakota's features.

It didn't matter if I wasn't looking at her, anyway.

I could still feel it.

Could sense the way she wanted to ask me what I meant.

She took a long drink of her wine like it could quell the questions that were dancing on her tongue all while the woman was watching me like I was a riddle to figure out.

"Are you sure I can't help?" she finally asked a couple minutes later.

"Nah, I've got it. You sit there and relax those pretty feet." I managed to find the teasing again.

She smirked. "I have news for you, Ryder. No one's feet are pretty." Then she curled up her nose. "Unless you have one of those foot fetishes?"

She leaned forward, tucking a loose strand of hair behind her ear, fighting a smile like she was horrified by the thought.

Only if they're your feet, sweet thing.

"What, you have a thing against fetishes? And here I thought you were into some *crazy kink?*"

A blaze of red rushed across her face when I gave voice to what had been eating at me for the last three days.

Visions constantly invading my mind and stirring my cock into greed.

I wanted to ask her what her fantasies were and then take her to them time and again.

"That was just Paisley trying to get a rise out of us." She muttered it below her breath.

"Yeah?" I asked as I drained the noodles in the sink, cutting her a glance as I did. "The kink or the dating app?"

Yeah. I'd come across as a misogynist prick Saturday morning.

But I couldn't stop the reaction, the way my stomach had sank and every nerve in my body had short circuited at the thought.

The thought of losing her.

Forever.

In a way I could never get her back.

She was leaned up close, both elbows on the counter as she nursed her wine, and she lifted one of those soft shoulders to her ear, though there was a tiny twitch of her lips. "The app, I guess."

"You're not interested in dating, huh?"

But the kink was a thing?

Noted.

I started working on scooping piles of noodles onto each of our plates and pouring a mountain of sauce over them.

Hesitation brimmed in Dakota, and out of the corner of my eye, I could see something creep through her features. Something that shouted reservation and doubt. "I actually have a date," she quietly admitted.

I nearly dropped the plate I was holding to the floor, and I had to set it on the counter so I could regain my bearings.

Heart thrashing.

Teeth grating.

I gave it my all to keep the asshole out of my voice. "Oh yeah? Who's the lucky guy?"

"Brad Geller. We're going to dinner on Wednesday," she added quickly.

"That's cool." Too bad the words sliced like spears.

I had to force myself to move. To focus on carrying our plates to the table rather than spitting out the thousand things that spiraled through my mind.

Rather than telling her the thought of it fucking killed me. Rather than begging her to give me some time.

Rather than promising I was going to fucking fix this.

But could I?

Was it ever really going to change?

And even then, it couldn't undo the stains. Couldn't erase the sins that I'd committed.

I went back to the counter and grabbed the small bowl I'd made for Kayden while Dakota stood from her stool and pulled Kayden from his playpen.

She buckled him into the highchair that I'd also picked up the day I'd gotten the crib.

The whole time, we moved around each other in this discomfort that made it feel like we were walking through sludge.

I was refilling her wine, my back to her, when her voice finally broke through the tension. "You don't think I deserve to find love, Ryder? Do you think I'm not desirable enough that someone would want me?"

Hurt wove into her words.

My chest felt like it was going to cave when I moved back to her. She stood in front of the table, facing out.

Lifting that quivering chin, so brave and fierce and sweet.

The sight of her hit me like a landslide.

Quicksand.

No way to get out.

I leaned around her and set her glass on the table, and when I eased back, she was right there, so close I could scent the sugar and vanilla that radiated from her skin.

I had the urge to lean forward and press my nose to it.

Inhale.

Trace my fingers over every slope and every curve.

I settled on touching her cheek before I took a little and dragged my fingertip over that divot at the side of her chin. "Do I think you're not desirable, Dakota? You're the most desirable woman I've ever met. And yeah, I think you're worthy of love. Worthy of it more than anyone I know. Don't ever mistake that."

I was just jealous that I wasn't worthy of receiving it from her.

She gulped, her throat bobbing, and that tension took new form.

New shape.

Growing thick and dense between us.

A clawing need.

"Ryder," she whispered.

Before I fumbled and let myself cross a line I couldn't, I stepped back and canted her a wayward grin. "I'll even watch Kayden for you."

A frown twisted across her brow, and it took everything I had not to reach out and smooth it.

To keep from telling her I wanted it to be me.

But I couldn't do that, could I?

"Now come on, let's eat, your food is going to get cold. I didn't work over the stove all afternoon to waste it."

The tease came easy. The way it always did.

But stomaching the food was an entirely different story.

Chapter Nineteen

Dakota

I PULLED THE BLANKET OVER KAYDEN'S LITTLE BODY. HIS BREATHS were even as he slept. Facedown and sprawled out the way he always did, his glowing bear hugged under his arm and his cheek pressed to it. Snuggled up.

Safe.

Loved.

All the things I hoped for my son.

I ran my fingers through his soft brown hair, whispering, "Sleep well, sweet boy," before I crept from his room, leaving the door open a fraction.

Muted light filtered into the hall, and the old wood groaned beneath my feet as I moved. I tried to keep my steps even quieter as I edged down the stairs to get a drink of water.

It was just past eleven o'clock, and the house was quiet. I'd finished reading a book in my room before I'd gone in to check on Kayden.

It wasn't like I was going to be able to sleep.

Not after whatever had happened between me and Ryder earlier tonight.

The man so thoughtful and sweet.

Making dinner so I wouldn't have to cook once I got home from the restaurant.

Taking care of me.

But then it'd gotten awkward, the air filling with a tension that had writhed between us.

I swore he'd been angry—jealous even—when I'd told him I was going on a date.

Then he'd just grinned and said he would babysit Kayden for me, then sat down at the table and joked with me throughout dinner like nothing had happened.

I thought I sustained whiplash every time we had a conversation.

This push and pull that tugged between us so fierce that I never could quite get my footing.

These were the times that made me think...*maybe.*

Maybe he did want me.

But then I remembered I needed to stop thinking of him that way. Let go of this fantasy that would never amount to anything.

It was pathetic, really, that I pined after him like he was the only man on Earth after he'd rejected me.

Paisley was right.

I did need to go on this date.

I needed to try.

I hit the bottom floor landing and crept across the living room and into the kitchen.

No question, I'd be paying for these rampant thoughts in the morning. Five o'clock would come early. But rather than tossing under the sheets, I'd decided to read to take my mind off things, and I'd allowed myself to get caught up in a love story that had pounded through my veins, the couple's connection so fierce and hot it'd left me a panty, sweaty mess by the end.

I figured a glass of ice water would douse the lingering steam.

This distraction? It hadn't helped. The only thing it'd done was make it disturbingly clear what I was missing.

What I needed.

My body throbbing and aching for something I'd gone without for so long.

I'd only gone and made it so much worse, unable to do anything but replace the hero's face with Ryder's, a masochist because my own kept slipping in, too.

And there went that dangerous fantasy.

Round and round.

A cycle I wasn't sure I'd ever get free of.

But it made it extra difficult when he was in the room two doors away.

I kept moving, the planks cool on the soles of my feet. Only a faint glow illuminated the kitchen, and I went directly to the cabinet, pulled out a glass, and filled it with ice and water from the dispenser.

I guzzled it down like I was trying to put out a fire, then I took a couple clearing breaths before I started back through the living room.

Creeping slowly, I tried to keep the wood from creaking as I ascended the stairs, my hand gliding up the smooth railing as I went.

Then I stilled when I got to the top and heard Ryder call my name.

Low and grumbly.

Crap.

As quiet as I'd been trying to be, I'd woken him. He kept saying we weren't a burden, but I had a hard time believing that when we constantly interrupted his routine. I shifted course so I could apologize.

"Ryder?" I whispered as my hand went to his doorknob, and I twisted it and pushed his door open.

Then I froze.

Completely froze.

Unable to move or form a coherent thought. Obviously, since the only logical one would have been slamming the door shut and running back to my room.

But no, I stood there holding onto the doorhandle.

My mouth gaping in shock.

Stomach tossed out somewhere on his floor.

Because Ryder was in his bed, a dark king where he was propped against black pillows and laid out on an expanse of black sheets.

No shirt, his chest bare.

He was still wearing the same pair of dark jeans he'd had on earlier, only the fly was open and they were shoved down enough that his cock was freed.

His enormous cock that he had fisted in his tattooed hand. He rode it up and down the stony, hard flesh.

Arousal flooded me, and my knees went weak, my heart beating so hard and fast I felt it like a storm battering the room.

Pulse running jagged, and my mind bending as I tried to process the sight.

His cock.

I was looking at his cock.

The head fat and purpled and pierced at the tip.

Some logical part of me was shouting to turn and go. To shut the door and pretend like I had not stumbled in on this.

But I was chained.

Held captive by those gunmetal eyes that watched me like he'd fully expected me to be standing there. As if they'd conjured me. Compelled me to this spot.

Lured and hypnotized.

He didn't stop stroking himself, he kept jerking his hand up and down his rigid length, his stomach bowing and flexing as he thrust up a little to meet his fist.

That gaze remained on me the whole time.

My pussy clenched in a pulse of need, and heat flash-fired over my skin, flames so intense and hot I wasn't sure how I hadn't combusted right there in his doorway.

"Dakota," he grunted.

It was the sound of his voice scraping through the air that finally jarred me out of the stupor.

What sent my eyes going wide and my mouth flapping in horror. "Oh my God, Ryder. I'm so sorry."

I pushed my hand out in front of me like it was a shield, obstructing my view, when I was pretty sure this moment was going to be emblazoned in my mind forever. "I'm so sorry. I didn't mean to just barge in...I just...I thought I heard you calling me...I thought..."

God. I was an idiot. A blabbering idiot.

I finally got my bearings enough that I backed out, stumbling as I went, and I slammed his door a little harder than I meant to. Then I dashed down the hall and into my room, where I slammed that door, too. I leaned against the wood, trying to catch my breath, to rein in the sense I'd lost somewhere in his room.

"Oh God," I whimpered. That horror began to thrum. It surged through me as I realized that I'd stood there watching him pump himself. For God knew how long.

I squeezed my eyes shut in an attempt to block it. The only thing it did was cause it to become even more vivid.

The way he'd said my name kept rolling through my brain, trembling through me in wisps of seduction that I knew better than to feel.

I'd misinterpreted it.

I had to have.

I blamed it on the stupid book. On the fantasy that I'd been a fool to give myself over to.

But knowing the truth didn't stop the tingles that raced. Did nothing to stop the flames that licked beneath the surface of my skin. Every cell in my body pulsated with need. With this desire I'd tried to subdue for years, and there it was, stronger than it had ever been before.

I shuffled to my bed and laid down, breathing hard as I stared through the darkness at the ceiling, praying I could tame what was stampeding out of control.

But it was too heavy and dense, and I was so turned on that my panties were drenched.

My hand was shaking when I gave in and let it wander down my stomach to slide under my sleep shorts, and I whimpered as my fingers grazed over my clit. As engorged and swollen as Ryder had been.

I had to suppress the moan that rolled up my throat when I began to rub myself, my fingertips swirling over the nub. Pleasure glinted, glowing behind my eyelids as I decided to fully give myself over to the fantasy.

Just one more time and then I would let him go.

It took all of five seconds for an orgasm to whip through my body. All I needed to do was imagine Ryder's head between my legs, black hair tickling the inside of my thighs as he ate me into oblivion.

I bowed with the moment's ecstasy, and I turned to the side to bury my face in a pillow to cover his name that whimpered from my tongue.

To hide it.

To pretend like I didn't want him anymore. Like he didn't matter the way I feared he would always matter to me.

Trembles rolled and reeled, this skewed rapture that continued to flicker through my limbs.

I startled when my phone lit up on my nightstand.

I grabbed for it probably a little too eagerly.

Ryder: Did you like watching me fuck my hand, Dakota?

A new shock of lust burst in my blood, so intense I could hardly think or see. I wanted to answer but was terrified at the same time. Another text came in before I could fathom how in the world I was supposed to reply.

> **Ryder: Did you touch yourself thinking of me when you got back to your room? With those sweet hands that are way too clean to get dirty with me?**

> **Ryder: You were a fucking vision standing in my door.**

> **Ryder: Like you'd been manifested in my dreams.**

I blinked, staring at the words.

Sure I had to be reading them all wrong.

Or maybe I was just dreaming.

Maybe I'd been knocked dumb by the sight of the man jerking himself on his bed.

The more likely possibility was that I'd made up the entire thing.

Except another text came through.

> **Ryder: Think it'd be a good idea for you to start locking your door, Dakota.**

My heart clattered against my ribs, and I strained to hear any movement or sound.

My breaths shallow.

This confusion so thick the room was filled with a haze.

Everything enclosed, the air and this tension that expanded in the space.

A whirring hum that echoed in the room.

Or maybe it was seeping in from the outside.

In it was this lingering need.

A call from down the hall.

If I followed it, I knew it would lead to his door.

A lure.

A trap.

My spirit ached to give it heed.

To give into the tugging that pulled at the center of me.

To see if this was real or if it was all a figment of my imagination.

Self-preservation kicked in.

I knew better than that.

Ryder would never really want me. Not the way I wanted him.

He'd told me, and I was a fool to believe anything else.

A fool to respond and beg him to make good on the last text.

So I forced myself to lie back in bed and ignore his messages.

Both terrified and thrilled by the exchange.

But I needed to remember that just looking at Ryder broke my heart.

And I could only imagine what would happen if he touched me—even if it was only once.

Chapter Twenty

Dakota

"**M**OM, IT'S ONLY A DINNER DATE. YOU'RE ACTING LIKE THE man asked me to marry him." My voice was hushed as I spoke to her on the phone and hurried around the kitchen getting Kayden's things ready, trying not to second-guess the choice I'd made to agree to this.

It was for the best.

Getting the heck out of this house before I completely lost my mind seemed like a really good idea right then.

"Well, he might not have asked you yet, but he seems like the kind of guy who is looking to settle down." My mom was as caring as they came, and there wasn't a mean or vapid bone in her body, but she also seemed to know all the gossip that made it through town. When Brad had moved into Time River, he'd been quite the topic of interest.

Suffice it to say my mother was most definitely interested now.

I sighed. "It's one date. That's all, so don't you start planning any weddings."

My nerves were rattled as it was.

My insides shredded from whatever had happened with Ryder two nights ago. All my edges frayed.

I didn't need her feeding anything else into the chaos.

Yesterday morning, neither Ryder nor I had mentioned the night before. We'd gone about our routine like everything was normal while a sticky tension had strained between us.

Not that I'd seen him all that much.

Once he'd gone into work, he hadn't returned. He had been gone long into the late-night hours doing God knew what. Things I didn't want to know about, that was for sure. Things that had kept me up tossing in bed, still awake when he'd come creeping up the stairs at close to three in the morning.

And that—that was the exact reason I couldn't allow myself to contemplate it.

If it weren't for the text messages that had still been sitting on my phone, I would have chalked the whole thing up to a dream.

But there they were.

Glaring and real.

The problem was, I had no idea what they meant, and deciphering them was a fool's game.

Ryder Nash could demolish me, and the last thing I needed was to get my heart shattered.

Mom huffed like I was ridiculous. "I'm not planning any weddings, Dakota. I'm excited that my daughter is going out. Is that such a bad thing?"

Affection swelled in my chest, and a soft smile pulled to my mouth. "No. It's not such a bad thing. I just don't want you getting ahead of yourself."

"I think the real question is if you want to go there?" She drew it out like life's most important question.

"I don't even really know him," I said as I poured milk into a sippy cup.

"Which is the whole point of a date," she reminded me, her easy encouragement knitted into the words. "It could be the beginning of something great."

"It's honestly not that big of a deal, Mom. He came into the café for lunch, and he asked me to dinner."

I left out the whole part where Paisley had instigated the whole thing.

"All I'm saying is you should keep your heart open to possibility."

I didn't have time to respond before the air got sucked from my lungs.

The presence covering me from behind was overwhelming.

Intense and harsh and so much stronger than it normally was.

The ground didn't just shift a fraction this time, but it tipped far enough it made it difficult to keep my balance.

To remain steady.

Compelled, I looked over my shoulder.

Ryder hovered at the entryway.

Midnight in the light of day.

All rigid lines and untamed hair and wicked eyes that stroked over me like a rough caress. One done with callused, needy hands.

A shiver rocked through, and I swallowed it down, trying my best to ignore this strange, new energy that had taken his house hostage.

Dense and deep.

So thick it was hard to move through it.

It'd grown even worse since I'd come downstairs after I'd showered and gotten ready. I'd decided on a high-waisted pink dress with a tulle skirt that lent itself to one of those childhood princess fantasies. I'd paired it with matching pink pumps and did my hair in a high ponytail, and each time I shifted my head, the curls bounced around my shoulders.

I'd finished the look with glimmery eyeshadow and glossy, pink lips.

I'd stood in the mirror for about three minutes looking at myself because I felt so pretty.

Felt beautiful and fierce and strong.

But I wasn't feeling all that strong when something that sounded like a groan emanated from Ryder, and I swore that he gnashed his teeth while he remained standing in the same spot staring at me.

"All right, Mom, I need to go so I can get Kayden settled before I leave." I basically choked it.

God, what was happening to me?

I could almost see her frowning from across the line. "Is Ryder sure he wants to watch him tonight? You know I don't mind having him here."

My stomach twisted, and I was answering quietly, still trapped under the weight of that glinty, silvered gaze. "He said there was no reason for me to drag him over there since it's already close to Kayden's bedtime, and he's going to be here anyway."

"Okay, then. Just let him know I'm here if he needs anything."

"I will. I'll see you when I drop Kayden off in the morning."

"You have *extra fun* tonight." There was no missing the teasing suggestion in her voice.

"Eww, Mom."

She cracked up like it was hysterical.

"Seriously, go and relax and enjoy yourself."

"I will. Love you."

I ended the call, and that same, unsure, anxious energy that had rained for the last two days began to pour down.

A torrent.

I cleared my throat and lifted the sippy cup I'd filled, hoping to distract from the strain that pulled between us. "Here's Kayden's sippy cup." I walked to the fridge and put it inside as I gave instructions, "He's already eaten so he should be good. He can drink that on the couch while you read him a story, but then he needs to brush his teeth after. He's going to try to convince you to refill it and let him take it into his crib, but don't let him swindle you into that."

There was no stopping the soft tug of affection when I said it.

There was no stopping the one that pulled at Ryder, either.

"Who knew a tiny tot could be such a manipulator. Kid has mad skills."

"Be careful not to let him use them on you." Why did my voice have to come out so shaky and hushed?

"I've got it, Dakota. You don't have to worry about him with me."

It wasn't like he'd never watched him before, on the nights when there'd been an issue at the café and I'd needed someone to watch him for a little while. That and the couple times I'd gone out with Paisley and the rest of our friends, and he'd offered to stay with him so I could have a night of fun.

Claiming that he didn't get to spend enough time with my son.

That was the thing about Ryder. He was always giving. So caring. Willing to drop whatever he was doing to help out when I needed it.

But tonight, it felt different. It wasn't close to being easy the way it used to be.

No, not when Ryder's eyes kept tracking over my dress, and my breaths had turned thin and shallow.

"I know. It's just...weird leaving him like this," I admitted.

"Is this what you want? To leave him like this? Do you want to go on this date?" It felt like a challenge.

A frown curled my brow, and a bit of that old anger and rejection rose to the surface. "Isn't it what I should do, Ryder? Move on with my life? Find someone to love me because I've been aching to love someone for a long, long time. You told me I deserved it."

Then a few hours later he'd been texting me asking me if I'd liked watching him fuck his hand before he'd told me to lock my door.

But he hadn't come, had he?

I had no way to make any sense of him. Of what he wanted. And I was finished letting these unfulfilled emotions master me.

Still, I hated the way my response had come out sounding like a plea. It felt a little too close to the way I'd opened myself to him once before, and I snapped my chin up like it could cover me in a hedge of protection.

A barricade around my heart that had sustained a crack Monday night.

I needed to reinforce it.

"You do deserve it, Dakota."

He pushed from where he leaned against the jamb.

That big, towering body slowly crossed the room.

The air vibrated when he approached.

Oxygen changing colors.

Vapors of blues and blacks and pinks.

Trembles rolled through me the closer he got. His face that was cut in all those severe angles was soft and intent and somehow razor sharp.

Everything about him at odds.

He reached out and touched my cheek.

His brutal hands so gentle that I whimpered.

I didn't mean to.

But when he touched me like this…?

"You deserve everything. Had once thought I'd be the one to give it to you."

What?

Confusion slammed me, bewilderment and distress, and my heart squeezed with the power of it.

I nearly jumped out of my skin when the doorbell suddenly rang.

Ryder jumped back, though he kept staring at me as if he were expecting me to say something else.

I was held in it. Staring back.

The doorbell rang again, and Ryder spat, "Fuck," toward his feet.

I swallowed around the disorder.

"I need to go," I managed, my hands shaking as I grabbed my clutch and started across the floor, shouting, "Coming," as I went.

Unfortunately, to get out, I had to go right past Ryder. His body burned hot, his arm grazing mine and his spirit swamping the space.

Tumult bound me in a fist, and I angled around him before I rushed to where Kayden was playing with his dinosaurs on the carpet. I knelt in front of him and brushed my fingers through his hair. "Mommy is going to go out for a little bit, and you're going to stay with Uncle Ryder."

"My Rye-Rye." Kayden patted his chest then threw out his arm to point at Ryder who'd shifted in the doorway. "You *pway wif* me, my Rye-Rye?"

"That's right, buddy, I'm going to stay here and play with you until your mommy gets back." His voice was gravel, though it had softened for my son's benefit.

"Yay. Bye, Mommy. You go now. I stay." Kayden patted both my cheeks.

Even through the turmoil, laughter puffed out, and I leaned in and pressed a kiss to the crown of Kayden's head. "I see how easily I can be replaced."

Ryder came striding our way, and he leaned down and scooped Kayden up, pulling him to his chest.

I stood at the same time as he did.

He was so close.

A raging fire.

Those arms so strong and sure as he held onto my son. "No, Dakota, you can't be replaced."

My knees knocked, and I wobbled on my feet, my breaths so shallow I couldn't speak.

But what was I supposed to say?

What, when he was saying all these things that I'd longed to hear him say for years?

The doorbell rang again.

Crap.

"I really appreciate you watching him," I finally forced out.

"No problem." The words barely made it through the grinding of his teeth, and I forced myself to move to the door. I had my hand on the handle when his voice stopped me from behind. "You look beautiful, Dakota."

I swallowed back the shattered whimper. "Thank you."

I forced myself to open the door. Brad stood on the other side with his hands shoved in the pockets of his dress pants. Although he didn't look all wickedly casual the way Ryder always did.

He looked like he was having second thoughts.

Especially when Ryder appeared in the doorway with my son in his arms. He held him protectively as he issued the words over the top of Kayden's head.

"Take care of my girl."

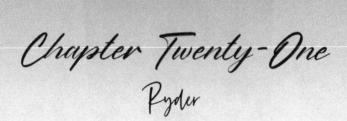

Chapter Twenty-One
Ryder

WATCHING HER STROLL DOWN THE WALKWAY WITH HER ELBOW hooked in Brad's was brutal.

Fucking brutal when he led her around to the passenger side of his car and helped her into the seat then jogged back around before they drove off.

While I stood on the porch staring like a stupid fuck who had no sense.

Had to beat down the urge to run after them.

On my feet like I could somehow manage to catch up to what was speeding away.

This was what I should want, though, wasn't it?

For her to go?

Move on?

Chase down whatever she wanted and take it for herself?

Except it was me standing there wanting to chase it down.

"Mommy go bye-bye." Kayden pointed at the taillights that faded in the distance.

"Yeah, buddy. Mommy went bye-bye, but she'll be back soon."

At least I fucking hoped so.

"Rye-Rye *pway* now." He dipped his head in all that excitement, cuteness dripping from him, enough that it pulled a short chuckle from me. I ran a hand over the back of his head before I pressed a kiss to the top.

"Let's go have fun, yeah?"

"I *wike* fun!"

I carried him into the house and back to the rug where his toys were dumped out.

Kid had basically confiscated the place, his shit strewn all over, and I couldn't help but think that's the way that it was supposed to be. That these walls were supposed to echo with this kind of love, with his giggles and sweetness and zest for life.

As I laid on the rug beside him, on my side and propped on my elbow while he sat fully up, babbling a million things in his little slur as he showed me every single one of his toys, I couldn't help but wonder if my mother had been in this very spot when I was little.

I had so many things I wanted to ask her about. Crawl inside her mind and heart and understand who she was because really, I hadn't been more than a kid when she'd gotten sick.

Had she watched me like this?

Had her heart been full?

Did it ache like mine did right then?

God, I missed her so fucking much.

So much that sometimes it was overwhelming. A pain so profound I felt it like a black hole inside me.

An abyss.

Bottomless.

No end.

There were times when I thought I might succumb to it, but I guessed on some part I had.

Shame billowed through me as I thought about the way I'd given up and given in.

What I'd caused.

Kayden suddenly threw himself at me, giggling as he went to wrestling around, and I rolled onto my back and tossed him high.

I stared up at his sweet face as his adorable laughter rolled, dimples deep, his arms and legs flailing as I zoomed him all over, making him fly and soar.

I pulled him down and squeezed him tight, and he rested his cheek on my chest. "Love is on house," he mumbled.

My spirit thrashed, pulsing so hard with *that kind of love* that I was feeling like I might succumb again, but in a wholly different way.

His mother's goodness rushed out of him on waves. This sweet, sweet thing who filled me up in a way I never should have let him.

But I accepted it then, my arms around him as I murmured, "Love you with everything I've got, K-Bear."

Wiggling all over, he snuggled deeper, and I felt his little yawn. "I get *mewlk* now."

I didn't let him go as I climbed to standing, and I carried him into the kitchen where I grabbed his sippy cup from the fridge, then carried him back out to his favorite chair in my living room where I sat him on my lap and grabbed one of his books.

He guzzled down the milk while I read him *The Very Hungry Caterpillar*, the kid counting along, though his words had gotten groggy and even more slurred with each minute that passed.

By the time I carried him upstairs and brushed his teeth, he was already close to sleep. I laid him down in his crib, tucked the glowing bear I'd gotten him for his birthday under his arm, and murmured, "Goodnight, sweet boy."

"I sweet boy," he agreed, nodding his cheek against the sheet.

Devotion pulsed, and I stood there staring at him for the longest time before I eased out, leaving his door open as I headed back downstairs.

I made myself a ham and cheese sandwich because I was fancy like that and grabbed a beer, sat down at the table, and ate by myself, watching the goddamn clock like it was a ticking timebomb. Like the later she was out, the closer we came to destruction.

To everything getting blown to shit.

She'd only been gone for two and a half hours when I heard the purr of the car pull up in front of my house, but it felt like a lifetime had passed.

Like the years had blurred, and I'd been looking back at them and knew they'd been a complete fucking waste.

That I'd squandered everything.

Anxiety curdled my blood as minutes dragged on and she didn't come inside, and I had to restrain myself from storming outside and stopping whatever might have been going down.

It wasn't my fucking business.

I needed to let Dakota do her thing.

Enjoy her life.

But this was the first time in all these years that she'd been out with another guy, that I knew of at least, except for whoever the asshole was who'd fathered Kayden, his identity something that she kept tight-lipped.

Just thinking about that prick sent me jolting to my feet, hands curling into fists as I paced, taking the kitchen floor like I could outrun the disorder that had taken me over.

My heart jackhammered.

Thoughts a goddamn stampede.

What the fuck would I do if she brought him in here? Took him up to her room?

I ripped at my hair knowing there wasn't a chance in hell I could handle that.

And I was sure I was going to go out of my mind when the front door quietly snapped open, and I stilled in the wake of it.

Her presence hit me like a balm, but it wasn't close to calming.

The door shut and I heard her turning the lock, felt her hesitation as she stood just inside my house, her sweet spirit clattering out for me.

I gathered myself enough to ease up to the kitchen entryway, refusing the urge to go flying out into the room to demand every answer that had been bouncing around in my head since she'd left.

Only she stole the breath from my lungs when I caught sight of her.

Left me staggered.

No way to even speak.

The woman in this pink, frilly dress that made her look like some kind of ballerina, pink pumps to match.

Had nearly died when she'd come downstairs earlier dressed that way.

"Hey." I managed to keep it cool like I hadn't been crawling the fucking walls waiting for her to get back.

"Hey." It was a murmur as she peeked up at me. She seemed to war for a second before she made the decision to start my way.

Slowly.

Carefully.

Her heels quietly clicking on the hardwood floors.

And there she was again.

A landslide.

Quicksand that immediately sucked me under.

No escape from her lure.

She stopped a foot away.

"How was Kayden?" she asked, keeping the words hushed.

"He was great," I told her, doing the same so we didn't wake him.

She let go of a tender smile. "Well, at least the house is still standing."

Affection bloomed, and my lips tugged with it. "Told you he was no problem at all. We played until he pretty much passed out. I read him a story, brushed his teeth, then tucked him into bed. Kid was out like a light."

Her teeth raked those shimmery pink lips. I did my best not to groan. "I really appreciate you doing it, even though it sounds like you two had a great time."

"We did. Love getting that kind of time with him."

Tension pulsed, curling and crackling through the dim light that closed us in.

Redness hit her cheeks, and she looked down. Apparently neither of us knew what to do right then.

"Do you want something to drink? Have a little of that wine left over from the other night."

She only hesitated for a beat before she nodded, and I turned and headed for the cabinet, knowing with the way I was feeling, I should have let her climb to her room and lock her door the way I'd warned her.

But I wasn't feeling so rational right then.

So I grabbed her a glass and emptied the bottle of wine into it, set it in front of her where she'd stopped at the end of the counter again.

"You're always taking care of me," she whispered. Cinnamon eyes glinted beneath the bare light.

So warm.

So real.

I'd gotten too close, and I was getting inundated with her scent. Sugar and vanilla and every fucking thing sweet.

I wanted to lean in and take a bite.

Desire hit me from all sides.

Lust gathered in my guts.

I needed to cool this fire before I did something stupid, so I sent her a grin and moved to the fridge and grabbed another beer for myself. I twisted off the cap and tossed it into the trash before I moved to lean against the far counter that ran against the back wall.

Ten feet separated us, but I could still feel her heat.

I took a sip, eyeing her over the bottle. "How was dinner?"

I shouldn't torture myself this way, but I never said I wasn't a masochist.

Another flush, and she dipped her chin for a second, not sure what to say, and fuck, I had to rough a hand through my hair to keep from demanding to know exactly what had gone down.

"It was nice."

My brows lifted. "Nice?"

She shrugged one of those delicate, bare shoulders. "We went to Sully's."

Sully's was an upscale steakhouse in town.

It was good he took her there. My girl deserved the best. But it still pissed me off. Made me cagey. A dull rage pumping through my veins.

"Let me guess…you had lobster scampi." I kept it a soft prodding. A teasing like this was any another night and I wasn't coming apart inside.

A light giggle rolled free, and she took a sip of her wine. "Am I that predictable?"

"No, Dakota, not predictable. I just know you."

The atmosphere throbbed when I said it, taking us back to those years when it was just me and Dakota. Way it'd been so easy and right.

And there was nothing I could do but move across the open area and to the counter where she stood, though I made sure to keep three feet separating us. Leaning an elbow on the countertop, I shifted to face her.

The air stirred. Heavy and dense.

She peeked at me again, her gaze softening, the swirl of brown flecked with red and gold mesmerizing. "I guess you know me better than anyone else."

It was quiet as it hit.

Issued like a secret.

"But that's about to change, yeah?" Keeping the spite out of it was difficult. Somehow, I managed it, following the question with a long pull of my beer.

She blinked. "I don't know what that means, Ryder."

"It means you're going to find someone who can treat you better than me. Someone you can get closer to. Someone you can fully trust."

Someone who could completely give themselves. Someone who wasn't about to end up dead or in jail.

Doubt puffed from her nose. "I'm not sure about that."

"Brad's a good guy."

He was.

Right then, I still hated the motherfucker.

"He's very nice." It was reedy.

I moved down the counter, around the stove until I was leaning on it a foot away from her.

A fiend who didn't know when to stop.

Reaching out, I traced my fingertip along the soft, plush ridges of her lips. "Did he kiss you?"

Trembles rolled through her body, lifting like tiny spikes on her flesh.

Her mouth parted, but she didn't answer.

What the hell I was doing, I didn't know, but there was no stopping myself from leaning in, crossing a line as I murmured close to her ear, "Did he touch you?"

Her head barely shook, the word a breath. "No."

"Did you want him to?"

"No," she whispered again, the word a short gasp.

"Why not?" My nose brushed her jaw when I asked it.

The air that had been crackling flamed.

She met my gaze, and she lifted that chin.

In it was both surrender and defiance.

"Because the only person I want to touch me is you."

Chapter Twenty-Two

Dakota

AT MY ADMISSION, RYDER HEAVED OUT A BREATH AGAINST THE side of my face, and he reached out and took the wineglass from my hand.

The glass clanked against the counter as he set it aside, then he straightened to his full height.

I released a raspy, frantic breath.

The man loomed over me.

A dark, towering storm.

Chaos.

Mayhem.

Midnight.

I felt like I was standing in it. Drenched in darkness and light and this simmering greed that I didn't understand.

"Is that what you want, Dakota? You want me to touch you?"

That time my nod was as frantic as my breath had been.

Terrified because this shouldn't be happening.

I shouldn't let it.

He and I were wrapped up in something that wasn't real.

But I couldn't find the logical response. Found no rationale. No sound

judgment when I whispered, "I've wanted you to touch me since I understood what desire meant."

He'd become the meaning of it.

The reason for it.

Shivers raced across my flesh when he set his beer aside and reached
up with both hands and dragged his fingertips from my jaw down my neck.

Like every single one of them had been aching to do it.

To touch and explore.

Tingles followed in their wake.

"I shouldn't be doing it though, should I?" he grumbled, the words scraping at the side of my face.

A shaky breath left me as I tipped my head back. That smoldering ball
of need that had forever simmered in the pit of my stomach flared.

"I would have to disagree." At least right then, I did. I couldn't find one
reason in the whole world for him not to be touching me.

He rumbled something that was a cross of a chuckle and pain, and he
dragged all those fingers lower, over my chest and to where my heart was
battering at my ribs.

I sagged against the counter.

No way to remain standing without the support.

Ryder followed, completely in sync, and his touch became light as he
continued down, over the fabric of my dress, just barely brushing over my
nipples that were peaked and pebbled.

A tiny mewl rolled up my throat, and Ryder leaned in and pressed his
mouth to the spot from where the sound had come, his lips parted like he'd
wanted to taste the reverberation.

The ground shifted, though this time, it was an earthquake below my
feet, and his name was rolling off my tongue in a desperate question. "Ryder?"

Because this couldn't be real.

I had no idea what had happened to the man who was always so protective and sweet and the one who overshadowed me now. What had happened
to the man who had told me he would love me forever, but *not that way*, and
the one who whispered against the sensitive curve of my neck, "What do
you need, Cookie?"

The flames in my stomach heightened. Licking up in a slow burn of
desire.

"I—" My tongue was too thick for me to answer.

"I think I know what you need. I'm the one who knows you best, remember?" It almost sounded of a warning, and he pressed his mouth back to that sensitive spot and murmured, "Might make me a fucking bastard, but I want to be the one to give it to you. I don't want to stop."

His confession was gravel. Stones that tumbled from his mouth.

"I don't want you to." It was a needy plea.

I didn't.

I might not know what this meant. I might be setting myself up to get crushed all over again.

Even if he only touched me once.

"I don't want you to stop," I rasped.

He whispered his lips along the angle of my jaw, and a groan rolled from his chest and off his tongue. "Cookie. Have been dying to touch you like this for so long."

He was suddenly on his knees in front of me, and he had me by the outside of each thigh, hot hands under the fabric of my skirt.

Gunmetal eyes raved as he looked up at me.

Sparks in the middle of the night.

Midnight at my feet.

"Cookie." The moan was torment, and my heart clattered, every inch of me shaking as I looked down at the man, my breaths so shallow and hard that they panted out into the dense air.

"You sure you want this?" he asked.

"Please," I whimpered.

That seemed to be the thing Ryder needed to give him the go because he was suddenly back on his feet. Before I could make sense of it, he'd spun me around and bent me over the counter.

Shock rocked from my lungs, and the cold of the metal countertop burned against my heated flesh. I felt disoriented, complicated and confounded as the room spun and spun as Ryder flipped up the skirt of my dress so it was around my waist.

Cool air hit my bottom, and I writhed, half in embarrassment at the way I was exposed and half in desperation for him to put me out of my misery.

"Fuck," Ryder hissed, and those big hands were suddenly on my butt cheeks, squeezing and kneading. "This ass, Dakota. Thing dreams are made of. Did you know that? The way I've wanted to get my hands all over it? Mark it? Claim it?"

Lust crashed through me, all mixed with the confusion. "I thought we were friends?"

Somehow, I was tossing out the weak designation we'd relegated ourselves to. Trying to make it a tease, only the last word cracked.

His rough chuckle scraped the air, just like his rough hands were scraping over my backside. "Oh, Dakota, we're friends. Really good friends."

I pushed back against him, the fire inside too intense not to beg. "Show me."

"So eager."

"What do you expect? I've been waiting half a lifetime." I tried to play it light. It didn't work. Not when it was the darkest confession of my soul. Everything I'd given him once and he'd rejected, and now...

The walls closed in and his aura possessed, my entire being quivering as he rode his palms up to the elastic band of my underwear that were fully lace and high-waisted. A pair that made me feel pretty and sexy and had given me the extra boost of courage before I'd come downstairs earlier tonight.

Not that I'd thought that I was going to let Brad see them, but a girl should always be prepared.

But what I hadn't been prepared for was this.

I honestly didn't think I'd ever really be when Ryder hooked his fingers in them and began to drag them down my trembling legs.

Everything whirled.

Shifting.

Pivoting.

Turning.

Like every thought and belief I'd possessed had been rearranged.

Old wants and new need and all the questions littered in between.

He angled all the way down so he could wind them free of the pink pumps I wore, and I writhed and squeezed my thighs together when I realized he was kneeling behind me, my ass propped in his face.

I knew I was dripping and soaking wet, and I moaned when Ryder brought attention to it. "You're drenched, Cookie," he muttered, dragging his fingertips up the back of my thigh as he slowly stood.

Shivers rolled through me at the tease.

Then he barely brushed his fingers through my pussy.

I jolted forward at his touch, my nails digging into the hard surface like it could keep me steady.

Keep me from floating away.

Because I'd imagined Ryder so many times, but it'd never been quite like this.

No way to anticipate the energy that thrummed. The desire that coated the air like an oil slick.

Electricity snapped within it.

In one heated instant, it felt like everything was going to blow.

"Please, Ryder. I don't think I can handle you teasing me."

Low laughter curled from him, and he angled over my back, off to my left side, his lips brushing the shell of my ear. "Do you need to come, Cookie?"

I whimpered, "Yes."

Even though I wasn't sure I *could* handle it.

This was already too much.

I was shivering and shuddering and couldn't see straight, and the man had barely touched me.

"Please, make me come."

The air stirred when he knelt behind me again. He spread my cheeks and licked me from my clit all the way to my ass. I lurched forward at the contact, and a choked breath escaped me. My breasts were pressed to the counter, my heart hammering so hard I was sure Ryder could hear it beating against the metal.

"Too much?" he asked, his voice so low.

"Not enough," I admitted.

Surprise jutted out of me when he suddenly had me spun back around and was hoisting me up into his arms, my legs wrapped around his waist.

My arms flew around his neck, and I wanted to complain. Warn him I was too heavy. Or maybe just die of embarrassment.

Except Ryder strode across the floor like I didn't weigh a thing, his hard cock covered by his jeans rubbing at my bare center. There were no words, nothing I could say, everything these incoherent, whimpering sounds as he carried me where he wanted me.

He propped me on the edge of the table.

And I was gasping again.

This man a whirlwind.

Whiplash.

"Ryder, no, I'm going to break it."

A growl ripped from him, and his hands cinched down on the tops of my thighs. "You're not going to fucking break it. And if it breaks, then we broke that shit together."

He stepped back an inch, and I shifted my bare bottom in a needy discomfort. But that bit of apprehension evaporated when Ryder slowly dragged his gaze over me. Heat seared every spot his eyes touched.

"So gorgeous, Dakota." His voice was hushed, dragging through the dense air. "Earth shatteringly beautiful. You make the world stop spinning every time I look at you."

My stupid heart threatened to burst from the confines of my chest, pressing against my ribs in a way I couldn't let it.

This was physical.

I knew it.

It's all it could be. Still, his words glided through me like praise. Like he was finally seeing me for the first time. The way I'd wanted him to before I'd lost him somewhere along the way.

But I didn't have time to contemplate all of that before that gruff voice was issuing another command. "Feet on the table, Cookie. Show me that pretty pussy."

And I think I'd always known Ryder would be a demanding lover.

That he liked it rough.

That he would tear me apart if I ever got the chance.

But that didn't mean I was equipped for it. That I could keep up.

That I wasn't letting go of the most mortifying sound when I complied and hooked my heels on the edge of the table. The tulle of my dress was fully bunched around my waist, and my knees dropped wide and exposed me in a way I'd never been exposed before.

Ryder's teeth snapped, and the words grated as he sat down in a chair in front of me. "Perfect, Dakota. Just like I knew you would be."

He ran both hands up the insides of my thighs, spreading me even farther as he watched me with that unrelenting gaze.

Like he was watching for any sign of discomfort.

For any reservation to show.

If there had been any, he'd eradicated them in the path of flames he left behind, his palms inciting a fire as they rose higher and higher.

I lifted my hips toward him, urging him into the same fantasy I'd had about him two nights ago.

He didn't hesitate.

He wrapped his arms under my legs and dragged me to the edge of the table and dove right in.

He suckled each of my lips before he drove his tongue deep. I shivered and shook as he angled up and swirled his tongue around my clit.

Pleasure sparked.

Tiny fireworks in the black-night sky.

"Is this what you needed, Cookie?" The reverberation of his words rolled through me. "You needed my mouth on you? Needed me to taste this sweet cunt?"

I barely wheezed a desperate, "Yes."

"Good girl," he mumbled against my engorged flesh.

He ate me like I was dessert, humming in rapture the way he always did when he ate something I'd baked for him.

Those sounds had always gotten me off, and tonight, they glided through me, that pleasure growing brighter and higher as he devoured me.

As he consumed me.

Drove me toward an ecstasy unlike anything else.

Because I might want to pretend like this was only physical, but I felt him like a life-beat speeding through my veins.

Like purpose.

Like reason.

All of it gathered and strengthened, and I began whimpering and jutting my hips, one hand holding me up on the table and the other going to the back of his head to keep him close, my nails digging into his scalp.

And if it was just one time, then I wanted it all, and the plea was raking up my throat as I yanked at his hair. "I want you to fuck me, Ryder. I want to feel you. All of you."

He groaned as he stalled for a fraction of a moment before he turned that intense gaze on me. Remorse or maybe it was guilt filled his eyes. "No. You don't want to go there. Not with me."

I wanted to tell him that he didn't get to tell me what I wanted, that I was tired of him protecting me, but he slowly drove two fingers into my body, cutting off my ability to speak.

He never looked away as he did.

My mouth parted and a helpless whine slid up my throat. I felt the warnings of an impending orgasm throb around his fingers.

"Fuck me, Cookie. You're going to kill me, sweetheart. Your cunt is so tight," he rumbled before he dipped back in. He swirled his tongue over my sensitive nub, thrusting his fingers deep and in sync.

Two pumps was all it took and I was going off. My walls spasming around his big fingers as an orgasm blew through my body.

Pleasure split me in two.

The blinding kind.

Splintering out.

Obliterating every cell.

Knocking through all the reservations that warned that I was setting myself up to get hurt.

But loving him had always hurt, and there was no stopping the surge of it right then.

The way it got carried on the rapture.

The way it was still rolling through me when I pushed him back, slid off the table, and got onto my knees.

And he was groaning the deepest sound. A sound that banged against the walls and reverberated back, amplifying the thunder that beat between us. His expression twisted in shame and gluttony, his words dragging like blades through the dense air. "What I would do to be good enough for you."

"You're wrong. Whatever you're thinking right now, you're wrong, Ryder Nash."

Because I saw it. That same sadness that he fell into sometimes. The grief that he covered with those easy smiles and that casual demeanor.

But the thing about me and Ryder was I thought I knew him best, too.

Was sure I was the only one who recognized those things.

The one who felt the darkness that poured out of him.

I wondered how I'd never fully noticed *this*, the lust that radiated from his body, or if I had just let my fears and insecurities cloud it, because there was no mistaking the desire that flooded from him now.

The way the designs inscribed on his flesh writhed over the corded muscle that flexed with restraint.

The way the gunmetal of his eyes had turned to pitch.

The way he strained at his jeans and his chest jutted with coarse, choppy pants.

"What I'm thinking right now is I have a goddess kneeling in front of me."

"I've always been here, Ryder. On my knees for you."

"No, Cookie. It's always been me. A beggar at your feet."

More questions flew through my mind, but I couldn't waste this time asking them. I leaned forward and yanked at the buttons of his fly, watching the way his face darkened with greed when I did.

Still, he was grating, "You don't have to do this, Dakota."

"No one implied that I did. I want to. I want to see you. I want to touch you. I want to taste you, too."

A tortured groan left him when I tugged at his jeans. He stood then, knocking the chair over as the man rose to tower over me.

A fortress of shadows.

I gulped when Ryder started shoving his jeans down until he was kicking them off his feet and pulling his tee over his head at the same time.

He straightened.

Completely bare.

A shudder rocked through me, and I wasn't even sure how I remained kneeling as I rushed to take in every inch of him.

Every carved, muscled edge, his skin covered in a canvas of ink. The strength that rippled and his dark beauty that bled from his pores.

My fingertips brushed over the chocolate chip cookie he had tattooed on his hip. Wondering if I'd been wrong. If he had thought about me like this.

I did my best to ignore the clock in the middle of his chest, not to contemplate it, refusing to allow it to rip open a wound.

Not when his penis was bobbing in front of my face, thick and long and hard, the veins visible this close. The head was fat, so heavy with need that I could almost see it throb, a metal rod running vertically through the middle of it.

My mouth watered, and my head spun, and I was vibrating like crazy when I reached out to gently run my hand along his shaft.

Ryder jolted, and his hips rocked forward. "Dakota."

I glanced up at him.

The man a shroud.

Midnight.

I tightened my hold around him before I lightly licked around his crown, the tip of my tongue flicking over the precum leaking out of his slit before I ran it up to do the same over the little metal ball.

He lurched, a harsh rasp raking from his lungs. "Who's teasing who now? Are you going to fuck me with that sweet mouth, Cookie?"

"Only if you want me to." It was the shakiest breath of a tease, and he choked out a sound that I wasn't even sure was a laugh or a threat, and he reached down to trace his thumb over the little divot at the side of my chin.

"Do I want you to? I've been dying to feel that sweet mouth around my cock for years. You don't have the first idea how fucking bad I want you, do you, Dakota? How many times I've imagined you just like this, getting ready to wrap those perfect pink lips around my dick?"

Lust tumbled through my being, and I leaned in and licked him again before I pulled only the head into my mouth. I rolled my tongue around it while Ryder wound my ponytail in his hand.

He gave it a slight tug. "Suck me like a good girl, Dakota."

A frenzy of nerves skittered, a rush of that energy that glowed, and I took him in as far as I could take him, his cock so hard and heavy in my mouth, so big it took everything in me not to instantly gag, the cool metal of the barbell piercing at odds with the heat that filled me.

A grunt drummed through his body. "Cookie. Fuck. Your mouth. So good, baby. Always knew you were going to wreck me."

I rode back up, picking up a rhythm, hoping I had a chance at giving him the kind of pleasure he'd ruined me with.

Because it wasn't me who was doing the wrecking.

It was the man who started to drive his hips forward with every stroke of my mouth, pressing in deeper like he wanted to overpower me.

Consume me.

But he'd already done it a long time ago.

So I was giving into it wholly.

I took him deeper with each thrust, and I wrapped both hands around the portion I couldn't take.

He hit the back of my throat each time.

And he was yanking harder at my ponytail, so hard it pricked at my scalp.

And I liked it.

God, I liked it, the way he was handling me.

Arousal spread through me again, slicking my thighs where I was on my knees, and I was pressing them together as he started to pound into my mouth.

"Look at me," he demanded. He tugged at my hair. "Look at me."

I did, and it tilted my head back, changing the angle, and his cock drove deeper into the back of my throat as he pushed in slower than he had been.

"Never thought I'd see something so perfect, Dakota. Look at you. So fucking gorgeous with my cock in your mouth."

I whined around him, and he sent me one of those smirks that sheared through me like a knife. Penetrating to the deepest places.

I vibrated with need. With joy. With the pleasure of what I was giving him.

And for a flash, his expression went tender.

So tender that it hurt to even look at him.

Then he touched the edge of my mouth. "Harder, Cookie. Show me how good you can give it."

He let go of my hair and took me by both sides of the face, and I angled up higher on my knees, holding on to the outside of his thighs as he took over, driving himself in deep, hard thrusts.

I felt it when he came apart.

When the glistening on his flesh somehow illuminated.

A flash of light.

A thunderbolt.

He rasped and grunted as he throbbed, as he poured into my mouth, holding me by both sides of my face while I swallowed around him, taking him deeper than I had before.

Ragged pants echoed from him, and he slowly withdrew.

Only he kept ahold of my face.

Big hands gentle.

Gunmetal eyes gazing down.

He ran the pad of his thumb over my swollen lips.

"Cookie," he whispered.

The faintest bit of shyness worked its way into my conscious. "Was that okay?"

I was a whole lot of years out of experience.

He didn't smirk, though.

He just pulled me up and onto my feet, curled an arm around my waist, and brushed the lock of hair that had gotten free from my face.

We were chest to chest, the fabric of my dress the only thing separating us as he held me to the heat of his body. "It wasn't okay, Dakota," he murmured. "It was more than I should ever ask you for."

He held me there for a minute before he blew out a sigh then stepped back to snag his underwear where they were wound in his jeans. He tugged them on, and I tried not to ogle him, but I couldn't help myself.

It was the first time I felt like I could really look at him without feeling like I was stealing something that wasn't mine.

That I wasn't creeping on what would forever be out of reach.

It still felt like gluttony.

Like decadence.

I remained in that spot while he wandered over to where he'd left my underwear on the floor, and that time he was smirking as he made his way back. "Never going to be able to look at you again without imagining these panties under your dress. You tryin' to wreck a man?"

A disconcerted laugh slipped off my tongue. "I do hope you imagine I change them every once in a while."

I was shocked that I was joking with him as he leaned down to help me back into them.

He stood, and he hooked his index finger under my chin, one of those grins playing all over those red, red lips. "Guess I'm just going to have to take a peek every now and again so we can be sure of that."

Butterflies went wild, flapping in my belly, way too excited by the prospect that we might do this again.

Only it made all those questions swirl to the surface.

Ryder's expression went soft, like he could read every one of them. "Would love you every day of my life if I could, Dakota."

"Why can't you?"

Dragging his fingers through his hair, he looked to the floor. His words were close to a mumble. "Your brother would kill me for one."

"My brother doesn't get to say who I can date or love or how I spend a single day of my life."

"No, but he will do everything he can to protect you from the monsters in this world."

Confusion drew my brow together.

Ryder dragged me back to him again, his arm around my waist and his heart banging at my chest. It wasn't tender that time, though. It was rough and powerful and filled with his grief. "Mean it when I tell you I'm not good enough for you."

"How could you ever say that?"

"Because it's the truth. You don't know the things I've done."

"I don't care."

Disbelief puffed from his nose, and he stared at me through the wisping darkness that curled through the kitchen. Right then, I wished all the lights were on so I could fully make out his expression.

"You would if you knew what they were."

Before I could assure him that he could tell me, trust me with it, he dragged me closer and mumbled at my neck, "And I'm the bastard who doesn't know if he can stay away from you."

"Then don't."

He pulled back, and his hand cinched down on my hip. "I don't want to hurt you, Dakota."

He seemed to swallow back whatever he was going to say before he turned to grab the rest of his clothes from the floor. "Come on, we'd better get some sleep. That tiny tornado is going to be up before you know it, and you have a long day at work tomorrow."

He took my hand.

A buzz rushed up my arm, and he squeezed like he'd felt it, too.

Slowly, he led me upstairs, through the shadows that played like ghosts on the walls of his house. Silence washed and shivered around us, an understanding without comprehension waving through the night.

He walked me to my bedroom door. He paused there, uncertainty in his eyes. "I don't want you to regret what happened tonight."

"I couldn't."

There was no chance.

"I should, but I don't think I can, either," he said.

"Maybe we should have been doing this for a long time."

That sweet wickedness gleamed in his eyes. "You are playing with fire, Dakota Cooper."

"Maybe I want to burn."

Greed hardened his features to stone, and he wavered before he brushed his fingertips down the edge of my face. "Go to bed, Dakota."

I couldn't say anything as he moved to his door, though I finally found my voice when he was turning the latch. "Your past doesn't define you, Ryder. No, I don't know the full circumstances, but I know you lost yourself after your mom died. I would never blame you or judge you for that."

I knew he'd gotten mixed up in some bad things.

When I'd been afraid he would forget me that night of her funeral, he had. Everything had changed after that.

For years, he'd detached himself from our family.

Had become reclusive.

A ghost.

The rumors had run rampant. The poor orphan who'd lost himself. The one who'd started hanging out with a rough crowd in the next town over.

I had seen it in the demons that had played in his eyes the few times I'd seen him during that time. The way his stare was too distant.

I had been certain of it when he'd started coming into the bakery where I'd worked during my senior year. When things had started to change between us again.

Plus, I'd known it for a fact when he'd been arrested for possession the night he'd stood for me.

The night he'd fought for me.

I'd left for college right after that, and by the time I'd returned, he had become so much more like the boy I'd once known back when we were kids.

Whole and happy.

He'd gone through a rough patch, but he'd made it through.

He stared at his door for the longest time before he finally looked back at me. "No one said it was in the past, Dakota."

Then he opened the door and shut himself in his room.

Chapter Twenty-Three
Ryder

I WAS A FUCKING BASTARD.

I had gone to sleep knowing it, the scent of her still all over me. On my fingers and on my tongue, my body painted in her ecstasy.

A fantasy that had come to life.

But Dakota was a whole lot more than a fuck.

She was everything, and I didn't know if giving into the greed had ruined that.

I didn't know where we were going to stand, or how the fuck I was going to be able to keep my hands to myself.

Not when all those fantasies had proven to be so much better than I ever could have imagined.

Her mouth was a fucking dream.

Her cunt perfection.

My dick throbbed in my jeans.

I'd been hard the whole goddamn day, since the second I'd woken up long before dawn and knew I had to get out of that house before I went stalking to her room and made good on the threat that she needed to lock her door.

Coming here to the shop hadn't changed it.

Instead, I was swamped with the memories. With the possibilities.

But how the hell did I consider any one of those with what I still had sitting on my shoulders? How could I even think about taking more of what I never should have taken in the first place? How could I drag her into what I was?

A deviant with a dark, ugly secret while she'd looked at me from her doorway like she'd believed in me. Accepted me as a whole.

But she couldn't. Not when she didn't have a clue.

I never should have touched her until I'd gotten free. Until I was sure.

But I hadn't known how to stop myself when she'd come through the door looking like that last night.

A fucking goddess dressed in pink.

Not when I had been so twisted up thinking about her out with that douchebag, losing my goddamned mind as I'd imagined every way Brad might be taking what was supposed to have been mine.

I scoffed at myself as I focused on trying to draw the line to make the cut on a piece of metal.

I'd spent so many years ignoring what I felt for her. Pretending it didn't exist. Had planned on doing it forever, but something inside me had snapped on Monday night when she'd walked in on me, and I'd spiraled into a deviancy that knew no bounds.

The barriers I'd erected had been demolished the second she'd stumbled into my room like an apparition of every warped, greedy fantasy I'd ever had.

Girl panting, eyes wide, standing there salivating over my dick.

So, I'd given into the depravity because I was exactly that.

A selfish bastard.

I had pushed into the space I shouldn't have gone.

She was good and right and fucking deserved the world laid at her feet, and she had no fucking clue who I really was or what I really did.

And until I fixed that shit? I had no right.

Putting on my facemask, I turned on the cutter. The motor whirred to life, sparks flying as I guided the sheet through the machine. The high-pitched screech of the diamond blade grinding against metal was deafening, and I struggled to focus on the task at hand rather than all the thoughts that kept charging through my brain.

I made the cut and turned off the blade, tossing off my mask so I could inspect the result. Satisfied, I set it aside, then stilled when I heard the rumble of a truck riding up to the side of the shop.

That was all it took to send agitation blistering through my blood.

I'd known he was coming, had gotten the text right after I'd arrived here.

I tossed my gloves to the worktable and weaved through the organized mess to the far bay. I pushed the button to raise the garage door.

Welcoming the wickedness.

The chains clanked as the door rolled up and Dare immediately started to back the trailer into the spot.

Hostility spiked, and I was still having the hardest time deciphering if it was directed at him or at myself. If this hate emerged from the days when I'd been so empty and lost that I'd wandered off course. So far out of line that I'd tumbled over the side.

Fallen straight to the bottom of the deep end.

Squandered away any goodness.

But how could I regret the last? The choice I'd made for her?

It was the consequences of it that left this bitterness writhing so deep that I could barely stand there and watch the fucker slip out of his truck.

Dare sauntered out, tossing out his burly intimidation while the rage steadily built inside.

"Look at you, being here when I expect you to." He sneered it like he was talking to an unruly teenager.

I wanted to pop him in the mouth. I shrugged like he didn't bother me. "It's noon on a Thursday. I have work to do, so where else would I be?"

Dismissal huffed from his nose, and he came forward and angled in close.

So close that I was itching to get my hands around his neck and squeeze until he could no longer breathe. "Nothing else going on under this roof matters. Think you know that by now."

Nash Metalwork Designs was a front.

Inconsequential.

But it fucking meant something to me.

"Whatever you say, Dare." I drew it out, way too placating like.

Fury burned in his eyes. Asshole hated me as much as I hated him.

"Don't fuck with me, Ryder. Warning you."

Rounding around me, he went to the trailer and quickly unlocked it. He dipped inside and started up the car, carefully rolling it back into its spot.

When he climbed out, he tossed the keys at me. "I'll be in touch about the date for the drop-off."

"And what if I'm busy?" I said it like a taunt.

He was in my face in a flash, voice curling with a threat. "You want to play games, Ryder? I own you, and I'm getting worried you might have forgotten it."

I cracked a smirk, but it was resolution that sank down to take possession of my soul. "Nah, Dare. Don't you worry. I haven't forgotten anything."

Chapter Twenty-Four
Ryder

Seventeen Years Old

"RYDER, WHERE ARE YOU GOING?" PAIN CURDLED HIS AUNT Linda's voice.

Desperation and fear.

He should have kept walking, but he turned to face where her plea had hit him from behind.

The house had been quiet enough that he'd thought it was safe to sneak out.

He'd thought no one would notice anyway because what the fuck did it matter?

But there she was, wearing a floral nightgown, standing on her stoop and wringing her fingers together.

"Just out," he said as casually as he could.

Grief broke across her features. "You don't have to run, Ryder. This is your home now."

Sorrow left him on a jolt of angry laughter. "My home? It's not my fucking home."

He backed away, shaking his head, while she took a step forward. "It could be. You just have to choose for it to be. You have to find peace here."

Peace?

What was that?

His mind flashed to the big tree beneath the stars and the tiny stream that trickled through.

There'd been peace there, he remembered.

When he'd go there while his mother was sick and just find the silence. When Cody's little sister would bring him treats that made him feel like someone had been thinking of him when he'd thought he'd die from feeling so alone.

But things like that were fleeting.

Because this emptiness was too great. Too broad and too profound.

He gulped around the clot of pain in his throat. "Thank you for letting me stay with you, Aunt Linda."

Then he turned and jumped into his car where it was parked on the street. The old engine roared to life when he turned the key. It'd been his mother's. The one thing he still had. The cloth seats were ripped, and the windshield was cracked, but he swore he could still feel the pulse of her hands where she'd held onto the steering wheel.

Through his bleary sight, he drove, winding through the darkness.

Aimlessly.

He shouldn't have been surprised when he ended up in front of the simple white two-story house.

The paint was peeling and cracked, and the flowers in the planters on the porch had wilted.

A vacancy echoed from the blackened windows, so stark and gutting he felt it howl through his being.

A *For Sale* sign swung in the breeze, and a *sold* sticker had been placed on the top left corner of it.

He ground his teeth and squeezed his eyes, but the pain didn't go away.

He took to the road again, driving through the night, and he ended up at the same house where he'd been last week. The place he'd sworn he was never going to return to.

If she knew, his mom would beat her fists on his chest. Scream at him that he was being a fool. Promise him that he had more to offer and there was so much more to this life. Beg him to make her proud.

But he couldn't hear her voice anymore.

Guilt pulled through his consciousness, a sickness in his stomach as he took the path to the door. He knew he shouldn't go inside.

Knew it.

But he didn't want to fucking hurt anymore.

So he walked in like he belonged, and he did three lines then fucked some girl named Amelia against the wall in the hallway.

And right then, he didn't feel so bad.

The pain wasn't so great.

And when he went back into the living room to do some more, this dude named Dare told him not to worry about the money. That he had his back.

It wasn't a biggie.

Ryder should have listened to the warning that went off deep in the recesses of his mind when the guy said all he asked was that Ryder do him one favor. But Amelia sat on his lap and kissed him.

He fell into the distraction.

Lost himself.

He'd just had no clue how far that spiral was going to go.

Chapter Twenty-Five

Dakota

MY STOMACH TWISTED AS I WROTE TODAY'S DESSERT SPECIAL on the board out front.

Midnight Temptation.

Maybe I'd been inspired when I'd come into the café this morning, or maybe I'd just needed something to do with my shaking hands, and I'd gone straight into the kitchen where I'd thrown myself into a new recipe. A concoction of dark chocolate and sweet cream swirled together in a decadent, flourless cake. It was served with a scoop of strawberry gelato since it was the closest color to the pink dress that I'd worn last night.

It was so rich that I was serving it as a smaller wedged slice, sure it could be consumed only in tiny amounts without the risk of becoming addicted.

At least I'd already felt that way when I'd awoken with boulders sitting in my stomach, a landslide of need crashing over me when my thoughts had immediately returned to last night. It was mixed with a tumble of worry and fear.

But I'd climbed out of bed resolved. Losing Ryder was not an option I could entertain, whether we went back to friends or decided to see where this went. Either way, we were going to have to suck it up and figure this thing out like adults.

It hadn't felt as easy as that, though, when I'd emerged from my room at five-thirty and he was already gone.

Anger had pulsed.

I wasn't about to stand for letting Ryder be a coward.

I wouldn't let him.

Wouldn't let him just…disappear like he had before.

We might have crossed a line, but we'd crossed it together.

I was so lost in my thoughts that I screeched when a hand landed on my arm.

I whirled around.

Paisley cracked up, pressing a hand over her mouth to try to stop the cackling that had everyone in the shop shifting their heads to see what the uproar was about.

"Oh my God, you should see your face right now." She pointed at me.

I attempted to straighten myself out. Gather all the stampeding thoughts up before they ran too far out of control.

I resituated the skirt of my red and black floral dress. "What did you expect when you snuck up on me like that? Are you trying to give me a heart attack?"

"Um, it's the light of day and there are fifty other people meandering around in here. But you were so lost in your thoughts I'm pretty sure you were here all by yourself. Or maybe you were with one special person…" She drew out the last.

Pure suggestion.

Heat flashed across my face before I could stop it.

Paisley's eyes went wide. "Wait, what, did you?"

I couldn't even speak she had me so flustered, my attention darting around to make sure no one could overhear.

When I didn't answer, Paisley grabbed me by the wrist, and she pulled me through the store and down the hall that ran the side to the restrooms.

It was quieter back here, no one around, but she still kept her voice muted when she started to speak. "I came in here to see how your date went, and I completely expected you to tell me it was kind of lame and you were in bed by nine. I was not expecting your face to light up like a Christmas tree."

"It did not light up like a Christmas tree."

Okay, maybe. A Christmas tree that had completely gone up in flames.

"You are the liariest liar ever. You think I don't see that blush. It's covering every inch of you. Fess it up right now."

A customer came out of the women's restroom, and neither of us spoke until she'd made it to the end of the hall and out into the store.

Then Paisley squeezed my wrist again. "Did you and Brad totally hit it off? Tell me he was good and took care of my bestie. The guy has big hands, so I was thinking that maybe there was going to be something good for you underneath those dress pants. I told you I was looking out for you. I want every detail."

Nerves rattled, and I bit down on my lip, my chest pressing full as I whispered, "Brad and I did not hit it off."

Dinner was nice, like I'd told Ryder, but there'd been no real connection, and when he'd dropped me off at Ryder's door, we'd both decided we'd be better off as friends.

Lines creased at the edges of her green eyes, and she angled in farther, attracted to the secret. "Well, something *hit* you off."

A war went down inside me. I'd kept my feelings for Ryder a secret for so long that admitting them somehow felt like a betrayal, but I didn't think I could physically keep the confession from Paisley.

Not after the way he'd made me feel.

I could still feel his touch burning through my senses.

I glanced down the hall before I returned my attention to her, voice so quiet I wasn't sure she could even hear. "Something happened with Ryder last night. After I got back."

"What?" She screeched it so loud I was pretty sure everyone clear out in the dining room had heard.

"Would you be quiet? I don't need the whole town to know."

"Right, right, sorry. But what do you expect me to do when you just *hit* me with that juicy detail from out of nowhere?"

"Well, it was definitely from out of nowhere."

"What happened? I am dying right now, Dakota." She flapped my arm all over.

I hesitated for a beat before I began to explain.

"I walked in on him the other night while he was…" I widened my eyes and tipped my head to the side twice, which I was pretty sure was the universal sign for masturbating.

"Oh my God, did you see his dick?" At least she kept that low enough that the entire restaurant didn't hear.

Heat rushed to the surface of my skin, and I yanked my arm away from her hold and covered my face with both hands, peeking at her through my fingers. "It's pierced, Paisley. Like, oh my God…how was I even supposed to handle it?"

She choked and grabbed me by both wrists that time. "I told you that you needed to go dick-hunting, and you landed yourself a prized stag? There is no handling that. No one could blame you for anything that happened after."

"Well, I stood there staring at him like a moron for about five minutes before I gathered my wits and went running back to my room. But then he texted me…and asked if I liked watching him."

"Holy crap, Dakota. I knew it. I freaking knew it. I knew that man has been dying to get in my Doodle-Boo."

"He acted like nothing happened the next day, but there was a tension between us that hadn't been there before. Like…I could just feel it. And after I got back from my date—"

A man who was unfamiliar and was giving tourist vibes rounded into the hall, and I clapped off my explanation, grinning wide as he passed like I wasn't over here confessing my most sordid secrets to my bestie in the middle of my restaurant when I should be working.

Paisley sent him daggers like he'd walked by with a pin and popped her balloon.

He hurried, quick to duck into the swinging door of the bathroom, and I giggled. "You're going to get me a bad review. *Food is great but watch out for the trolls loitering outside the bathroom.*"

Her grin was manic. "Um, tell me a bad review isn't worth *this*?"

"It'd be worth a thousand bad reviews."

And that was a problem. What I was willing to give for him. But I'd been willing all along. I'd wanted to share this life with him, and we had, in a way, but so different than I'd hoped it would be.

I'd spent the last years thinking I'd been a complete fool. A lovestruck little girl with stars in her eyes who didn't get it.

One who wanted something far above her reach.

But now…

"So…you looked crazy hot, just like I knew you would, because hello, my bestie is a stunner, and you came back, and he was crazy jealous, and he hauled you upstairs and ravaged you the entire night with that pierced dick?" Paisley urged, tugging at my arm again, supplying all the details like she'd been there.

A needy wash fluttered through my belly.

God. I wished.

I was also kind of terrified of it at the same time.

The little that had happened had left me unanchored.

Still, I laughed a low sound, shaking my head. "No."

"Then what?" she whined. "Tell me I don't have to gut him and bury him in a shallow grave out on the ranch. Because I will if he left you wanting."

Flames licked. "He didn't leave me wanting."

Truth was, I'd always be wanting...but still.

"He set me on his table and he..." I did that whole tipping my head thing again. Apparently, it worked for all sexual acts.

She squealed and flung my arms all over. "Yes! Thank God. It's about time my Doodle-Boo got herself the yummy O that wasn't compliments of her own hands. Now it's time for the good D."

Desire barreled through me, but I had to be careful not to let myself get carried away.

Ryder had made those barriers clear, his feelings pronounced as he'd gone back to his room like him touching me had been a mortal sin.

I shook my head. "I doubt that. I think it was a one-time thing. We both got caught up in what happened that night when I walked in on him, and we had to get it out of our systems."

"And aren't you asking why it was in your systems in the first place?" she challenged.

I'd spent way too much time asking myself about it.

I hesitated, then said, "I think who we are got confused for a minute."

"Confused?" Paisley rocked back on her boots and crossed her arms over her chest.

"Yeah."

She tossed a lock of her white hair over her shoulder. "Are you joking with me right now, Dakota?"

A soft puff of air blew from my nose. "It's what makes the most sense."

After everything, it's what added up.

Except for the things he'd been saying last night. The way he'd murmured that he wanted to be good enough. The way he'd said he'd love me every day if he could.

"And what makes the most sense? That morbid belief you've always had that there is something about you that Ryder might not be attracted to?"

Paisley was the best kind of friend I could ask for, but she never hesitated to push me up against a wall, either.

Relentless when she believed something was right.

"I didn't say that."

Her arms tightened across her chest, her love and belief and some kind of disappointment leaking into her voice. "Um, yes you did, Dakota. Maybe not in those words, but you told me when I got back that you weren't *delusional*. I didn't press you then, but I want you to tell me right now what that means."

The men's restroom door swung open, and the same gentleman stepped out. This time, Paisley sent him a ridiculous grin as he passed by. "Thanks for coming into Time River Market and Café," she called behind him. "Be sure to leave us a 5-star review."

"Paisley." I giggled.

Her smile softened when she looked at me, everything about her going tender as she reached out and fiddled with a lock of my hair. "You are the most amazing person I know, Dakota Cooper. Talented and smart and hardworking and stunning in a way that leaves the rest of us in your shadow. And I know you see it when you look in the mirror. But it doesn't show when you stand in front of him. And it's time you stood up and felt it. Let go of whatever he did in the past that made you think you are anything less than incredible."

"He didn't—" I cut the denial off myself.

Because he had.

He hadn't meant to. But he'd hurt me.

"I know you two have some sort of history. You've tried to keep it hidden, but it's obvious, Dakota, and whatever it was you two tried to bury has floated to the surface."

"That's the thing, though, Paisley. I tried once. I told him how I felt, and he told me he didn't feel the same way."

I glanced around the restaurant, vibrating with appreciation for the gift that he'd given me despite it.

"Just because he didn't feel that way then doesn't mean he doesn't feel it now. Feelings develop. Hell, I hated Caleb the first time I saw him."

"You only hated him because of how bad you wanted to hump him." I cocked my head with the tease.

"True. That man drove me insane with just a look."

I laughed, and she wrapped me in her arms, rocking me back and forth. "If you want him? Then go for him, Dakota. I know there's history. I know there's pain and your brother and all these voices that are telling you it's a bad idea. But if *you* want it? Then you go for it, and you do it unafraid."

My fearless, wild friend.

But I wasn't sure I could fully lay myself on the line again. Wasn't sure my heart could take it if Ryder rejected me again.

Still, I hugged her back and whispered, "Thank you so much for being here for me."

She eased back with a soft smile. "Um, hello, what do you think I'm here for? You've always been there for me during my hard times, and you can bet I'm going to be there for you. You can trust me, you know? With whatever you need to talk about."

"I know that, and I'm so thankful for it."

She squeezed me tight again before she laughed and pulled all the way back, taking my hand and swinging it between us as she led us down the hall. "I need to get back to the ranch. I was at the store and wanted to swing in to see how everything went, plus Grandpa is demanding I bring him home one of your pot pies."

Affection pulled at my chest. "He's always loved those."

"Reminds him of my grandma's."

"That makes me happy."

"Well, you make a whole lot of people happy, Dakota. I hope you know that. What you've created here is something special."

She slowed as we stepped out into the store where a ton of people milled around, waiting for their names to be called since the dining room was already full for lunch.

Pride swelled, and I couldn't help but remember how it'd been made possible.

And maybe that should have been enough.

His care for me.

But with Ryder, being friends with him...or family...or whatever we were? It just had never been enough. I wondered how I hadn't recognized it all along because a moment later, that energy pulsed through the air.

The ground shifted.

It wasn't a slight tilting.

It was an earthquake below my feet.

A crack right through our shaky foundation.

I'd worried it was going to be awkward or weird when we saw each other again, or worse, he was going to freak and totally shut down since he'd been gone this morning when I'd awoken.

But instead, an easy smirk pulled to the severe contours of his face, and he sauntered forward, all cool and casual the way he usually wore himself.

If I didn't know better, I would have thought nothing had happened between us last night.

Except the glint in those gunmetal eyes promised he wasn't soon to forget.

"Paisley-Cakes," he drawled, slanting Paisley a grin as he eased up to us.

"Hey, Ryder, what have you been up to?" She fully exaggerated it.

God, she was obvious, and Ryder's gaze skated my way, the hint of something playful edging his mouth. "Just hanging out with Dakota here."

His voice twisted through me like the knitting of greed.

"Oh, you don't mind her and Kayden hanging out at your place? I was just telling her she should come and stay at the ranch instead, just until Ezra finds this creep. You know we have a ton of extra rooms. That way they can get out of your hair."

And I was the liariest liar ever?

Hardly.

Still, I tried not to let go of the laugh that wanted to erupt with the way she was toying with Ryder.

Or maybe I just loved the way a growly sound rumbled from him, and he stuffed those tattooed hands into his jeans as he cocked his head. "Nah, I think Dakota might want to stick around. It's closer to the café and all."

"The offer is open." She shrugged, though I could see her internally dancing with glee.

Ryder looked at the specials board before he leaned in close to me. "Besides, how am I supposed to get myself more of those Midnight Temptations if you aren't there to offer it?"

It was gruff and smooth as silk.

Then he pulled back like he hadn't just left my knees weak, voice easy as he said, "I better get going. Ezra is already waiting for me at a booth. Nice to see you, Paisley. Dakota." He drew my name out a little longer before he turned and strolled through the open double doors, leaving me standing there gaping behind him.

Paisley was suddenly there, whispering at the side of my face. "There it is. The good D. I see it in your future. I sure hope you can handle all of that."

She waved a hand in the direction of where Ryder had been.

Jostled from the daze, I swatted at her. "Would you stop it?"

She laughed too loud. "Absolutely not. Not until my Doodle-Boo gets all the good stuff she deserves. And judging by that? It's going to be good."

Chapter Twenty-Six

Dakota

I PULLED UP IN FRONT OF MY MOTHER'S HOUSE AT JUST AFTER FOUR. I should be dead on my feet, but there was enough anxious anticipation pulsing through me that I thought I could run a marathon and it still wouldn't be enough to escape the buzzy need that pounded through my veins.

But I wasn't distracted enough for my heart not to pang when I started up the walkway and saw Kayden's little face pressed to the mesh, his nose and lips smooshed as he grinned out at me.

Love pressed hard against my ribs.

Joy profound.

"Mommy! I see you!"

"I see you, too," I called back, my footsteps light as I climbed the steps. Mom was already unlocking the screen door in welcome by the time I made it there. I went right for Kayden, scooping him up, tossing him high without letting him go before I brought him down to smother his chubby cheeks in smacking kisses. "There's my sweet boy. I missed you."

He giggled and squealed, arms and legs flailing as he tried to wiggle out of my hold all while fisting both his hands in my hair. "Mommy go work?"

"I did, but now I'm all finished."

"Go Rye-Rye's house now?" He dipped his head twice in those deep, emphatic nods, his grin splitting wide and showing off two straight rows of his tiny teeth.

A thread of worry tugged at my spirit. I had to be careful with this. It wasn't only my heart that was on the line. Kayden adored Ryder, and I couldn't stand the idea of stealing that bond from him over a stupid choice on my part.

But how could it be stupid?

How when Ryder had grinned at me in that sly way the whole time he and Ezra had been sharing their lunch? Not when he'd stolen a secret touch, brushing his fingertips along the outside of my thigh under my dress when I'd placed his food in front of him.

Trembles rocked at the memory.

God, it sure felt like something.

"That's right. We're going to go to Uncle Ryder's house." It came out a little breathier than it should.

My mother caught it, care woven into every line on her face. "How is it going over there?"

"Good."

Worry followed it. "Has Ezra heard anything more about this break-in?"

"No. I really think it was someone who was looking for something easy to steal, and they took off once they realized it was actually an occupied house they were breaking into. I don't think we need to worry about it."

Except not worrying about it meant that it was safe for us to go back.

Rejection billowed through.

I wasn't ready for that yet.

The problem was, it didn't have anything to do with being cautious about returning to my house.

It had everything to do with the man who would be waiting for us at his place.

Mom's head angled a fraction to the side. Barely enough to notice, but enough to know she'd picked up on something. "And how was your date last night?"

"Good."

A throaty chuckle rolled from her. "My, my, aren't you just full of the adjectives this afternoon? Don't you think you could do a little better than that? You did promise to tell me all about it this morning, and then you dropped Kayden off so fast I barely caught sight of your face."

I let go of a slight giggle. "Sorry, it was just a long day. The date was... fine."

Her brows lifted, and that time I laughed. "Brad's a nice guy, but I don't think there are going to be any wedding bells in our future."

"No sparks, huh?"

"Not even one."

But I sure had felt one later. I had to bite back the flush that threatened to steal across my skin.

"Well, that's too bad, but I'm glad that you at least got out and tried. It's been a long time since you went on a date."

She looked at Kayden then.

I hated how all of them speculated. How I'd kept it like a dirty secret.

It wasn't like I thought of sex as that. It was just where my mental state had been at that time. How it'd left me feeling gross after.

The depths of the heartache that I'd been lost in, how desperate I'd been to erase it and fill it.

"I guess now that the café is on its feet and Kayden is getting a little older, it's time for me to have a little fun." I managed to keep it light.

She hooked her shoulder on the wall and crossed her arms over her chest. "I'm thinking it's time for a lot of fun."

"Mom." I laughed, shaking my head as I set Kayden on his feet, then I sent her a wry arch of my brow. "As if you're one to talk. I don't think I've ever known you to go on a date in my entire life."

"You never know, this old girl might get a wild hair and decide to start looking for a man herself."

"I hope you do. You deserve to be happy."

Her smile was soft. "I am happy, Dakota. You and your brother and sister make me happy. Our little man right here who loves to keep his gammy company makes me happy."

Her gaze was tender as she looked at my son.

"And I'm happy, too," I promised her.

"You are, but I've also seen the hole inside you, Dakota. One that clearly is longing to be filled. It's the only reason I've been pushing you."

I didn't know that vacancy had been so obvious.

"I'm trying, Mom, and I'll be okay, no matter what. I don't want you to worry about me. I'm stronger than you think."

She clucked a gentle sound. "Not worry about you? Impossible. And

I know how strong you are. You make me so proud. I don't think you have the first idea. How I see my fierce, brave, kind girl. You're the whole package, Dakota."

I choked over the affection. "Thank you. For everything. I couldn't do any of this without you. I don't know how I could ever repay you."

She brushed her thumb under my eye. "Love is on the house."

Everything swelled and rushed. "Thank you for teaching me that. What it means."

"It's who we Coopers are."

I swiped a tear that got loose from my eye. "And now that I'm crying, thank you very much…" I drew out, forcing as much lightness as I could into it.

I blamed it on the whirlwind that was Ryder, all these emotions that were simmering at the top.

"Sorry about that."

"No you're not," I told her around a grin.

Her laughter was easy. "You're right. I'm not. I'll forever be telling you how great you are."

Sniffling, I turned back to the living room that was a complete disaster. Ryder was right. My son was nothing but a tiny tornado.

"You'd better pick up your toys if you want to go to Ryder's house."

Kayden jumped into action, running around and tossing all his toys back into the bin. "Watch me. I fast, Mommy."

"Hmm, someone sure loves that Ryder, don't they?" Mom mused from behind.

Yeah, we definitely did.

"He spoils him rotten, that's why."

"Only because someone loves Kayden, too."

More moisture threatened at my eyes, but I bit it back. The last thing I wanted was my mom to pick up on the scent. She would hound me until I confessed, and I was most definitely not ready for that.

"All done!" In victory, Kayden threw his arms into the air. "We go right now."

He came bounding my way, and I scooped him up, laughing with a flurry of emotions.

Happiness and anticipation and the flutterings of fear because I was afraid I might be a fool for allowing myself to feel any of these things.

But I didn't want to put up walls.

Didn't want my questions and insecurities and the what-ifs to steal the seeds of joy that had just begun to sprout. "Well, I guess we are out of here since someone is really super fast."

"Me!"

"You two have fun tonight. I'll see you in the morning."

Mom handed me Kayden's bag, and with a wave, we were heading down her sidewalk. I buckled Kayden in, my son babbling on about his day, how he'd played with the hose in the backyard, his little hands animated, grin and dimples so sweet. "I got *aww* wet."

"You got all wet?"

He giggled and kicked his feet. "Gammy spray me, Mommy!"

"She's a stinker."

"No, I a stinker." He squished up his button nose, making little snorting noises.

"The best little stinker around."

I shut his door and climbed into the driver's seat, eased out, and drove down her quaint street. The long branches of the trees stretched out over the road, nearly touching. Glittering rays of light broke through the crown, tossing the afternoon in a cover of peace.

I came to a stop at the stop sign at Manchester before I pulled out onto the main road and wound the rest of the way to Ryder's neighborhood.

It took all of five minutes for us to make it there, and I pulled into the spot behind his car and was quick to get Kayden out. I tossed the strap of his bag over my shoulder and started up the walkway with my son attached to my hip.

I was climbing the porch steps when something stalled me. When a feeling crawled over me, lifting the hairs at the nape of my neck.

Slowly, I shifted to peer over my shoulder, eyes moving over the street. Riding over the houses that sat farther back from the road and the lines of dense trees that gave each of the lots privacy.

More of the late summer afternoon peace hung in the air. Birds chirping as they flitted through the branches and a calm that whispered on the light breeze.

But it was hard to hold onto it when I went to the door and unlocked it.

Because it didn't matter that I saw no movement or anything out of place.

I was sure we were being watched.

Chapter Twenty-Seven

Dakota

I STEPPED INTO THE SANCTUARY OF RYDER'S HOUSE AND CLOSED THE door behind us. The turn of the lock was enough to shut out the unsettled feeling that had followed me, my thoughts instantly jumping toward the man when I was hit with the smell of onions and garlic that wafted from the kitchen.

My stomach rolled in a tumble of nerves and excitement.

"Down, Mommy, down!" Kayden wiggled in my arms, and I set him on his feet, his tiny shoes a thunder on the hardwood floors as he raced that direction.

"Hi, my Rye-Rye!" he shouted as he blazed through the opening, his arms thrown over his head. "I here!"

"Hey, there, K-Bear." Ryder's voice echoed through the house, all rumbly and low, sending tremors through my body. I let Kayden's bag fall to the floor near the door, and I slowly eased across the room, stopping at the threshold.

The sight of him hit me like a shockwave.

A sonic boom that reverberated through my senses. Shaking me all the way to the bone.

He was tossing Kayden into the air without letting him go, holding onto him to keep him safe while my son assuredly thought he was being launched to the moon.

Ryder wore dark jeans and a gray tee stretched tight across his solid chest, that shock of black hair flying back as he looked up.

His profile severe, carved in masculine beauty and edged in darkness.

It was his expression that weakened my limbs.

The sheer devotion that lined his features. The love that seeped from the razor-sharp angles.

And I was nearly dropping to my knees when he pulled Kayden to him and turned his attention on me.

Gunmetal eyes blazed, dragging over me in a slow slide of appreciation where I stood shaking like I was standing beside a freight train barreling through.

Chest rattling and legs quivering.

That intense gaze darkened, and a hazy fog of lust curled through the air. Disorienting.

Both anticipated and unexpected.

I finally got myself together enough to offer him a smile. "Are you making dinner again? You really are trying to spoil me, Ryder. Keep it up, and you won't be able to get rid of me."

"That's the plan." He sent me the softest smirk, the man letting some of that easy cockiness into his tone. A slight razzing that touched his words.

My heart wouldn't make it through if I dug too deeply into it.

I forced myself to raise a brow and casually stroll deeper into the kitchen like he wasn't systematically plucking out every chink in my armor.

Not that there was a whole lot of that to begin with when it came to him.

"The plan, huh? It sounds like you've been giving it a lot of thought," I teased.

"A whole lot of thought." It was rough. Scraping the air.

I exhaled a shallow breath, and he seemed to shake himself from the direction we were going.

"I hope you're hungry."

"I *hungee!*" Kayden offered.

Ryder chuckled. "Good thing, little man. I made enough to feed a small army."

He set Kayden in his playpen before he turned back to me.

"What are we having?" I chanced, edging closer and coming to a stop at the end of the counter. It was usually a safe spot. Where I could stand to put some distance between us.

But my mind was slammed with the memories of what had happened in that very spot last night.

The way my breasts had been pressed to the cold surface as he had knelt behind me.

The way his big hands had felt touching me for the first time.

I was pretty sure all those same thoughts hit Ryder because he groaned before he raked a hand over his face, winding around me as he went to the stove. "Chicken fajitas."

"It smells delicious."

He quirked me a playful grin as he added sliced red bell peppers into the onions. "Are you trying to flatter me, Dakota?"

A soft giggle skated out. "No. I mean it. It smells really good."

"Can't compare to what hits me when I walk into your restaurant."

"I think you might be biased."

He hummed. "Maybe. Have to admit, every time I go through the café's door, I feel like you're making something special, just for me. That you're thinking about me."

He peeked my way, like he was looking for a hidden truth. And I wondered if he knew. If he'd known all this time that whenever I wrote a special on the board, it was a memory of him. That I kept them like a secret diary.

But he was owed that gratitude either way, wasn't he?

Before I could respond, he gestured to the stool across from him. "Why don't you sit and get off your feet? I picked up another bottle of wine if you want a glass."

My spirit buzzed, and I fought the giddy smile that wanted to take hold of my face. "I think you're the one who's been thinking about me, Ryder Nash."

He set aside the spoon he'd been stirring the vegetables with.

He came my way, that energy crackling, and he pressed his hand to the side of my face.

Heat flamed at the connection, and he stared at me with those eyes as he murmured, "The entire day, Dakota. The entire fucking day I was thinking about you. Couldn't get you off my mind. Not for a second."

A ragged breath left me when he suddenly went back to the stove. "Shouldn't be, I don't have a right to be, but it's the truth."

I wanted to argue with him.

Press him.

Ask him why he thought he didn't deserve me.

Instead, I gave him a shaky nod and glanced at Kayden. "It has been a long day. I think I'll go upstairs and get changed. Do you mind if I leave him down here for a few minutes?"

I needed a breath. A moment to clear my head. He was so much, and I felt like I was being hauled one direction before I was being pushed in the other.

"You don't have to ask, Dakota."

"But he's my child. My responsibility."

When I said it, his jaw clenched. A flash of anger that shifted into determination. His voice grated as he dumped the sliced chicken into the skillet. "That doesn't mean you can't rely on me."

And I did. Probably too much. "I have relied on you, Ryder. For so long. It makes me feel like I've taken advantage. I almost have the money—" I started to rush, only the words clipped off when he suddenly moved.

In front of me so fast I nearly fell on my butt.

He got angry every time I mentioned it, but it needed to be addressed.

He gripped me by both sides of the face. Ferocity blazed from his hold, but in it was this trembling softness that reached down to touch my spirit that made me want to dig my fingers into him and never let go. He dropped his forehead to mine. "You think I give a fuck about that money, Dakota? That I want it back?"

I shifted so I was looking into his eyes, blinking through the disorder and the hammering that thundered from my heart. "Then what do you want?"

I needed to know. I had no idea where we stood or what any of this meant.

A ragged sigh rolled up his throat, and his entire body vibrated, rolling with uncertainty, before he peeled himself away and took a step back, his thick throat bobbing when he swallowed. "Go upstairs and change. Dinner will be ready in five."

I blinked.

Caught in the whirlwind.

No clue where it was going to spit me out.

⌇

"Are you sure I can't help with the dishes?" I asked as I placed Kayden's bowl and sippy cup into the sink.

"Nah, I have them. Get that one a bath and I'll handle this."

I'd have thought things might have been awkward between us when I'd gone up and changed and come back down, but no, Ryder had shifted into that same role he'd stood in for years.

My friend.

Easy and light.

Casual and teasing.

There was a flirtiness to it that hadn't existed before, though, or maybe there had always been, and I'd just been too fearful to see it for what it was.

But we'd both sank into it.

Enjoying the meal which really was delicious.

Now, I hesitated, and he lifted his brows as he rinsed our plates under the faucet. "And don't you start about me doing too much. Not unless you want me to take you over my knee for complaining."

He tried to hide his smirk when a blast of red jumped to my cheeks.

"You're awful bossy, Ryder Nash." The taunt was my attempt at distracting him.

Only that redness flamed when he warned, "You don't know bossy, Dakota. Now go before I make good on it."

Shivers rolled.

Excitement at the prospect.

I bit down on my lip to tame it, and I snatched Kayden out of his highchair and hurried upstairs before I stuck around to tempt him into showing me what that might be like.

I was treading into dangerous territory. I knew it. The way he kept getting close then pushing me away promised that. But I was having a hard time convincing myself to care.

Self-preservation didn't seem to exist under Ryder's roof.

"I take a bath?" Kayden asked as I carried him into the bathroom. I went right to the bathtub and turned on the faucet to heat it.

"Yep, you have to take a bath to get you all cleaned up after you played all day then ate up your dinner."

"Big boys eat lots," he told me, his little hand clinging to my pajama shirt to keep steady as I leaned over the side of the tub with him still in my arms.

"And just how big do you think you're going to be?" I asked him, tenderness in my voice.

"*Dis* tall." He threw his free hand into the air, reaching for the ceiling.

I feigned shock. "That tall? I think that's way too big. How am I supposed to carry you around if you get that big?"

Kayden giggled. "I carry Mommy."

Love rushed, and I pecked a kiss to his chubby cheek before I plugged the tub when the water had reached the right temperature.

Kneeling on the bathmat, I quickly undressed him before I picked him up from under the arms and lifted him over the side. "In you go."

He started splashing, drenching me in a flash.

"You're getting Mommy all wet."

"*Aww* wet *wike* me."

"Stinker," I told him, laughing under my breath as I leaned forward and grabbed the baby shampoo from where it sat on the ledge. He flailed and kicked as I washed his hair then his body. There was more water on the floor and soaking my pajamas than what was left in the bathtub.

"Tiny Tornado." The words rumbled through the small room, heavy and light, and I barely could glance over my shoulder at Ryder who stood in the doorway, something sly lining the edge of his mouth as he took us in.

I was quick to return my attention to Kayden, rinsing the suds off as I whispered, "That he is."

"I get Mommy *aww* wet," he told Ryder, tossing his arms and splashing more water over the side.

Ryder chuckled. So low it skated over me like a rough caress. "Looks like she's the one getting the bath rather than you."

I felt him move. The stir of the air as he pressed into the cramped space.

His footsteps heavy.

His presence overpowering.

Ryder leaned down beside me. "Like this?" he asked Kayden.

He reached into the tub and dragged his hand across the surface, splashing me over the side.

I gasped, and my mouth dropped open. "Ryder."

He laughed. Laughed a free, satisfied sound that was so sexy my knees went weak.

Stomach tipping at what was dancing across his face.

Greed.

Like he'd given into the restraint he'd been trying to show earlier tonight. I'd recognized it for what it'd been, and now, it was missing, and with it, I had no idea what was going to be left of me.

"What, you don't want to get *wet* with me, Cookie?"

"Ryder," I chastised like I hadn't given it the first thought when I could feel the dampness soaking my panties.

I pressed my thighs together.

"That's what I thought, sweet thing." He leaned in and rumbled it near my ear before he moved to grab a towel from the cabinet and held it open.

Did he expect me to stand after that?

I reached in and scooped up some water and tossed it his way. Only a few droplets made it to the mark of his face.

"What was that for?" He didn't attempt to stop the smirk lighting all over that mouth.

"For teasing me."

A coarse chuckle vibrated out of him. "You're in trouble for that, Dakota."

"How much trouble?" I wheezed it.

God, and I was, in so much trouble as that dark, hungry gaze dragged over me.

"Give me a minute and you're going to find out. Now give me that kid."

"Me!" Kayden giggled and kicked his feet in the water that by then wasn't deeper than an inch.

Shivers rocked, head to toe, and my arms were shaking as I picked Kayden up and passed him to Ryder who wrapped him in the towel. Kayden squirmed all over as Ryder sat him on the counter and dried him off then helped him brush his teeth.

The whole time, I could feel the man cutting his attention to me, sneaking peeks while I leaned into the tub and pulled out the plug.

His heated stare devouring me.

"Sight of you right now."

Butterflies flapped, and the man was doing stupid things to my heart as I looked back at him, on my knees and bent over, my shorts so short I was pretty sure he was getting an eyeful.

He groaned. "Trying to wreck a man."

And still, I played it off like this hadn't become very real between us. "I guess I'm nothing but a troublemaker."

I kept telling Paisley that I didn't need this kind of trouble in my life, but how much I wanted it right then.

I wanted the teasing and the tempting and the playing.

I wanted his body and that mouth and those hands.

And I guessed I'd been staring up at him with all of it written on my face because Ryder's teeth ground. "Warning you, Cookie. You don't want to go looking at me like that."

"And what am I looking at you like?"

I asked it as I mopped up the mess we'd made on the floor and stood with a pile of wet towels. I went to angle by him so I could go downstairs and put the load into the washing machine. Only Ryder's hand shot out to stop me, landing on my waist, his mouth going to my ear. "You're looking at me like you want me to wreck you, too."

"You wrecked me a long time ago." I didn't mean for the confession to whisper free, and Ryder looked like I might have hit him. Regret swam through his dark, dark eyes before he pulled away and turned back to my son.

Blowing out a sigh, I hurried around him and went downstairs where I started the load of towels. By the time I'd climbed back up, Ryder had taken Kayden into his makeshift room. He had him sitting on the bed and was dressing him in a pair of pajamas printed with monster trucks.

Kayden was making a bunch of engine noises, pointing at each one. "*Dis* and *dis* and *dis.*"

"I like that one, but I think I like the red one even better," Ryder told Kayden.

"I wike bwue," Kayden told him in his sweet slur.

"Blue is super cool." Ryder finished tugging on his pants. "Alright, little man, story time."

Ryder grabbed a book from the stack, and he climbed up onto the mattress beside him and leaned against the headboard.

Kayden curled up at his side, tucked in the crook of his arm so he could see the pages.

And I found I couldn't move into the space. Found I was rooted to the spot, standing there in the doorway watching Ryder read my son a story, lost to the infectious laughter that rolled from Kayden as Ryder changed his voice with the different characters. Lifting it high and dropping it low, making the sound of a racing car and the beep of a horn.

Lost to everything Ryder kept saying.

To the greed that kept surfacing and the hidden shame that would shut him down.

And I wanted to sink into it. Disappear into those hidden places. Dip my fingers in and invade.

Understand where it was coming from and why.

Show him it didn't matter. Whatever he'd done, it didn't matter. The only thing that mattered was the man in front of me.

When he turned the last page, he picked up Kayden and carried him over. "Tell Mommy goodnight."

"Night-night, Mommy!"

Kayden threw his little arms around my neck, though Ryder still held him, and I squeezed him tight and whispered, "Goodnight, sweet boy. I love you so much."

Then Ryder swooped and soared him across the room until he was laying him in his crib. "Sleep tight, K-Bear."

"Night, my Rye-Rye."

Love crushed into the room.

Pressing at the walls and pushing out.

Or maybe it was just a landslide of everything that had happened in the last few days when Ryder slowly turned and was facing me.

Because the air deepened, a shiver blowing through. An arrow of warmth and a quiver of need.

And a second later, Ryder was coming for me.

Chapter Twenty-Eight
Ryder

RESTRAINT WASN'T EXACTLY MY STRONG SUIT, AND I HAD NONE of it then. Every ounce of it obliterated when I turned around to Dakota standing in the doorway.

Wearing black sleep shorts made of thin sweats material and a matching pajama top that kept falling off one shoulder.

Still soaked from her son's bath.

In her expression was something I'd never dared allow myself to recognize before.

Like she was imagining what it might be like if this was our truth. If we did this every night, and I didn't have a lifetime of garbage strewn between us.

They were obstacles that I should heed.

What should have me diverging.

Changing course.

But I didn't think there was a goddamn thing in this world that could keep me from her right then.

"Dakota." Her name left me like a plea, and my hand was going to the side of her face and pushing up into her hair as I backed her out of the doorway and into the dim-lit hall.

A short gasp left her, and she blinked at me. Cinnamon eyes swirled with so many things.

Confusion and need and questions I didn't know if I had the strength to answer.

"I keep trying to stay away from you. Don't think I know how to do it any longer. Don't think I can."

I spun her into the hallway wall, pinning her back to it. My nose went to the slope of her neck, breathing her in.

Sugar and vanilla. The sweetest thing.

"Cookie," I murmured into the night.

"Who said I wanted you to stay away from me?" The challenge was back, her chin lifted.

Guilt constricted, and I let my fingertips wander the angle of her jaw. "I keep trying to do the right thing, Dakota. Keep trying to be the good guy, but I don't want to be him right now."

A glutton stealing more. Taking what I shouldn't have all while knowing she should have belonged to me.

Cody's warning kept rolling through my mind. Hitting me on a circuit. Because I knew he was right.

But I was stuck on this girl who had me on a hook.

"And who do you want to be?"

"I want to be the guy who's pleasing you. The one who's making you come. Over and over again. I want to make you beg my name."

A flood of desire coated the atmosphere. Dakota released a wispy breath, and her fingers curled in my shirt, needing something to hang on to.

"Want to be the one who's showing you how gorgeous you are," I murmured as I wound my hand into her hair. "How beautiful you are. The way you steal my breath every time you walk into the room."

She exhaled, shaky and long as I pulled her head to the side to expose her neck. I pressed my mouth there, to the silky, smooth skin, and I rolled my lips along the delicate slope. "Do you have any idea, Dakota? What you do to me?"

There was a tiny shake of her head. "No. Not with you." Hesitation brimmed before she shifted to meet my eyes, this fierce girl whispering her truth into the lapping night. "You were the one person I wanted to be something different for."

It fucking gutted me.

Seared me through with the hot blade of a knife.

"How could you ever think that?"

A trembling sound rolled up her throat. "How could I not, Ryder? How could I not think that you didn't want me? That you didn't desire me? That you wanted something different? Because I spent a whole lot of years questioning, *what* was it about me that you didn't want. What weren't you attracted to. My personality? Because I was pretty sure you liked that. Or was it my body?"

Pain leached into her voice, and she looked away when she asked, "Do you think I didn't notice the type of women you went after?"

I reached out, taking her by the chin, prying those eyes back to mine. "I went after them because I couldn't have the one woman that I wanted. Because I knew I would never be worthy of you, Dakota. Because I knew I'd never be good enough. And I'm still not, and here I stand, a fucking bastard for even thinking about touching you."

I shouldn't be.

Not yet.

Not until I fixed this.

And still I was sliding my arm around her waist, tugging her against me and walking her backward into the closest room which happened to be hers. The lamp glowed from her nightstand, and I edged her back until we were in front of the full-length mirror that was leaned against the wall.

Slowly, I shifted her around, and my hand slid around and came to rest on her stomach as I turned her to face the mirror. I looked at her reflection from over her shoulder.

Her chest heaved, and I could feel the shivers rolling through her. Shivers of need and ones that were coming from whatever wounds I'd unknowingly inflicted.

"Look at you," I muttered at her ear, tugging her closer against me.

My cock was stone, pressing into the small of her back, and our breaths had gone ragged.

I watched as her gaze traced over herself.

Over us.

This gorgeous girl in front of me, all her beauty up against the hard planes of me where I towered over her.

My fingertips pressed into her stomach, needing her closer.

Dakota whimpered.

"Look at you," I said again, voice so low.

"Do you see what I see? Because what I see is this fuckin' stunning woman who's got me so hard I can hardly think straight. So twisted up, I might black out. A woman who walks into the room and every head turns, drawn to her beauty."

My hand wandered, gliding up her quivering stomach to come to just below her breasts.

"A goddess." I breathed it at her ear.

Whimpering, she pressed back against me. "Ryder."

I kept going, my voice low in the confines of the room. "Look at her. This woman who is so strong and fierce. One who strives for what she wants. Fights for it. But she's also good, through and through. So thoughtful and kind that it breaks my heart looking at her because I know I could never be a match to who she is."

I smoothed both my palms down the front of the pajama top and dipped them under, riding them back up, taking the material with me as I went.

And I was the one who was fucking trembling because I couldn't wait to get to those gorgeous tits I knew were hiding underneath. Tits she'd driven me to madness with over all these years. Chills lifted on her flesh as I dragged the damp fabric up and pulled it over her head.

I grunted at the sight. "Fuck, look at you, Dakota."

She wasn't wearing a bra, and her breasts were heavy, dusky pink nipples peaked and hard.

I cupped them from the underside and dragged the pad of my thumbs over the pebbled tips, trying not to come in my pants because fuck, the number of times I'd imagined touching her like this.

She gasped and sagged against me, a tiny moan getting free of her delicious mouth as I continued to rub circles. "Ryder. God, I don't think I can take this."

"You can't take it, Dakota?" My mouth returned to her ear. "Do you have any idea the way you teased me with these gorgeous tits? Wearing all those sweet dresses? Knowing how perfect you were underneath. Did you know, Dakota?"

The back of her head shook against my chest.

"Well listen now and don't ever forget it. You are everything. Inside and out."

I nipped my teeth over her earlobe before I kissed down her neck, gliding lower, before I fully knelt. I angled around the side so I could continue to watch her through the mirror. The way she shivered and shook as I hooked my fingers in the waistband of her sleep shorts and peeled them down her legs, taking her underwear with me as I went.

I unwound them from her ankles.

It left her completely bare in front of me.

A sight I'd only dreamed of seeing.

Rich brown hair streaked in honey cascaded around her shoulders, draping down to brush over her tits.

Hips full and wide.

The girl nothing but delicious curves and tempting frame.

"Told you last night that you're the one who's had me on my knees, Dakota. A beggar at your feet. Do you get it now?"

"Yes."

"Good."

Still behind her, I slowly pushed to standing, fingers sinking into her hips and dragging her back against me.

All that soft against all my hard.

I wanted to bury myself in it. Get lost in it.

And I knew I was treading a thin line. That I was teetering. Getting ready to fall off the side. But I couldn't go on without her knowing what I saw when I looked at her.

How I felt.

That was the confession that threatened to erupt, and terror locked up my throat.

It was an admission I couldn't give. Not until I was sure I could promise her everything.

That I wouldn't be issuing a lie if I admitted what thrummed in my veins.

I slowly rounded her, placing soft kisses on every curve.

Her shoulders.

The swell of her breasts.

Riding down to her belly.

Her hips.

Her thighs.

Needy fingers dove into my hair, yanking at me.

I looked up, catching those eyes staring down at me. "Ryder, I don't know what you're trying to do to me, but you'd better do it fast."

A rough chuckle scraped free. "Eager girl."

"I already told you I've been waiting for too long. I need it. I need you."

She yanked me toward her pussy that was right in my face. I sent her a smirk as I nudged my hand between her thighs and pressed two fingers into her cunt.

Her walls throbbed around me, woman dripping into the palm of my hand.

"Soaked," I grunted.

"Did you think I wouldn't be? With the way you're teasing me? I want—"

Standing fast, I cut her off before she could get out the plea because I knew what she was asking for. I picked her up by the waist and tossed her onto the center of her bed.

Surprise left her on a gasp, then she giggled as she bounced, and God, she was a fucking sight.

Mesmerizing.

Entrancing.

A dream I was fading into.

The way she was watching me, long locks of hair strewn around her, every inch of her bare.

"I want to see you," she murmured.

It was a terrible, bad idea because my restraint was fraying with every second that passed, but I figured she'd seen me that way last night, anyway. And if she'd let me strip her down to nothing, the only gentlemanly thing to do would be to return the favor. So I peeled myself out of my tee then went to work on my fly, shoving my jeans down my legs until I was naked in front of her.

She pushed up onto her elbows, and she took me in the same way as I'd been watching her through the mirror. But unlike her, I had everything to hide. A reason to cower and cover.

Except she was murmuring her praise like I wasn't a monster standing in front of her. "I've never seen anything as beautiful as you, Ryder. You think it was me driving you insane? Couldn't you feel it coming off me every time you came in the room? I don't know how one man can make me shake the way you do. The way you make my heart race. The way I…"

She trailed off, unable to say it.

Confessions locked in the tension. Bound by the past. Because we'd be fools to go there when I'd already warned her that I wasn't sure that I could stay.

But I was still climbing onto the bed, a fiend crawling over her, hovering in all her heat.

Getting lost in her warmth.

In those eyes.

Her hand slipped up to cup my cheek.

"Ryder." She whispered my name. A question. A plea. And I eased back so I was kneeling between her thighs, watching her close as I pressed two fingers deep into the well of her body.

Her back arched from the bed, her nipples so hard they peaked toward the ceiling, and I couldn't do anything but ease forward so I could draw one tight bud into my mouth. I ran my tongue around the nub while I started to drive my fingers into her heat.

Fingers burrowed in my hair, tugging hard. "Ryder."

"I've got you," I rumbled at her flesh, moving to lick at the opposite tit, laving my tongue over her sensitive flesh that had her squirming below me.

"I want to feel you," she wheezed.

A pained groan rolled out of me because the only thing I wanted was to sink into her.

My dick pulsing, raging with need.

But I knew I'd already taken this too far. That she was going to hate me in the end. And still I was taking a little more, and I grabbed my cock and ran just the tip through the lips of her pussy, dragging it up until I was rubbing the metal ball of my piercing against her clit.

Dakota bucked, and the sound coming out of her was so desperate that I nearly gave in and thrust into her. Instead, I started rocking over her like a teenager who was hunting down his first orgasm.

Rubbing my dick in all her sweetness without fully giving in.

She was slick, coating my flesh. I propped my hands on either side of her head and looked down at her while I angled so the head of my cock was rubbing against her with each erratic thrust.

Blunt fingernails raked at my chest and up to my shoulders, trying to draw me closer while she gasped and whimpered my name.

"If I could have you, Dakota. If I could have you…" It panted out of my mouth as that energy banged through the room. Hitting the walls and bouncing back. Rising up and growing higher.

Pleasure gathered, running my spine, and I could feel the tension wind in her, and I rocked faster, creating a friction that flickered and flared in the space between us.

She split at the same second as I did.

The girl fireworks.

Flashes of colors and light as she clung to my shoulders as the orgasm tore through her. I could feel it rush like a flashfire across her skin.

Consuming every inch.

Right as everything inside me burst.

Racing out.

Flames that licked and blazed and incinerated.

And I knew it was never going to be enough as I dumped my cum all over her stomach. That this ache was going to remain as she gasped and tremored.

Knew it as I gazed down at the girl who had the ability to snatch my heart right out of my chest.

I couldn't give it. Not like this.

But she dragged her fingers over that achy spot like she could get to it anyway, and I knew what was in her eyes as she looked up at me. I grabbed her hand that she balled in a fist and pressed her knuckles to my lips, air wheezing in jagged heaves from my lungs. "Cookie."

Had to beat back the urge to confess it all right then.

Just fucking tell her.

Lay it out.

But I couldn't accept her rejection yet, not before I'd set it in motion and there was no turning back.

I guessed I was a coward like that.

So, I whispered to her hand instead, "Let me get something to clean you up."

Slipping off the bed, I went into the bathroom and wet a washcloth under the sink, then I stole back into her room like a thief.

I took her in where she still slowly writhed on the bed. Satisfied, but it wasn't quite enough.

So pretty.

So perfect.

So close and so far out of reach.

I ran the warm cloth between her thighs, making her jolt, before I moved to clean her stomach. "I'm sorry," I muttered, glancing up at her.

"What are you sorry for, Ryder?"

"That I'm not who I want to be. Not yet. But I promise you, I'm trying to be."

And I prayed it was enough.

Chapter Twenty-Nine
Ryder

Twenty Years Old

SUNLIGHT SEEPED THROUGH A SLIT IN THE BLACK-OUT DRAPE THAT covered the window. Blowing out a strained sigh, Ryder sat up on the side of the bed, scraping a hand over his face like it could wipe away the exhaustion. The bone-deep weight that sat on him like he'd awoken beneath a landslide of boulders.

Erase the night before and the thousand others that had looked just like it. Scramble things up so when he looked in the mirror he was a different person.

But shit couldn't so easily be scrubbed away, could it?

Couldn't be rectified or changed.

Glancing at the clock that said it was half past noon, he reached to the nightstand littered with half empty beer bottles, wrappers, a baggie that he'd dusted last night, in search of a pack of cigarettes. He shook one out then rummaged through the mess for a lighter, and he angled his head, lighting it, filling his lungs before he tossed a glance over his shoulder when he heard the dull groan behind him.

He squinted through the bare light at the shape passed out in his bed. Long, blonde hair, a pretty face he couldn't even recall.

Because it was always a fucking blur even though everything remained the same. Night after night and day after day.

He blew the smoke out into the air, watching the vapor twirl and spin and disappear over his head, evaporating into the nothingness.

How many times he wondered if he would do the same.

Stubbing out the butt, he stood and dragged on his boxers that'd been discarded on the side of his bed. How he even found them in the piles of dirty clothes and the shit strewn on the floor, he didn't know. In an instant, one of those thoughts infiltrated. A memory that caught him unaware.

His mother standing at his bedroom door with her hip propped on the jamb.

Ryder, it's a disaster in here. It looks like a tornado hit. And when I mean tornado, I'm talkin' about you.

It was the kind of memory that pierced him.

A blade driven into his spirit he did his best to numb so he didn't have to feel.

His mother's voice firm yet teasing, a soft prodding that echoed at his ear. Touching his mind and gripping his heart in a fist of guilt.

Her voice wouldn't be soft if she stumbled in on this, that was for damned sure.

She'd be disgusted. Disgusted and ashamed of him.

He couldn't shake it as he opened his bedroom door and stumbled out into the duplex apartment he called *home*. The blinds were still closed out in the living room, but it was brighter out there, and he blinked against the intrusion, taking in the remnants of the chaos still scattered about the room. The bodies tangled on the two worn couches and the three people passed out in the middle of the floor.

He wandered into the kitchen and flipped on the light. The counters were covered in empty bottles, trash on the floor, the sink overflowing with dirty dishes that almost made him puke.

But he didn't worry about any of that. He went to the cannisters that sat on the counter next to the fridge, and he pulled off the lid of the largest one, tossing out the bag of sugar he kept on top, relief flooding him when he found that he had at least enough to keep the thoughts at bay.

Enough to get him through the day.

Enough to make it.

Because he saw the message that was waiting for him on his phone, and he knew it was the one thing that would have truly made his mother hate him. What made him hate himself.

Dare: You're on tonight.

∞

Ryder

Twenty-Two Years Old

The bell dinged overhead as he walked through the door to the small bakery on the corner of Manchester and Elm. He'd been strolling down the sidewalk when he'd seen the board sitting out front proclaiming baked goods in a swirly font, but he guessed it was the scent radiating out of the darkened panes of glass that fronted the shop that had stopped him in his tracks.

What had hit him like a thunderclap.

A million memories surged, slamming him from out of nowhere. Good ones, and not the ones that had stacked up like bad omens over the last five years.

He tossed open the door without giving it a second thought and strode inside, then he nearly toppled over when the girl who'd been obstructed behind the glass display case suddenly stood and came into view behind the cash register.

Her eyes went wide at the sight of him, surprise catching her up and parting her lips as he stood there, trapped by the scent of sugar and vanilla that filled the air, a moron who couldn't speak because he was too busy getting lost in thoughts of the good days.

Back when he'd wander into that small kitchen at Cody's house. Back when life was simple and right. Before he'd squandered away every good thing in his life.

"Dakota," he finally managed, shaking his head to clear the daze. He sent her a soft smile. "Is that you?"

Obviously.

There was no missing the unique shade of her eyes. The brown flecked with reds that reminded him of cinnamon. Her heart-shaped face, her full cheeks, that same soft expression she'd forever worn.

But she was different.

Older.

God, close to nineteen, he guessed she had to be. Time fucking flew when you were always high, he supposed.

Redness climbed from the collar of her shirt, and she dipped her head before she cleared her throat. "Ryder. Oh my gosh, it's so good to see you. How are you?"

It wasn't like he wasn't around, but he'd been missing. A phantom that haunted the night. He talked to Cody every now and again, had hung out with him and Ezra a few times over the years, but it wasn't the same.

Not even close.

And the last time he'd met up with Cody, his oldest friend had backed him into a corner, shoving him against the wall and demanding he come *clean*. He had told him he was fucking sorry about his mom, but it wasn't a valid excuse any longer.

He'd told him he was pathetic.

That his mom would be ashamed of what he'd become.

Like he didn't know every single one of those things.

So, he'd made himself scarce, drifting through the shadows of this town like he didn't exist.

"Good," he finally managed the lie. "How about you?"

That blush kept lighting her cheeks, a timidness surrounding her, an unease that hadn't been there before, even though there was still that same familiarity that had always been between them tugging at him somewhere deep.

That comfort that had always come with looking at her.

She shrugged a shoulder. "I'm good. Finishing up my senior year in a couple months and working here on the weekends and afternoons. At least as much as I can without failing my classes."

He remembered she'd always been close to a year older than the rest of her class. She'd repeated first grade because she'd had some speech difficulties, but once she'd overcome that, he couldn't remember a time that her mom hadn't had one of her honor-roll certificates pinned to their fridge.

"I doubt there's much risk in that. You always were the smart one."

He took a couple steps deeper into the bakery, part of himself warning him not to get too close, that he didn't belong, while the other part couldn't resist.

Because he'd missed her.

Her smile and her sweetness and just how cool she'd always been. He couldn't stop the grin from cracking at the edge of his mouth. "Smells good in here. Knew you were going to conquer the world with your baking." He let a small tease wind into his tone.

More of that redness, and she let go of a self-conscious giggle. "It's not my baking. I mean, I put the cookies in the oven, but it's not my recipes or anything. I just work here."

"But you're going to own it one day. No one does it quite like you."

She dropped her head between her shoulders, flushing all over the place, though she kept peeking out at him. "Someday, maybe, but I have a long way to go."

"I know it will happen for you. You've always been like that. Going after what you want. All of my memories of you are in that kitchen, mixing up something amazing."

A long silence passed between them before she glanced down for a beat, wary when she looked back at him. Sadness flashed in her eyes. "What about you?"

He roughed an agitated hand through his hair. "You know, just living."

If that's what it could be considered.

Her gaze narrowed, studying him from over the counter. "We miss you, you know?"

He pushed out a heavy sigh. "Things change, yeah?"

"Yeah, in ways I wished they didn't." Then she cleared her throat and sent him a big smile that panged through his chest. Because it was real and genuine and so much like the little girl he'd once known yet so different.

Regret slammed him hard.

She'd been like a sister to him.

More than that, even.

Someone who'd just gotten him the same way as he'd thought he'd gotten her.

And now, they had all that fucking time lost. An ocean between them. No way to cross it or to get back to the way things had been. He didn't know a thing about her anymore, and that was all on him.

"Would you like something?" she finally asked.

"Uh…yeah…sure," he mumbled, moving through the awkwardness to the display and peering inside. It was stocked with a ton of different types of cookies, chocolate chip and sugar and everything in between. Elaborately decorated cupcakes. Pies and cakes. One of them caught his eye, a dark chocolate cake already cut into slices and set on plates. It had three pieces of white chocolate candy in the shape of stars decorating each.

"I'll have one of those." He pointed at it through the glass.

Dakota giggled a shy sound and pulled one out, and she carefully placed it into a white pastry box. She closed the lid and carried it to the register where he waited. She surprised him when she leaned a little his direction, her voice held low. "It looks like you still have good taste, Ryder Nash. That's my one recipe in that case."

"Really?" Satisfaction pulled at him.

"Yeah." Her smile was soft, and he thought some of that understanding they used to share was still there. And it reminded him that maybe he wasn't fully gone. That maybe he could find his way back.

"What do I owe you?" he asked, digging into his back pocket for his wallet.

She bit down on her lip and pushed the box toward him, her words a whisper, "Love is on the house."

$$\infty$$

He kept seeing her after that.

By mistake or on purpose, he wasn't sure.

He just…wasn't hiding the way he usually did. He was coming out in the light of day, and he wasn't fucked up as much because the last thing he wanted was for her to see him in that state.

He'd hung out with Cody and Ezra a couple of times, too.

Normal.

Like old friends.

Close to the way they used to be, but a discomfort remained, like they didn't quite know what to say to each other.

Or maybe they just didn't fully trust him.

It wasn't like he could blame them.

He was still in deep, chained, even though there was no chance that they knew the circumstances or the depth. He figured they could just feel the slime radiating off him, the corruption seeping from his pores.

But he didn't feel it so much as he entered that tiny bakery on the corner, the scent of sugar and vanilla smacking him in the face.

Or maybe it was the way his stomach tightened a fraction when he found

Dakota on the other side of the counter, smiling back. "And to what do I owe this pleasure?" she teased. Easy the way she'd become. The way they used to be.

"I was just passing by and smelled something good."

"Just passing by, huh?"

He shrugged, all nonchalant as he strolled in deeper. "It is a small town."

"Not that small of a town." A smirk hinted at the edge of her mouth, and he couldn't help but let go of a full one, and he pulled the big gift bag out from behind his back and set it on the counter. "I heard it's someone's birthday."

Surprise jutted across her face, and redness splashed her cheeks. "You remembered."

"Of course, I remembered, Dakota. How could I forget about you?"

Except for all those years that he had.

Guilt clawed at his throat, and fuck, he wished he could take it back.

She stared across at him. There was something new that hummed in the familiarity. An energy that buzzed. Or maybe it was just the faint flickering of joy that had started to shimmer inside him. Something that had been missing for so long that now it felt foreign.

"Are you going to open it, or what?" he pressed, nudging the bag her direction.

She exhaled before she grinned and rushed to toss out the tissue paper, then a frown was forming on her brow when she pulled out what was tucked inside.

It was a metal box, twelve by eight inches and four inches deep. The lid was engraved, the nickname he'd given her years ago carved deep into the metal.

Cookie.

"What's this?" she asked, her breath short.

Ryder roughed a hand down the back of his neck, trying not to itch in discomfort. "I made it."

That line between her eyes deepened. "Made it?"

He shrugged even though he felt like he might come out of his skin. "I've been playing around with welding and shit. I don't know…it's dumb… but I thought you could put your recipes in it or something."

He looked to his boots because fuck, this was stupid, putting himself out there like this. He had no idea what he was doing or why he was doing it or what made him think he had the right, but all those questions were getting crushed when her soft voice hit the air. "It's not stupid, Ryder. It's the most thoughtful, beautiful gift anyone has ever given me. I love it."

He looked back at her. "Yeah?"

"Yeah."

"That's good then."

He jolted when the bell dinged over the door, and he twisted to find some douche sauntering in, arrogance riding out on his weaselly smirk.

Dakota startled, and she cleared her throat and tucked a piece of shiny brown hair behind her ear. "Seaton, hey."

"What's up, Dakota?" The asshole cut Ryder a sneer as he passed before he returned his focus on Dakota. "Picking you up at seven on Saturday. Make sure you're ready and wear something hot."

Was he serious?

Ryder had the urge to reach out and throttle this punk.

But he had no right to do that, either. No reason to get in the way if hanging out with this asshole was what she wanted, though he was sure Dakota could do a million times better than him.

She nodded, though there was something about it that didn't sit right, and she seemed to force a smile. "Yeah. Of course. I'll be ready."

Cinnamon eyes flashed to Ryder as he backed away.

He suddenly had to get the hell out of there.

The air clotted, too thick for him to breathe.

Dakota looked like she wanted to stop him, and he turned and pushed open the door before she could say anything, though he paused long enough to mutter, "Happy birthday, Cookie," before he strode out and disappeared up the street.

⌒❧⌒

"It's really good to see you this way."

Cody took a swig from his beer, eyeing Ryder over the top where he sat across from him in a booth at Time & Tap Tavern. The place gave off a pub vibe, and it sat on the farthest end of town, away from the tourist shops and restaurants that had popped up over the years.

It was still packed. People occupied every stool around the big horseshoe shaped bar that took up the middle of the cramped space. The two walls on either side were lined with elevated booths that you had to take a single step onto, and a few small round tables sat by the front at the entrance.

Country music played from the jukebox and a rumble of inaudible voices mixed with the din.

When Cody had texted and suggested they meet up for a beer, they'd decided to come here.

Ryder wasn't in the mood to hit a spot like Mack's, the bar people flocked to for dancing and live music.

Less chance of running into anyone he knew.

"It's good to see you, too, man," Ryder told him, taking a sip from his tumbler of whiskey.

They'd been reminiscing about all the dumb shit they used to do for the last two hours, and it was the first time Ryder thought he felt fully comfortable in Cody's space, though in that easiness, there was no question Cody had a bunch of shit he wanted to say.

Cody's giant body was rested back in the booth, angled a bit to the side. "Thought I'd lost you, if I'm being honest."

Discomfort shook Ryder's head, and he kept his cool as he slouched back in the booth. "Was worried I'd lost myself, too."

He still was.

But things had started to feel different.

Like he was coming up for a breath after drowning in the darkest waters.

"But here you are." Cody leaned over to tap the neck of his bottle against Ryder's glass.

"Here I am."

A girl Ryder recognized from high school sauntered up, her eye on Cody.

A smirk took to his face when he saw her coming.

"Hey, Cody."

"What's up, Luce?"

"Just saw my favorite cowboy over here and thought I'd better say hi."

She all but crawled onto his lap, and he gave her ass a squeeze when she leaned in to hug him. He muttered something in her ear that Ryder couldn't hear, and he was laughing under his breath as he nursed at his whiskey, doing his best to act like he wasn't there.

"Only if you'll call me back tomorrow," she answered to whatever proposition Cody had made, her mouth puckered in a flirty pout as she pulled away, hands pushing against his chest.

"No promises, darlin'." Cody's grin was easy, dude charming the panties off the girl without even touching her.

"Well, I might make an exception. I'm hanging out with my friends in that booth over there." She pointed to the other side of the bar. "You know where to find me."

She waltzed off and Cody watched her go.

Ryder chuckled, a grin taking hold. "Some things never change."

"Why would you change them when they're so damned good?"

"Cocky asshole." Amusement pulled around Ryder's mouth. "That's going to catch up to you one day."

"Me, cocky? Nah. I just love giving the ladies what they need, and what they usually need is a little bit of me."

His smirk spread as he sat back farther in the booth, and he lifted his beer and gestured with it out into the crowd. "And don't tell me you haven't been balls deep in half the women here. Rumor has it, you have a different chick stumbling out of your apartment every morning. Sometimes two."

Cody's brow lifted, daring him to deny it.

Ryder laughed an uneasy sound.

The guy wasn't off-base, but that shit was getting old.

Guilt climbed his throat when Dakota's face flashed through his mind. The thought of her out with that little prick tonight had him in a stranglehold.

Still, he hiked an indifferent shoulder. "What can I say, I'm a man who likes to indulge."

Cody chuckled, smiling slowly. "And I'm the cocky one?"

The mood shifted as his oldest friend sat forward to fully face him. "So, what are you doing with your life, Ryder?"

A gust of disquiet blew through him. The two baggies he had left in his front pocket burned like an admission of guilt. Before he'd met up with Cody, he'd gotten rid of enough to appease Dare, but that *appeasing* had left him covered in a sticky slick of contempt.

"What is this? Some kind of intervention?" Ryder tossed it out light. A joke.

Cody laughed, but there wasn't anything playful about it. "Nah, man, just want to make sure you're good. I want you to know that I'm always here, no matter what is going on in your life. What you're going through or dealing with."

No doubt, Cody hadn't been blind to the deviance Ryder had devolved into.

"I appreciate it, man, but I'm all good. And I hope you know the same stands for you."

"I know you've always got my back. Just…" He let his attention wander over the crowd before he returned his focus to Ryder. "Be careful out there, yeah? Take care of yourself. Don't want to have to hunt some shady motherfucker down for messing with my best friend."

He tacked a tease on the last.

"Don't you know I'm the shady motherfucker?" Ryder grinned, all teeth.

Cody cracked up. "Hell yeah, man. If I didn't know you, I'd cross the street if I saw you coming. Why do you always look like you're about to commit murder?"

"Now you're just hurting my feelings."

It felt good. Joking with Cody this way. Easy the way it used to be.

He could feel the change coming. The fact he hadn't been high in two weeks was proof of that.

Ryder had come to realize there was no outrunning the shame. He couldn't cover it or distort it, and he knew there was no fucking way to blot out the sound of his mother's voice. He'd tried, but it didn't work, and it might fucking destroy him to let himself feel the full force of it, the grief of losing her, but it was time.

The truth left agitation clamoring through his spirit.

Because it wasn't like he could dust off his hands and walk away from the life he'd been living, but however it went down, he was going to find a way.

Cody drained his beer and slammed it down on the table. "Now, if you don't mind, I think I'm going to go take Luce up on her offer."

"Ah, I see how it is, ditch me to get your dick wet."

"Don't blame a man. Have you seen her?" Cody pushed out of the booth, dug into his wallet, and tossed two twenties onto the table. "Do you want to join me? Her friends are usually game for a good time."

Ryder polished off the last dregs of his whiskey. "Nah, man, think I'm going to call it."

"Your loss."

"I'm doing you a favor. Luce gets a closer look at me, and we know it's your ass that's going to be getting ditched." He grinned as he slid out.

Chuckling, Cody leaned in and clapped him on the back, the teasing going nonexistent. "Fuckin' missed you, brother. Thank fuck you're coming through."

Ryder clapped him back. "I'm right here, man."

Ryder pushed out the swinging door and into the night. The sound of country music and the clatter of voices faded behind him as he crossed the lot and took the side street, heading in the direction of his duplex.

He stuffed his hands into the pockets of his jeans, enjoying the feel of the cool breeze on his face.

He'd walked since he was only a couple blocks over.

It was about eleven-thirty, and most of the town was sleeping, only a few intermittent cars passing by, a peace in the air as he took a turn at Elm. He was almost to Manchester when something drew his attention to a deserted parking lot.

The glare of red taillights where a car was parked beneath a big tree and hidden in the shadows. He didn't know what it was, but a stir of energy cut through the tranquility.

Tossed it into chaos.

A feeling that beat like a drum in the middle of his chest.

And he guessed he wasn't even all that surprised when the front passenger door suddenly burst open and Dakota stumbled out, barely able to catch her balance as she wheezed, clutching at the top of her dress that was ripped at one side.

"Stay away from me. I said no," she gasped through the jagged words.

Ryder was already moving that way by the time the prick climbed out from the driver's side, the slur of his words that he spat over the top of the car dumping acid into Ryder's veins.

"You think I'm going to let you play me like that? You bitch. You should be thanking me for even asking you out."

A horrified sound scraped out of her lungs. "You're such an asshole, Seaton. Screw you, I don't want anything to do with you. Stay away from me," she tossed back.

But it was already too late for poor Seaton.

Ryder descended before the bastard knew he was there, coming out of the darkness like the monster that he was.

Rage tore through his bloodstream.

Aggression breaking him in two.

He took the asshole by the back of the head and smashed his face into the edge of the roof.

Shock raked from Dakota, the attack coming from out of nowhere, while the prick wailed in agony. "What the fuck?"

It earned no sympathy from Ryder.

He kept him upright by the back of his shirt, spinning him around. "You think you can touch her when she said no, you fuckin' pussy?"

Ryder tossed a blow to his already busted face. The asshole cried out, and he stumbled back from the force of the hit.

Ryder went after him, throwing another punch that sent him wheeling back before he dropped to his ass.

"Ryder, oh my God." Dakota rushed around the car, her heels clattering on the pavement. "Ryder," she begged. "Just leave him."

There was no leaving him for Ryder, and he dove for him, pinning him to the ground. "Little fucker, I'm going to make you regret ever speaking her name."

The asshole writhing on the ground spat blood in Ryder's face. "Do you know who I am? You can't touch me. I'll destroy you for this. Over a fat fucking whore who's terrible at sucking dick."

Fury clouded Ryder's sight. Darkness seeping in at the edges. Taking over.

Every time he'd ever sat with Dakota under the cover of that tree while she'd cried over something one of these ignorant pricks had said burst through the dam.

An assault of memories.

The comfort she'd found in him.

The way he'd always wanted to be there. Protect her. Every vain promise he had made.

The shame over walking away.

Every bit of it got taken out on this asshole.

Ryder threw fist after fist.

Dakota's pleas barely dented into the mayhem.

"I'll kill you, you piece of shit."

And he probably would have, too, the way the bastard went limp and stopped fighting back, if it wasn't for the blip of the siren and the blinding glare of the headlights and spotlight that cut into the madness.

It was an SUV pulling into the lot. *Sheriff* was painted on the side, and a crackled voice shouted from the speaker. "Hands in the air. Right now."

Lungs heaving for air, he sat back, his knees digging into the pitted pavement as he slowly lifted his hands above his head.

"Oh, God, Ryder." Dakota wept from somewhere behind him, and he could feel her fear. Her confusion. The horror of what had just gone down whirling around her sweet spirit.

Both doors on the SUV cranked open, and the sheriff on the driver's side came around the front. He had his gun drawn and aimed at Ryder. "Slowly move to the side and lay down on the ground. Facedown."

Ryder complied, nerves clattering through him as he did. He'd always been so careful. So fucking careful. But protecting Dakota was worth any cost.

Any consequence.

Except he cringed when the second officer came into view.

Ezra.

His cousin who'd just graduated from the academy and had gotten hired on at the department two weeks ago.

Shame poured down.

He knew what they were going to find when the older officer stepped over him and handcuffed his arms behind his back, before the officer began to pat him down, digging into his pockets.

He pulled out the two baggies.

It wasn't much.

But it was enough to have Dakota whimpering and Ezra wheezing, "Fuck, Ryder," under his breath.

It was bad enough there was an asshole with a smashed face unconscious off to his side, and in the distance, the shout of another siren echoed through the air.

A minute later, an ambulance and another sheriff's patrol pulled into the lot.

Ryder was dragged onto his feet and turned, and his gaze tangled with Dakota's.

Cinnamon eyes were wide and full of fear. Terror and disbelief. Shock rolled through her body. The girl shaking so hard you'd think she'd been rescued out of a frozen lake.

A paramedic wrapped a blanket around her while the others tended to the fucker who was currently moaning on the opposite side of the lot.

Ezra was the one who guided Ryder to the back of the SUV and forced him into the backseat. "What the fuck were you thinking, Ryder?" Remorse leached into his tone, and he kept his voice low so only Ryder could hear. "You know I can't cover for this."

"I wouldn't ask you to." He would never get him involved in his mess. His attention skated to where Dakota numbly nodded at whatever the paramedic was saying.

His chest pulled tight.

Heavy with that feeling.

And for the first time, he recognized what it really meant.

"Even if it means you just landed your ass behind bars?" Ezra pressed.

"She's worth it."

Dakota

Nineteen Years Old

Dakota slipped from her house under the cover of night. She clutched the plastic container to her chest as she quietly edged down the steps. She kept low as she crept along the side of the house, before she increased her pace when she hit the once worn path that had now become overgrown.

Darkness hung low, strewn with stars that speckled the sky.

She trudged through the high grasses, and she slowed when she came to the edge of the woods. It was quiet save for the babbling of the stream and the drone of the bugs that hummed from the trees.

Her heart crashed against her ribs when she saw the shape of the silhouette sitting on their favorite branch.

Black hair waved in the slight breeze that whispered through, and she gathered her nerves and weaved farther down the path.

How she knew he would be there, she didn't know.

It'd been years.

Years since he'd met her there, but she'd been unable to fall asleep, her body alive with an awareness that had kept her tossing in bed.

A lure that had pulled at her.

Tugged at that place that had always been reserved for him.

She ducked under the low-hanging branch, and he didn't flinch or acknowledge her presence as she began to climb.

She felt his acknowledgement, though.

Felt the shiver that crackled through the air and caressed her flesh like a forbidden embrace.

The branch swayed a little as she settled down in the deep notch that made for the perfect seat, and she stared out at the same nothingness as Ryder did.

That same awareness hummed between them. A safety she had sought for so long, though now, it was riddled with danger and velocity.

"I brought you something." She mumbled it into the dense stillness that echoed around them, and she popped off the lid.

Ryder choked a disbelieving sound, though there was the softest tug at the corner of his lips. "Of course, you did."

Inside were chocolate brownies with a thick chocolate bar melted in the middle.

Ryder reached in and took one. He groaned as he took a bite.

Dakota couldn't do anything but watch him chew. Eyes tracing the rough contours of his jaw, the way his throat bobbed as he swallowed.

How powerful and broken he looked.

He ate another and she turned and forced herself to look ahead while they floated in the unsettled silence.

How much time had passed while they sat like that, she didn't know, the two of them drifting on the night, like they were suspended on a cloud, lifted above all the pain and circumstances and questions littered below them while Ryder ate half the brownies in the container like he was never going to get the chance to taste one again.

Except Ryder wasn't removed from the torment, and his grumbly, low voice cut into their solitude. "I'm not sorry, Dakota."

Her attention remained focused ahead while she felt the weight of his gaze burning into the side of her face. "I'm not sorry for what I did last night."

She finally gathered the courage to look at him.

And it was like she was looking at midnight.

Falling into it.

Getting lost in it.

A storm raged through his expression, and he scraped the back of his hand over his mouth like he was wiping away a bad taste. "I won't apologize for hurting him when he hurt you."

His teeth ground. "I would have ended him if that's what it required. Gladly." Then he blew a puff of air through his nose as he admitted, "Hell, it took everything in me not to hunt him down and do exactly that after Cody bailed me out this morning, asshole thinking he could touch you when you didn't want him to."

A disorder blustered through her senses.

Gratitude.

Fear.

That fluttering in her belly that had risen all the way up to infiltrate her chest.

There was hatred, too.

Hatred toward the jerk who'd ripped her dress when she'd struggled to get out of his car because he thought he could reach out and take whatever he wanted.

Hatred that her word hadn't mattered.

Hatred that Seaton was going to get away with it since his father was a doctor in town, and it was his word against hers. His word against Ryder's. Ryder who'd also been charged with possession and had beaten him so bloody it looked like he'd been attacked by a madman.

"It's me who should apologize. You're the one who got arrested for me."

He scoffed. "A small price to pay for putting that fucker in his place. He needed to know if he ever comes around you again, things aren't going to land in his favor."

"I hardly think things landed in his favor last night." Her brow lifted, her voice barely twining with a thread of lightness.

Paisley had called her this morning. Her boyfriend, Jeremy, was one of Seaton's best friends. Paisley had told her that Seaton's jaw had been broken and he'd lost two teeth.

Paisley had been horrified, ranting and saying she was going to kick Seaton's ass, too.

Dakota kept studying Ryder from the side.

Carefully.

Any ease they'd found in the last few weeks was hard to find tonight.

"It didn't land in yours, either," she whispered.

Leaning forward, Ryder blew out a sigh. "I hate that you saw that. Who I am."

Dread filled up the hole where he'd gone missing all those years before.

"What's going to happen?"

Apprehension shook his head. "I don't know. I could go to jail for a few months, but Ezra thinks I'll most likely get probation."

She nodded around the lump that filled her throat. "I'm sorry."

"Don't be, Dakota. I deserve it. It's a long time coming."

Tension strained on the breeze, and the branch groaned beneath their weight.

"Why do you do that to yourself, Ryder?" Broaching it felt insurmountable, pushing into his darkness.

He wavered in it, pain rolling through his body, shadows haunting his eyes when he finally looked at her.

"It was easier. Not feeling it. The hole my mother left." The words hitched in his throat, and he sniffed like he was trying to hold back the grief, but Dakota felt the shockwave of suffering, anyway. "It hurt so fucking bad that I just…" His head dropped in shame. "I just couldn't, Dakota. I couldn't. It's like I've spent the last six years terrified of loving and terrified of never feeling it again."

Sorrow drenched her heart, and she wanted to reach out and touch him so badly. Wrap her arms around him. Promise him it would be okay.

"But that has a way of spinning out of control, you know?" he continued. "Running from something you don't think you can face, but the only thing you do is end up running straight into the grips of something so much worse. And before you know it, those claws are so deep in you, you can't get free."

"I would have been here for you. I…I waited here for you. For years, I waited out here for you." She refused the embarrassment at the admission.

Low-pitched anguish vibrated from his chest, and he scrubbed both hands over the top of his head as he bent over. "It was better I didn't come, Dakota. You couldn't reach me then, and the last person you should have been around is someone like me."

Contempt huffed from his nose. "You still shouldn't be. You learned the proof of that last night."

"I don't care."

He laughed a hollow sound, and he looked up through the branches at the star-speckled night. "You should, Dakota. You should."

Then he dropped his attention to her. "But I promise you that I'm going to make a change. It's going to take me some time to crawl out of the disaster I've created, but I promise that I'm going to be better."

Peeking at him, she chewed at her bottom lip. "That's good, Ryder. You deserve a good life. I want you to have one. Even though I know it hurts, thinking about your mom. But not remembering her will be the biggest regret of your life."

He stared at her with an expression that knotted her stomach in fists. "I have so many regrets, Dakota. But I'm going to stop adding to them."

He kept watching her for the longest time before he took her by surprise when he suddenly hopped off the branch. Standing on the ground, he turned his gaze up to her, and he crept so close that she felt his heat seep into her bare legs.

"I'm leaving soon." Why it shot out of her like a desperate plea, she didn't know. All she knew was it felt necessary. Like she was begging him for something.

"I know, Dakota. It's good that you are. I want you to go to college. Gain all those experiences. Chase after everything that makes you happy."

She wanted to go, too. Was excited for it. She had so many dreams, and she was going to own that bakery one day, but she needed the skills to make it come to fruition.

Plus, she craved those experiences, too.

But there was something that held her in this hesitation, the buzzy sensation that fluttered in her chest. She felt hinged on this boy that she'd hardly begun to know again.

"What are you going to do?" she asked.

Air huffed from his nose. "Get clean. Maybe pursue this welding thing. Find a way to buy back my mother's house."

The last wheezed out of him like he was afraid of voicing his own dream.

"She'd like that," Dakota whispered.

Ryder raked his teeth over his bottom lip. "Yeah. I think she would."

Ryder shifted in indecision before he looked back up at her, and shivers raced through her when he slowly lifted his arms and planted his hands on the branch on either side of her body. He leaned in so close to her that she was inundated.

Inundated with his aura.

Warm leather and deep, decadent spice. She wondered if she could recreate the flavor in the kitchen. Box it and label it.

But she doubted there would be any way to reproduce this feeling.

The urge she had to drag her fingers through his hair.

"What that bastard said to you last night?" He let the implication trail off.

Mortification threatened to close off the flow of air. Her entire life people had made those comments. Jabs at her just because she didn't fit into their perfect mold.

But lately, she'd started to feel different about them. They didn't pierce so deep, and they didn't hurt so much. And she figured if they didn't like her for who she was, then fuck them. There were plenty of people who did.

Her mother called it healing, but Dakota thought it was growing.

That she was coming to recognize who she was.

But all those old wounds throbbed inside her right then.

Because Ryder had heard it.

She hated that it stung.

That it made her want to cover herself up and hide.

"He's a fool, Dakota. A fucking fool. You're beautiful. Everything about you. The inside. The outside. That smile and the way you light up the room. Don't fucking listen to anyone who ever tells you otherwise."

Heat blistered through her at his words, lighting her insides in a full glow. It pulsed where it met with the vibrating in her chest and became something so profound it was difficult to breathe.

Her throat felt thick, sticky with the tension that pulled between them. The man so close, she could feel the hammering of his heart.

She gasped when he suddenly stepped away. "I've got to go."

Warily she nodded, and she murmured around the thickness of her tongue, "You're a good person, Ryder. Don't fucking listen to anyone who ever tells you otherwise."

A small smile quirked on her mouth when she returned his words, and Ryder's split into a full grin.

God, it hurt just looking at him.

"Deal," he said as he backed away with his hands stuffed in his pockets, then he spun around and started for the trail that cut through the woods.

"Don't forget about me while I'm gone?" she couldn't help but call to his retreating form.

He stalled, and he looked back at her through the wisps of the night. "No, Cookie, I could never forget about you."

Chapter Thirty

Dakota

LIGHT BARELY LEAKED IN THROUGH THE WINDOW, SENDING A HAZE of glittering gold through the room and pulling me from sleep. Heat saturated my flesh, his strength seeping into me where he held me from behind, and his deep, slumbering breaths puffed into my hair.

I felt hedged in a sanctuary.

Shielded by a fortress.

It was a comfort that I'd craved for so long. One that I wanted to trust in. To believe would still be there tomorrow. That he wasn't going to steal away the way he'd done before. Not that things had ever been like this between us before.

But after everything he'd confessed last night, how he looked at me, how he saw me, how he'd wanted me for all these years, I realized there was a part of me that had always known.

A part that had felt something so much bigger between us. Something I'd seen in his eyes and felt in his care.

The way I sensed him when he came into the room, my axis tilting a fraction each time, drawn toward something that he'd fought to keep hidden.

He couldn't hide it now.

Not with the tattooed arm he had wrapped around my waist, keeping me snug against his body.

Both of us were still naked, and I relished in the press of his bare skin.

After he'd tended to me last night, he'd pulled back the covers and ordered me to get in. It'd only shocked me a little that he'd climbed in behind me, and he'd tucked me close and pressed a tender kiss to the back of my head and murmured, "Sleep."

Now, he grumbled from the depths of it, and his hand glided down from my waist to take a handful of my hip. He tucked me even closer, and his hard, rigid cock dug into the small of my back. The sting of the cold metal against my skin was a shivery contrast to the flames that burned from him.

And those flames leapt when he muttered my name. "Dakota."

His hand tightened on my hip, fingers dipping in, like he was terrified of letting go. His nose burrowed into my hair at the back of my head, and his rumbled words glided through me like a dream. "Love you."

Emotion cinched down so tight around my heart, a desperate squeeze that contracted before it expanded out and unfurled with the truth.

And I felt entranced by it.

By the deafening quiet and the roaring that shouted in my heart and in my ears.

I love you. I love you.

My soul chanted it. Demanded it.

I slowly shifted around. A pained breath left me at the sight of him asleep on my pillow, on his side facing me.

It'd always hurt looking at him.

A blade driven through to the spot that had always been reserved for him. Each time, it had carved it out. Scored it deeper. Only this morning, it throbbed with something new.

Something beautiful as my eyes caressed the sharp contours of his face. The man a perfect sculpture with the faint glimmering of light caressing his features.

Everything about him harsh and severe.

Midnight in the breaking day.

And that truth shouted louder, clamoring through the room, bouncing against the walls and ricocheting back.

Shoving off any insecurities, I shifted to straddle him. Sensing me in his sleep, he followed the motion and rolled onto his back. A rumbly groan filtered between his full, red lips.

I kept most of my weight on my knees, and I eased down just a fraction.

Enough to rub myself against his cock that was hard between us, so long that the tip nearly touched his belly button.

Sparks zapped at the contact, and Ryder's hands flew to my hips as those gunmetal eyes snapped open.

Shocked.

Wild.

One second later, they darkened with greed.

They dragged over me where I hovered over him, my hips barely moving, but it was enough to stoke the friction that flamed.

"Cookie." It was a grumble. So rough and low that it sent chills racing my flesh. "What are you doing?"

"I need you." It was a gluttonous sound that curled in the air. The connection tugged hard between us.

I felt his dick twitch, hardening even more, and his fingers dug deeper into my waist, close to painful as he warred with restraint.

But I didn't want that between us anymore.

Restraint.

Walls.

Boundaries.

I wanted to crush them all.

Lay them at our feet.

"Please," I whispered, and I angled up, taking his cock in my hand and stroking up.

Ryder nearly bowed from the bed, his hips arching up as he moaned. "Cookie. Fuck."

"Please," I said again, and I shifted to align the fat head of him at my center.

The muscles of his abdomen flexed, corded and ripped. Strength quivered beneath the designs he had painted on his flesh.

"I'm on the pill. Please let me feel you." It was a frantic rasp as the slight pressure of him nudged at my entrance, and that time when he murmured, "Cookie," it was pure lust.

I braced my hands on his stomach as I began to sink onto him, and his fingers burrowed in possession.

A sound so needy it was almost embarrassing got free when I shifted so I could watch myself taking him in.

Inch by inch of him spreading me.

Filling me.

A pleasure so close to pain that I cried out with it, and a tremble rocked through when I had him to the hilt.

I felt ripped apart.

Sewn together.

Pierced.

Healed.

Whole.

So much. Everything. Never enough.

A growl escaped him, and he wound his big hands around my waist. "Fuck, Cookie. I have to be dreaming. You feel so good. So fucking good. Your sweet, perfect cunt hugging my cock. Show me how good you can take it."

He was the one who began to guide me, taking me by the outside of the thighs and urging me up before he slowly pressed me back down on him.

The burn of him speared through me. Pinpricks of pleasure pulsed from my center.

A moan coasted up my throat, shivers skating far and wide.

Emotion rose, lifting up from that vacant space and crawling into the cavity of my chest.

"Ride me, Cookie."

I began to move over him, rolling my hips as I took him in again and again, slowly at first before I quickened as the intensity swelled around us.

He touched me everywhere, gripping my curves, riding up my sides, cupping my breasts, the rough pads of his thumbs rubbing circles on my nipples before he grabbed me by the bottom to drive me harder onto him.

He left a trail of fire, the man the flame.

The one who held the power to leave me nothing but ash.

He watched me the entire time, his eyes on my face, his lips parted as praises tumbled from his mouth. "Look at you, Dakota. Do you have any idea what I see when I'm looking at you? A goddess in the morning. The light breaking inside me."

And those words glided as deep as the ones he'd admitted in his sleep, and I jolted when he began to swirl his thumb over my clit.

Sensation rushed.

Building and glowing.

I threw my head back as I gave myself over to it.

To everything we'd both needed for so long.

Overwhelmed and overtaken.

Bouncing on him, taking him so deep and hard that each thrust forced a pleasured cry out of me, and Ryder was grunting and pushing me down as he bucked up.

The sound of us meeting filled the room.

Pants and groans and the slapping of skin.

And it grew so intense. Wild and frantic as we clawed at each other.

My nails raking into his skin. His abdomen. His shoulders. Dragging over the broken clock he had tattooed in the middle of his chest.

And I refused to let it hurt. Refused the old pain.

Instead, I stared down into those molten eyes.

Believed in what they said.

And it gathered like a swirling storm.

Swooping in.

Pleasure.

A rapture I knew I could only find in Ryder.

It stirred the glittering gold that held fast to the air.

"Ryder, it's so good. So go—"

Ryder suddenly shot up, bringing us chest to chest, and with the change in the position, that bar on his cock hit me somewhere deep. The band stretched so tight inside me snapped.

Pleasure splintered apart.

An inundating rush.

Ecstasy.

Wave after wave.

I clawed at his shoulders as bliss kept rolling through me, and Ryder was burrowing his face in my throat to bury the roar as he came apart.

A current rocked through his body as he throbbed inside me.

Sweat covered us as we remained like that, plastered together, our arms wrapped so tightly around each other that I didn't think we could ever let go.

It was Ryder who eased back a fraction to meet my face, and he reached up and tucked a lock of my hair behind my ear, his fingers trembling as he did. "Dakota."

The roaring in my heart and in my ears shouted louder.

The chant of my soul.

I love you. I love you.

"I love you, Ryder." There was no stopping it from seeping out and crawling into the air. No hesitation as I found the courage to finally voice my truth.

I loved him, and I always had.

Gunmetal eyes flashed.

Possession and devotion.

But the guilt in them was so much greater and turned everything grim.

That sliced through me, sharper than any knife.

"Dakota." My name shook with fear, even though he tried to play it off like a warning.

"Tell me you feel it, too," I demanded.

He didn't say anything, he only swallowed with that halo of shame dropping his head between his shoulders.

Hurt disbelief echoed through that vacant spot, and I rushed to climb off him. I yanked the sheet free, wrapping it around me before I slid off the side of the bed, hugging it as I turned to stare at him.

But it wasn't me who was covering.

"You're a coward, Ryder. A coward. And I don't need one of those in my life."

I started for the door.

"Dakota." My name grated behind me.

A plea.

I only stalled for one second before I opened the door and walked out.

Because I knew what I needed. What I deserved. And if he couldn't meet me there? Give me his truth?

Then I was only setting myself up to get destroyed.

And I didn't need that kind of destruction.

Chapter Thirty-One
Ryder

Twenty-Two Years Old

RYDER CREPT DOWN THE HALL, AGITATION FIZZING THROUGH HIM as he walked toward the back office of the run-down dry cleaners that sat in a seedy part of the city that was an hour outside of Time River. Ryder had dragged the filth of this place back into his small town for the last five years.

Guilt gnawed at his conscience.

He was finished with it.

That didn't mean he wasn't shaking, and the first real fear he'd felt in years brimmed inside him when he saw Lenny and Pete, the two assholes standing guard outside the door today.

Anxiety slicked his skin with sweat and pounded his heart in frantic beats.

He guessed it was the first time he'd realized he had something worth living for, his spirit coming alive with something new.

Two weeks ago, he'd promised Dakota he would make a change, and he was going to see it through.

Whatever it took.

He lifted his chin as Pete and Lenny pushed off the wall they lounged against.

"I need to talk to him." Ryder's words were low and emphatic.

Speculation moved through Lenny's expression. "Does he know you're coming?"

"No."

Lenny wavered before he moved to the door and tapped it lightly with his knuckles. "Boss, Ryder is here. He wants to talk to you."

"Let him in." It echoed through the door, and Ryder tried to play it cool as he squeezed between Lenny and Pete and stepped into the office.

It was dusky inside, a single, dull lamp setting it aglow from where it sat on the cluttered desk.

Dare clasped his hands over his stomach and rocked back in the chair, bastard eyeing him from across the desk.

Ryder tried not to shrink or shift on his feet.

The fucker was dangerous.

He'd seen it.

Witnessed it.

Knew it from experience.

"How did it go?"

Ryder swallowed over the lump in his throat. "Three months of probation and a hundred hours of community service."

Unruffled, Dare nodded. "And you claimed it as yours?"

Dare's only concern was that his ass was covered. That Ryder hadn't leaked when he'd been squeezed.

"Said I bought it off someone I'd never seen before on the outskirts of town."

He nodded again. "Good."

Good.

It wasn't fucking good.

None of it was good.

Dare took a long drag of his cigarette that was burning in his ashtray before he stubbed it out, blowing the smoke out the side of his mouth like it wouldn't cloud the dank space. "Lay low for a bit."

"I'm done with it," Ryder said rather than agreeing.

Dare cracked a menacing grin like he wasn't surprised, rocking farther back, so casual though it was cut with a threat. "Is that so?"

"I was seventeen. A fucked-up kid who didn't have a clue. I want out."

Air puffed from Dare's nose, and he sat forward, his arms rested on the desk as he shrugged. "Seems you still don't have a clue because you should know by now that's not the way it works."

Ryder's molars ground. "I won't keep taking that poison into my town."

"I see." Dare's grin was back, and a second later, the door burst open and Lenny and Pete rushed in. Ryder didn't have time to prepare himself before Pete grabbed him by the shoulders and drew up a knee, ramming it into Ryder's stomach.

He choked on the shock of pain, the air knocked from his lungs. A second later, he was on the ground, getting pummeled in a flash. Fists and feet and a flurry of pain that made his sight blur in and out.

His consciousness came at him like the spinning beacon from a lighthouse.

He could barely process the presence that came to stand over him while he lay face down on the soiled, grimy floor with blood pouring out of his mouth.

The wickedness that slithered over him.

Dare leaned down close, getting in the line of Ryder's fuzzy sight. "Don't worry, Ryder. You won't have to drag it into your town anymore. I have something much better planned for you."

Chapter Thirty-Two

Dakota

I T WAS AFTER SEVEN WHEN I PULLED INTO THE DRIVEWAY OF RYDER'S house. I could feel the emptiness radiating from the walls, and for a moment, I was pinned by the weight of it. The boulder sitting on my chest was so heavy that I wasn't sure how I managed to breathe.

He'd been gone when I'd come out of the bathroom after taking a shower this morning.

I hadn't meant to cry, but I had. I'd broken down right in the middle of the room where I'd left him twenty minutes before because this was the man I loved.

The man I'd loved since I was nineteen.

Probably longer than that if I was being honest with myself.

But he was right—I deserved better than what he was offering me.

Blowing out a sigh, I shut off the car and glanced through the rearview mirror at my son who had fallen asleep on the drive over.

I'd stayed at my mom's for dinner. I hadn't been ready to come back here and face him yet, but he wasn't here, anyway, so I guessed it didn't matter much.

I opened my door and stepped into the twilight.

The air was tinged in that iridescent pink that was so thick it felt like you could reach out and touch it.

Run your fingers through the color.

Paint yourself in its beauty.

I went to the back and unbuckled Kayden, careful not to wake him as I pulled him into my arms.

It would be a whole lot easier to pack our things without him running around the house demolishing it.

He mumbled a tiny sound as he snuggled into my chest, and I released a strained breath as I carried him up the walkway and onto the porch.

I nearly tripped when I got that same gross feeling again.

A sticky awareness that lifted the hairs at the nape of my neck and turned my stomach sour.

I shifted around and peered into the fading light. Into the quiet peace of Ryder's neighborhood.

There was no movement.

Nothing other than the breeze stirring through the trees.

God, I was letting the disorder get the best of me. Letting the haunting echoes inside me turn into something they were not.

I shook it off and angled so I could get the key into the lock while keeping Kayden carefully balanced in my arms. I locked the door behind us, climbed the stairs, and went into Kayden's room where I laid him in his crib.

My chest squeezed as I looked at his sweet face as he slept. Hating that he was going to get his heart shattered, too. This morning, it hadn't just been my heart on the line.

I hurried into the room that I'd come to think of as mine, ignoring the bed rumpled with linens and missing a sheet.

I dragged the suitcase from under the bed and opened it on the floor, and I began tugging the dresses I'd hung in the closet from their hangers and tossing them into the case.

With each one, my movements became more frantic, a blur of desperation. A bedlam of pain and sorrow and disappointment.

By the time I moved to the dresser and opened the top drawer, I could barely see through the sheets of tears that blanketed my face.

I dragged my hand over my eyes to try to clear it, tried even harder to suppress the sob that climbed my throat, but it erupted, anyway.

Another came behind it, and another as the misery rushed me, ripping from my mouth and banging from the walls.

I had gotten to the point where I was barely able to stand beneath the weight of it when I felt the presence emerge behind me.

I froze beneath its gravity.

Held in the potency that ripped through the room and slammed into my spirit.

My hands shot to the dresser for support, unable to look at him.

He stood there for the longest time, as if he wasn't able to move, either. Unable to speak. Trapped by this connection that had become the most painful thing I'd ever felt.

When he spoke, I nearly broke.

"Do you think I don't love you, Dakota?"

The words were gravel, shards that sent a shiver rolling down my spine.

I gasped for the oxygen that had grown too thick, and I dug my nails into the wood of the dresser, trying to hold on, to keep from falling to my knees.

"Look at me, Cookie." His voice scuffed the dense air. Low and desperate. "Look at me."

Maybe I was a fool.

Maybe I shouldn't give in.

But I slowly shuffled around to face him, drawn to a man who'd held me for so long I couldn't recognize what not loving him looked like.

Ryder stood in the doorway.

Towering.

So tall and powerful.

Covered in all that ink.

Midnight.

Those silvered, gunmetal eyes flashed, and his throat bobbed heavily when he swallowed.

Severity crackled. The energy alive. Pulling and pressing as he stared at me from across the room.

"Do you think I'm not in love with you?"

My eyes slammed closed, and my body bowed forward with his admission.

Part of me wanted to fight it. The other wanted to savor in hearing him say it.

He didn't speak again until I opened them.

Pain lancinated through his expression, and his head canted to the side in supplication.

"I love you, Dakota. I'm gone for you. Since I was twenty-two fucking years old, I've been gone for you. Since you became the one thing in this world that could soothe the ache inside me. Since you became the reason to look beyond my circumstances. Since you reminded me of the good things this world might have to offer."

He took a step forward.

The ground trembled below my feet.

"You saved me, Dakota. Saved me when I was lost. When I'd given up. And I keep trying to push you away because I know I don't deserve you. But I can't do that any longer. I can't fucking deny that you are the one thing in this life that I've been living for. You are the light breaking the darkness inside me. And I'm begging you, please don't walk away."

Chapter Thirty-Three
Ryder

DAKOTA STARED AT ME FROM ACROSS THE ROOM AS THE LAST OF the light faded away through the window behind her.

It cast her in a silhouette.

The faintest glow slipped across her precious face from the dull glow coming from the closet.

Her breaths were short and shallow. Hair a mess. Cheeks soaked and splotchy with her tears.

So fucking gorgeous I couldn't breathe.

My heart pounded out between us. Pleading for her to see. To get it. To understand when I hadn't given her a reason to, not when there was all this bullshit I had to keep hidden in the shadows. But the shame I felt over the corruption hadn't come close to the kind I'd felt when she'd walked out on me this morning.

The shame I'd felt when I couldn't speak it.

When I'd rejected the gift that Dakota had offered. When I'd refused our truth.

I wouldn't refuse it any longer.

A tear streaked from the corner of her eye, and I groaned a pained sound as the energy shifted.

The room enclosed and the air grew dense.

"Cookie," I murmured. "Tell me I'm not too late. Tell me you still love me, too."

"Do you think I could ever stop loving you?"

The second she said it, I snapped, and I was across the room.

I crashed into her in a landslide of greed.

One hand dove into her hair and the other curled around the side of her neck as I crushed my mouth against hers, kissing her for the first time.

Nothing had ever felt quite like kissing Dakota Cooper.

Her lips against mine.

It was flames and heat and pure relief.

I sucked it in, imbibing the feeling as I devoured her mouth.

Sugar and vanilla and all things sweet.

My chest nearly blew with the power of it. With the way my heart thrashed violently at my ribs. With the devotion that surged from the sacred place that had always been meant for her.

Our tongues tangled in a clash of desperation, and she clawed at the fabric of my shirt, pushing up onto her toes to get closer.

I spun her as I kissed her, lips plucking and rolling over her plush bottom lip before they did the same to the top, urgent in their plea, unable to break for a second as I backed her toward the bed.

"I love you, Ryder, I love you," she mumbled at our connection. The sound of it reverberated through me, slipping down my throat and spreading through my cells. It seeped all the way down to my spirit because this woman would always possess my soul.

We stumbled and spun, and I kissed her deeper, hands on her face so I could get her closer. "I love you, Dakota. So fucking much."

The back of her legs knocked into the side of the bed, and she giggled a blissful sound, and I was smiling against her mouth, whispering, "I love you," again.

My palms smoothed down her neck, and I wrapped my arms around her so I could get to the zipper at the back of her dress. I dragged it down, then spread my hands flat, riding them up the soft skin of her back and over her shoulders to push the dress out of our way.

It skimmed down her body, landing in a pool at her feet.

Dakota was in a black bra and another pair of those high-waisted underwear that had made me lose my mind the other night. Back when I should have known everything was getting ready to hit a boiling point. There would no longer be any resisting this.

"Goddess," I rumbled as I kissed down her throat, and I reached around her back to unlatch her bra and dragged it free of her arms.

Shivers rolled beneath my touch, and Dakota's hands slipped under my shirt, lighting a fire as she pushed it up. I eased back for the flash of a second so I could rip it over my head.

Then I was back on her.

Skin on skin.

Her pebbled nipples pressed against my chest.

Her warmth and her sweetness and her soft against all my hard.

Lust spun with the devotion.

A need unlike anything that should exist.

Greater, more powerful than any sin I could ever commit.

And I was kissing her again.

Frantic.

Frenzied.

Dakota's fingers fumbled at my jeans, tugging my fly loose as I kicked off my shoes. She pushed my jeans down around my waist and took my briefs at the same time.

"I need you," she wheezed, her hands grabbing at my ass while I shoved my jeans the rest of the way down with one hand while I backed her onto the bed.

She edged onto the mattress, and I twisted free of the heavy fabric around my ankles. Without missing a beat, I angled in to grab the edges of her panties and ripped them down her legs.

Dakota whimpered, her hips coming off the mattress. "Ryder."

"Fuck. The sight of you, Cookie. Sweet thing." The words rolled off my tongue.

Praise.

Adoration.

A fire raged at the center.

I rushed to crawl over her and made a spot for myself between her thighs.

Urgency spiraled around us as she kept lifting her hips to mine.

I grabbed my dick and drove into her in one deep thrust.

Possession.

It splintered through the middle of me.

Shattering out in surrender.

Dakota cried out, her words ragged as she raked her blunt nails down my back. "How is it possible you feel so good inside me?"

I slipped my arm around her back so I could hold her close, staring down at the one who'd found me in the dark. Called me out of the barren desert where I'd lost myself. The one who'd made me believe again. "Because this is the way we're supposed to be, Dakota. You were meant for me. You're mine, Cookie, mine."

But it was me who belonged to her.

Knew it as I pulled almost all the way out and sank back in.

I nearly blacked out with the way her walls hugged my cock.

So tight.

So perfect.

I groaned her name, my forehead dropping to hers as I drew back and thrust in deep. "Dakota."

It was so different than it'd been this morning. It'd been so fucking good, but it'd still felt like torture. I'd felt like a thief taking something that he wasn't supposed to have.

But Dakota and I were always meant for something more.

And I couldn't do anything but keep kissing her as I moved in her. Because I wasn't stealing but giving her everything that I had.

Dakota met me thrust for thrust, giving it, too.

"I love you," she kept whispering.

Touching my cheek.

My brow.

My jaw.

Our bodies roiled, liquid in the middle of the bed.

Swelling and surging.

A tide.

An ebb and flow that always crested at the perfect time.

Her hands were all over me and mine were all over her.

Touching.

Worshipping.

Loving her in a way I never thought I would get lucky enough to do.

The connection I'd always shared with her glowed in the room.

Covered me in her bright, blinding light.

Dakota whimpered and begged as I drove us higher, and I could feel the tension gather at her middle.

Her gasps and her pleas.

I drove into her harder, deeper and faster, and I swallowed her cry with a desperate kiss when the orgasm blazed through her body.

Her nails sank into my shoulders, digging in as she rolled beneath me, clinging to me like she might float away if she didn't.

And I gave her mine as I split, the roar of rapture that burst in my blood.

The streaks of pleasure that whipped out to touch every nerve in my body.

My cock throbbed as I poured inside her, and both of us were gasping as we rode that high.

A high I was never going to come down from.

I held her like that as we trembled and shook, both of us relishing the aftershocks, before I eased back a fraction so I could look down at her face.

Cinnamon eyes watched me with the kind of tenderness I couldn't fathom.

I ran my knuckles down the soft curve of her cheek and down to her chin. "Nothing could ever feel as good as being loved by you, Dakota Cooper."

"That's good, Ryder, because I promise you, I'm going to be doing it my whole life."

Chapter Thirty-Four

Dakota

"YOU MIGHT AS WELL NOT BOTHER GETTING DRESSED."

At his words, I stumbled to a stop just inside the doorway.

I had the same sheet wrapped around me as I'd had this morning, but this time when I'd slipped off the bed to go into the bathroom, I'd promised I'd be right back.

Redness flushed across my skin as I looked at the man propped on a pillow against the headboard, a blanket coming up to cover him just to his hip bones that jutted out from his waist, his arms tucked behind his head.

A cool, casual king.

One that dripped midnight.

Covered in all those colors and designs.

Imposing with all that corded strength.

Every inch of his gorgeous body rippled with power, except I felt no threat as he laid there smirking at me.

"Is that why you want me to stay? So you have me naked and ready for you?" I remained in the doorway as I tossed out the tease.

Clearly, I was only teasing myself because I was so ready for him.

My insides throbbed at the sight of him.

Gunmetal eyes raked over me where I stood hugging the sheet. They left a scorching path in their wake.

My knees wobbled, and his gaze gleamed as he quirked a dark brow. "Tell me you're going to complain about that?"

It was purely a challenge.

"Do you want me to lie to you, or do you want the truth?"

"The truth, Cookie, always the truth."

Only we had never really given that to each other, had we? It was time, though. Time to come out from behind the veils where we'd kept our feelings secreted.

"Then I'd have to say that you can have me any time and any way that you want."

A growl rolled through the room, and those dark eyes gleamed with greed. "That's a dangerous proposition to make to a man like me."

Even though I shivered, I cocked my head. "I think you might underestimate me."

Ryder chuckled a low, disbelieving sound, and that grin cracked at the edge of his mouth. "Get over here."

Biting down hard on my bottom lip, I shuffled toward him, the worn, wooden planks cool on my bare feet. I attempted not to trip on the fabric that draped around my legs and brushed the floor.

I made it to the side of the bed then yelped when he suddenly reached out, grabbed me around the waist, and hauled me onto his lap. It left me straddling him with only the thin sheet separating us.

"You're ridiculously strong, Ryder." It came out sounding like I was scolding him for picking me up.

He leaned forward, buried his face at the side of my neck, and murmured, "Nah, baby, these arms were just made for you."

I might as well have been melting in those arms as he wound them around me and pulled me tight against his chest.

My own looped around his neck, and I played with a short lock of his hair as we stayed like that for the longest time, both of us just breathing in the moment.

"Then why did you wait so long to hold me with them?" My question broke into the stillness that had descended, a whisper that fell in sync with the ghosts that played along the walls of the room.

Ryder barely tensed, the muscles on his back going rigid, and he slowly eased back. Enough that he was leaning fully against the headboard. Enough that he could lay the full intent of his gaze on me. "I knew I wasn't close to being worthy of you when you were going away to college, Dakota. I was barely finding myself, thanks to you, but I had a lot of shit to work out in my life. Problem is, when you live a life like mine, working that shit out isn't so easy."

Dread dripped into my bloodstream.

I'd always known there was something that Ryder was hiding beneath the easiness. The way he walked into a room so casually, tossing out smiles and grins, all while he always seemed to be looking over his shoulder.

I'd turned a blind eye to it, no doubt because I didn't want to see.

Didn't want to know.

I wanted to go on happily delusional that my friend was just fine. That he'd overcome the demons of his past.

I knew better now.

I just prayed they weren't the kind that could destroy him.

The kind that could destroy us.

I had to curl my arms back around his neck and press my mouth to his ear because I was too terrified to look at him when I got the answer. "Are you still…using?"

I didn't believe that, though.

Never once in all the years after I'd returned from Boulder had I ever thought he'd been messed up like that. The drugs that numbed him into oblivion.

No.

Not when those eyes had always remained so vigilant.

So raw and real.

His head shook against my chest. "No, baby, it's not that."

"Then what is it?" I drew back so I could see his face, and he reached up and threaded his fingers through my hair at the side of my head.

I leaned into his touch.

"It's the one thing I can't give you, Dakota."

Hurt stabbed into my chest. "You don't trust me?"

He only hesitated for a beat before the words began to flood, quiet and hard and riddled with a torment that I didn't understand.

"No. Because it's dangerous, and I can't involve you in it. It's why I'm going to have to go on pretending like you're not mine when we're in public because I can't risk someone knowing who you are to me or what you mean to me. Just for a little while, until I find a way to get out from under this."

Terror must have slashed through my expression. I doubted there would have been any missing it with the chill that slipped down my spine. An ice slick that froze everything in its path.

Because he framed my jaw in both of his big hands, angling up so he brought us face to face.

His breaths mine.

His promise was gravel. "I will never let anything happen to you or Kayden, Dakota. I won't. I will protect you with everything I have. Fight for you, but in that, I have to fight *this*. I have to finally put it behind me, and I don't know what that looks like, but I promise you that everything I'm going to do is for you. For us. For this family. The family that should have been mine from the beginning."

Surprise widened my eyes. Was he implying what I thought he was? Had he felt it then, too?

I'd thought I'd been a fool for putting my heart on the chopping block that day. When I'd garnered the courage to finally tell him what I'd felt.

But then why would he have said what he'd said? Why had he been so devastated when he'd told me Amelia was dead?

I'd thought he'd been…heartbroken.

That question locked in my throat, a gnarl of old pain, and Ryder tightened his hold like he'd heard every question on the current of our connection.

"It stole our chance, Dakota, and I succumbed to the belief that I was never going to get to have you, and I refuse to believe it for any longer."

"You told me you loved me…but not like that." An accusation slipped into the confusion.

He'd told me.

Had gently destroyed me as he'd murmured the words.

I'd thought he was trying to save my feelings. Let me down easy.

Shame crested through his features, words so aggrieved they cut through the air. "It was the greatest lie I've ever told, Dakota. Seeing your face when I told you that? It fucking killed me. Breaking your heart while I was breaking mine, too."

"I don't understand."

"I know, and that's on me, and I promise one day I will explain it, but not until I know it's safe. Please trust me on this."

My attention dropped to the broken clock on his chest. The fractured hands stuck at five o' four. I'd always thought it'd marked the moment he'd lost Amelia.

I'd witnessed his pain that day.

I'd thought he'd been devastated over Amelia's death.

I'd thought he'd lost the one he'd been in love with.

He suddenly gripped my hand and spread my palm over the tattoo, pressing it hard, like his soul was desperate to tell me something but his tongue was locked.

"Give me time to make it right."

Alarms were going off somewhere in my mind. They should have been deafening, but it was only faint, blotted out by the sincerity of his eyes.

"Okay," I agreed, and he sighed then leaned forward and kissed me hard.

Kissed me into a puddle, until I was on my back on the bed and his hand was smoothing up the sheet, over my hip and up my side, though he paused when he was pressing his palm over my trembling stomach.

He edged back and looked down at me. "I nearly lost my mind when I found out you were pregnant. Destroyed me to think of you with somebody else."

It wasn't regret that I felt. It was the vestiges of the pain that had driven me that night.

How I'd felt so raw, and the only thing I could do was seek some kind of comfort. Unfortunately, it'd only left me feeling worse. Like I'd used myself up, trying to cover what I really felt with something else.

"Watching you with other women destroyed me, too."

Remorse dimmed his eyes, and he brushed his thumb under the hollow of my eye. "I did my best to put as much space and history between us. Thinking one day, it would finally kill what I really felt for you. That one day I'd look at you and we'd really just be friends. But I don't think that's even possible, Dakota. There's no chance of not feeling this."

He curled his fingers deeper into my stomach. Clinging to me. Like he was terrified I might get away.

"Why don't we know anything about Kayden's father?" he pressed.

I knew this would be coming. Keeping that story a secret was a choice I'd made. I hadn't wanted anyone else to have it, only because there was no chance anyone else would understand. But I wanted Ryder to hold it now. "I was blinded by how hurt I was that evening, Ryder, when I came to you and admitted how I felt, and you didn't return it."

My tongue stroked over my bottom lip. "I just…drove. For hours. Away. I ended up in Poplar at this crowded bar. I couldn't be here in this town around anyone I knew, but I also felt like I couldn't be alone. I met some random guy there. He was attractive, I guess, though I don't know that I really even processed that. But he smiled at me, talked to me, and in the middle of my pain, it made me feel something other than the misery over you. So I had sex with him in his truck out in the parking lot. I never mentioned him because I barely caught his name."

Regret dimmed those dark eyes, and I hesitated beneath the weight before I forced myself to continue. "Trey. We didn't exchange numbers or anything. It wasn't like that for either of us. We were both looking for something to make us feel good for a little while."

Inhaling, I pressed on through the torment seeping out of Ryder. "When I found out I was pregnant, I went back to the bar where I'd met him. A bunch of times. I didn't know if I hoped to find him or hoped that I wouldn't, but I guessed in the end, I was relieved when I never found him. Thankful he'd been my comfort that once, and he'd left me with this little gift that I never anticipated."

It'd been reckless, I knew.

But sometimes things worked out the way they were supposed to.

"I don't regret it," I admitted.

Affection slipped through Ryder's expression, and a tender smile edged his mouth as he hovered over me and brushed back the hair from my face. "How could you regret that tiny tornado?"

"I couldn't."

Every part of Ryder billowed with intensity. "I love him, too. Love him with everything I've got."

"I know that," I told him.

It was the truth.

I'd always seen Ryder's love for Kayden. I'd just missed out on what that love had really meant for me.

"So, it's the three of us now." He tipped up my chin with his index finger, staring down at me. A promise blazed in those midnight eyes.

"Is that what this is, Ryder?" I could barely speak.

"I told you that I'm fighting for this family. For you and Kayden. For us."

Warmth spread, expanding my heart. I reached up and scratched my nails through the stubble on his jaw. "I always prayed you wouldn't forget us."

"Forget you, Dakota? That's not possible."

The smirk was back on his face, and he shifted so he was on his knees, the gorgeous man rising high, every inch of him on display.

He peeled away the sheet with a wicked grin pulling at his mouth.

A shiver rolled through me, and I could feel the flush cover my entire body.

Need consumed me in an instant.

"Cookie, what I'm going to do to you."

Tingles spread, and my teeth raked my bottom lip. "I hope it's good."

He rumbled a low laugh before he shifted me onto my hands and knees, his mouth dropping kisses down my spine as he muttered, "Oh, it's going to be."

Chapter Thirty-Five
Ryder

I SAT UP IN BED JUST…STARING DOWN WHERE SHE SLEPT. DAKOTA'S soft breaths drifted into the wisping darkness of the room, and my fingers swirled in her hair as I struggled to process what had happened tonight.

Where I'd taken her to.

The promises I'd made, the confessions I'd given, even though they were shallow and obscured, and the belief and trust she'd turned around and placed in my hands.

My eyes traced every curve of her face. Her brow and her nose and her cheeks. Her jaw and those lush lips and that tiny dimple on the left of her chin that drove me to disorder.

Everything about her was a hook in my soul.

There was no not making good on that promise now. I'd known I was coming up to it. That I was finished with Dare. I had to find a way out of his snares, and there was no way I could continue cowering to his threats.

He'd manipulated me for years, and yeah, I might have been a dumb kid then, but I wasn't close to being that same man now.

I had no idea what the consequences were going to be. If I was signing my own death certificate or where it was going to land me.

In jail, maybe.

Or maybe the reputation I'd carried like a false brand would be tainted, and I'd be shunned by Dakota and her family once and for all.

The only thing I knew was I was going to fight.

Ruin him, the same way as the bastard had ruined me.

Resolved, I eased off the bed, careful not to disturb Dakota, and I crept out into the hall with my cell in my hand. I dialed the number with my heart in my throat.

Ezra's voice was groggy with sleep when he answered. "Ryder? Is everything okay?"

I blew out a sigh and pushed through. "Hey. Yeah. But I need to talk to you."

Chapter Thirty-Six

Dakota

"**C**OME BACK TO BED." THE RUMBLY VOICE COVERED ME FROM behind.

Redness flushed my skin in an instant rush of heat, and I shifted to look back at the man who was facedown, a single eye peeking at me just as I was starting to slide out of bed. He stretched his arm out over the mattress, hand reaching my direction.

I couldn't do anything but shift around and get onto my hands and knees as I crawled to him. I had that sheet wrapped around me again, hugging it to my naked flesh.

At this rate, it was making a run for my favorite dress.

Ryder shifted and rolled onto his back as I came. The second I got close enough, his fingers dove into my hair, and I dipped down to press a soft kiss to his mouth.

He hummed against the connection, and I eased back, no stopping the tender smile that spread as I gazed down at him.

Reaching up, he caressed his thumb along my cheek. "Now this is exactly the way I want to wake up every morning for the rest of my life."

Giddiness blazed through my veins, and my teeth clamped down on my bottom lip. "With my bed head and morning breath and mascara smeared on my face?" I teased.

A rough chuckle skated from his lips. "That's right, Cookie. You think I'm scared of you raw? Uncovered and unmasked? Besides, you always smell like sugar and vanilla."

He sent me a smirk.

That redness deepened, and my heart swelled so fierce and fast that I could feel it pressing at my ribs. "You think I smell like sugar and vanilla?"

"That's right." He angled up and pecked a kiss to my mouth. "Cookie."

Oh.

"That's what that means? I always thought it was because you liked my cookies."

I could almost see the guttural sound roll up his throat. "Oh, I like your *cookies*, Dakota."

Both his hands latched onto my hips, and he pressed himself against me.

Butterflies swarmed. I'd thought I was too old for them, but they fluttered and flapped, sending tingles rushing through my body. I sighed, and I leaned down to kiss him a little longer before I forced myself back before I got lost in him again. "I need to get Kayden up and ready. It's Saturday… family breakfast at my mom's."

I hesitated. It wasn't like Ryder had never attended before, but I wasn't sure that I could face him in front of my family this morning without revealing what had happened between us. Without it being written all over me.

I thought he was probably thinking the same thing because he tipped up my chin. "How I'm supposed to keep my hands off you in front of your family and this town is beyond me. Now that I've touched you, Dakota, it's the only thing I want to do."

Everything squeezed. My heart and my stomach and the achy spot between my thighs.

"But I imagine if your brother even sees us in the same room together, he's going to catch the trail. Not sure I'm that good of an actor, and now that we've finally just begun to make good use of my dick, I doubt it would be in our best interest for me to lose it now." His joke was soft, woven with something more, a quiet intensity that whispered of his secrets that he continued to keep locked on his tongue.

"I might have an issue with you losing it," I murmured back, the faintest smile pulling around my lips.

Ryder's gaze turned serious, and he brushed back the lock of hair that kept falling in my face. "Your brother is going to be against this, Dakota.

He's going to lose it, kick my ass, and I mean it in the most literal way, and I'm going to deserve it."

"Why?" How could he? Not when he and Cody were so close.

His thumb skimmed the hollow beneath my eye. "Because he knows me."

Disquiet blustered through, and Ryder's voice became a little rougher when he said, "I am supposed to meet up with Ezra this morning. I need to get going, too."

"Okay." Hesitation brimmed, and I stayed there staring down at him, like I could get behind his mask. See everything he kept shrouded. Questions burned where I held them in my chest.

He'd asked me to trust him. To give him this. So I forced it aside and kissed him quickly again before I slid off the bed and went to the suitcase still opened on the floor. I snagged a dress off the top. It was short and red and always made me feel pretty.

Ryder groaned. "You're really trying to wreck a man, aren't you?"

From over my shoulder, I frowned at him.

His brow lifted like it should be obvious. "The number of times you'd be wearing that dress when I'd come into the café and the only thing that I could do was imagine following you into your office and pushing my hands up under it. Bending you over your desk so I could get to all the goodness hidden underneath."

How hadn't I known?

"I wished you would have, but I guess we're going to have to make up for lost time, aren't we?" How I managed to get it out flirty, I didn't know, but Ryder was rumbling again as he climbed out of bed.

Naked and gorgeous and stealing my breath.

The floor rocked beneath my feet as he ambled my way.

He plastered himself to my backside and buried his face in the side of my neck. "Oh, Dakota, we'll be making up for it. I promise you. I'm making up for everything."

Then he sauntered out the bedroom door, leaving me gaping behind him.

Forty minutes later, I pulled into the driveway at my mother's house. Kayla's car was already there, and I quickly went to the back and unbuckled Kayden. I set him on the ground, taking his hand as we headed up the walkway. He trotted along at my side, pointing at the house. "We go Gammy's house? I get Auntie *Kaywa*? I get *bwekfast*?"

His sweet little slur traveled on the morning air, his adorable face tipped up toward me as we went, and I thought I might feel lighter than I ever had before. This hope that had come seeping out from the walls where I'd shored it away, filling me up, a faith as bright as the sun that had begun to climb the sky.

All while there was a brand-new pressure gliding through my bloodstream. It felt as if I were carrying a new burden. One that was faceless and obscure. One that Ryder had entrusted me with without giving it a name.

It left me unsettled and unsure, a sour dread that festered in my stomach, but the one thing I was sure about was Ryder, so I pushed it down and promised myself that I wasn't going to allow my imagination to get carried away.

Resolved to let Ryder handle it the way he'd asked me, I gave a quick knock to the door before I turned the knob, finding it unlocked.

"Hello!" I called as we stepped into my childhood home that I loved so much.

I could almost feel the memories hovering like ghosts in the room. Vestiges of voices that still whispered and embraced.

My mother's support and belief. The way she'd encouraged and whispered her faith into her children, gave us the confidence to pursue anything we wanted. The way she'd so patiently taught me everything I knew.

The love and hard work that she'd instilled.

A giggle that I recognized as my sister's rolled from the kitchen. At the sound of us entering, she showed in the entryway, sipping from a mug of coffee. Her brown hair that was a shade lighter than mine was done in a long braid, and she smiled softly as we entered.

Kayden bounced on his toes. "Auntie *Kaywa*, I see you!"

Kayla let go of the softest laugh, so much affection in it that I could feel it travel through the air. "I see you, too, my sweet boy. I've been missing you."

"I miss you!" He grinned that dimpled grin and pointed at her with his chubby finger. He started hopping her way, making froggy sounds as he went.

A giggle slipped from her, and she sent me a knowing smile just as our mother came to stand at her side, using a hand towel to dry her hands.

"Well, what do we have here?" Mom asked, forever playing along.

"I a *fwoggy!*"

"The cutest froggy I ever did see."

Welcome covered her expression, her love for us so fervent it might as well have hung on the wall with the rest of the pictures.

Mom's attention landed on me.

"Good morning. How are you today?"

Yeah, there was worry there, too. No question, my mother had picked up on the fact that I was distraught yesterday evening. I'd barely been able to eat, and I'd been fighting tears through the entire meal.

The difference one night could make.

"I'm feeling much better this morning. I guess I just needed a good night's sleep."

Okay, I'd slept all of two hours.

But I felt alive.

Awake.

Running on the remnants of Ryder's touch.

"That's good," she said, though I could tell she was still appraising.

"We get *bwekfast?*" Kayden's question distracted from whatever she'd been about to ask, and he patted his belly before he lifted his arms for Kayla to pick him up, bouncing on his knees like he was contemplating jumping into her arms. "Auntie *hungee?*"

She set her mug aside and picked him up. "Starving."

"That's good because it's just about ready," Mom said, still eyeing me.

I gave her a bright smile, praying I could keep my nerves settled and I wouldn't slip and say something I couldn't.

The scent of bacon wafted through the air, mixed with the aroma of dough and sugar and frosting—a smell that could only mean cinnamon rolls.

"Well, I'm definitely hungry," I said.

"Since you ate three bites of your dinner last night, I can only imagine why."

I waved her off as I treaded deeper into her house. "It's been a long week and I was tired last night. I'm fine. Really."

The door suddenly burst open behind me, and Cody came striding through.

Anxiety blistered across my flesh, reddening my neck and cheeks. There was no way to stop it.

God, could he see Ryder written all over me? Was it obvious I'd been taken time and time again last night? *Loved up* so right my knees were still knocking with the aftershocks?

Keep it cool, Dakota.

You'd think I'd never been kissed before.

But the truth was, I'd never been kissed like *that*.

"Mornin', everyone." He pulled the cap from his head and tossed it to the table next to the door.

"Little sister." He pecked a kiss to my temple as he passed.

"Good morning." Wow, I managed it without it shaking.

Go me.

He went for Kayla and Kayden, dropping a kiss to the crown of our younger sister's head before he turned and did the same to Kayden's cheek, though he made a raspberry when he did.

Kayden squealed. "I see you, Uncle."

Cody ruffled a hand through his hair. "How could you miss me? I'm as big as this house," he teased.

"I big," Kayden told him, giving him two of those deep nods that always panged at the center of my chest.

Cody turned to our mom, and she yelped when he swept her off her feet and hugged her hard, swinging her around.

"What in the world, Cody?" She swatted at him, even though she was laughing as he set her back onto her feet.

"What, can't I be excited to see my family this morning?"

"A little too excited if you ask me." She tsked, completely a tease. "Don't tell me you've been off getting yourself into trouble."

"Who me?" He exaggerated it with one of his big grins.

I finally gathered myself and started the rest of the way across the room. "Cody's always covered his guilt with those grins. He's definitely been up to something."

There.

Deflection.

If I put the attention on Cody, no one would be looking at me.

He crossed his arms over his chest, brow arching for the sky. "Um, says little miss Dakota who I have on good word had a date with Brad Geller this week."

Date?

Brad?

Right.

That felt like a million years ago.

The catalyst that had tossed Ryder and I together.

I bit down on my bottom lip.

"Now who's looking guilty?" he challenged.

I huffed. "It was just dinner."

"Just dinner? Think I'm going to need a few more details about how this dinner actually went."

Kayla scoffed. "Who Dakota and I date and how it goes are none of your concern unless we offer up the information. I swear, there isn't a single guy in this town who will even ask me out because of you."

He grinned. "Great. Sounds like I'm doing my job right."

"Yet, he dips it in every girl he meets." Kayla's eyes widened as they met mine.

Mom choked. "That is a visual I don't need, thank you very much. But your sister is right. It's high time you stop going around chasing off anyone who even looks their way. They don't need you hovering over them."

"Just looking out for them, Ma. The way I was taught to do when I was young."

A flash of grief ran beneath the casual cloak he wore, gone so fast I wasn't sure if I'd made it up.

Somewhere in that messed up brain of my brother's, I knew he did think it was his duty.

To protect Kayla and me. To protect our mom.

"I'm not saying it's not a good thing for you all to look after each other, but I think Kayla and Dakota deserve a little breathing room, don't you? I think they can make that decision on their own."

She dipped back into the kitchen.

"Don't want any assholes doing my sisters wrong."

"*Asshoe.*" Kayden pointed at Cody, leaning that way as he said it.

Kayla's hand shot to her mouth to cover her laugh as she balanced Kayden in the other. "Oh my God."

"Um, do you think you could watch what you say around my son? The last thing I need is him learning any of your bad habits."

He covered his guilt with another of those grins. "Just teaching our Kayden over here the ones to watch out for."

"Yeah, you," I said, smacking his chest when I got to him. I pulled Kayden out of Kayla's arms.

"Don't listen to a thing that comes out of Uncle Cody's mouth," I told him.

"*Asshoe?*" He looked up at me when he asked it.

Cody cracked up.

I pressed one of Kayden's ears to my chest and covered the other with my hand. "I am going to murder you. Don't expect Cody to show up for breakfast next week, Mom," I hollered in her direction. "He's going to be buried somewhere out on Paisley and Caleb's ranch. No one is ever going to find his body."

He laughed harder as both he and Kayla followed me into the kitchen. "Since when did my sister get violent?"

"I don't know…since I was thirteen and you saw Timmy Brunhill kiss me at the front door, and you told him if you ever saw him again you were going to drown him in the stream out back. He took off running so fast he tripped when he got to the street, and he never talked to me again. I've been plotting your death ever since."

"You're seriously going to blame me when that little *asshole* was trying to get his hand under your shirt?"

"Maybe I wanted him to. I was totally into it."

Okay, I hadn't been, but I figured it served Cody right if he thought he'd interfered with the love of my life.

"Gross, Dakota. That guy wasn't anything but a little weasel."

I sent him a scowl, and he softened as he reached out and gave a tiny tug to my ponytail. "Never meant to be a jerk. I mean it. I just can't stand the idea of someone doing you wrong."

I didn't miss the way his attention flashed to Kayden for the barest beat.

"In my mind, I can't see how anyone is ever going to be good enough for you. Not for you or Kayla."

"How about you let us decide who's going to be good enough?" Kayla shot at him as she wound around the small island in the middle of the kitchen and went to the toaster on the far counter. She placed four pieces of bread into the slots and pushed down the button.

"And trust your judgment?" It was purely a razzing out of Cody's mouth.

"Hit him for me, Dakota. You're closer," she said.

I swatted him again. "Like I said…violent," he drew out as he clung to the spot as if I'd inflicted a mortal wound.

An amused smile was on my face as I rounded the island, and I sidled up to my mom where she'd cracked a bunch of eggs in the same skillet that she'd cooked the bacon in. "What can I do to help?"

"It's your day off…sit. And even if you say you feel better this morning, you look tired." She cut me a glance, her brown eyes sparking in interest, warmth, and a tease. Mom had a way of processing everything in a beat, showing her care and concern and doing it all with this lightness that always gave you the sense you were in a safe place.

"You know I don't mind helping out."

A grin pulled to the edge of her mouth. "What, are you worried I don't do it as well as you? Don't forget I taught you everything you know."

I laughed. "You know it's not that… I just don't know what to do with myself if someone else is cooking and I'm not a part of it."

"Hang onto that home wrecker, that's what you do." Her grin spread as she gestured with her head to the squirming child in my arms.

"Well, I can do both if—" I was cut off by the loud rapping at the front door.

It wasn't a knock that was asking for permission to enter.

It was an announcement.

An announcement that had always sent my heart skittering and the blood chugging through my veins when he'd come in. And today that skittering heart went sprinting when I whirled around, my mouth dropping open as Ryder came sauntering in like he lived there.

So freaking sexy wearing jeans, a tee, and boots. Every angle of that striking face lit in the rays of sunlight that slanted in through the window as he crossed the living room.

But it was the way those eyes took me in, slithering down in a slow slide of appreciation that heated my flesh, that knowing glint behind his gaze sending trembles rocking me to the core.

I was pretty sure the imprints of everywhere he'd touched me last night lit in a glow of red.

How in the world was I ever supposed to keep this contained?

He roughed a hand through the mess of his hair, pitching me a smirk before he said, "Mornin', everyone."

So casual and sly.

My belly tipped.

Crap. What did he think he was doing here? I mean, I knew that we'd eventually be in the same place with others present, but I hadn't been prepared for it yet.

The way he stole my breath and every thought in my mind. Since my heart and body were already his, I felt unsteady on my feet.

Drawn.

Hungering for a way to get closer.

I dug in my heels to keep from moving for him, and I did my best to reel in the reaction.

Hold it back.

Hide it.

It didn't help things when Kayden went wild in my arms, reaching in Ryder's direction as he kicked his little feet. "My Rye-Rye! You come see me?"

Emotion struck through the easiness that had been pinned on Ryder's expression. Something soft and profound.

The same devotion he'd promised me last night.

Us.

This family.

He covered it as fast as it'd shown, but he still came around the island and whipped Kayden out of my arms. He soared him through the air.

Delight rolled from Kayden, his shrieks full of joy.

"Of course, I came to see you. I was missing my favorite tiny tornado."

I bit down on my lip to keep the rush of affection at bay.

It'd been an hour.

With the way that gaze slanted down to me for the barest flash, I knew he'd been missing me, too.

"I a good boy," Kayden told him right as he was trying to get fistfuls of Ryder's hair.

Ryder laughed, though his voice turned gentle as he cupped the back of Kayden's head, pressed his lips to his temple, and murmured, "That's right. You are my good boy."

I had to reach out to the counter to support myself.

To keep from falling to my knees with the earthquake that rocked me through.

Staggering.

And I wondered if every-single-person there felt it, the way everyone went quiet and watched them like they were watching a spring flower blooming to life.

Or had it been there all along and I'd had myself so guarded that I hadn't allowed myself to see it?

Mom cleared her throat. "I didn't know you were coming this morning, Ryder. What a nice surprise."

"Hope you don't mind. I'd had to swing by Ezra's earlier, and I knew you'd all be here, so I thought I'd stop in."

"You know you're always welcome here."

A flicker of sorrow traipsed through his expression. "You've always welcomed me. I appreciate it more than you could ever know."

She set her hand on his cheek. "You're family, Ryder. Always have been, and you're always going to be."

He swallowed hard, and I knew he'd gotten swept in a memory of his mother. I wanted to touch him.

Wrap my arms around him.

Murmur that he wasn't alone.

"What have you been up to, Ryder?" Kayla asked as she pulled out the slices of toast that popped up from the toaster and refilled the slots.

"Not much other than work and hanging out with these two while they stay at my house for a bit."

I couldn't decipher the look that Ryder gave me.

All I knew was it traveled through me in an avalanche of possession.

Chills skated, and I focused on grabbing plates from the cabinet and setting them around the table.

A grunt of discomfort left Cody as he poured himself a mug of coffee from the carafe. "Any word from Ezra about the break-in?"

Ryder grimaced. "Guess there was another incident at the hardware store two nights ago. Someone busted open the back door and stole a bunch of expensive equipment."

"Heard about that. He thinks it's related?"

Ryder scraped a hand through his hair. "Yeah."

"Scumbags need to get caught." Cody's jaw clamped.

"Guess there was some footage from the security cameras. Thinks he finally has something to go on."

Cody breathed out in relief. "That's good."

I forced myself to walk around the island, tiptoeing back into Ryder's orbit, the man a black hole I could get sucked into.

Lost forever.

I focused on gathering both a plate of bacon and another stacked high with toast.

Ryder was suddenly there, towering over me.

Midnight in the middle of the day.

I had the intense urge to push up onto my toes and press my face into his throat.

"Let me." He took the plate of bacon while I struggled to keep my breaths under control.

"Bacon!" Kayden shouted, smacking at Ryder's cheek and trying to get in his line of sight like the man had just given my child the best gift in the world.

Ryder turned one of those adoring smiles down at him as he spun and started for the table in the corner. "Your favorite, next to pancakes, am I right?"

"Pancakes!"

My chest tightened, and I had to take a second to gather myself before I headed that direction.

Leave it to my mother to be watching me with that same intuition as I leaned over to place the toast onto the table.

Her attention drifted over me like those handprints really were glowing on my skin.

We all settled into chairs, Kayden's highchair pulled between me and Ryder. Ryder buckled him into it and placed a small pile of scrambled eggs and a piece of bacon that he'd crumbled onto his plate. I buttered and put jam on a piece of toast, setting it on Kayden's plate, too, while Ryder kept cutting me glances over the top of my son's head as I did.

Nerves scattered.

Anticipation and joy and that secret shame I didn't want to feel any longer.

I'd held it for such a long time. Now, it'd taken on new form. Had become something real. Something beautiful.

I wanted to shout it. Wanted him to shout it.

But it was Ryder who was keeping the secrets that he wouldn't give me insight into, only his vague warnings that had left a snarl of dread and worry in the pit of my stomach.

But that snarl was completely distorted and skewed by the amount of elation gliding through my veins. Like the worry didn't have anything on the bliss. Everything else was clouded by the relief that Ryder had finally, finally come to me.

That we finally *were*, however awkward it remained to be.

"So, tell us about that date," Cody said as he bit into a piece of toast.

I wondered if anyone else felt the way Ryder flinched.

I took a sip of piping hot coffee before I cleared my throat and gave a half shrug. "It was fine. Brad is a really nice guy."

I could feel my mom's attention. The way she angled her head as she studied me, waiting on me to let on more than I had the other afternoon.

"Nice guy? He's crazy hot." Kayla moaned toward the ceiling. "Those dress pants and button-downs he's always wearing."

I would have told her to go for him if Cody's grumble hadn't beaten me to the punch. "Dude's a fuckin' wet noodle, is what he is."

"I *wike* noodles," Kayden shouted as he crammed a fistful of egg into his mouth.

My eyes narrowed at my brother. "Again, Cody? You seriously need to watch what you say around him."

"Yeah, man, language," Ryder added, like it was his job to do it.

"Sorry...keep forgetting that kid is nothing but a sponge. Smart as a whip, just like his uncle." Cody's smirk grew at that.

"Please don't compare my son's intelligence to yours since you're nothing but a giant oaf."

Cody set his hand over his heart. "You wound me."

"I will wound you if Kayden starts muttering unmentionables." I waved my butter knife at him.

"Deadly." He whistled. "And this coming from the woman whose best friend swears like a freaking sailor."

A light laugh got free. Paisley definitely had a mouth on her. "At least she has the foresight to cover the kids' ears before she goes spilling it."

"Well, you sure aren't *spilling* any details." Kayla nudged her elbow into mine.

"There's not a lot to spill. He picked me up, we went to dinner, and he dropped me back at Ryder's place. That was it."

"Boring," she drawled. "When is my big sister going to have herself a little fun? If I'd been out with that delicious hunk of a man, I would have climbed him like—"

Cody making a retching noise cut her off.

Glee filled her giggle. No question, she was fully egging him on.

I couldn't help but laugh. "I guess I should have climbed him, too. Just for the pleasure of making Cody squirm."

Under the table, a hand clamped down on my upper thigh, fingers digging into my flesh, possession dripping from the tips.

A haggard breath left me, and I was shaking when I looked at him from over Kayden's head, the air growing so thin that the only thing I was breathing was him.

It didn't seem to matter to Ryder that everyone was staring at us when he growled under his breath, "Not gonna happen, Cookie. Not unless poor Brad wants to lose his hands."

⌒⚬⌒

"That was delicious." Ryder wiped his mouth with a napkin after he'd just demolished three cinnamon rolls once he'd finished his main meal.

The man liked his sweets.

"Second that," Cody agreed.

"I need to watch out…Mom opens her own restaurant and she's going to run me out of business," I said as I stood to unbuckle Kayden from his highchair.

"Pssh." She waved her hand in the air. "Charmers. The lot of you."

I carried Kayden to the kitchen sink so I could wash his face and hands. He howled and fought me the whole time like I was putting him through the worst kind of torture, then he took off running out the sliding back door the second I set him on his feet.

"I'll go out with him so he can play a bit," Cody offered, pushing up from his chair and tossing his napkin to his plate.

"I just brewed some fresh iced tea. Why don't we all go out for a while and enjoy the fresh air? It's a gorgeous day," Mom offered.

"Sounds good to me." Kayla stood, too, gathering plates and plunking them into the sink.

"I need to use the restroom then I'll meet you all out there," I said.

I did my best to ignore the energy that pounded through the room when Ryder pushed to standing.

The man a shockwave.

I could feel those eyes tracking me the whole way as I turned and made a beeline for the hall. I rushed down it, quick to lock myself in the bathroom.

How was I supposed to manage this? That severity that crashed into me every time he looked my direction? The way it felt like I couldn't fully move when I was in his space? The way he kept watching me like he wanted to rip me out of this dress?

He made me feel like I was the only person he could see, all while knowing he would deny me if anyone asked.

But this denying thing felt impossible.

This connection.

This bond that seared and flamed.

I used the restroom then washed my hands, and I glanced at myself in the mirror. My cheeks were flushed, and I swore there was something different in my eyes. Something that shined bright, arising from the depths, something that could no longer be contained.

Blowing out a sigh, I dried my hands, unlocked the door, and turned the knob. I gasped when it suddenly swung open from the other side. Ryder was there, pushing through, so tall that he loomed over me.

A force of nature that made my knees knock.

Caught off guard, I stumbled back two steps.

Ryder shut and locked the door behind him.

"What in the world do you think you're doing?" I finally managed through the surprise.

A breath later, he was in front of me, and he set both his palms on the sides of my face. He tilted it up as he angled down. "I can't go one more second without touching you."

"Someone's going to know you followed me in here. I thought we needed to keep this thing quiet?"

"We do," he grated.

"Then you're being reckless." The words were hushed.

I thought they only tugged him closer because he leaned down and barely brushed his lips over mine before he angled back, that severity covering me like a shroud. "This whole thing is reckless, Dakota. But how am I supposed to resist when you're wearing this dress?"

Playfulness edged into the seriousness, and his hands tightened on my jaw.

So sweetly possessive my heart careened in my chest.

"If you keep looking at me like that while I'm wearing it, then I'm never going to take it off."

"Oh, you're going to be taking it off, Dakota." He backed me deeper into the tiny room, and my back hit the wall.

Desire poured, flooding the confined space.

"Especially after you put that fucking deplorable image of you with Brad into my mind. Was bad enough the night you were out with him."

A slight giggle got free, and I let the tease wind into my voice. "Are you jealous, Ryder Nash?"

"At the thought of another man touching you? Fuck yeah, I'm jealous, Dakota. Then you had to go rubbing it in. You're really trying to drive me out of my mind, aren't you?"

"And what was I supposed to say?" I got entranced by the energy that swept the atmosphere, mesmerized by Ryder here, looking at me this way.

My spirit light and my heart pounding so heavily I was sure the rest of the house could hear it.

"You were supposed to say that you wouldn't dream of touching him. Of touching anyone." It was a soft growl, a razzing that slipped from his delicious mouth.

His mouth I was fast becoming addicted to.

I feigned regret. "Oops, I guess I didn't get the script."

Possession reverberated in his wide chest, and he pressed me harder against the wall. That big body covered mine.

So powerful.

So protective.

It was everything I'd craved for so long that a needy whimper slipped out.

Ryder only tightened his hold. "Script goes like this, Dakota...you're mine, and I'm yours. You got it?"

"I'll try to remember." I whispered the tease.

"You better," he rumbled back, pecking his lips to mine.

I moaned that time.

That was all it took for him to deepen the kiss.

A crackle that sparked.

Our mouths moved in a desperate dance, and his hand came around to the back of my neck to angle me just right. His lips plucked and pulled at mine before his tongue swept into my mouth.

Tangling.

Licking.

Commanding.

My hands shot out, diving into his hair as he rubbed himself against me.

Gasping, I writhed back, my breath instantly gone.

My pulse crashed as it thundered.

I nearly cried when he peeled himself away. He dropped his forehead to mine, panting with his hands still gripping my face. "You're everything, Dakota Cooper. The most important thing in this world. Whatever happens, promise me that you won't forget that."

"I won't."

He gulped then nodded as he stepped back, then he sent me a cocky grin. "Do you have any idea the number of times I've considered following you into this bathroom, wondering if you'd let me kiss the hell out of you? Wanting to push past that line?"

A surprised laugh ripped from my throat, and I shook my head, my grin coming slow. "Probably as many times as I imagined you doing it."

His hand slipped under the skirt of my dress and took a handful of my left butt cheek. "I blame it on this dress."

Shivers raced, a collision of this love and the playfulness and the edge of the darkness that kept seeping into the atmosphere.

"I guess I'm going to have to order one in every color."

"You do, and I can't be held accountable for my actions. All of them are going to end up tattered shreds on my bedroom floor."

"Oh, and here I thought it was going to be on my office floor?"

"Whatever floor is below us at the time. The bedroom. The kitchen. Your office. This bathroom is seeming like a mighty fine place."

"Sorry to break it to you, but I think my family might notice if I come out and my dress is torn to bits."

"We can blame it on a pack of wild dogs that came through."

"I'm pretty sure a wild dog would be the one to blame." My fingers plucked at the fabric of his shirt.

Amusement traipsed through his features, this fierce affection that pulsed so thick when he reached out and stroked his thumb over my bottom lip. "I love you, Cookie."

"I don't think I'm ever going to get tired of hearing that."

"Good, because you're going to be hearing it forever."

Emotion dumped into my chest.

All the years of holding it back and there was no chance of keeping it checked any longer.

"You're the only person I've ever loved, Ryder."

He rushed forward, pressing his lips to my forehead, breathing me in before he forced himself back to the door. He set his hand on the knob and glanced back. "This pretending bit is fuckin' painful."

My bottom lip caught between my teeth. "We won't have to do it forever, will we?"

"No, baby, not when I want to shout your name from every rooftop in this town."

My spirit glowed, and I gave him a nod. He returned one before he slipped out.

I waited for a minute before I followed, and I started to slink down the hall.

All stealth mode.

Only I startled when I heard the movement behind me, and I whipped around to find my mother coming out of her room with a bottle of sunscreen.

I was pretty sure I was painted in guilt with the way I gulped and fidgeted and tried to smile around the discomfort.

Her gaze turned knowing. "While you didn't hit things off with Brad, it appears to me that you might have hit it off with somebody else."

"Mom." I warred with what to say, almost pleading with her to drop it, but I remained frozen as she stepped forward and set her hand on my cheek.

"The only thing I want is for you to be happy, Dakota. Fully happy and fulfilled. I pray every day that this life gives you everything you deserve. That you find the one who makes your heart and body sing, holds you up when you need uplifting and cheers you on when you're standing fine on your own. And I'm not blind...I know your heart made its pick a long, long time ago."

Uneasiness wobbled through my being. I thought to deny it, but what was the use?

It was already written all over me.

I was marked by it.

Scarred by it.

Held by it.

Tender eyes flicked over my face. "And I love that boy like my own son, but I also know there is something in his life that is far more complicated than he lets on. And more than that, there is a pain...*a fear* there," she corrected, "that scares me. And I won't ever tell you what to do, but I will ask that you be careful."

My nod was shaky against her hand.

She stared at me for a beat before she pulled away and walked to the end of the hall. She paused to look back. "And for the record, your brother doesn't get to decide who's good enough for you. Only you can decide that."

Without saying anything else, she disappeared around the corner, leaving me standing there trembling against the wall.

Chapter Thirty-Seven
Ryder

HATRED CLAWED THROUGH MY SPIRIT, SQUEEZING IT IN A FIST as I stared at the bastard who sat in that same chair where he'd sat doling out my sentence for so many years. Where he'd wielded his power, twisting me up in a seedy grip of manipulation.

I shook with the brutalness of it. At the lengths he'd gone to keep me under his thumb. The sins he'd piled on top of me like they were my own when I'd wanted to get out from beneath them for so long.

It was time.

Fucking time.

"Have it ready by next Tuesday night. Marc and I will be at the safe-house at midnight."

Agitation lifted a sheen of sweat on my skin, and I did my best to keep the anxiety from showing. I had to play it cool. It was just another job out of hundreds of others that I'd done for him. I couldn't give him any indication otherwise. I was dead if I did.

"I'll be there."

Dare rocked back in his chair, a smirk lighting on his pompous face. "So agreeable."

Air puffed from my nose. "Don't see much of a point in arguing it."

"Easy money in your pocket, Ryder. Not sure why you ever did in the first place. I've always taken care of you."

He said it with zero conscience. Like he really didn't see a problem with it. Like he was the one doing me a solid.

Like any of this was okay.

Amelia's face flashed through my mind.

Grief over her fate.

That hatred burned hotter, singeing my skin. I had to grit my molars to keep from reaching across the desk and wrapping my hands around his throat until the life drained out of him.

But I had to be patient.

Play this right.

My shoulder lifted like I didn't give a fuck. I couldn't act too compliant, either. "Just want to get the fucking job done and over with. Have other things at the shop I want to be focused on."

He laughed a sound of disbelief. "Fucking waste of time, but I guess your hard work provides a good cover, so I'm not gonna complain."

I wanted to tell him to fuck off. Remind him it was something I'd built. With my own hands. It was one of the things I was most proud of.

He was the one who'd swooped in and used it in his favor, seizing it as his own opportunity.

But that shop was mine.

The art was mine.

Dakota was *mine*.

And this time, I wasn't going to let her go.

Chapter Thirty-Eight
Ryder

Twenty-Six Years Old

COUNTRY MUSIC BLARED FROM THE SPEAKERS AS THE BAND PLAYED from the stage at Mack's.

Mack's used to be a giant barn that had been converted into the bar that half the town of Time River had to be crammed into tonight. People were packed wall to wall, taking up the huge dance floor in the center of the cavernous space. Not a single one of the high-top tables that surrounded it were unoccupied.

Ryder sipped at a tumbler of whiskey where he and his crew had managed to pull a couple tables together. Cody broke through the crowd, carrying two pitchers of beer. Ezra was behind him, carrying another two, plus he had a stack of plastic cups tucked under his arm.

Ryder cocked a grin. "You two look like you have some sort of expectations for tonight."

Cody chuckled as he set the pitchers down. "While I normally would be taking advantage of an opportunity like this…"

He waved a hand at the women in a line on the dance floor, tossing their hips as they spun and kicked to the choreographed dance. Most of them wore cowgirl boots and were in varying states of dress. Cut-offs and jeans and dainty dresses.

Mack's was never in short supply of the fairer sex, and it'd become the place Ryder and Cody hung out most. Ezra had, too, until he'd fallen hard and gotten married a couple years ago. Brianna was home with their little girl, so Ryder's cousin was flying solo tonight.

"Tonight is all about my sister," Cody finished.

Ryder's stomach tightened in a fist, though he kept grinning like he was completely unaffected. "When did she get back into town?"

"This morning. Graduation and birthday in the same week." Awe shook Cody's head as he slipped onto a stool. "She graduated with honors all while managing a bakery off campus the entire time. I figure we have some celebrating to do."

Of course, she had.

This was Dakota they were talking about. Ryder wouldn't have expected anything less. She was crazy smart and crazy talented, and he knew she was going to be crazy successful.

Pride filled his chest, all while it got mixed with something unsettled. This shaky anticipation gliding through his nerves that he needed to shuck.

It wasn't like he hadn't seen her over the years when she'd come back to visit. But it'd always been quick. In passing. He'd been sure to keep his distance because he'd never fully squashed what she'd triggered in him four years ago.

Gratitude, he guessed it was. The fact Dakota had seen him when he'd been at his lowest. Pulled him out of the dark place he'd thought he'd be a prisoner to forever.

Lit a path.

The girl a beacon he couldn't help but follow.

Because of her, he was different. Fighting for something better.

But that didn't mean he wasn't still trapped, so he knew he had to maintain that distance. Go on pretending everything was just fine while his soul crawled with the filth of what he'd succumbed to.

A frenzy suddenly broke through the crush.

Paisley, Beth, and Chloe, Dakota's three best friends, were pure smiles, tossing their arms in the air and squealing with their excitement as they clambered for the table. "We're here! It's party time, baby!"

A smirk tugged at Ryder's mouth. They were all fucking cute. Living this life the way it should be lived. Happy and free and with a zest that traveled out ahead of them.

"Looks like we're in for a bit of trouble tonight," Ryder said, standing so he could give them a round of hugs.

"That's right, Ryder. No one here is going to know what hit them," Paisley said as she swept in for a massive hug. He picked her up and shook her around. "Good to see you, Paisley-Cakes."

But it was who cut in behind them that stole his breath and sent his stupid heart pounding, what had him setting Paisley onto her feet because he didn't think he could physically hold her up any longer.

Dakota looked like she'd aged a decade, and not in a bad way, either. She was all woman now, the angles of her face growing more defined, her waist cinching down, her hips fuller. There was a confidence to her that she hadn't worn before, and she wore it well in this babydoll dress that was long-sleeved but short as fuck, exposing her thighs.

She was still soft, though, delicate in every way, that sweetness radiating around her as she gave Ezra and Cody hugs. Ryder tried not to tremble as she slowly inched his way, and he wondered if he was the only one who felt the air cloud and grow dense.

She bit down on her plump bottom lip as she approached, and she seemed almost careful as she wrapped her arms around his neck. He stalled for only a second before he curled his around her waist and tugged her close, a fool who was breathing out in some kind of twisted relief.

The scent he could never erase from his mind inundated him.

Sugar and vanilla and all things sweet.

"I'm so glad you came." She whispered it like it was their secret.

He forced himself to untangle himself from her body and sent her a gentle grin. "Like I was going to miss your party? This has been four years in the making. I wouldn't be anywhere else. Congrats, Dakota."

Redness splashed her cheeks. It was a bitch resisting the urge to reach out to trace the color with his fingertips.

"It was a great experience," she said, like she was purposefully taking them back to the night when they'd shared their last real conversation. When their connection had been so powerful that it'd struck a chord inside him, a resonation that had shifted his insides around, made him sure he was going to earn the right for her to be looking at him the way she had then.

"And now she's back!" Paisley slipped her arm around Dakota's waist and leaned her head on her shoulder.

It seemed to yank Dakota out of the trance that had fallen over them.

"Now that you're leaving. I can't believe that you're moving to Scottsdale. Gross." Dakota sent Paisley a pout and a curl of her nose.

Paisley laughed an uneasy sound. "You make it sound like I'm taking a trip to Hell."

"Do you know how hot it gets there? I'd say that's exactly where you're going," Dakota teased.

Paisley squeezed her. "Jeremy thinks we can really make it happen there. It's a great opportunity. I think we have to take the chance."

Yeah, and Ryder was pretty sure she was actually making a deal with the devil. The dude was a prick.

"I'm just going to miss you now that I'm back," Dakota told her.

"Don't worry. You know I'll be back a ton to visit my grandma and grandpa."

"I'm going to hold you to that."

"All right, enough of the sappy stuff." Beth snapped her fingers between them. "This is supposed to be a celebration, not some kind of boo-fest."

"Oh, you know you're going to be crying over me leaving, too," Paisley told her.

"Tears of joy," Beth deadpanned, her razzing sly.

Chuckling low, Ryder looked between the four friends. "Why don't I hit the bar. First round's on me." Ryder needed the excuse to get out of there. Gain some of that distance.

Paisley asked for a Moscow Mule, Beth one of those trendy beers, and Chloe a margarita.

"I'll have a cosmo," Dakota said, swaying in that fucking dress that was going to make him lose his mind. His mind that had traveled to places he couldn't let it go.

Still, a grin was kicking at the edge of his mouth, loving that Dakota ordered something sweet.

"On it. I'll be right back," he promised.

Ezra went with him to help carry their drinks, and by the time they returned, the girls were already on the dance floor, stealing the attention of every eye in the place.

He and Ezra set their drinks down and Ryder reclaimed his stool.

For the longest time, he sat there, taking it in, happy that Dakota was having a blast.

Her eyes shined and her skin was slick with a sheen of sweat when they came racing back to the table, all of them laughing, giggling under their breaths, at what, he wasn't sure. All he knew was he couldn't look away as Dakota hopped onto the stool next to him and took a big gulp of her drink.

"Mmm," she hummed into the glass like it was the best thing she'd ever tasted. "Thank you."

He couldn't help but lean into her, his shoulder touching hers, his voice just loud enough that only she could hear over the din. "That drink is the same color as your cheeks."

That flush only heated more, and she dipped her head, that old shyness winding with something bold as she smiled back at him.

And fuck, he wanted to reach out again.

Touch it.

See if what he'd kept suppressed for the last four years was real, only he was tripping up when Amelia suddenly showed up at their table.

All sly grins, her black hair curled in fat waves, dressed like she was on the hunt.

Unease skittered through Ryder. He knew what she was hunting was him. He knew Dare used her to keep tabs on him. Another fucking trap he'd been a fool to fall into.

She sauntered up, all hips, her fingertips going to his chest as he sat back in his stool. She angled down to his ear. "I've been looking for you."

A scowl took to his brow and that hatred that'd been simmering for years bubbled up from the depths. "I'm busy."

"Too busy for me?" she purred.

"It's a family celebration." He let an edge of warning slip into his tone.

Her gaze bounced around the table. No one else was paying them any mind or found it out of character. It wasn't like he didn't have women crawling all over him half the time. He'd gained that reputation.

The only one who seemed to notice was Dakota who he could feel shifting in discomfort on her stool.

Amelia immediately zeroed in on her before she cut a wicked smirk back at him. "Call me later, then. I'll be waiting."

She touched her fingertips to his lips.

Disgust pumped through his system, this shame as Dakota peeked at them before she jerked away, turned her attention to Beth, and jumped into a conversation with her.

It was for the best.

He needed to maintain those boundaries.

Keep up the walls.

He and Dakota were friends. They'd always been. She was like a sister to him and that was the only thing she could ever be. It was already reckless that he came around this way.

Creeping too close.

An outsider drawn to this normalcy.

Wanting to be a part of it, dipping his fingers into something good when his feet were solidly cemented in immorality.

Except something inside him clutched when a cowboy who worked one of the local ranches strolled up and asked Dakota to dance.

She didn't hesitate.

She slipped off her stool, her hand in his as he led her to the floor. The song that was playing was fast, and the guy led her in a quick two-step, and Dakota's face was lighting up again as he spun her round and round.

All while Ryder sat there feeling like he was going to suffocate. This feeling snaking over him that he just couldn't shake.

The night went on like that. Different guys asking Dakota to dance, which she was all too eager to oblige. The girl having the best time.

It was growing late when he finally found the balls to cut in.

Surprise rolled through Dakota's expression when she found him standing there, and she warily let him pull her into his arms as the guy she'd been dancing with disappeared into the fray.

"What are you doing, Ryder?" She said it like she couldn't believe he was standing there. Like maybe she'd felt him physically trying to push her away.

But when it came to Dakota, he found those walls didn't stand.

"Thought it was time I danced with the birthday girl since every guy in the place has gotten the chance to." He fought for a smirk as he began to sway them, the beat of the song slowed.

"Isn't your girlfriend going to mind if you're dancing with me?"

His chest pinched. "She's not my girlfriend."

Dakota's brows lifted as she looked up at him, no hesitation when she asked, "Are you telling me you've never had sex with her?"

"Didn't say that."

"Ah, so you are the player Cody tells me you are." He couldn't tell if she meant it as a tease or if it was an accusation, not with the way those cinnamon eyes glinted beneath the strobing light.

He fought to keep it easy. Playful. Refusing the thing he could feel brewing between them. "I see how it is. My best friend is spreading rumors about me."

"Is that what they are? Rumors?"

He couldn't do anything but tug her to him, and he breathed out the words too close to her ear. "I wish they weren't."

⌒⸎⌒

Giggles floated on the night air as they went stumbling out at closing.

Ryder had his arm looped around Dakota's waist, supporting her, and the other was around Paisley's as he guided them to his truck parked in the lot.

The two of them had done it up, tossing back three rounds of shots during the last hour they'd been there. Their laughter had started to come easier just as their words had started to slur.

Chloe, Beth, and Ezra had bailed two hours before, and Cody had ended up slinking off with some girl he'd met from the next town over.

Turned out when it came to Cody, this hadn't just been about Dakota after all.

But Ryder didn't mind watching out for her.

It felt like something intrinsic. Something he'd been purposed to do.

Clicking the locks to his truck, he opened the door. "In you go, drunkie-drunks," he razzed, his voice soft.

Dakota climbed in first, flashing him a glimpse of her perfect ass as she did, then Paisley hopped in behind her. Dakota's best friend reached out and patted him on the cheek. "You are the best, Ryder. You really know how to take care of a woman. And look at the size of those hands."

Dakota giggled like it was the funniest thing she'd ever heard.

Ryder all but rolled his eyes. "Yeah, yeah. Just don't puke in my truck."

"Wouldn't dream of it, Captain." Paisley gave him a sloppy salute.

He was chuckling as he shut their door and rounded the front, then he was losing his breath all over again when he slipped into the driver's side.

The scent of Dakota smacked him in the face.

Sugar and vanilla and all things sweet.

Her body was pressed against his as he put the truck in drive and pulled out of the lot.

Neither Paisley nor Dakota stopped laughing the entire ride.

He dropped off Paisley at her grandparents' house where she'd grown up. He walked her to the door, and she fumbled inside, insisting that she didn't need help and that he should go take care of her, "Doodle-Boo," and to make sure that he did it well.

He jogged back to the truck and jumped back in.

Dakota had moved to sit on the main seat, like she'd become aware that they needed to keep the distance between them, too.

A few minutes later, he pulled up in front of her mother's house.

A swarm of memories rushed him. He thought they were likely some of the best of his life.

He shut off his truck and led her to the front door.

Dakota turned and stared up at him.

The air between them hummed.

An energy he fought to recognize.

"Welcome home, Dakota. I'm glad you're back," he said rather than admitting the thousand things that were on his mind.

"I'm glad I am, too," she whispered.

He hesitated then dragged his fingers through his hair. "You need help inside?"

She giggled again. "I think I'm capable of making it inside on my own. It's not like I didn't stumble my way back to my apartment by myself for the last four years."

A wave of protectiveness slammed him. He hated the idea of her out there like that, wandering on her own. He knew full well the twisted fucks that roamed, looking for prey. "Maybe I just want to look out for you."

More of that redness splashed her cheeks. "I think I can manage."

"Maybe I'm the one who can't." He meant it to come out a joke, but it rang too true.

He wasn't sure he could handle this.

This insane thing she made him feel.

Confusion knitted her brow, and he couldn't do anything but reach out with the pad of his thumb and smooth it out.

He swore he felt the air come alive, and Dakota gulped before she cleared her throat and took a step back. "I should get in."

He nodded, trying to rein it in. "Yeah."

Dakota sent him a soft smile and dipped inside, and she clicked the door shut behind her.

Ryder blew out a sigh, and once the lock clicked, he turned to head in the direction of his truck.

Only he found he couldn't force himself to go to it. He diverted paths. Drawn.

Unable to go anywhere but the single place that had forever called to him.

He climbed the tree and sat under the peace of the stars.

And maybe he shouldn't have been surprised when he felt her presence emerge from behind. The way she'd done so many times before.

The way it soothed and coaxed and made him feel like he was exactly where he was supposed to be.

She climbed to the spot beside him and handed him a tin of cookies.

Satisfaction thudded through his bloodstream that she'd been thinking of him. That she just got it.

And they sat like that in that tree beneath the star-speckled sky.

For the whole fucking summer.

Every night they met there.

Talking.

Sometimes just sitting in the silence.

Trusting each other with their fears and their beliefs.

Their hopes and their failures.

One night, Dakota showed up giddy that the local diner had gone up for sale. She dreamed of buying it, and she whispered a thousand ideas of how she was going to turn it into something magical.

A week later, he held her in his arms when she'd been crushed that the bank had rejected her application for the loan because she couldn't get enough money down.

A few days later, she'd turned around and encouraged him when he'd admitted he'd rented a warehouse that he was going to turn into his own custom welding shop.

They spent all those months getting to know each other, while he was sure no one had ever known him better.

All except for the one thing he could never share with her.

This was his best friend's little sister, and he knew better than to drag her into that sordid world.

Except she was the best thing that had ever happened to him.

And he knew if he was going to take this where he wanted it, where he was desperate to go, he had to fix it.

End it.

Because he understood the feeling that had taken him over. What had been simmering in him for years.

He was in love with Dakota Cooper.

So, when he went into Dare's office late that night, he didn't let old fear stop him. He simply strode in and spat, "I want out."

Dare rocked back in his chair, chuckling under his breath. "I thought you would have learned your lesson the last time you came in here spouting off about walking away."

"Yeah, I did learn something, and that's that I don't give a fuck about what you have to say any longer."

Dare tsked, so fucking pompous when he drawled, "Awful brave."

Ryder planted his hands on Dare's desk. "I figure one of us is going to end up dead. You shouldn't be so confident which one of us that's going to be."

Dare laughed again, so low that it curdled Ryder's blood, but he refused to stand down.

Sitting forward, Dare stubbed out his cigarette. "I'll tell you what, Ryder, I have a job. It's big. Bigger than anything I've ever done before. You get this shipment to the East Coast, it's 250k in your pocket and a whole fucking ton more in mine. You do it, and we'll call this thing even."

Alarms went off in every one of his senses. Warnings clamoring through his cells. Shaking him to his core.

He knew it would be a risk. One bigger than he'd ever taken. But Dakota was worth it.

Dakota who dreamed and believed and with every day that passed made him want to be something better.

He wanted to give her that dream, too.

That fucking diner that had broken her heart when she didn't have enough cash to put down to get the loan.

So Ryder leaned forward and sold his soul again.

Just for a little while more.

"I want half right now. When it's complete, I walk. You forget you ever fucking knew my name."

Dare bit down on his lip before he grinned. "It sounds like we have a deal."

Chapter Thirty-Nine

Dakota

I WONDERED WHAT PEOPLE WOULD THINK IF THEY COULD SEE INTO my mind as I stood at the chalkboard writing today's specials on the board.

It wasn't the chicken breast stuffed with cheese, artichokes, and capers that had me blushing and grinning all over the place.

It was the *Sugar Cookie Addiction* that had my thoughts traipsing into the obscene. What had heat flaming across my skin and my stomach tightening with desire.

The way Ryder had taken me once we'd gotten back to his place Saturday afternoon while Kayden had been taking his nap.

He'd licked every inch of my body, murmuring that I tasted of sugar and vanilla, promising he wanted to eat me for every meal.

He'd made me come four times like that before I'd slumped onto the mattress, begging for mercy. That night and all day yesterday he'd come back to me time and again, then I'd woken this morning with his head between my thighs, the man driving me to oblivion with his tongue.

He'd popped up with a smirk on his face, wiping his mouth clean with the back of his hand, claiming I was his new favorite addiction.

You weren't going to find me complaining. I didn't think either of us were ever going to get enough.

I started back for the main dining room to check on things when my phone buzzed from the pocket in my dress. I pulled it out, and a giddy grin spread across my face when I saw it was a text from Ryder.

Ryder: I wish you were in my bed right now.

I wondered if I might float away from the joy that had taken me over, the swell of euphoria that ballooned, filling me with a lightness unlike anything I'd experienced.

I glanced around the dining room like I was going to be caught doing something salacious before I quickly tapped out a response.

Me: And what would you do to me if you had me there?

Ryder: Tie you to it, that way you can't get away from me.

I moved around the high counter and leaned on it since no one was sitting there.

Me: Who said I wanted to get away? But I think I might get a little bored if you simply tied me to your headboard. Surely you could come up with something better than that.

I could almost hear the lust smack the air, a thunderclap that echoed all the way from his shop. The only thing I could do was picture him there amid all that metal, pressing his fist to his mouth like he was trying to control himself.

I loved being the one who got him unhinged.

Ryder: You're making it tough to stay gentle with you, Cookie.

Me: What made you think I wanted you to be gentle?

I couldn't help but prod him, wondering if I had half the effect on him as he had on me.

Ryder: I have half a mind to come down to that restaurant and show you exactly what I'd do to you.

Me: I hope you plan on making good on it.

Ryder: Oh, Cookie. You are playing with fire. I have four appointments back-to-back, so you're going to have to settle for me showing you after I get home tonight.

My stomach fluttered with need.

> **Me:** Why do I get the feeling I need to prepare myself for what you have in store?
>
> **Ryder:** Because I've lost all restraint when it comes to you.
>
> **Me:** Good.
>
> **Ryder:** Fuck me, Cookie. You're really trying to kill me.

Another text came in right behind it.

> **Ryder:** I'm going to be late. That sweet ass is mine tonight. I expect you to be ready.
>
> **Me:** You already have me soaked.
>
> **Ryder:** Don't even know how I'm going to make it through the rest of the day.
>
> **Me:** By thinking about all the ways you're going to have me.

"What are you doing over there grinning like a cat who just caught herself a big fat rat?"

A shocked yelp escaped when my phone was suddenly plucked out of my hand. My attention whipped up to find Paisley sitting in the stool across from me.

"Give me that." I reached over the counter, trying to snatch it as she held it above her head.

"Why? Have something you're hiding?" she teased.

"Ugh, why do you always show up when I'm in the middle of something? I think you're half bloodhound."

"Pssh. Bloodhound? Call it a sixth sense." Her voice lowered as she leaned my direction. "Or maybe it's just because you didn't text me the entire weekend, and the last thing you told me was things had gotten a little spicy between you and Ryder, and my bestie intuition kicked in telling me things went from hot to boiling with you two."

She sat back like she was just going to casually peruse the texts before her green eyes went wide. "Nope. Wait. I stand corrected. Not boiling. Scalding. Holy crap, Dakota."

She turned the screen toward me and pointed at it.

Groaning, I buried my face in my hands.

"Tell me you two did the dirty deed. Emphasis on the *dirty*."

At her prodding, I dropped my hands and glanced around the restaurant, ensuring we were out of earshot of anyone around us. My staff was busy, and the customers seemed satisfied and well taken care of, so I edged forward, feeling a sudden rush of gratitude for Paisley.

That she just knew and was always there for me when I needed her, showing up before I even realized how badly I did.

"We did. So many times, I've already lost count," I admitted below my breath.

Except every one of them was scored inside me. Memories I would forever cling to as the best of my life.

She squealed, and I shot her a look to be quiet.

"Right, right," she whispered, glee lighting all over her face. "But how in the world do you expect me to stay quiet when my bestie finally got herself some of the good D?" She gripped the edge of the counter. "Tell me it was good. This is Ryder Nash we're talking about. I mean, those hands."

Tipping her head back, she issued a greedy groan toward the ceiling.

"If I didn't know you better, I'd tell you to keep yours off my man." It was purely a tease.

One that sent that glee striking like a sun flare. "Your man?" she challenged.

All those emotions rushed me at once, and a shudder rocked me through, my tongue growing thick as I whispered, "He told me he's in love with me."

Paisley was suddenly holding both my hands from over the top of the counter, leaning my direction as she squeezed. "Of course, he's in love with you, Dakota. If I had to make bets about it, I'd say he's been for a long, long time."

My nod was erratic. "He keeps confessing all these things. About how he's been since he was twenty-two, but he didn't think he was good enough. How could he ever think that?"

"I think both of you have walked around for far too long thinking you weren't good enough for the other while it was plainly obvious to the rest of us that you were meant to be together. But sometimes the heart has to take its time to figure out what that means."

I warred, usure of what to admit. "He said we have to keep it between us for now. There's something going on in his life that he's afraid of. What's held him back all this time."

A frown marred her brow, and she squeezed my hands tighter. "Is he in trouble?"

Worry bottled at the base of my throat. "Maybe. I don't know. He just said he needs to take care of something in his life before we can tell anyone."

Paisley scowled, not liking the sounds of it. "If that's a woman he needs to cut loose before then, I will literally chop off his dick and cram it down his throat. I don't even care how good it is."

My head shook, and I blinked through everything he'd told me. "No...I don't think it's that."

Her frown deepened. "Do you trust him?"

I didn't have to search too deep inside myself for the answer. "I do."

"And you love him back?"

"So much."

"Then you hold onto that. But just..." Her frown deepened more. "Be careful, okay?"

Unease quivered through me at her statement. It reminded me too much of the warning my mother had given.

Before I had time to answer, she smirked. "And enjoy that D. Based on this..." She glanced down at the phone she'd set on the counter. "...I'd say you are."

"That is a very safe assumption."

She giggled and squeezed my hands again. "I'm so happy for you, Dakota."

"I'm happy, too."

"Then that's all that matters."

Moisture stung my eyes, and I wiped at it and inhaled the emotion down and straightened. "Okay, enough about me. We need to make some final decisions about this party. I've worked up a sample menu, and I'd like to come by the ranch to check out the area you want to set up in so we can figure out what we have space for and what we need to order."

"That would be great."

"I'm off Saturday, so I thought I'd swing by then."

"But that's your day off."

"Please, I'm happy to do it. Besides, it gives us a chance to hang out a little bit. I feel like I haven't seen my sweet Evelyn in forever."

"Why don't you bring Kayden with you and we'll make a day out of it?"

"I'd love that."

She squealed again, but this time I didn't shush her. "I can't wait to surprise Caleb with this. I know he's going to get all grumbly and act like he doesn't need us making a fuss over him, but I think he's going to love it."

"Because he *loves* you."

"That's right. He does. Speaking of..." She glanced at the watch on her wrist. "I need to get to the bank. He had some meetings this morning, and he wanted me to meet him to get me on some accounts."

I quirked a brow. "Who would have ever thought my bestie would end up with a billionaire?"

She giggled as she hopped off the stool and slung the strap of her bag over her shoulder. "Not me. Not that I care a bit about that money except for all the horses that man keeps buying me."

She winked, then she clambered around the bar and threw her arms around my neck. "Love you, Doodle-Boo. I'm so happy for you."

I hugged her tight. "Thank you for always knowing when I need someone to talk to."

She edged back and tapped her finger to her temple. "Sixth sense."

I laughed. "See you Saturday."

"Bye."

I watched her strut through the double doors in her pink boots and cut-offs, laughing under my breath at my whirlwind of a best friend, before I blew out a sigh, figuring I'd better go check on things in the back.

The kitchen was chaos the way it always was but done in an order that always seemed to work. Beth was back there shouting orders at the cooks.

"All good back here?" I asked.

She sent me a waggish grin. "Do you even need to ask? I have it under control, the way I always do."

I chuckled under my breath. "Are you implying you have no need for me?"

"Just keep coming up with the recipes and we'll be just fine."

"I see what I'm good for," I drew out.

She pulled one of the specials out from under the warming lamp. "It's good all right."

Pride pulsed, and I gave a smile before I went into my office. I quickly went through emails and returned a couple that needed to be addressed, though my thoughts kept drifting to Ryder.

To everything that had happened in such a short time.

I finished what I needed to in my office, and feeling like I was floating again, I headed back for the dining room and pushed through the swinging door.

Only I froze the second I stepped out. All the blood in my head drained, leaving me dizzy and covered in a cold slick of dread.

It was impossible to breathe.

Impossible to move.

My legs lead as I stood gaping at the man sitting in the same stool that Paisley had been sitting in earlier.

Because in a flash, I knew my life was never going to be the same.

Chapter Forty

Dakota

I CAREFULLY EDGED UP TO THE COUNTER, MY FEET SO HEAVY AND MY heart thundering so hard that everything had gone fuzzy.

Throat thick.

My chest about to cave.

I attempted to swallow it down and act like nothing was out of the ordinary as I gauged the man's purpose who sat with both his elbows resting on the counter, his gaze wary.

It was that instant I was sure that he wasn't there because he was interested in today's special. Knew it in the way he looked like he was covered in a sheen of dread, too.

Like he was questioning coming, all while knowing that he had to be there.

He wore a white button-down with blue pinstripes, and the top two buttons were undone like he'd been sweating so bad he needed to loosen it so he could breathe.

Trey.

"Hi," I barely managed when I made it opposite him.

He scrubbed an agitated palm over his face before he was eyeing me in speculation again. "Hey."

"Can I...get you something?"

He shrugged a small gesture that affirmed the reason he was there. "I, uh, sure. An iced tea would be nice."

My hands shook out of control while I poured him a glass, and it clanked on the counter as I passed it to him.

"Thanks."

"You're welcome." I smoothed my damp hands over my dress, anxiety riding so high I was about to drown in it.

He hesitated before he blew out a sigh that spoke of his discomfort. "I think we need to talk."

I gave him the slightest nod. "Okay."

"You remember me?" he asked.

I choked out a disturbed sound, realizing this guy didn't know a thing about me, only the tiniest tidbits we'd shared that night. "Yeah. I remember you."

He nodded quickly, and he looked to the tea glass like he was reading tea leaves, searching for answers through the anxiety that weaved around us. "I…I was in town about a month ago. I'd stopped by the grocery store to grab something to drink on my way back out to Poplar. I saw you in the parking lot as I was leaving."

He peeked up at me.

A barbed-wire ball rolled in my stomach.

I could barely nod.

He roughed a shaky hand over the top of his head. "I'm going to be honest…it took me a second to place you. Where I knew you from, but the second I did, it punched me in the gut because you had this little boy hooked to your hip, and my mind instantly started calculating."

He stalled out, his throat bobbing as he swallowed. "I was too shocked to do anything. I just sat there like an idiot as I watched you drive away. I tried to shake it off, but I couldn't stop the nagging at the back of my head telling me that little boy might be mine."

A shiver rolled, head to toe, and I tried to form a response, but he kept going like he was trying to fill the discomfort with words.

"You have a sign in the back window of your car. I had some business back here in Time River again today, and when I drove by, I…I couldn't do anything but stop because I need to know."

I gulped around the razors in my throat. "I tried to find you. After I found out I was pregnant. I went back to the bar where we'd met at least ten times, but I never saw you."

He nodded like he accepted the confirmation. "I don't hit bars all that much. It'd just been a bad day and I hadn't wanted to be alone. Same as you, I suppose."

"Yeah."

He looked down, his fingers slipping over the condensation that dripped down the sides of his glass, a war in the way his shoulders tensed and his entire being clenched.

"He's cute," he finally rumbled toward his tea.

I thought it might have ripped my heart out of my chest. "He's my world."

He still wasn't looking at me when he mumbled, "Can I...take some time to process this? I don't know..."

"You don't have any obligation—"

"But I might like to meet him." His claim sliced through the middle of me, stilling the words on my tongue, and the only thing I could do was give him a trembling bob of my head that was spinning with so many things it'd become a blur of dread.

Would he want to become a part of Kayden's life?

Try to get custody?

Change everything that we knew?

And would it be better for Kayden if he did?

Was I being selfish by wanting to protect what we had, this life that we'd built? Selfish because this was Kayden's father and he had a right, even if I didn't want him to have it?

God, I was getting ahead of myself, but I didn't know how to stop the spiral.

Trey stood and dug a five out of his wallet for the tea he hadn't even taken a sip of.

"That's not necessary." It was hoarse.

He shrugged a shoulder as he studied me. "Thanks for being honest with me. I didn't know what I was going to find when I came in here. Good to know you're just as sweet as you were that night."

Disquiet gusted, and I couldn't say anything else as he ambled out. The second he disappeared, I turned, raced into my office, and slammed the door shut.

I covered my mouth with my hand, but it wasn't enough to silence the cry that erupted.

Chapter Forty-One

Ryder

I T WAS AFTER NINE BY THE TIME I PULLED MY BIKE UP IN FRONT OF my mother's old house. My childhood home. Warm lights glowed from the windows, and a comfort hit me like none other. Eagerness and anticipation bubbled in my blood, thinking about Dakota waiting inside.

I couldn't wait to get to her.

I'd had a couple actual legitimate meetings, and the joy and pride I found in my work thudded through me in a beat of satisfaction, while the rest of me had wanted to say fuck it all and get to her as fast as I could. Bummed that Kayden would already be down for the night but also excited that meant I had Dakota to myself.

I figured if I felt this way every day of my life, then things weren't going to turn out so bad.

I hurried up the walkway and put my key in the lock, calling out, "Honey, I'm home," as I opened the door.

Then the tease was replaced with a loud groan when I was hit with the smells that permeated the walls.

Sugar and vanilla and coconut, a doughy heaven that glided through the room and had my nose in the air following the scent.

And my heart got all fucked up again when I hit the doorway to the kitchen and found Dakota at the counter frosting some kind of giant cookies.

Brown hair twisted up in a messy knot and wearing a black baggy sweat-shirt with the neck cut out that draped off one shoulder.

Matching sleep shorts.

Her legs and feet bare.

Her plump lips shiny and those cinnamon eyes glinting when she looked at me where I hovered at the archway.

My mouth watered, and it wasn't just from the cookies she was baking.

"What are you doing in here?" It was a rumble of greed.

The faintest smile hitched at the edge of her mouth, though it was leaden with something that tugged at my spirit. That place that wanted to forever protect her from anything or anyone that would threaten to do her harm.

"What does it look like I'm doing? Baking."

Any glimpse of dejection evaporated when she lifted the knife and licked the white frosting from the tip.

My dick jumped in my jeans, and I strolled in, so casual, while the house quivered around us.

Like it was subject to the same gravity.

The awareness that spun, whirring and whipping up a storm of need that cracked in the air.

A frisson that flickered and leapt with each step that I took.

I edged up behind her, slipped my arms around her waist, and pressed my lips to the exposed skin at her neck. "The way it makes me feel to find you in my kitchen like this."

Goosebumps lifted in the spot where I mumbled the words.

"And what does it make you feel like?" Her question was raspy.

I tightened my hold, my lips riding up her neck in the barest kiss until I was murmuring in her ear, "Like I just stumbled into paradise. Heaven. Except it's more than that, Dakota. It's like I'm coming home for the first time after I've been missing for an eternity."

A soft gasp whispered from her mouth, and she leaned into my hold.

"That's what you are, Cookie. Home. You've always been my safe place. The place my heart was called to. The only place I wanted to be. Sitting in that tree with you."

She let go of the smallest whimper as she admitted, "I never could wait to get out there to find you."

Pressing my nose into her hair, I inhaled. "It's like you always knew I was there. Enticing me with those treats and hypnotizing me with this body."

"I loved the sound you would make when you took your first bite. The way your eyes would close like you were savoring the best thing you'd ever tasted."

Shifting around in my arms, she picked up a cookie and brought it to my mouth.

I kept my eyes on hers as I took a bite, but then they were rolling back in my head as the flavors hit my tongue. Sugar and vanilla. White chocolate and coconut. And I was sure I was looking so much the same as I did then because I moaned, overcome with the taste.

Then I opened my eyes to find hers locked on my mouth.

"Ecstasy," I told her. "Like I was getting a taste of what I really wanted, all while thinking I would forever be craving you."

She lifted the cookie to my mouth again, and I chewed while she whispered, "And now that you have me, I hope you never get your fill."

"Never, Cookie. I could never get enough of you."

Energy crackled, so intense it lifted the hairs on my arms, my guts a tangle of want as I pinned her back to the counter. I propped myself up with one hand and leaned in close. I pushed my other hand between her legs so I could cup her center over her sleep shorts.

Dakota gasped, and her thighs trembled.

"Are you still soaked for me?"

Her nod was erratic, and she curled her fingers into my shirt, gripping it for support, her knees nearly buckling as I pressed my hand harder against her heat.

"You told me to be ready for you," she breathed.

"Thought I was going to lose my mind thinking about getting home, but it gave me plenty of time to dream up what I want to do to you."

I sent her a smirk as I dipped my fingers into the bowl of frosting then pressed them deep into her mouth.

She moaned around my fingers, the reverberation riding up my arm and taking hold of every cell in my body.

Each of them coming alive.

"Suck, sweet girl."

She did, those eyes big and bright but with a challenge in them that sent lust scattering through my being. "Is that what you think? That I'm sweet? Because I'm going to need you not to be gentle with me tonight. Not when I need you in a way I've never needed you before."

Chapter Forty-Two

Dakota

I WONDERED IF I EVEN KNEW WHAT I WAS ASKING FOR WITH THE WAY those gunmetal eyes both dimmed in possession and flashed in a lightning bolt of lust.

The only thing I knew was I needed to feel him.

Feel him everywhere.

Taking me.

Owning me.

I needed to be stripped bare, pared down to the place that was only Ryder and me. Desperate hands and frantic bodies. Where he'd strip me of the new weight that now rested on my shoulders.

I just needed…*this*.

A distraction.

A reprieve.

A moment to remind me that everything would be okay. We were going to make it through this. We had each other.

Only a surprised yelp got free when he suddenly leaned down and tossed me over his shoulder.

"Ryder," I rasped, fingers scraping into his back, half terrified I was going to fall and the other mortified that he thought he could carry me like this. "What do you think you're doing?"

"Carrying my woman to my bed, where she belongs."

"You're going to drop me."

"You keep forgetting these arms were made for you. Think it's time we make sure you remember." He had one arm wrapped around my waist, and he reached up with the other and smacked my bottom before he dug his fingers into my butt cheek, gripping a handful.

I choked around the shocked breath, and a rush of arousal flooded.

He started to walk before he snatched the jar of coconut oil I'd used for the new cookie recipe from the counter.

"Think we're going to need this." He gave it a small toss, catching it before he started through the kitchen and across the living room.

My insides tumbled in a wash of desire, and I felt half delirious as I clawed at his back, holding onto his shirt.

I bounced against his shoulder as he carried me.

Giddiness pulsed, for a moment overpowering the fear, giving me a reprieve from the dread that I'd stewed in all day. Light as he climbed the stairs, a thrill racing through me, need clattering through my senses.

A muddle of desire.

He didn't carry me into my room that we'd been sharing for the last few nights. He turned left into the gauzy darkness of his, and I was instantly back to when I'd walked in on him. When I'd been so confused. Riddled with questions.

But his need no longer remained a mystery as he went directly to the side of his bed and dumped me onto the mattress.

Mischief glinted in his gaze as he watched me bounce on his bed, something sly cutting into the sharpened angles of his face.

He never looked away as he set the jar on the nightstand.

Midnight standing over me.

Darkness and gravity.

But it was a giggle that was skipping up my throat.

Joy and trust and need.

My hips followed it, arching toward him in their own plea.

"Always so eager," he rumbled.

"I need it, I need you," I rushed, unashamed to admit it.

"I'm going to take care of you, Cookie. Promise you."

He reached in and hooked his fingers in the waistband of my sleep shorts and ripped them down my legs, taking my underwear with them.

Cool air hit my heated flesh.

"Now who's eager?" I spouted the tease.

He rewarded me by shoving two fingers into my throbbing center.

A cry jutted free, and he stroked them in twice, so deep before he withdrew, climbed up to straddle me still wearing all his clothes, then pressed them into my mouth.

His fingers still tasted sweet, though they were coated with my arousal, and I groaned at the mix. At the man who hovered over me, knees on either side, a gorgeous silhouette that towered in the night.

"Are you mine, Cookie?" he asked as he dragged his fingers out, raking them over my bottom lip and down my chin.

"Yes. All of me. Everything. It's yours."

He inched back a fraction so he could gather the hem of my sweatshirt and ripped that off, too.

It left me a bare, writhing mess of desire below him.

Slowly, he eased off the bed, and I was shaking beneath his deliberation. The way his gaze went predatory.

Mad with hunger.

A frenzy that he barely kept in check.

"On your hands and knees." The command scraped the dense air.

I didn't hesitate. I scrambled to meet his demand.

"Good girl," he said right before his hand cracked against my bottom. A second later he was smoothing his palm over the cheek.

I cried out in surprise, not because the sting really hurt but because I was shocked by how much I liked it. How my hips were rocking back in a bid to meet with him in any way I could get him.

"This ass, Dakota. So fucking perfect, always teasing me beneath those dresses, driving me out of my mind."

He dipped down and whispered his lips over the spot where his hand had been before, murmuring, "And now it's mine."

He spread me wide and dragged the tip of his tongue from my clit to my asshole.

I didn't have time to be shy or question what he was doing because he began to rub my clit with the pads of two fingers while he swirled his tongue in the most private place.

I was struck with a surge of sensation. Coming at me from all sides. Pleasure lit in an instant, something so seductive and powerful that I was sucking for oxygen, and my fingers curled into his bedspread, hanging on as he whipped me into a dripping ball of need.

"Ryder." I didn't even care that I was begging it.

That I wanted him.

That I wanted him everywhere.

I whimpered when he pulled away, though my gaze caught on the mirror that was situated in the corner of his room. Caught on his reflection as he moved to stand on his feet behind me. Those eyes tangled with mine as he watched my expression, and my blood pounded through my veins as he slowly dragged his shirt over his head.

His chest bare, the designs coiling and undulating in the lapping shadows.

It felt like the hands on that broken clock might be able to move again.

The sound of him rustling out of his jeans echoed from behind, and my lungs were locked as he reached over to his nightstand and dipped his fingers in the jar.

"Do you want to feel my cock in that tight, sweet ass, Dakota?"

My nod was erratic.

Frantic.

While nerves skittered across my flesh and coated me in a sheen of sweat.

I heard him stroking himself with the oil, coating himself, before his fingertips were teasing at my hole.

I moaned as he slowly pressed two inside.

My fingers tightened in the bedspread. "Ryder."

"I have you, sweet girl. You need to tell me if you don't feel right about something. If it's too much or if it hurts. Otherwise, I'm going to make you feel the best you've ever felt. Do you understand?"

Another nod, and Ryder was climbing onto the bed behind me, on his knees as he took me by the hips. He watched me through the mirror.

Severity flashed through his features, and he slipped his hand around to my trembling belly and rode it up until his palm was flat against the hammering in my chest.

He guided me up, pressing my back to the thunder that ravaged at his.

The rhythm of our hearts was violent but in sync. Thrumming and thrumming as he gazed at me from over my shoulder, his hand riding up higher until he was lightly holding me by the throat. "Look at you, Dakota."

I couldn't do anything but take myself in where he had me exposed.

Pared down, exactly the way I'd wanted to be.

My hair wild.

My eyes shining.

My hips wide and my belly quivering and my nipples beaded into hard peaks.

His mouth was at my ear. "The light breaking inside me."

He picked me up the way he seemed to love to do, shifting me around so I was holding onto his headboard. The change in position happened so quickly I didn't even know what'd hit me. He used his knee to spread my legs farther, and he angled my hips back, his breath still in my hair as he murmured, "I love you so fucking much, Dakota."

A sharp jolt of air wheezed up my throat when he shifted and pressed the head of his cock to my ass. Apprehension scattered with the lust, a ravenous ache that echoed inside me.

Like I wanted everything, but it would never be enough.

The cool metal of his piercing sent a chill coiling up my spine, and Ryder held me closer as he began to slowly nudge inside me.

My legs trembled and my body shook as he carefully filled me in a way I'd never allowed anyone to fill me before.

And it was so much, the crash of pleasure that verged on pain, the way it sparked and flashed, skittering through my nerves and lighting a brand-new fire in my veins.

Ryder choked the lowest sound.

Guttural.

Gluttony and greed.

"Fuck, Dakota. The way you feel like this. Hugging my cock. So fucking tight. So perfect." He rambled it on a haggard breath as he curled an arm tighter around my waist and braced his other on the headboard. "Swear you were made for me. This body. This heart. Can you feel it?"

"I feel it. I need it. I need you."

"You have me, Cookie. Always. Forever. I could never forget you."

Emotion swam, amplified as he began to move.

He took me in a way that was completely consuming. His body scored into mine.

I clung to the headboard, shaking and gasping and tremoring as he took me as deep as he could.

As he filled me.

Possessed me.

I moved with him, rising up before I sank down to meet him.

We arched and curved and rolled.

Our bodies as in sync as the thrashing of our hearts.

And I fell completely into him.

Lost in his darkness.

Covered in midnight.

"Ryder." I whispered his name in adoration.

"Dakota." He murmured mine in praise.

His fingers moved to my clit, strumming light, and the pleasure that blazed gathered to a pinpoint.

A flash.

A spark.

A scattering of light.

"Come for me, sweet girl."

Ecstasy split through me with the force beyond anything I'd experienced before.

A complete sundering.

Only this time, that earthquake I always felt when Ryder came into the room?

It fully cracked.

And I was no longer spinning on the same axis.

A new orbit had come into existence. Time and space and location setting on this man.

He burrowed his face in the back of my neck as he let go. Every muscle in his body went rigid as he pulsed. "Dakota. Fuck. So good. You feel so good. Everything. Everything."

We both struggled for air.

Oxygen held.

A moment given to us as we remained like that for the longest time.

It felt as if the last wall had been demolished between us.

The last chink undone.

Nothing to keep us apart but the fear if we let it.

And I wouldn't let the unknowns keep me from this.

This connection that hummed in his room.

A sated song.

A silence brimming with so much meaning that neither of us could speak.

Ryder never let go, he just shifted me in his arms and carried me into the bathroom.

His touch so tender. His care so fierce.

He turned on the shower, and once it warmed, he stepped into the stream, only then placing me onto my feet.

He angled me under the fall, urging my head back so he could wet my hair. Chills lifted as the hot water rushed over my body.

His hair was wet and the water pounded into his skin and those eyes never looked away as he tended to me.

And my spirit resounded with truth.

With us.

With the promises we'd made.

Both the unspoken and the ones that had fallen from our lips.

He didn't need to say anything as he wrapped me in a towel and carried me back to his bed. He situated me in the middle and didn't hesitate to climb in and wrap me in his arms.

His fingertips played through the wet locks of my hair as we both lay facing each other.

Staring for the longest time.

Finally, I broke through the bated stillness. "I need to tell you something."

His sharp brow furrowed, but he kept gentling his fingers through my hair.

Sure encouragement.

"What is it?"

My mouth suddenly felt dry, and my pulse quickened in a fray of anxiety. "Kayden's biological father came into the restaurant today."

Every molecule in Ryder tensed, worry treading through his features, though he set his hand on my hip, his thumb running circles in an effort to chase my apprehension away.

"How?" The single word cracked down the middle.

I inhaled a shattered breath, forcing myself to speak through the fractured peace. "He saw me with Kayden at the store a month ago. He said he didn't recognize me at first, but when he did, he realized Kayden might be his child. He'd seen the Time River Market & Café sign on the back window of my car, and when he came back into town, he came in."

Ryder flinched, but he kept running those circles on my hip. "Did he tell you what he wants?"

My head shook on the pillow. "He'd come to find out if his suspicions were true. When I confirmed them, he said he needed time to process it."

I stalled, then whispered the fear. "I'm terrified he might want custody or something, and I know that makes me selfish, but I got so used to the idea of him not being a part of our lives."

"You don't have to feel guilty for that, Dakota. You don't even know this guy." I could feel the protectiveness well in Ryder.

A rising tide.

One that would demolish when it hit land.

"I know." My teeth plucked at my bottom lip. "I'm scared of what this means."

"You're allowed to be. But the only thing we can do is take it as it comes. And know that no matter what, we're always there for Kayden. He has us, and that love will never fail him."

My spirit thrashed, and a tear slipped free. Ryder reached out and gathered it with his thumb before he pulled me closer to him, strong arms wrapping me in their protection as he pressed his lips to my forehead when he whispered, "This life is for you two now. Whatever that looks like. Whatever that means. I promise you, Dakota."

Chapter Forty-Three
Ryder

"I watch *Wion King*." Kayden patted his chest and dipped his chin real deep, shooting me one of those dimpled smiles that completely slayed.

The one that cut to the core and guaranteed the choice I had made was the right one. One that affirmed I wasn't just taking this action to get myself free, but because our kids deserved better. A safer place to grow up. A safer place to live and learn. One that didn't fester with greed and prey on their innocence.

On their pain and their grief.

It wasn't like I was going to change the world or shake up the order of things, but it was the one small footprint I could make.

Because I could see myself standing in that very spot at Kayden's age, and there wasn't a question in my mind that my mother had looked at me the exact same way as I was looking at him now.

With a love so fierce that she felt like she might explode with the magnitude of it. Ribs hardly strong enough to contain it. With a hope so fervent that I would grow into a good man. That I'd find joy and peace and all the things in this life that made it worth living.

But I'd followed my grief down the wrong path. It was insane that I could go back all those years and pin it on one reckless, foolish decision made in a place of desperation. A choice to walk through a door I never should have walked through.

There was no choice left now but the one I'd made to end it. Consequences be damned. Gazing down at Dakota's son was all the proof I needed.

"You want to watch the *Lion King*, huh? We just watched that two nights ago."

"Again, my Rye-Rye." Another dip of that chin, and that love was pounding wild.

"*Lion King* it is."

"Old or new?"

At the sultry voice hitting my ears, I shifted to find Dakota in the arch between the two rooms, wearing that soft affection on her gorgeous face as she watched where Kayden and I stood in front of the television flipping through the options on the screen.

Kayden pointed a chubby finger up at where the TV hung on the wall, jumping in place. "*Dis* one, Mommy!"

Dakota giggled. "My son is one for the classics."

"Watch yourself, woman. I was born the year this movie was made."

A flirty grin ticked up at the edge of that seductive mouth, but because it was Dakota, it dripped this sweetness that slipped through my veins.

A straight shot of honey.

"Don't worry, Ryder, I always thought it would be sexy to date an older man."

"Older man?" I let the growl of a warning glide into the words, though it was a lightness that possessed. An easiness that had taken us over.

"That's right." She purposefully bit at her lip because the little tease knew exactly how to get me hard.

There she was. Sweet with all that sass.

I stalked her way, real slow. Swore that the air actually trembled around us.

The glow of gravity as it pulled and lured, tugging so deep at my soul there was nowhere else I could go. I looped an arm around her waist and jerked her against me, and I let my palm splay down over her ass as I pressed my cock against her belly.

Her heart thudded, but the flirty smile only grew.

"You're going to pay for that, Cookie."

"I do hope that's a promise."

With a groan, I buried my face in her throat. "What you do to me, Dakota."

"I'm pretty sure it's what you do to me."

I almost got lost there, except a little hand yanked at the leg of my jeans, vying for his own attention. "Now, my Rye-Rye."

I pulled back and swooped my tiny tornado into my arms, making him giggle with all that life, little arms flying around my neck as I carried him toward the couch.

"For the record, it is a promise," I tossed over my shoulder before I sat with Kayden, the kid instantly climbing all over me like he thought I was a jungle gym. I smirked back at her as she hovered across the room then patted the spot next to me. "Now get over here where you belong."

Dakota came prancing over on her bare feet, so goddamn pretty she stole the breath right out of me. She snuggled into my side, and I wrapped my arm around her shoulder and flicked off the lights before I pressed play.

The movie came to life, and Kayden was immediately immersed, but I was the one who was mesmerized.

By the both of them.

The way it felt with them in my arms and the calm and peace that surrounded us.

The rest of the week had gone by without Dakota hearing anything more from Kayden's biological father. It made me hopeful that the prick would just disappear, all while feeling a stab of guilt that I felt that way.

But I wanted to protect this. Shield it. Keep it from any outside threat.

Maybe I felt it even more because the bullshit I was in was coming up quick. What I'd set into motion was getting ready to play out. A squall of agitation thrashed at my spirit because I didn't know what that was going to look like, but there was no other option.

Not when the choice I'd made was the only one I could make.

By the time the movie had made it halfway through, Kayden was asleep in the crook of my arm with his cheek pressed to my chest, his breaths deep and his little mouth parted where his precious face was tipped up toward me.

Dakota was wrapped in the other, and she'd fallen asleep, too.

I wondered if I'd ever felt a greater significance than I did right then.

Recognizing the treasure that I was holding.

One I could never deserve, but one I would defend for the rest of my life.

Careful not to disturb Dakota, I shifted her around and rested her head against a pillow then stood and carried Kayden upstairs. I laid him in his crib and spread my hand over his back. "Tiny Tornado. The perfect kind of havoc in my life. I'm going to do everything in my power to do right by you. By your mom. I love you more than should be possible. With the kind of love that doesn't exist. Not until the two of you created it."

I crept back downstairs with plans to carry Dakota to my bed. Only I stilled when I heard the clank of what sounded like metal from the backyard. It wasn't loud, but it was enough to make me still and incline my ear, listening through the muted volume of the movie that continued to play.

I swore I heard shuffling and a creak over the wind rustling through the branches of the trees.

I moved quickly but quietly through the living room and into the kitchen where I went to the back door. I peered out through the square window that took up the upper section. Darkness howled back, only the faintest illumination from the slivered moon seeping into the shadows that danced through the yard.

When I couldn't make out anything amiss, I flipped on the light switch, flooding the porch and three feet into the lawn with light. It was at the edge of it that I saw the outline of a shape—one that shouldn't be there, one that suddenly dashed deeper into the cover of the trees.

Without wavering, I fumbled through the lock and flung open the door, and I darted out, taking the porch steps in one leap and racing into the lapping darkness.

"Hey!" I shouted, not sure what I was shouting at.

It took me a second to be sure it was a person.

The shape of the shadow that raced through the night.

Footsteps thudded in a frantic beat, and the sound of them pounded through me like a drum, driving me faster. I wasn't about to let whoever this bastard lurking in my yard was get away.

Part of me wished I'd taken the time to get my gun from the safe in my room, while the other knew this might be my only chance to stop what was creeping over me like an omen.

The sticky awareness that made my stomach bottom out.

Did Dare know? Had he found out? We'd been so fucking careful. It couldn't be. It couldn't. Still, I pushed myself harder, barreling across the soft grasses that dented below my feet.

"Stop right there!" I shouted.

The fucker didn't slow. He tossed himself right over the top of the wooden fence at the back of my property.

Behind my house was a section of woods before it opened up into another neighborhood on the other side. I only had a split second before he would disappear, a million places for him to hide in the overgrown bushes and brush, and I threw myself over the top of the fence, too.

I landed crouched on my feet, ready to spring back into the hunt, only when I propelled myself forward, I was met with the blunt force of a metal rod. It whirred through the air so fast that I had no time to prepare myself.

Pain splintered through my brain.

Piercing.

Blinding.

It dropped me straight to my knees.

Blood poured from the wound at the side of my head, weaving an erratic web across my face.

Another crack landed low on my back. I cried out as it bowed me forward, and I slumped onto the ground on my stomach.

I struggled to stay lucid.

To fight the darkness that pressed in at the edges of my sight.

Consciousness ebbing in and out.

My nostrils filled with the acrid smell of damp soil and newly fallen leaves that had just begun to decay.

But it was the scent of the foul and the filthy that crawled over me, the treacherous voice that uttered the warning at my ear. "Just a friendly reminder from Dare not to forget your place."

The boot that landed in my side came swift and from out of nowhere, and I wheezed in agony as the breath was knocked from my lungs.

As the world spun and the darkness enclosed.

Terror clamored over me like demons. Specters that played over my body.

The metal bar cracked down once more in the center of my upper back, and I couldn't stop the agony from gurgling out of my mouth.

A second later, heavy footsteps faded into the distance while I struggled to breathe, to force the air into my lungs.

Lungs that were on fire.

Every part of my body in flames.

And my eyes kept drifting closed.

Succumbing.

Falling toward unconsciousness.

"Ryder? Ryder?" Dakota's frantic voice suddenly carried through the night. "Ryder? Are you out here?"

Her name bubbled in my chest, but it bottled in my throat, silenced on the torment that congealed all hope.

Except that hope didn't give up, and I could only faintly make out the clattering of the back gate before she was croaking, "Oh my God, Ryder!"

Fumbling to my side over the fallen branches and exposed roots, she dropped to her knees. Her fingers trembled and trembled as she brushed back the hair stuck to my face.

An anguished cry gushed from between her lips. "Oh God. Ryder. What happened? I'm…I'm going to call an ambulance."

She went to stand, but somehow, I managed to grasp her around the wrist. "No."

"You're…bleeding." She said it like she didn't want to let on how bad it was.

But I already knew how bad it was.

So much worse than she could ever imagine.

Chapter Forty-Four

Dakota

HORROR CHUGGED THROUGH MY SENSES, A DISORIENTING PANIC as he pulled at my arm.

"You're bleeding." I could barely force it out.

God. He was bleeding, and there was so much of it, his face covered in rivulets that streamed in cragged lines from a gaping gash at the side of his head.

Dirt and hair were caked in it, and even beneath the bare light, I could see glistening, dark fluid continue to ooze from the wound.

But it was his eyes that pierced me.

The whites exaggerated in the night. Filled with so much fear that it spurred a riot inside me.

"Are you okay? Oh, God. Ryder. What happened? Are you okay?"

He didn't respond, and instead he pushed up onto his hands and knees. A discordant moan rolled from him as he tried to get his bearings. To climb to his feet.

"Let me help you." Frantic, I leaned down so I could get an arm around his waist and help him the rest of the way up. He swayed when he stood. His entire being swerving and lurching as he struggled to find balance.

"Lean on me," I told him, and I knew the shape he was in when he did. His big body was heavy as we staggered back over the rutted terrain and through the gate. How we managed to get across the lawn, I didn't know, our movements slowed as we trudged through the violent foreboding that saturated the atmosphere.

I could feel it.

Feel it pulsing and throbbing around us. Could feel it as Ryder was bent at the waist as we stumbled up the porch steps and through the back door.

Felt the oppression of the ghosts that tormented his being.

"Lock it." It ricocheted a warning. The sliding metal a gunshot in the night as I engaged the deadbolt.

"Let me call Ezra."

"No," he said again.

I gulped the words down because I wanted to argue but somehow, I knew Ryder meant it.

That he wasn't acting like this wasn't a big deal.

It was just something bigger than anyone else could help with.

And that trepidation only increased as we moved through his house and up the stairs, both of us clinging to either railing while I tried to support him as we took each laborious step. We finally made it into the bathroom, and I flicked on the light and helped him sit on the lid of the toilet.

A cry sprang from my spirit when I got a good look at his face, and I smacked my hand over my mouth like I could revoke its passage. Take it back. But tears streamed free, the pain and confusion at finding Ryder like this so intense I didn't know how to process it.

Because there was no evading that sense that covered the air.

I sucked it down and tried to focus because standing there losing my shit wasn't going to solve anything. I went to the sink and grabbed a washcloth from the cabinet then wet it under cool water.

I returned to stand between his knees. Carefully, I dabbed the cloth at the wound. Gathering the blood and debris. I rinsed it then continued the ministrations, neither of us saying anything while that feeling simmered and grew.

Ryder kept looking up at me while I tended to him.

And it was too difficult to breathe in the confined space. Too difficult to get out any of the questions that bottled. Too difficult to say anything at all.

"I think you really need stitches, Ryder." I managed that, a haggard whisper issued at the top of his head as I focused on the wound that was two inches long, gaping enough that I could see the meat inside. And judging by whatever had caused it, I would worry that he might have a concussion, too.

But Ryder didn't seem concerned with himself at all right then.

He curled his hand around my outer thigh, and he tipped his head back to look up at me. I froze there, locked in the grimness of his stare.

"I need to tell you something, Dakota."

The last time I'd told him that, I was confiding in him that Kayden's biological father had come on the scene, but I had a hunch whatever Ryder was about to tell me was so much worse than that.

That it might be something we couldn't figure out or overcome.

Because devastation was written there.

Complete obliteration.

"What is it?" I wanted to take the question back because I didn't want to know. Didn't want to hear the answer when Ryder pushed to his feet.

The man came to tower over me.

"You need to sit down and rest."

His head barely shook. "I need you to listen to me, Dakota."

The words were so low they crawled over me like the scattering of bugs. Chills lifted, and a cold dread slipped down my spine and sank to the pit of my stomach.

"I always knew that I wasn't good enough. A fool to take a chance with you."

He came closer.

Hovering.

I managed to mumble, "That's not true."

"It's true, Dakota. You asked me what I was in, and I couldn't tell you because I was trying to solve it myself. Take care of it. End it."

I blinked, fighting the way my knees felt weak.

"You asked if I was still using."

That cold dread sloshed, and I couldn't speak, I just stood there waiting for him to deliver whatever blow he was going to inflict.

Because I could already feel it pressing down. A frenzy of desperation that clawed between us.

"It wasn't a lie. I've been clean since I was twenty-two."

Relief gusted, and I exhaled, but it clipped off when he pressed on, his confession so quiet, like he was offering me a secret and he was terrified someone else was going to hear. "But what I never got free of was that life. I became indebted to this small-time dealer when I was seventeen."

Shivers rolled, dread that crashed through my being.

Ryder only pressed closer, and my back hit the wall. "He asked me for one favor, and I was the dumb fucking kid who fell into that trap. Wound in his chains so quickly that I didn't know what hit me. I tried for years to get free of him, Dakota. For us. So we could have a chance. And every fucking time, he's been one step ahead of me. Manipulating me. Threatening me. Tightening the shackles that chain me."

My throat closed off, and I swore the room spun.

Ryder's tongue swept across his chapped lips. "But small-time crooks never want to stay that way. They're fucking greedy, and he pushed that greed on me. He made me a deal when I was twenty-six."

Twenty-six.

Dread slithered through my consciousness. Vipers slipping beneath my skin.

It was the summer I'd come back. The summer I'd thought…

"I had to do this big job for him, earn us both a shit-ton of money, then he'd cut me loose."

I blinked, struggling to process. To understand exactly what he was saying.

"But he double crossed me, Dakota. I got the money, but I also got sucked deeper into his sordid world. He made it clear what would happen to the people I cared about if I ever tried to walk. That I knew I was finished if I even thought about getting away from him."

Misery flashed through his features.

Guttural and bleak.

On his tongue was a secret so sharp and deep and ugly that I couldn't ask what he meant. Couldn't stomach whatever it might be.

"He's been using my shop as a front, Dakota. For all these fucking years," he continued, his voice cracking through the confession. "I modify the cars so they can be loaded down with whatever shit he's trying to get to the East Coast, and it's on me to drive it there. Meet up with whatever slimy fuck is going to distribute it in that area."

Disbelief pulled through the disorder, and my breaths turned choppy and shallow.

Fear covered, what he was saying, what this meant.

I tried to blink through it.

Process it.

This man who I loved. He was a…drug trafficker? Is that what he was saying?

No.

I gulped.

"No." That time I said it aloud, refusing it. My hands fisted in his tattered shirt. "No. You're lying. You're lying. Tell me you're lying to me, Ryder. Please."

He took me by both sides of the face and forced me to look at him. "It's not a lie, Dakota. It's who I am. It's who I've been trying to protect you from for all these years. But something happened when you came here." His voice was raw. "And I knew I couldn't keep running from you any longer. That I had to stop this. Change it because there was no life worth living if I wasn't living it for you. So, I called Ezra. I set them up, Dakota. When I go to load the car next week, the DEA is going to be there."

Fear pounded, so loud, battering my brain and churning my stomach. Disgust and disbelief wound with it.

No.

"I think Dare knows something is up. One of his men was in the backyard. I chased after him to pin him down, but he got to me first. Sent a warning that I needed to remember my place."

No.

There was no stopping the spiral of thoughts. The questions. Everything I thought I'd known.

My eyes squeezed closed as my mind whirred through the things he'd told me. The things he'd done.

And it all started to fall on me.

Adding up to a sum I couldn't endure.

"How did you buy this house?" I stammered.

Guilt struck through his expression. "It was my mother's house, Dakota. I had to—"

I choked, cutting him off. "My restaurant? The money you lent me? The money you said came from a life insurance policy of your mother's that you hadn't known about?"

Shame blasted from his conscience. So palpable that I could feel it coating my fingertips that were wound in his shirt.

No.

"Dakota." My name was a plea.

A confession. "Please tell me you didn't give me drug money to start my restaurant, Ryder. Please tell me everything I built isn't tainted. Please."

His jaw clenched, and disgrace rushed from his pores.

The betrayal smacked me across the face.

The truth of what he'd done.

Of what he'd made me an unknowing accomplice in.

He tightened his hold. "Dakota."

I'd thought I could handle it. Anything he was holding. But how could he ask me to hold this?

Sickness churned in my guts. "Let go of me."

"Dakota, please."

"Let go!" I screamed it, and he dropped his hands.

I stumbled back, hugging my middle. Nausea spun, and the burn of bile lifted in my throat.

Tears coated my face. "How could you? How could you?"

My back hit the door, and the fear and disbelief broke, sending a shock-wave of horror through my being.

It crashed through my spirit and annihilated my heart. A frenzy lit, and I turned and ran from the bathroom and into the bedroom where my things were, even though I hadn't slept in there in almost a week. I grabbed a duffel bag and started to shove whatever I could into it.

I felt him emerge in the doorway behind me. "Dakota."

"Don't. Stay right there. Don't come near me." I barely gasped out the words, my sight so bleary I couldn't see. Couldn't think. Couldn't breathe.

The only thing I could feel was the betrayal.

The agony.

It was too much. Too much of him to ask of me.

I slipped my feet into flats, and I pushed out around him and raced into Kayden's room. I didn't slow. I went directly to his crib and scooped him out of it, praying he'd remain asleep.

Ryder was right there. "Dakota, please, listen to me."

"I don't want to hear anything else you have to say, Ryder." I elbowed out around him, my flats clacking on the floor as I rushed back down the hall and hit the stairs. I hugged Kayden to my chest as I took the stairs as fast as I could. I grabbed my purse from the entry table before I whipped out the door, never slowing as I ran across the porch and down the pathway.

Ryder followed, gritting his teeth against the pain.

His presence big.

Profound.

Horrible.

Perfect.

My love.

My demise.

Revulsion slammed with it all. My restaurant. What I'd built. And it'd been built on *this*.

And Ryder…how could he remain involved in something so horrible? How could he? Did I know him at all?

Because he felt like a stranger right then. Someone I couldn't recognize. All while that familiarity tugged through the connection.

I fumbled to get my keys so I could unlock the doors, barely able to get my trembling hands to cooperate as I buckled Kayden.

Kayden who murmured, "Mommy," in his disrupted sleep.

"It's okay, sweet boy. It's okay."

The whole time Ryder kept begging me from behind, "Dakota, please don't do this. Come inside. I need to know you're safe."

I choked over an incredulous laugh as I shut Kayden's door and scrambled to mine. "Yeah, well I don't feel *safe* here."

Jumping into the driver's seat, I slammed the door and locked it, gasping as I pushed the button to start the engine. Ryder pressed his palms to the window. "Dakota! Please!"

I threw the car into reverse and flew backward down his drive. I rammed on the brakes when I hit the road.

The man stood in the spray of the headlights staring at me.

Broken.

Grieved.

Midnight.

Darkness I'd allowed to cover me. To take me whole. Possess me.

I put the car in drive, refusing the lure that called me back as I gunned it and flew down the street. I swiped at the tears that kept streaming from my eyes as I made it to the stop sign, and I carefully eased out onto Manchester, trying to keep from throwing up as I passed by Time River Market & Café.

I couldn't go there.

Couldn't go home.

Couldn't go to my mother's.

So I went to the one place where someone would truly understand. Driving under the blanket of stars thirty miles outside of town on the desolate two-lane road.

I slowed when I got to the turn-off to Hutchins Ranch, and I took the dirt road over the pastures that led to the main area of the property.

My lights cut through the darkness, brightening against the front of the mansion where I came to a stop in the circular drive.

Paisley was already opening the front door by the time I made it up the porch steps with Kayden in my arms.

"Dakota, what's wrong? Are you okay?"

And I gave myself over to the sobs that wracked me when she pulled us into her embrace.

Because no.

I was not okay.

And I wasn't sure I was ever going to be.

Chapter Forty-Five

Dakota

Twenty-Three Years Old

DAKOTA GOT TO THE TREE FIRST THAT NIGHT, AND SHE LET HER legs dangle where she sat swaying on the branch. Cool air caressed her flesh as a mild breeze murmured through, though she felt an instant heat when awareness suddenly flashed over her from behind.

A comfort that left her so unsettled she felt her nerves scatter beneath her flesh.

She shifted so she could look at him. The man stood at the end of the path with his hands stuffed in his pockets and that black hair gently waving in the wind.

Something so stark and fierce about him though there was a softness that floated around him like an embrace.

He eased forward, and she couldn't help but notice there seemed to be something hesitant about him tonight. Something that slowed his steps, like maybe he was questioning coming there.

But she swallowed the insecurities down because she was past being a hostage to them. Her confidence had grown so much while she'd been away at college, but there was something about Ryder that always set her off-kilter.

Made her feel shy and fluttery.

Beautiful but somehow indistinct.

It probably had a lot to do with the fact that she'd seen Amelia coming out of his shop three days ago when she'd swung by to say hello. But he'd denied them being together the whole summer. Had said they'd had sex before, but he'd ended it more than four months ago.

She had to trust in it.

She didn't have any reason not to believe him.

And it wasn't like she had a right to be angry with him if he was sleeping with someone, anyway.

But she couldn't deny that he felt like hers.

Like her own perfect secret.

Without saying anything, he hoisted himself onto the branch, all his sleek muscles coiling in the smooth, quick motion, and he plopped down beside her.

Nerves skittered and crashed, and tingles spread up her arm when their skin brushed.

Flames at the contact.

"Hey," she finally murmured, and she handed him the tin that contained the lemon bars she'd spent the evening preparing for him. "I brought something for you."

"You always have something for me, Cookie." His voice was so gruff. A scrape of seduction.

That's the way she'd begun to feel. Like he was slowly seducing her.

Turning her to putty.

Leaving her a puddle of need.

And she'd started to wonder if it wasn't the same for him.

The way he'd look at her. The way the air sparked between them. The way he'd stay for so long, like he couldn't bring himself to leave, though there was something in his gaze that always made him shut down.

So close, but just out of reach.

He popped off the lid and let go of a small moan when he saw what was inside.

"It's a twist on a classic. Lemon bars though it's whipped in cream. They're sweeter. Less tart."

He reached out and ran his thumb at the tiny dimple at the edge of her mouth. "Sweet like you."

Shivers rocked her through, and she couldn't stop the whimper that whispered from between her lips with him touching her like that.

He didn't look away, he just kept watching her.

His stare penetrating and complex.

"I have something for you, too, Dakota."

Her brow furrowed, and her heart beat in a fit of anticipation.

"What's that?"

"I talked to Todd at the bank."

The frown between her eyes deepened.

"You're going to get that loan."

"What do you mean?"

He looked out over the stream, the water stained a shimmery black as it babbled over the rocks. "I came into some money."

It was so rough when he said it. Like it pained him to admit it.

She waited for him to explain.

Patient while she felt like she was going to rattle apart.

Because she felt his agony all while there was a thrill that bubbled in her blood.

"A life insurance policy of my mother's that I didn't know about. One that came to maturity when I turned twenty-six."

He shuddered, and she couldn't do anything but reach out and grip onto his upper arm. Unable to sit still beneath the torment that raged through him. "I'm so sorry, Ryder. I...you can't give me that money. It's yours. You need to—"

"I'm getting mine and my mom's old house back with it, too. It's a wreck, but the owners are letting it go cheap. The rest? It belongs to you."

"I can't accept it."

Surprise jutted through her when he suddenly hopped off the branch, and he set the tin aside. Her head spun when he reached up and grabbed her by the waist and placed her on her feet.

An inch from him.

And the sparks in the air started to shoot.

So bright they blinded her eyes and sent her heart battering at her ribs.

He framed her face in his hands, and a fire burned from his palms. "You can accept it, Dakota. Because I want to give you everything you deserve in this world. I want to watch you soar. Fly. Take hold of every dream you've ever wished. And I want to be worthy of watching you do it."

Her lips parted on a shaky gasp. "Ryder."

"I mean it, Dakota. Run after this dream. Because it's good and right, and you'll be offering this town something that is beautiful. Something that is so uniquely you it would be a fucking sin not to bring it to life." In emphasis, he tightened his hold on her face. "Love is on the house."

A war went down in his dark eyes, then she nearly dropped to her knees when he pressed the softest kiss to her closed lips. It was the barest brush.

Innocent.

But in it, she felt a promise.

He drew back, gazing at her for the longest time, before he murmured, "I have to go."

Turning, he disappeared into the shadows, and Dakota touched her lips with her fingertips.

Never so sure of anything in her life than she was right then.

⌒∞⌒

Ryder

Twenty-Six Years Old

Ryder took the twenty-four-hour drive straight through with Amelia in the passenger seat.

"I'm honestly shocked you agreed to this," she said, angled to the side so she could study him.

He tried to ditch the cloud of disgust and shame that wept in a hazy fog from his conscience. The feeling that it was all wrong. Something afoot and amiss. "It's my ticket out. It's the only thing I can do."

She laughed, only partially at his expense, like she truly couldn't make sense of him. "Why do you want out?"

"Because this isn't the kind of life I want to lead."

"I never knew a hard man could be so soft."

"I'm not soft." He spat it like it could protect from her getting into his thoughts. Into the sacred places that he had to keep guarded.

"Yes, you are, Ryder. And not the kind you should be ashamed of. You're the only person in this world who's ever treated me like I'm more than a tool. A weapon that Dare uses on both his friends and his enemies."

It was the first time he'd ever heard the regret in her voice. A haunted misery that she'd covered and suppressed.

"Maybe it's time you got out, too."

"I'm pretty sure it's too late for some of us."

There was something in her voice. Something that left him itching more than he had been.

"It's never too late to become something better."

He'd never been so sure of it as they made the trade with twelve men surrounding them with automatic rifles. As he'd looked down at death and knew he wanted to live.

These men got to decide his fate right then, and a true sense of terror covered him as he and Amelia gathered the four duffels stuffed with money.

But they let them walk, and Ryder promised himself he would never be in that position again. He silently chanted it as they picked up the rental car that had already been arranged for them and took turns driving back to Colorado.

He couldn't sleep on his break, though.

He was riddled with too many thoughts.

Too many emotions.

Grief and hope.

Fear and love.

Guilt and the belief that he could be better.

And he held onto that belief when they pulled into the alley behind the dank dry cleaner's office at just before dawn. Knew it as they went inside and tossed the bags to Dare's feet.

As he grated, "It's done, and so am I."

A smile split across Dare's face. The menacing kind. The kind that froze the blood in Ryder's veins.

"Oh, Ryder, you're just beginning."

Pete stepped forward and brought the butt of his gun down at the back of Ryder's neck. It dropped him to his knees. Dare came forward and leaned over him so he was holding onto his shoulder and muttering near his ear, "I own you, Ryder. Who is going to have to die for you to remember it?"

That was right before another blow landed at the side of his head. A blow that completely knocked him out.

He woke with pain splitting his head in two. Agonizing as he blinked open his eyes to the glaring light and tried to get his bearings.

The house he rented. He was in the bed in his house.

Dread seeped deeper when his arm brushed against something, and he shifted to find Amelia in bed beside him.

And the dread blasted cold when he realized she was too still. That it was too quiet. He flew onto his knees, taking her by the face and shaking her. "Amelia. Wake up. Please, wake up."

Her body bounced as he shook her. No response. No resistance.

His fingers trembled where he pressed them to her neck. There was no pulse. And her skin was too pale. Too white.

He fumbled for his phone and dialed 9-1-1, begged them to hurry before he started blowing breaths into her mouth.

Frantic as he pumped at her chest.

Tears blurred his eyes as the paramedics came in, and he stumbled off the bed as they took over.

He watched like he was detached.

Floating.

Suffering a near-death experience and he was watching his body below him.

But he guessed a piece of him died right then.

When they took her away in the ambulance, even though he knew she was already gone.

He still went to the hospital in Poplar where they'd taken her. He waited in the waiting room, claiming her as his fiancée, knowing she had no one else. No family. More alone than he could ever be.

And the doctor gave no sympathies when he came out and told him they couldn't bring her back. She'd OD'd. So many opioids in her system there was no way for her heart to beat.

Ryder buried his head in his arms and choked over a shattered, "What?"

As if he was in shock.

As if he didn't know.

As if he couldn't believe what she had been involved in.

But it was shock.

Shock over what Dare had done. The lengths he'd gone to keep Ryder trapped.

A warning.

A threat.

One that had cost Amelia her life.

Chains rattled around him. Cinching down tight.

He wandered out of the hospital.

And he dropped to his knees and wailed toward the sky.

⌒⋇⌒

Dakota

Same Day

Dakota looked at her reflection in the mirror where she sat at the dressing table in her childhood room. She slicked a shimmery gloss across her lips while nerves fluttered like the flapping of wings in her belly and chest.

Today was the day.

No more reservations.

No more holding back.

He'd encouraged her to chase a dream, had given her the gift of making that dream a reality, and she was going to chase this one, too.

She wouldn't wait for the cover of night. When the world whispered around them. When they were held in a sanctuary where no harm could befall them.

She was going to go to him and tell him how she felt and pray he felt it back.

Inhaling a steeling breath, she stood and smoothed out the red dress she'd picked for the occasion. The one that made her feel pretty and confident. The one she was sure Ryder loved when she wore it.

Giving herself another quick pep talk, she grabbed her purse from the bed and headed down the hall. She went into the kitchen and grabbed the tin filled with what she'd dubbed *Mounds of Joy*. Cookies made with Ryder's favorite candy.

She was quick to hurry out the front door and to her car.

Ten minutes later, with the late afternoon sun shining around her, she pulled up in front of the little house he rented on the far side of town.

Joy filled her that he was chasing a new dream, too.

One of reclaiming his childhood home. She was excited for the memories that would be waiting for him there, and she prayed he would find a semblance of peace within those walls. And she hoped she would get to be a piece of that, too.

Snatching the tin from the passenger seat, she climbed out and rushed to his door.

Anticipation hastened her steps.

She rapped at the door, those butterflies flying through her stomach and lighting in her chest.

She was doing this.

She was really doing this.

Dakota frowned a little when a minute passed, and he didn't answer. Shifting on her feet, she glanced around. His motorcycle was in the spot where he always parked it.

He had to be there.

Besides the bike being there, she *felt* him. That sense she got whenever he came near. The hum that buzzed in her blood and the way her feet never quite felt like they were on solid ground.

She knocked again, this time louder.

Nerves rattled through her as she waited.

Anticipation.

Excitement.

In it was also a sticky discomfort.

It grew as she finally heard the lumbered footsteps echo from the other side of the door, and the air locked in her throat when the lock disengaged and he pulled it open.

She gasped when he came into view.

His hair was disheveled, his face ashen, and the deepest grief was carved into the gray of his eyes.

"Ryder?" She could barely get his name to form on her tongue. "What's wrong? What happened?"

Blankly, he stared at her before he whispered, "She's dead."

The words were hollow, though they tumbled through her with the weight of a thousand boulders.

"Who?" She barely got it out.

Fear clamored through her senses.

Dread thick.

"Amelia." Ryder heaved it, another stone.

The tin she held slipped from her fingers and crashed at her feet, knocking the lid free.

Mounds of Joy spilled out onto the ground.

Guilt struck her hard in the middle of it.

She had to be the most horrible, selfish human with her heart clattering. Fumbling in a jolt of jealousy with the way Ryder looked absolutely broken.

As if he'd lost a piece of himself.

All she could do was silently pray that the expression on his face didn't mean what she thought it might.

Through the disorder, she murmured, "Oh my God, Ryder. I'm so sorry. What happened?"

Because she was. It didn't matter that her spirit squeezed, it was terrible news.

Ryder stumbled back as if he couldn't stand, and she followed him, taking a single step into the tiny foyer of the house.

"I…" The word clotted off, and he kept blinking as he sagged against the wall, and she was sure he was in shock.

She wanted to erase his pain. Take it away. Give him everything he'd given to her. So she pushed farther into his space, and she set her hand on his wet cheek.

"I don't know what's happening right now, but I need you to know that I'm here. You're not alone. I'm right here."

"Dakota." He rumbled her name.

So deep.

He pressed his cheek deeper into her hand.

Like touching her gave him the barest flash of relief in a barren cold.

"Dakota."

He needed her.

She knew it.

And she couldn't stop the confession that rushed. "I'm right here, Ryder. I'm right here. I'm right here because I love you. Because I'm in love with you. God, Ryder, I love you so much. I don't know what's happening, but what I do know is that I love you. That I'm here for you."

Dakota felt a surge of relief in finally admitting it.

Laying her heart at his feet. Asking him to hold it in his hands.

She felt terrified. This love she'd held for so long no longer her dirty secret.

That she was offering it at such an awful time.

But she had to believe that he felt it, too.

She had to believe in *this*.

Had to believe in them.

It couldn't be possible for it to be one-sided. Not when it was so beautiful and strong.

Ryder emitted a groan.

Guttural.

Languished in its affliction.

He took her hand that was on his cheek, and he held it between both of his. He brought her knuckles to his lips, his voice so strained that she struggled to understand what he said. "I love you, Dakota. So fucking much."

He looked away, to the wall, away from her face. "But not like that."

The last of his admission cracked, so jagged it cut into her soul. Her knees went weak as his rejection cut her in two.

She couldn't stand beneath his pity. The way he hadn't even been able to look her in the eye when he said it.

But not like that.

She choked and tried to suppress a sob.

To hold her heartbreak back. It busted out, anyway, a cry of misery that she couldn't contain. She squeezed her eyes closed and tried to reel it in.

To stand as his friend.

Because what kind of monster was she if she made this about her?

But she couldn't help but feel a part of it was.

It was about her.

About him.

About them.

Who they were supposed to be together.

"Please don't cry, Dakota." Every sharp angle of Ryder's face pinched in misery as he whispered the words against her knuckles. "Don't cry. I'm not worth it. You're so much better than giving that love to me. You deserve the world. Everything in it. Everything it has to offer. I want you to chase it. Every good thing. Please."

She wanted to curl her fingers into his shirt.

Tell him he was wrong.

That what she wanted was him.

Beg him to love her back.

But he didn't.

He didn't love her.

Not like *that*.

Dizziness spun as her chest cracked wide open.

Stricken.

Grieved.

Oh, God, Dakota thought she was going to puke. Because she'd just confessed it all and the man she loved was devastated by the loss of someone else.

Amelia.

How hadn't she known?

Why didn't she see it?

She was a fool. Such a fool.

"I…I'm sorry for your loss." She forced it out, the words riding out on a shattered sob.

Before she could make it any worse, she turned and ran down his walkway.

She needed to get away before she completely broke apart.

By the time she got into her car, she couldn't breathe, and her chest was squeezing so badly that the little air she could get wheezed up her raw throat.

She started it, her tires squealing as she sped from the curb.

Tears blurred her sight as she drove.

She had to get away.

She choked out an aggrieved sob when she realized she really had nowhere to go.

No one to rely on.

No one who would understand.

Paisley had moved a month ago, and Ryder had been the one person she could always go to. The one who would hold her secrets.

Her truths and her fears.

A cry ripped from her soul.

She drove out of Time River like it could leave the heartbreak behind.

Like she might be able to pretend she hadn't been shattered.

That she hadn't been such a fool to put herself on the line.

She ended up at a bar in Poplar.

It was loud and packed with people.

She didn't know any of them, but she didn't want to be alone.

She couldn't bear going back to her empty room.

Couldn't bear to think of the vacant branch that would sway beneath the moon.

Her mother had always warned them about the risks of drowning their miseries in alcohol, but it was the only solution she could find right then.

Just for one night.

For one night she had to numb this pain because it was too great.

And maybe it was stupid and desperate when the guy took the stool beside her. Pathetic that the way he looked at her felt nice.

And when he set his hand on her knee, she didn't flinch.

She didn't want to be herself.

Just for one night, she didn't want to be the girl who would love Ryder Nash for the rest of her life.

For one night, she wanted to forget about him.

Because she knew tomorrow, it would be Ryder she remembered.

Chapter Forty-Six

Dakota

TEARS STREAMED DOWN MY CHEEKS, AND I SNIFFLED, WIPING them away as I stared out the rambling wall of windows that overlooked the back of Caleb and Paisley's property from where I sat curled in the banquette table.

A sprawling lawn rolled out from the back of the house, running all the way to the river and woods in the distance. Beyond the copse of towering trees, the stunning mountains that hedged Time River touched the endless blue sky.

I couldn't imagine a more breathtaking view.

But I was having a really hard time recognizing the beauty right then. Not when everything had soured.

My mind wouldn't stop running through the torment of everything he'd revealed.

After Amelia had died, after I'd confessed to him how I really felt, it had taken a long time for Ryder and me to get back to a place where we could be friends. To a place where we were comfortable around each other. Where looking at him didn't ache so horribly that I felt like I couldn't breathe.

He'd stayed away from me for months. During that period, we'd only seen each other in passing, and every single time I'd felt cracked wide open.

Like I was missing an intrinsic piece of myself.

What had made it even worse was when the lender had called and told me my loan was going to go through. It was the one time I'd gone to Ryder to speak with him. I'd told him I couldn't accept it. It was the first time he'd ever shown any anger around me. Rage clouding his eyes before he'd simply refused.

So, I'd taken it.

Poured myself into renovating the restaurant and making it mine.

I had made an oath to myself that I would repay him as quickly as I could. Considered it a loan and tried to compartmentalize it as that.

It was the most I'd spoken to him until the day Kayden had been born. There'd been a light knocking at my hospital room door, and it'd been Ryder who had poked his head through the crack.

He'd said he couldn't go on with the way things were between us. He said it wasn't supposed to be like that. We were family, and he cared about me, and he wanted to be a part of my life.

That day, he'd held my newborn son in his arms and whispered that he was beautiful. Promised he'd always love him, and he was there for both of us, no matter what we needed.

We'd never discussed any of the things I'd admitted that day in his foyer.

And now that I understood it, why he'd turned me away, the reason he'd lied and told me that he didn't love me, I wished that I didn't.

I jolted when Paisley's voice broke into my thoughts. "More coffee?"

"Sure."

She grabbed the carafe from the coffee maker and carried it over, eyeing me as she refilled my mug that I'd been nursing for what had to have been the last six hours. I felt like I couldn't physically move.

Stagnant and stuck.

The fact I'd even managed to make it out of bed had to be considered a miracle.

"Thank you," I told her.

She sank into the chair next to me. "How are you doing?"

I brought the steaming mug to my lips, inhaling the scent more than actually tasting the coffee. "As good as can be expected."

I turned back to look through the windows. Lost. In a trance that I didn't know how to pull myself from. Because this whole thing had to be a bad dream.

A nightmare I'd fallen into.

"I don't expect you to be feeling a whole lot of good right now, Dakota."

More tears clouded my sight before they fell. Frustrated, I swiped them away. "I can't believe he kept that from me for all these years."

Paisley's hair was twisted in a loose, messy knot on top of her head. It fell over the side when she reached for me from over the top of the table. She set her hand over mine that I had fisted on the wood and squeezed. "But if he thought that money was getting him out and it was used for a valid purpose? For something good?"

"Drug money, Paisley?" A high-pitched sound came out with the whisper. "He gave me *drug money.*"

Agony slayed, slicing through my middle. I tried to suppress another cry, but it ripped out, anyway.

Sympathy pinched Paisley's face. "I don't believe Ryder is a bad person. He's not greedy, Dakota. He's not, and you know it. And if he said he was trapped? Then I have to believe that."

"Does it make it any better, though?"

She blinked at me as she squeezed my hand tighter. "I guess only you can decide that, but the one thing I do know is that we all have things in our lives that we regret. Things we would take back. And most of the time we get lucky enough that there is good that comes from it. A silver lining that we couldn't see. We learn a lesson we needed. Find out what's important. It teaches us how to walk better in the future. And I need to believe the same of Ryder."

I sniffled, blinking as I turned my gaze back to the soaring panes of glass. "He put us in danger."

The pad of her thumb rubbed over the back of my hand. "Which is why he stayed away from you for all these years. He can't help it that my bestie is irresistible."

She tacked a tease on the last.

A pained chuckle slid off my tongue. "I guess he and I were inevitable."

A magnetism that couldn't be avoided.

Gravity.

My words narrowed in pained emphasis. "I wish he would have told me. Confided in me then. We could have figured something out."

Speculation pulled through Paisley's expression. "He told you they made it clear what would happen to anyone he cared about if he left. And I might not know the details, but I can only imagine what that might have looked like. He was probably terrified, Dakota. Terrified of putting someone he loved in harm's way. Put yourself in those shoes. I doubt you would have been able to confess it, either. But he's also a good man who knows he can't allow it to continue, so he's taken the step."

Fear spiraled.

A battering of horror.

What if that step cost him his life?

I couldn't even let myself contemplate it.

Couldn't handle the idea.

"He lied to me," I told her, hating how bad it hurt that he had. That I'd been so gullible. So deceivable. That my dream had been built on something so ugly and vile.

A clatter of pounding footsteps cut off our conversation, and we both turned to see Evelyn come barreling into the kitchen.

All messy brown hair that was in her face, the little girl wearing a pink tee, jeans, and matching pink cowgirl boots. "Mommy! I took Kayden to the barn to see the horses, and he got to sit on Mazzy. He loved it!"

She threw her hands in the air and planted her feet in a lunge, like she was calling a touchdown.

Paisley's grandfather wandered in behind her, chuckling under his breath. "Those two would have spent the entire day out in that barn if we would have let them. Had to drag them back in so we could get some lunch."

"That's because the barn is my very favorite place in the whole world, Grandpa," Evelyn told him, perfectly nonchalant.

The old man's face lit in staggering joy, and his eyes moved between Paisley and the child, cherishing every moment he had with them.

Paisley was actually his granddaughter, and he and his wife had raised her from when she was little. Paisley and Caleb had moved him here into the house so he could be near them. So he wouldn't be alone.

Caleb sauntered in last, carrying Kayden.

"Mommy! I see the horsey!" Kayden pointed his little finger toward the wall like I could see into the barn.

I swallowed the misery down and forced myself to smile at the treasure that was my son.

"You saw the horses? That is amazing."

Caleb set him onto his feet, and he went bouncing up to Evelyn's side.

"I ride horsey, my Evie?" He patted his chest, and she giggled like mad as she reached out to take his hand.

"Not right now. We have to eat lunch, and then maybe we can again."

"How about Grandpa makes us some sandwiches, and then we'll go back out for a bit?" Paisley's grandfather suggested.

"Yes!" Evelyn shouted.

"Yes!" Kayden copied her, dancing on his feet when it made her laugh.

"These two," Caleb rumbled as he came deeper into the room, easing our way. Worry was written in his expression as he approached. He came up behind Paisley's chair and pressed a soft kiss to the crown of her head, but it was me he was looking at.

Concern weighed heavy in his eyes. He'd told me last night that he had known Ryder was involved in something just because he'd been involved in enough corruption in his own life that he knew when something shady was going down.

But he had no idea how bad it was. That Ryder was in that much trouble.

Ryder had kept it from everyone who was important to him. Except for when he'd finally hit a breaking point and had gone to Ezra.

Another wave of alarm went off.

Caleb touched my arm. "We're here for you, Dakota. Both you and your son. And I know I don't have the details or know exactly what is going on, but the one thing I know, for certain and without fail, is my cousin loves you, and he would do absolutely anything for you."

But that was the problem, wasn't it?

What he'd done for me, and the lies he'd told to cover it.

⁂

"Do you think we should just postpone the party?" Paisley asked as she followed me to the door. She chewed at her nail in contemplation, at war with how to proceed.

I shrugged even though I was in the middle of that war, too.

A war that conflicted and raged, so many questions at odds with each other I didn't know how I was even standing beneath the barrage of bombs.

I'd spent the entire day yesterday crying, both numb and feeling too much, and I knew I had to at least get up and do something with myself today. I couldn't let it fester.

"I don't know," I told her. "I think we just…continue to plan it and then you can make the decision how you want to proceed based on what happens."

Based on what happens.

I nearly choked over a sob.

I had no idea what any of this would mean.

What was going to happen to Ryder.

What danger he was in both with whoever he was trying to get away from and legally.

I couldn't just call up Ezra and ask what kind of deal had been made, and I'd fled from Ryder's house long before any of those questions had arisen.

Now they came at me perpetually.

Relentlessly.

"Are you sure you want to deal with it?"

"I honestly need something to do to take my mind off things."

The pain and the torment that continually wound through me. Because I missed him, so much, and it was brutal not to answer the texts that he continually sent.

Begging me to talk to him.

To listen.

But I'd listened for so long, and now I didn't know if I could ever believe what he had to say again.

"Only if you're positive."

"I am. And besides, Caleb deserves his day," I promised her.

She swallowed hard. "And you're sure you don't want to stay here for a couple more days?"

I flinched, hating the idea of being alone, but I still had a dream to follow. A restaurant to run. The life I'd built for Kayden. I couldn't allow this to destroy any of that, even though the clot of guilt inside me was so big I was sure it was obstructing the flow of blood.

But I would figure out something.

How to make this right.

How to pay restitution for a sin that had been made on my part.

"I need to be at the café by six in the morning. I think it's best if I go home."

Home.

The thought of it juddered through me. I'd only been staying with Ryder for a short time, but his house had come to feel that way. Like it was where we belonged.

Those walls safety and love.

"Okay, but if you need anything at all, I want you to call me. Caleb meant what he said. You and Kayden always have a place here."

"I know. Thank you so much for being there for me."

Paisley wrapped me in her arms. "Um, hello, you're my Doodle-Boo. You think I wouldn't be?"

A wave of appreciation billowed. "I know, and I'm so grateful for that."

She stepped back, but she continued to hold me by the outside of the arms. "Call me tonight before you go to sleep, okay? I'm going to be worried about you."

"I will. But you don't have to worry. I'm going to be okay."

"I know you are, but that doesn't mean you're not in pain right now, and I'd do anything to take that away."

"Which is why I love you so much." I forced a smile.

"What's not to love?" She let the razzing wind into her voice, and I chuckled through the waves of sorrow as I opened the door to step out into the late afternoon light. Warmth saturated the air, the fading summer still holding on, though the color of the leaves on the trees had begun to change.

Kayden was with Evelyn on the lawn that fronted the house. He squealed as his little feet padded the ground, and she chased him, her giggles riding free as they played.

The second Kayden saw me, he changed course and ran my direction. "Mommy, help me! Evie is a horsey monster!"

I scooped him up and hugged him close. "Oh, no, a horsey monster? I'll protect you."

Evelyn cracked up, and she used both her hands to push the thick locks of her hair out of her face. "I'm not even really a monster, Auntie Dakota. Did you know that?"

I ran my hand over the top of her head. "Are you sure?" I teased.

"If I was really a horse, I'd be a nice horse, like Mazzy."

Affection rippled, and I leaned down and kissed her cheek. "You are the sweetest, Evie. We'll see you soon. Thank you for helping to take care of Kayden while we were here."

"I really liked it and I can be a babysitter and I don't even need any money."

"Well, that's an offer that's too hard to pass up," I told her, glancing at Paisley who watched her with a crush of devotion.

They all walked us to our car, hovering as I strapped in Kayden, and Paisley hugged me again once he was safely buckled. "If you need me, I'll come running," she said as I sat in the driver's seat.

I pushed the button to start it. "I know."

She nodded, shut my door, and took Evelyn's hand. I put the car into drive, fighting the swell of trepidation that rolled over the top of me when I caught sight of Caleb where he stood against a pillar on the front porch.

I knew he'd spoken to Ryder. Knew he'd been wrought with a brand-new turmoil after, even though he hadn't offered me any more details.

I forced myself to drive.

Kayden fell asleep during the thirty-mile trip back into town, while I silently cried, unable to keep the worries or thoughts or heartbreak at bay.

I was thankful when I finally pulled into the café parking lot. It was already packed with Sunday evening dinner guests. I drove through and rounded the small road that led to my house.

The second I turned off the car to the overbearing silence, I decided to run to the restaurant to make sure things were going smoothly. Or maybe it was just that it made me sick to think of going into the vacancy of my little house.

Nauseous to think of returning to the way things had been before I'd left here two weeks ago.

Only things would never be the same, would they? I'd forever be marked with Ryder's love and eternally scarred by his betrayal.

I pulled Kayden out of his seat and carried him into the café. Everyone always fawned over him whenever he came in, and Beth took him while I went into the office so I could print out the recipe for the breakfast special tomorrow so the cooks would have it first thing in the morning.

I found I wasn't settled being in the restaurant, either, so I quickly worked through a few tasks and headed back out into the main dining room, promising my staff I would see them in the morning.

By the time I stepped back out, the sun had begun its descent toward the west. The air cooled even farther, a gentle breeze gliding through that tickled across my skin.

Somehow, it churned as an unease in my senses.

A sticky sensation that nothing was right.

Or maybe it was just what was waiting on me that sent queasiness rushing through my body.

A dread I'd all but forgotten over the last couple days.

Because when I opened the gate, I found Trey sitting on the single step of my stoop, resting his elbows on his thighs, bent over like he was torn between two worlds, too.

I froze while his head snapped up. He blinked through uncertainty while I fought the urge to turn and run. To refuse him the right to Kayden because I didn't think I could handle losing anything else right then. Not moments or days or peace because I didn't know this man at all, and I had no idea what kind of father he would be.

But I couldn't move, and it felt like my feet had grown roots as I stared across at him for the longest time. But his attention wasn't on me. It was on Kayden who pointed at him from where he was in my arms. "Look it, Mommy. A man."

And that man slowly stood, itching, roughing a hand over the top of his head. "I'm sorry to show like this. I just…took the chance you might be home." He let go of a self-deprecating laugh. "Of course, I've been sitting here for the last three hours after I knocked and no one answered."

I finally got myself together enough that I moved, though I inched down the pathway like I was tiptoeing through landmines. "You should have gotten in contact with me first."

He dipped his head, scruffing a palm over his face before he returned his gaze to us. "I know. I just…couldn't stop thinking about him. Couldn't get him off my mind. And I knew I had to meet him."

Reservations gusted, but I still kept walking. Two feet away from him, I stopped, staring at the stranger's face. "Okay. But anything beyond this has to be planned if we're going to figure this out."

"Thank you."

My throat felt thick as I wound around him and took the one step onto the stoop where I pushed the key into the lock and opened the door. Emptiness echoed back, and I had to brace myself against the impact of it.

I stepped in and Trey came in behind me. He shut the door, and I frowned when he reached out and locked it. Disquiet pressed at my senses, the blunt force of a dull, rusted blade.

"I always knew you were the key," he rumbled when he turned back to me.

I took a step backward, hugging Kayden tighter against my chest. "What are you talking about?"

"I couldn't have hoped for a better outcome when you got pregnant," he continued. "I figured the day would come when you became useful. I knew Ryder would forget the warning I'd given him that day. You know, I just had a sense that he was about to get up to no good. I'm good with foresight like that. Can tell when people are questioning their loyalty. It's why no one can touch me. So I sent one of my guys to sniff things out over here. Stir things up to see what Ryder would do."

Sickness clawed as realization sank down deep. All the way to the bone.

It was one of his men who'd broken in here?

They'd been...watching us?

"I can tell by the way he's acting that he's getting foolish enough to think about double crossing me, and I think the two of you are the only thing that can remind him of the mistake he would be making."

All the uncertainty and reservations had bled from his features.

In their place was malice.

Without hesitating, I turned on my heel and darted through the small space toward the door on the opposite side of the kitchen.

It was our only chance of escape.

I made it across the room, frantic as I tried to turn the deadbolt.

But he was already there, taking a fistful of my hair and yanking me back. I cried out, and Kayden wailed, and a second later he had Kayden ripped out of my arms and I was shoved to the floor. I landed hard on my hip. Pain fractured up my side, but I scrambled onto my hands and knees, ready to push to my feet, only I stalled out when I was met with the barrel of a gun.

Terror pinned me to the spot. A glacier that had frozen me over.

I looked up at him where he had my squirming son held against him in a vise grip.

The man who'd manipulated Ryder. One who'd manipulated me. Some *random guy* who'd talked me up in a bar.

And I knew. And I knew. He'd followed me that night. Used me. A pawn to be exacted whenever the time arose.

It was *time* that had just started for Ryder and me.

Time we never should have wasted.

Time I was terrified had just run out.

Chapter Forty-Seven
Ryder

"**YOU HAVE TO LIE LOW, RYDER.**"

Ezra's voice barely cut into the mayhem that had infiltrated. Heart and body and mind.

I couldn't sit still. I kept raking my hands through my hair as I paced my shop, trying to calm the disorder. But it didn't matter what I did, I couldn't shake it.

Agitation ran through me on a circuit.

It'd been racing since the moment Dakota had left my house Friday night. It'd only grown into something insufferable after Caleb had texted to let me know she'd left the ranch to return home.

It wasn't like I expected her to take up residence there, but fuck, I couldn't stand the thought of her on her own right then.

Not when the evidence of how quickly things could go south was clear. The proof of it was in the fact my body was covered in bruises from that fucking metal rod. The left side of my face black and blue. The warning one of Dare's men had issued in my ear.

But at least any time the subject of Dakota had ever come up between me and Dare, I'd maintained that she was just my best friend's little sister. Played it off like she was more of a nuisance than anything because I couldn't take the risk that he might know that she was more.

It left me sick that her staying at my house for the last couple weeks might have made it obvious.

"Fuck, it was stupid for me to insist that she come to my place," I spat, pacing the other direction.

I should have known.

I should have fucking known.

It was the whole reason I'd stayed away from her for all these years.

"We have two days until this goes down, Ryder, and you need to keep your shit together between now and then." Leaning forward, Ezra clasped his hands together where he sat on a metal chair at one of the desks. He'd been trying to talk some sense into me for the last hour when there was no sense to be found.

Worry hunted me. Stalked me. But it was me who felt like the beast.

"The best thing Dakota can do right now is return to her normal routine," Ezra said. "Go home. Work the restaurant. If you don't want to draw more attention to her, then you have to stop giving it to her."

I bit out a sound of disgust. "It's not like she wants anything to do with me, anyway."

And I deserved it. Deserved it after what I'd done.

"You kept something from her that was huge, Ryder. Something that she's likely feeling guilty for. You need to give her time to process through it and understand why you did it. And *you* need this time away from her. We can't afford this thing falling apart."

"And if Dare already knows?"

Ezra blew out a sigh. "Dare's going down, Ryder. You know this. When you came to me, the DEA had already been watching him for two years. You just gave them the extra evidence to make this happen sooner. He's not getting away with any of this. We just need to see this through so you're safe from the fallout. Make sure you're on the right side of it."

The smallest fraction of relief eased inside me. The only thing I wanted was to put Dare behind bars, where he belonged.

As for me, I'd struck a deal. I was giving them the safehouse location, and they were going to raid while I was there loading the car Tuesday night.

I'd be arrested, too, but I'd get off on a technicality.

My immunity for setting this up.

Ezra looked at his phone when a text went off. A small smile tugged at the edge of his mouth.

"Who is it?" I asked.

"Olivia. She said she just helped her grandma make dinner for us, and it's Sunday and it's family day and I'd better hurry up and get home."

His little girl was adorable. A year older than Evelyn. I figured she'd taken the role of mothering since her own mother had been killed a couple years ago.

And I realized as Ezra stood, all massive muscle and hulking height, ghosts forever writhing deep in his eyes, that I was fucking lucky.

Dakota was safe and we were going to make sure we put this threat away permanently so Dare couldn't hurt anyone ever again.

Ezra hadn't gotten that chance.

His wife had been stolen from him, and he'd never even had a warning.

"You should get back to them."

"Yeah." He reached out and squeezed my shoulder. "This is for the best right now, Ryder. Let her be and let's get this behind us and then you two can figure out your shit."

I gave him a tight nod. "Okay."

"Give him a little shit for the attack, play it that you didn't see it coming."

"Already did."

Ezra cracked a smile. "Don't need to coach you, do I?"

I scoffed. "I've had to survive this life for years."

Air puffed from his nose. "See you Tuesday, brother."

A promise came with it.

A wedge of hope slashed through the turmoil.

I was finally going to get my life back. I just prayed it wasn't too late to get Dakota back, too.

Ezra dipped out, and I blew out a sigh, snagged my keys from the table, and jogged out of the shop. I locked the door behind me before I hopped into my car, deciding to head home, the way I would any other night.

I was halfway there when a call rang through the Bluetooth.

Rage blistered my insides when I saw Dare's name lighting the screen.

"What?" It wasn't like his calls weren't always met with animosity. I was all about keeping it consistent.

Except a wail echoed through the background. A wail that stabbed through my heart. A wail I would recognize anywhere.

Kayden.

Dare tsked. "It seems my son doesn't like me very much."

Ice froze over my soul, and a bolt of fury cracked through the middle of it.

There was shuffling in the background, and the gagged whimper that curled through the line tore me in two.

"Dakota doesn't like me much, either, though she liked me plenty the night she let me fuck her in my truck."

Bile erupted in my throat. "You fucking bastard. I will kill you."

He tsked again. "I don't think you're in the position to be making threats, now, are you? Be at my office in one hour, and you get to choose which one lives. Come alone, or neither of them do."

Without saying anything else, the line went dead.

Terror ricocheted, pumping my blood into chaos.

My mind twisted through what he'd said. What he'd implied.

He'd fathered Kayden, which meant he'd known all along. Had planned to use them as bait. As pawns for whenever the time arose.

And it wouldn't matter if Kayden's blood did run through his veins.

He had no fealty or morality.

He'd gladly hurt Kayden if it won him what he wanted.

My sight turned red, and my knuckles blanched white as I held onto the steering wheel. I made a U in the middle of the road, the tires squealing as my car fishtailed. The second it righted, I gunned it and flew in the other direction.

I hit the desolate two-lane road that I'd taken so many times. Each time I felt like I was cutting out a piece of myself. Leaving it behind. But this time, I was getting it back.

The only things that mattered.

I wavered, contemplating, every scenario curling through my thoughts. I finally tapped the button and dialed Ezra.

"Miss me already?" He tossed out the razzing.

Only I croaked around the terror and fury that clotted my throat. "He has them."

Silence resounded for a beat before Ezra heaved out a sound of horror that he attempted to quell. "Stay calm, Ryder."

"I'm not staying fucking calm, Ezra. He has them. He told me to be at his office in an hour. To come alone. He said they both were dead if I didn't. Otherwise, I got to choose which one would live."

"Shit," he hissed. "Where are you?"

"On my way."

"Fuck, Ryder, you can't take off over there. Pull over."

I could hear his tires squealing as he turned around, his engine roaring as he rammed on the accelerator.

"You know that's not going to happen. He wants me there, and I'm going. You can't call anyone to come in blazing. No sirens."

"I'm going to be right behind you. Just wait and don't do anything stupid."

The laughter that rolled out of me was hard. Close to deranged. Because I'd done a million stupid things in my life. Made uncountable mistakes. Had stumbled and failed.

But this time wasn't going to be one of them.

⁓⁂⁓

My heart battered at my ribs as I came careening to a stop in the alley behind the dry cleaners. I'd forced myself to slow, knowing it would close the gap between mine and Ezra's arrival.

Now, I felt like I was going to tremble out of my skin. My blood pulsing so hard that it thundered in my ears. Could feel it in my fingertips that raged with the need to end anyone who would ever think about harming Dakota.

About harming Kayden.

But this bastard always preyed on the innocent. Wielded his rancid power over the blameless.

I should have known that he would have been watching closer. That there'd been no way to hide what I felt for Dakota.

Not then and not now.

Should have known he would have twisted it in his favor. Hunted her, used her, shored it away like blackmail until its fitted time.

I was shaking with the weight of it as I tapped at the heavy door at the back.

It cracked open, and Pete peered at me through the narrow slit. Rage clouded my sight, and my fists curled just as a sick, satisfied laugh rolled from him when he saw my busted to shit face. "Looks like you ran into some trouble."

"Fuck off, Pete."

He only laughed lower as he widened the door for me to step in. He pushed me against the wall and patted me down to make sure I wasn't carrying, his voice in my ear when he warned, "If I were you, I would have already left town. Left no trail. Disappeared."

Yeah, because he was a fucking coward. All of them were. Out for themselves, willing to hurt anyone if it protected their asses.

I bit it back because my issue wasn't with Pete right then.

My only concern was the torment that rode through the air. Stagnant terror that coursed through the descending night.

I had to force myself to keep my cool and not go rushing the door, and I swallowed around the razors in my throat as Pete led me the rest of the way down the hall.

Two more of Dare's guards rested against the walls, watching me like I was a dead man walking.

With each step, Kayden's cries grew louder.

Pete tapped at the door with the barrel of his gun before he cracked it open. "He's here."

"Alone?"

"Yes."

"Bring him in."

The door opened the rest of the way. All the oxygen punched from my lungs as I scanned the room.

Dakota faced me where she was against the far wall, bound to a chair, her arms behind its back and a gag in her mouth.

She whimpered when she saw me, cinnamon eyes flashing in terror.

In pain and relief.

Dare had Kayden sitting on his desk, and he had an arm around him. In his other hand was a knife, and he dug the tip of it into the wood, turning it round and round like he was bored.

Kayden's little face was soaked with tears, and he flailed when he saw me, stretching his arms out to me. "My Rye-Rye."

He smacked his chest, giving me one of those emphatic nods, urging me to come to him.

To help him.

Save him.

I toiled in the agony of it, while Dare tightened his arm around him and cracked one of those sinister smiles. "Ah, Ryder, so nice of you to join in on this little family reunion."

Shifting, Dare took the tip of the knife and barely dragged it down

Kayden's thigh. Not deep enough to cut but enough to send horror ricocheting against the walls.

Dakota wailed into her gag and thrashed in the confines of the chair, making the legs bang on the floor.

I curled my hands into fists, every part of me wanting to fly forward and rip Kayden from his arms. But that was too risky. Too much of a chance. And I had to play this right if everyone was going to make it out of this.

I let a scoff puff from my nose, hoping to draw his full attention to me. "You're that pathetic that you need to prey on my best friend's sister? Going to those lengths to coerce me? Seems awful desperate to me."

He wasn't biting, though. The smug-fucking-smirk he always used when he had someone trapped emerged on his revolting face. He rocked back in the chair, just a fraction, enough that it let a tiny bit of air into my lungs since he didn't have Kayden completely curled against him. "Do you think I didn't know you wanted to get out because of her? You think I couldn't see it in your eyes? You think we didn't know you were sneaking off to meet her every night? Your obsession with her was clear to me. It was clear to Amelia."

He shrugged. "So, I figured I should check out what all the fuss was about."

Dakota whimpered while Kayden continued to cry, "I go my Rye-Rye's house. I go, my Rye-Rye. *Pease.*"

Agony cut and slayed. The truth that I was the one who had gotten them into this. That I was responsible.

I'd gladly spend my last breath getting them out of it.

"You know, it was a shame that I had to let Amelia go. She was so in tune with you. You two could have been so great together."

Let Amelia go?

Hatred burned hot.

"But you needed to know what betraying me would cost, which was why I had to follow our sweet Dakota that night." He tsked it like the sleazy fuck he was. "It was simply precautionary, added insurance." He shrugged. "I'd hoped I'd never have to tap into that resource."

His voice came out like he had an ounce of regret as he pressed the tip of the knife a little deeper into Kayden's thigh.

Resource.

As if that little boy meant nothing.

Nothing when that monster had fathered him.

"And now you've forced me into this."

"You touch either of them, and it will be your last day." It came out shards.

A rough chuckle fumbled up his throat. "Big words to be spouting when you're surrounded by my guards."

"What the hell do you want from me?"

"What I've wanted all along. For you to understand that you belong to me. I molded you. I picked you up from a sniveling, pathetic kid and made you who you are today. And who you are is mine. I've always demanded loyalty of my men, Ryder, and you make me more money than all of them combined. So no, I won't kill you like you deserve, but I will pluck off the people you care about, one by one, until you understand your place. Because I know you're plotting something, and I won't let you derail the plans I have for you."

It occurred to me that he didn't know the actual details. That he had no idea how deep *my plans* went. That I was set on destroying him.

I refused to stop until I saw that through. Until Dakota and Kayden would be safe forever.

I just had to wait for the right moment.

The right moment came one second later when there was a thud outside somewhere in the hall.

It was enough to distract Dare for the flash of a second. For his attention to dart to the door. Enough for me to be sure that Ezra was there and handling the guards.

"What the fuck is going on?" He frowned toward the commotion, like he was just catching on to the fact that things were about to go sideways for him.

That his reign was about to come to an end.

I took the chance, and I dove forward and grabbed him by the wrist of the hand that held the knife.

I bent it back hard.

Hard enough that he roared in pain, and the knife clattered to the ground.

"You piece of shit, you betrayed me," he spat.

I kept his wrist bent back, making him twist to the side, while I delivered a punch so hard to his face that he flailed backward.

It tipped the chair over and sent him toppling with it.

Kayden wailed, and my soul shattered with it because I fucking hated putting him through this. I swooped him off the desk just as I heard a barrage of gunshots go off in the hall.

A frenzy lit.

Chaos.

And I knew I only had one minute.

One fucking minute to get them out of this.

Running around the desk, I dipped down to snag the knife from the floor.

Dakota's eyes were wide, like she was trying to express a thousand things as I rushed for her, my heart battering at my ribs as I scrambled to get behind the chair so I could cut her free while still trying to hold onto Kayden. I sawed the blade over the thick rope.

Sweat beaded on my brow, a sticky heat rushing through my veins as I tried to hurry, desperate, needing to get them out of there and to safety.

Dakota kept whimpering, and I was mumbling, "I have you, I have you, I have you."

Finally, I cut through her bindings and freed her arms. She reached up and yanked the gag from her mouth, heaving for oxygen as she jumped to her feet.

Only there was no relief.

Because she screamed, "Ryder!" just as the blow came from out of nowhere. The office chair cracked against the back of my head. It sent me to my knees, knocking the knife from my hand and sending the metal clattering against the floor. I fought to hold Kayden against me, fully wrapping myself around him, trying to protect him from the attack while Dare jumped onto me from behind.

Fists kept cracking against the back of my skull and my temples. Doing their best to black me out.

I managed to get Kayden to his feet, yelling, "Dakota! Get Kayden and get out of here!" at the same time as I threw an elbow into Dare's gut.

It knocked him back enough that I was able to turn around, though he was on me again in a flash, pushing me to the ground as he threw a fist into my face.

It cracked into my jaw. Pain screamed, but I didn't care. I rammed my forehead into his nose.

He howled as blood gushed, and he came back at me full strength. "You think you can play me? Have you forgotten who I am?" he wheezed. I think it was then he knew the depths that I had gone. That his building was now surrounded by a slew of agents.

That he had no way out.

I kicked and punched, but the fucker was huge, and he got his hands around my neck.

He squeezed, and I clawed at his hands while dragging up a knee, trying to hit in any spot that would make him lose hold.

Another round of gunshots rang out, this time so many, a blitz going down on the other side of the wall.

And I prayed that Ezra was holding his own. That he was safe. That he was razing the depraved assholes that roamed this city.

"You piece of shit. I will kill you," Dare grumbled through the exertion, squeezing tighter. "You betrayed me, after everything I did for you."

My consciousness ebbed, coherency fading as he cinched his hands tighter around my neck.

Suddenly, his eyes went wide, and he roared, releasing me as he whipped around and climbed to his feet.

I rolled over, choking and gasping for air, desperate to draw it into my lungs.

In my blurred sight, I registered that Dakota was backing away, pushing Kayden behind her, her hand trembling as she held up the knife. A knife that dripped with blood.

She'd stabbed him.

Saved me.

"Stay back. Stay away from us." She could barely get the words out around the quivering of her mouth.

Dare lumbered that way, injured, though the aggression and adrenaline kept him standing. "You fucking bitch. I should have killed you years ago. Slit your fucking throat while you were riding my cock."

She jabbed at him when he got close, missing, and his hand swung out, cracking her against the face. The momentum slammed her against the wall. She hit it hard and tumbled onto the ground.

Kayden wailed.

Fury pounded through me, and he went to go for her again, but I was already on my feet, jumping onto his back. My arm locked around his throat that time, and I pulled so hard that he dropped to his knees.

And I didn't let go.

I squeezed as his nails raked at my arms. As he gurgled and fought. As he tried to toss me off.

"This is for every kid you ever got addicted," I growled at his ear. "For every person you've ever hurt. For Amelia. But most of all, for Dakota and Kayden, so they never have to spend one second of their lives worried about you."

The fingers clawing at my arms began to fail, and his arms dropped to his sides.

I held fast until the blood ceased to beat in his body.

One second later, the door burst open, and Ezra came through with his gun drawn, followed by three DEA agents.

I let the fucker go.

He flopped face-first onto the ground.

I went to go for Kayden and Dakota, but Ezra put his hand out, stopping me. "Don't move, Ryder. Stay right there."

I gulped, helpless to do anything as Ezra and the agents cleared the room before a group of paramedics descended.

A minute later the agent I'd met with after I'd contacted Ezra appeared in the doorway. "Come with me."

Chapter Forty-Eight

Ryder

How many hours I'd spent in the office the size of a tissue box, I didn't know. The only thing I knew was I'd itched, continually scrubbing my palms over my face and yanking at my hair as they asked me the same fucking questions over and over again.

My story needed to be straight.

I thought the only question worthy of being answered right then was the one I kept asking. "Are they okay? Someone tell me if they're fucking okay."

I didn't care if they charged me.

If they put me behind bars for the rest of my life.

If the deal I'd struck was a trap they'd set.

The only thing that mattered was if Dakota and Kayden were okay.

Except it wasn't a trap.

I was free.

I wasn't in danger.

Anyone who knew me in Dare's ring was dead. His close circle of men slain during the shootout.

The raid currently happening at the safehouse would be attributed to the two-year-long investigation that had been conducted by the DEA. They'd finally gathered enough evidence that they'd made their move, even though I had been the one to provide that last bit of *evidence* they had been lacking.

My name would never be mentioned. I had to believe Ezra had a whole lot to do with that.

But the only thing that mattered was Dakota and Kayden, so even though they'd instructed I go home and lay low, I was walking through the sliding double doors that led into the emergency room in Poplar.

It was the same hospital where Amelia had been taken, and I could still feel the hopelessness and despair I'd felt that day. Ghosts that hung from the walls.

I went straight to the reception desk, her name haggard when it slipped from my tongue. "Dakota Cooper?"

The man behind the counter looked up. Surprise covered his expression. No question, I looked like I could use some medical attention myself.

But I couldn't feel anything except for the desperate need to ensure they were fine.

To go to them.

To see them safe and whole.

He finally turned away and tapped into his computer.

"I need your ID so I can make you a visitor badge."

I fumbled to get out my license, trying to breathe as I waited for him to fill out the information. He passed me a sticker. "Put that on your shirt. It's room E-16."

"Thank you."

He buzzed me through the double doors that led into an open room. A nurses' station was in the middle, and there were a bunch of curtained off areas on each side.

A hall branched off at the back, and a sign indicated rooms E-11 – E-20.

I hurried that way, turning the corner and hitting the hall that had private rooms with sliding doors. I increased my pace when I saw Cody, Kayla, and Dakota's mom loitering outside a door halfway down.

"Are they okay?" It heaved out of me when I got close enough.

At the sound of my voice, Cody whirled around just as I was making it to them.

And I shouldn't have been surprised when he threw a fist and clocked me in the jaw. I didn't deflect it or fight back because I knew I deserved it.

Kayla yelped and Dakota's mother gasped. "Oh my God, Cody."

Cody ignored them both when he took me by the shirt and yanked me toward him, spitting in my face, "You don't get to ask if they're okay, Ryder.

Not when they are in this mess because of you. Because of what you've done. You think I don't know you've been touching her? Feeding her those lies you love to tell? I warned you to stay away from her. I told you. You think you're good enough for my sister? I think tonight has proven to us all that you're nothing but trash. You're supposed to be my best-fucking-friend. And you did this? I can't fucking believe you. After you promised to stay away from her. Get the fuck out of here."

"I need to see her." Guilt strangling, I tried to angle around him, to get loose of his hands.

I needed to see her.

Just once.

Tell her I was sorry.

That I wanted her to live whole and free and find every joy that this world had to offer.

He shoved me back and pointed in my face. "Stay the hell away from her."

"I need to see that she's okay."

He edged forward, his teeth grinding as he snarled, "Stay the fuck away from my sister, do you understand me? You are no longer a part of this family. I don't want to see you ever again."

Tears burned down his face. And fuck, I hated that I'd destroyed this, too. This friendship. The guy who'd stuck by me, through thick and thin.

He'd asked me one thing.

To stay away from his sister.

Because he loved her. Wanted her safe.

And if I'd listened? She wouldn't be here.

I gulped around the torment, trying to suck it down. I looked between the members of her family who were caught in a swill of torment. "I'm sorry. I never meant to hurt her. Never meant to hurt any of you. And I know it's not worth anything, but I love her. I always have. She's the best thing that has ever happened to me, and the only thing I want is her safety and happiness. And I pray that she and Kayden are okay."

I turned and rushed back down the hall, needing to get the hell out of there before I did something stupid like fight my best friend to get to her.

I'd already caused enough grief. I couldn't keep doing it.

But I couldn't stop the swelling inside me. The one that promised that I would. That I would fight for her with everything I had.

I rounded the corner, out the double doors, and into the lobby. I was out in the parking lot, trudging through the night when the voice hit me from behind. "Ryder."

I slowly turned to find Dakota's mother standing ten feet away. Her face was mottled and reddened with tears. She twisted her fingers, hesitant before she said, "They're both fine. Dakota's injuries were only minimal, but they are taking her for a CT scan just to be sure. Kayden is unharmed and Paisley took him to the ranch."

Relief slammed me, and I bent in two, all the strain I'd been holding coming out of me in a whoosh. I gathered it and forced myself to look at her. "Thank you for letting me know."

Another tear streamed down her cheek. "I'm so angry with you, Ryder. Angry that my daughter and grandson got stuck in your mess. But I also know you, and I know you would never purposefully or carelessly put them in danger. I know you had your fears. Your losses. Your mistakes. But I also know you were brave enough to set Dakota free of it, so for that, I thank you."

Without saying anything else, she turned and hurried back into the emergency room.

Leaving me standing there alone.

Chapter Forty-Nine

Dakota

I N THE BARE LIGHT GLOWING FROM THE OVEN VENT, NIGHT COVERING the house in a shroud, I stood in my mother's kitchen slowly whisking the mixture in a metal bowl.

Sugar, flour, eggs, vanilla.

Butter, brown sugar, baking powder.

I added the chunks of the candy bars I'd already cut up, blending them into the gooey mix. I heaped the balls onto the cookie sheet, put them into the oven, and waited while the timer counted down until they were done, then transferred them onto the cooling rack.

I always thought of baking as therapeutic.

The way you could get absorbed in the motions. Your thoughts and fears still alive and plaguing you, but it was like you could churn through them as you churned through the ingredients. Process each one until they were diluted and reshaped, meshing to become a part of something greater.

Because the pain would always be a part of me, but it became a piece of the bigger picture. A piece of the whole. Every experience we had shaped us into who we were, we just had to make sure the bitter parts came out sweeter on the other side.

Once the cookies had cooled, I used a spatula to transfer them into a tin, my chest heavy and achy when I covered it with a lid.

The house creaked in the silence as I tiptoed across the floor. My mom and Kayden had both been long asleep. I'd asked her if I could move Kayden's portable crib into her room tonight because I had something I needed to do.

We'd been staying here while we convalesced.

While we rested.

There weren't really any physical wounds to recover from other than a bruise on the side of my face.

It was the discovery of Ryder's past that required some healing.

What he'd been involved in, who Trey was, the trauma Kayden and I had both been through, and the million other things that I'd had to meld into that mixture to fully see everything as a whole.

What it meant.

I held my breath as I opened the door and stepped out into the cover of night. I'd done it so many times before, slinked around the edge of the house and quietly raced down the path to the edge of the woods to the tree beneath the star-speckled skies.

Drawn because I'd always been able to feel when he was there.

Intrinsically pulled his direction in his time of need.

Meet me in the place of the forgotten.

It was overgrown now, unused, but I could never forget the path.

One that had always led me to the man who'd be waiting on our branch.

Tonight, his black hair rustled with the breeze, his energy so thick that I always felt it as the rumbling of the ground.

It trembled then, this foundation that hadn't had the time to set.

Held, I stayed there for a long moment. My pulse thundered so wildly that it echoed through the cool air, and my breaths were shallow and hard.

Finally, he shifted to look at me from over his shoulder.

Darkness rained around him.

Midnight.

His pain was so stark and intense that it was difficult to walk through the surge of it.

But I did because I finally could see what that mixture had become on the other side.

And it was so much sweeter than I ever could have imagined.

I approached, moving through the night until I was climbing onto the branch so I could sit at his side. In the same place where we'd fallen in love, even though it had taken so long to truly understand what that really meant.

Our obstacles had been so great, they should have been insurmountable.

But this love was greater than that.

We both faced forward, staring into the darkness that weaved through the woods.

The connection hummed between us.

Wrapped and soothed.

It'd been a week since everything had happened, but I'd felt him out here, every night.

I had known he was waiting. Waiting on me to make the choice.

"The number of times I've sat on this branch," he finally mumbled in that low, deep voice.

It covered me in chills.

"For all those years after I'd ruined my chance with you."

Self-deprecating laughter rolled from him, and he rubbed his hands together like he could squash the tension that strained between us. "You weren't even living here at your mom's any longer, and I'd still come, just because I ached to be close to you. So I could get lost in the memories of you."

Pain lancinated through my chest. "And I couldn't come because it hurt too bad to sit here in the amount of love I felt for you and know you didn't love me back."

Regret left him on a slow sigh. "I don't know how I even forced out that lie, but hurting you that way? Seeing the evidence of what I inflicted on your face? It was the moment that fully broke me. The moment I marked on myself as a reminder of what I had lost. Standing at my door, having to break both of our hearts."

He fisted a hand over the spot where the broken clock sat on his chest.

Its fractured hands unable to move.

I'd never asked him what the broken clock on his chest had meant, sure I'd already known its meaning.

Now, my spirit toiled with its truth.

Those hands were an affliction.

They were his chains.

They were his lost hopes.

They were *me*.

Grief clouded his voice. "He killed Amelia, Dakota. Killed her as a warning of what would happen to those I loved if I tried to break away from him.

And I knew I couldn't have you a part of that life. So I tried to stay away from you. Tried to put as much distance between us as I could."

I'd known about Amelia. Ezra had told me when he'd come to check on me the next day after I'd been released from the hospital. He'd given me the barest insight, more ingredients to process into the convoluted mix.

It was sickening, knowing what that monster had done to her. What he had done to Ryder. What he had done to *us*.

His chuckle was hollow. "Seems I'm not so good about staying away from you, though, am I? And when I'd heard you'd had a son, I came crawling back, thinking if I could just have that small part of you, I would be satisfied. Thought it wouldn't hurt so fucking bad if I at least had you as a small part of my life. But it was never enough, was it? I wanted more and more of you when I never should have asked for it."

His hand shook as he roughed it over the top of his head. "I'm fucking sorry, Dakota. I'm sorry for hurting you. I'm sorry for lying to you. I'm sorry for betraying your trust. For giving you that money without you knowing where it came from. For dragging you into something that wasn't yours."

Incredulity seeped into his laugh. "I thought I was doing something right—for the both of us, but Dare played me a fool again and again, always a step ahead of me, destroying every chance of joy that anyone around me could get."

"Except he couldn't destroy it, could he?"

His harsh brow pinched when he looked at me. "Did he, Dakota? Did he destroy it? Did I destroy it? I kept telling you I wasn't a good man, and now you see the fullness of that. What I put you and Kayden through…"

A broken sound clawed from his throat, and he looked away as he scrubbed a hand over his face. "It kills me, Dakota. It kills me to know what you both went through. It will forever be the greatest regret of my life."

He inhaled a shaky breath. "But I don't want to live my life regretting my choices any longer. When I look at you? When I look at Kayden? I see the man I want to be. The one I should have been all along. The one I'm going to strive to be every day of my life."

Emotion pressed at my chest, and tears blurred my eyes.

He reached out and ran his thumb over the tiny divot on my chin. "You're the light breaking inside me, Dakota Cooper. You were the one who taught me what goodness meant. Can you forgive me? Can you look at me and see the man who wants to live for you? Because I choose you, Dakota, and I'm praying you can choose me back."

I didn't answer that question.

Instead, I cleared my throat and lifted the tin. "I made something for you."

Wistfulness gusted through his features, the smallest smile tweaking at the edge of his big red lips. "Of course, you did."

He took the tin and carefully lifted the lid to the cookies sitting inside. He groaned but didn't take one, like he was afraid he hadn't earned the right.

"I made these for you that day. When I came to you to confess my love," I whispered into the lapping shadows. "I called them Mounds of Joy because you filled me with joy, Ryder, and you still fill me with that same joy. We all deserve to have that person in our lives."

The air shivered and shook, and Ryder kept looking at me with those gunmetal eyes that pierced and slayed.

"My mom told me recently that the only thing she wanted was for me to be happy. That she wanted me to be fulfilled. That she hoped I would find the one who made my heart and body sing. The one who holds me up when I need lifted, and the one who cheers me on when I'm standing fine on my own. My own heart told me that man would be the one who would stand in the fire for me. Fight for me. Love me with everything he had."

I took his hand, gathered it up in both of mine, and pulled it against my chest. "My heart made its pick a long, long time ago, and now, after everything, I've never been so sure. It's you, Ryder. It's always been you. And I see it now—everything you did—your mistakes and your hopes. Your failures and your love. I forgive you because I see you, Ryder—I see you through all of it, and I know your heart is beautiful despite everything that you've done."

His breaths came ragged and short, and he suddenly hopped off the branch and set the tin aside before he approached.

Slowly.

With purpose and care.

He never looked away from my face as he curled his hands around my waist and pulled me down to set me on my feet.

Energy crashed as he framed my face in his big hands.

"Cookie," he murmured, his thumbs tracing my cheeks. "I love you, and I'm going to for the rest of my days. For as long as these stars shine above us. And I promise you, I won't ever give you a reason to question that again."

He took my hand and placed it over the clock that sat on his chest. "And this heart? It is always going to beat for you. Because there aren't enough days in eternity that could make me forget about you."

Then he kissed me.

Slowly and powerfully and without any secrets lingering between us.

Because we had become each other's truths.

No, we didn't make it here by perfection. It was messy and ugly and riddled with regrets.

But my mother was right—only I could make the decision of who was worthy of me.

And for me, Ryder had earned that right.

Pulling back, he gazed down at me with those dark eyes, but the blackened pools were the clearest I'd ever seen. "It's our time, Cookie."

I gave him the softest smile. "It's our time."

Ryder threaded our fingers together then reached down and snagged the tin, slanting me a smirk as he did. "I'm going to need these."

A giggle got free, and I snuggled up to his side as we started back down the path. "I think you only want me for my sweets."

He pressed his lips to my temple. "That's right, I want all the *sweets*."

Suggestion filled his voice, and I giggled again as he shifted to curl his arm around my shoulder and tucked me closer to his side. His tone grew somber. "Your brother is going to want to kill me, Dakota. And I know it's going to take time to prove to him who I really am and how much I really love you, but I will. I'm going to show this whole fucking town that you belong with me, Dakota Cooper. I'm going to give you everything."

I stilled, shifting so I was standing in front of him, my eyes on the unforgettable lines of his face as I set my palm on his cheek. "I don't need everything, Ryder. I just need your honesty. I need your truth. Your devotion and your love."

"You have it, Dakota." His thumb swiped over my bottom lip. "Love is on the house."

Epilogues

Dakota

Six Months Later

THE CLATTER OF DISHES AND VOICES FILLED THE RESTAURANT. Every table and booth were taken during the lunch rush, except for one of the long tables in the middle that sat twenty that had been reserved for a large party scheduled to arrive in ten minutes.

Satisfaction pushed at my ribs as I wandered through the dining room, ensuring the guests were happy and well fed.

Their smiling faces and their mumbled praise over the food never failed to send me soaring.

I was proud of Time River Market & Café. What I had built and what it offered our small community. From such a young age, I'd known this was what I wanted to do, and it filled me with pride at what it had become.

I'd found a speck of shame in it, but it had been on Ryder and me to eradicate it, to do something good in its place, and I'd found joy in that, too.

A foundation had been started in Amelia's name in Poplar. It was a shelter for at risk teens, and Ryder and I had doubled the money he'd given me to fund its opening.

Ryder volunteered there every weekend, and he would take the cookies I'd bake and share them while he shared pieces of his story. How one choice could have a devastating ripple effect, but how each of us have the power to walk a good path. That sometimes we stumble, but we have to fight our way back onto the right track.

Fight for health and joy and security.

He'd fought for his, and I was so proud of him for that.

I glanced up to find Beth smirking at me from the other side of the counter. "You look like you're over there daydreaming again. That man must be something in bed because every day you're walking around here on a cloud. It's kind of annoying," she teased.

I swatted at her as I rounded the counter, redness hitting my cheeks. "Would you stop it?"

"Never, not when you turn to mush any time I mention his name."

I saw no point in denying it since every thought of him made me all squishy inside.

"Do you need any help?" I figured I'd do best to change the subject before she got carried away.

She ducked her head into the short refrigerator under the counter. "Would you mind double checking the dairy order is coming in tomorrow? We are running super low on whipped cream, and you know how the town considers that a local tragedy."

A slight giggle got free. "That they do. But I just checked this morning and everything is in order."

"Do you mind checking again?"

"Um…sure. If I didn't know better, I'd think you were trying to get me out of your way."

Beth waved a teasing hand at me. "You are in the way. You know I have things handled out here."

"Fine, fine, I see what I'm good for. Ordering supplies," I told her as I started for the swinging door.

"And recipes. Don't forget the recipes," she called behind me. I was laughing under my breath as I headed back into my office. I added three more cases of whipped cream just to make sure.

The truth was the bakery portion of the business had been booming.

It wasn't a bad problem to have.

While I was back there, I decided to check emails to make sure everything was handled.

A few minutes later, I looked up to find Beth standing in my doorway. "Hey, would you mind coming out to help fill the drink orders for the big reservation? They're an unruly bunch and Chloe is having a hard time keeping up."

"Oh, I see how it is—you do need me."

"I'll never admit it." She sent me a playful smirk as I edged past her and started down the hall.

I pushed out the swinging door, only I stalled out when I saw the people who had gathered at the large table.

Everyone I knew and loved. Paisley, her grandfather, Caleb, and Evelyn. Ezra and his kids and his mother Linda. My brother and sister, and Kayden was in my mother's arms.

But it was the man standing in front with his hands stuffed into his pockets and grinning at me that sent shockwaves rolling beneath my feet.

The air shimmered with light, and my consciousness got pulled toward his darkness.

Drawn in a swelling of need.

A blaze of love that scorched me to the bone.

I slowly eased forward, moving through my restaurant toward the people who meant the most to me.

"What are you all doing here?" It trembled out of my mouth. It wasn't like they didn't frequent the café. But they didn't usually come together, and if we did a big family thing, I knew about it.

No, this was different.

It was palpable and alive.

A buzz in the atmosphere that shivered and flashed and sent nerves scattering through my senses.

The rest of my staff began to gather around us, as well as a few friends and acquaintances who had been sitting at other tables.

It took me a second to realize that Ryder had stolen my chalkboard sign from the front. The one where I wrote the daily specials.

It was standing right beside him, and the dessert special was now written in his strong print.

My eyes traced it, seeing what it said.

Marry Me Muffins.

It was at the same second that he dropped to his knee.

Ryder

There she was again.

A landslide.

Quicksand that immediately sucked me under.

I dropped to my knee, no escape from her lure, which was a good fucking thing because I didn't have to fight it any longer.

What we were supposed to be.

This love.

This devotion.

This thing that burned inside me so bright it could never be put out.

Tears slipped from the edges of her eyes, and she pressed her hands to her mouth to cover the tiny cry that slipped out.

"Cookie." I rumbled it around the thickness in my throat.

More tears fell down her gorgeous face, cinnamon eyes filled with so much adoration that my words choked around the force of it.

"My love for you was a secret for too long. Hidden in the shadows. But your love was big enough and bright enough for the both of us that it never could burn out. Because of it, I will forever burn for you. For so long, I've wanted to shout my love for you from the roof of every building in this town. And I figured there is no better place to start than right here, in front of our friends and family, in this place that you built out of your love and devotion and dreams."

I took in a ragged breath, overcome by what I felt.

"I love you, Cookie, and I want to share all those things with you. This love. This devotion. Every dream we could ever conjure. I want us to chase them together. Today, tomorrow, and always. Be my wife. My partner. The one who believes in me as much as I believe in you. Because I want to share every single day with you."

Dakota came the rest of the way forward, no longer trying to slow or hide her tears. She knelt in front of me. Reaching out with those tender fingers, she dragged them down the side of my face.

A tremble rolled, and I couldn't do anything but stare at the woman who had changed everything. The one who'd filled me up when I was empty. The one who'd given me faith when I'd lost all hope.

The one who'd shown me I could believe in myself.

344 | A.L. JACKSON

"Nothing could make me happier than spending every day with you, Ryder Nash. All our todays and all our tomorrows."

I crashed my mouth against hers because I couldn't keep from touching her for a second longer, kissing her mad through our tears and laughter and the cheers that rose up from our family.

I curled my arm around her waist, guiding us both to stand, and Dakota's mom set Kayden on his feet. He tottered over, this other piece of my soul, that devotion that could never end, his face full of that dimpled grin as he held the ring over his head.

"I got *somefing* for you, Mommy."

Dakota choked, her love so fierce as her son placed the ring in her palm. It was unique and every bit as beautiful as Dakota, made of metal I had forged in my shop, and the stone was a Red Tiger's Eye.

The same color as that knowing gaze that flashed up to me.

Joy pushed so hard at my chest that it overflowed.

She held her palm out to me, and I took the ring so I could slide it onto her trembling finger, and I whispered, "All our todays and all our tomorrows."

The End

I hope you loved reading Ryder and Dakota's story as much as I loved writing it. Their love story was so powerful, and I'm so thankful to get to give them their happily ever after.

Curious if Dakota and Paisley were able to pull off Caleb's surprise party? Visit my website to get a free bonus scene.

About the Author

A.L. Jackson is the *New York Times* & *USA Today* Bestselling author of contemporary romance. She writes emotional, sexy, heart-filled stories about boys who usually like to be a little bit bad.

Her bestselling series include THE REGRET SERIES, CLOSER TO YOU, BLEEDING STARS, FIGHT FOR ME, CONFESSIONS OF THE HEART, FALLING STARS, REDEMPTION HILLS, and TIME RIVER.

If she's not writing, you can find her hanging out by the pool with her family, sipping cocktails with her friends, or of course with her nose buried in a book.

Be sure not to miss new releases and sales from A.L. Jackson - Sign up to receive her newsletter http://smarturl.it/NewsFromALJackson or text "aljackson" to 33222 to receive short but sweet updates on all the important news.

Connect with A.L. Jackson online:

FB Page https://geni.us/ALJacksonFB
A.L. Jackson Bookclub https://geni.us/ALJacksonBookClub
Angels https://geni.us/AmysAngels
Amazon https://geni.us/ALJacksonAmzn
Book Bub https://geni.us/ALJacksonBookbub

Text "aljackson" to 33222 to receive short but sweet
updates on all the important news.

Printed in the USA
CPSIA information can be obtained
at www.ICGtesting.com
LVHW091113171023
761338LV00020B/55/J